Anne Hart lives in St John's, Newfoundland where she is a librarian at Memorial University of Newfoundland and the author of a number of short stories, poems and plays. Her much-acclaimed first book, *Agatha Christie's Miss Marple*, was hailed as 'the perfect companion . . . an engaging work with much of the fascination of an Agatha Christie mystery and a charm of its own.' She is the mother of a daughter and two sons.

Also by Anne Hart

AGATHA CHRISTIE'S MARPLE

Poirot books by Agatha Christie

THE MYSTERIOUS AFFAIR AT STYLES
THE MURDER ON THE LINKS
POIROT INVESTIGATES
THE MURDER OF ROGER ACKROYD
THE BIG FOUR
THE MYSTERY OF THE BLUE TRAIN
BLACK COFFEE *(adapted by Charles Osborne)*
PERIL AT END HOUSE
LORD EDGWARE DIES
MURDER ON THE ORIENT EXPRESS
THREE-ACT TRAGEDY
DEATH IN THE CLOUDS
THE ABC MURDERS
MURDER IN MESOPOTAMIA
CARDS ON THE TABLE
MURDER IN THE MEWS
DUMB WITNESS
DEATH ON THE NILE
APPOINTMENT WITH DEATH
HERCULE POIROT'S CHRISTMAS
SAD CYPRESS
ONE, TWO, BUCKLE MY SHOE
EVIL UNDER THE SUN
FIVE LITTLE PIGS
THE HOLLOW
THE LABOURS OF HERCULES
TAKEN AT THE FLOOD
MRS MCGINTY'S DEAD
AFTER THE FUNERAL
HICKORY DICKORY DOCK
DEAD MAN'S FOLLY
CAT AMONG THE PIGEONS
THE ADVENTURE OF THE CHRISTMAS PUDDING
THE CLOCKS
THIRD GIRL
HALLOWE'EN PARTY
ELEPHANTS CAN REMEMBER
POIROT'S EARLY CASES
CURTAIN: POIROT'S LAST CASE

Agatha Christie's Poirot

The Life and Times of Hercule Poirot

Anne Hart

HarperCollins*Publishers*

HarperCollins*Publishers*
77–85 Fulham Palace Road,
Hammersmith, London W6 8JB
www.harpercollins.co.uk

This edition published 1997
10 9 8 7 6 5 4 3

Previously published in paperback by
Sphere Books Ltd 1991
First published in Great Britain by Pavilion Books Ltd 1990

With thanks to Agatha Christie Limited
(a Chorion company)
www.agathachristie.com

ISBN 13: 978-0-00-728246-3

Set in Goudy Old Style by
Palimpsest Book Production Limited,
Polmont, Stirlingshire

Printe d and bound in India by
Gopsons Papers Ltd., Noida 201301

For Susan, Peter and Stephen

CONTENTS

Preface

This is a biography of the illustrious Hercule Poirot who, behind a façade of dandyisms and mannerisms, was as shrewd and subtle a detective as ever walked the streets of London. For his creator, the incomparable Agatha Christie, he was at times a torment. In 1938, a mere twenty-two years after his genesis, she exclaimed in an interview: 'There are moments when I have felt: "Why-Why-Why did I ever invent this detestable, bombastic, tiresome little creature? . . . Eternally straightening things, eternally boasting, eternally twirling his moustaches and tilting his egg-shaped head" . . . I point out that by a few strokes of the pen . . . I could destroy him utterly. He replies, grandiloquently: "Impossible to get rid of Poirot like that! He is much too clever."' Indeed he was. Poirot knew a supreme story-teller when he found one and never let go. For him she set her most perfect puzzles, thereby achieving immortality for them both.

As with my biography of Agatha Christie's other major detective, Miss Jane Marple, I owe a great debt of thanks to Rosalind Hicks, Agatha Christie's daughter, for her kind permission to use her mother's writing in this way. In working on this second book I have also received the benefit and pleasure of her direct encouragement and hospitality, for which I am immensely grateful. I would also like to thank Anthony Hicks for his lively and helpful comments at the early stages, particularly on the ever controversial matter of Hercule Poirot's age.

Two people have helped me enormously in the writing of this book. Peter Hart's knowledgeable, rigorous and witty editing has saved me from many a pitfall (the ones that remain are entirely of my own digging), and Vernon Barber's encouragement and assistance from the very beginning made the whole enterprise possible. I am grateful as well to Debbie Edgecombe for her heroic and intelligent deciphering of a seemingly interminable number of drafts and revisions. I would also like to thank Brian Stone, my astute and encouraging agent, Bob Comber, his assistant, Nancy Grenville, who gave discerning attention to the final draft, Christopher Burton, who kindly pursued the mystery of Poirot's telephone numbers in the archives of British Telecom, and Pamela Hodgson who helped so much in the final stages.

Finally, at risk of appearing precious, I would like to thank Hercule Poirot. In my preoccupation for almost two years with this endearing and elegant little detective, there have been many moments of trepidation and exasperation. At the end of it all Poirot is firmly in my heart, a delightful condition I share with millions of readers. All of us are indebted to his inspired creator and sternest critic, Agatha Christie.

Anne Hart

I

The Curtain Rises

'My name,' said Poirot, contriving as usual to make the simple statement sound like the curtain of the first act of a play, 'my name is Hercule Poirot.'

—The Labours of Hercules

That benevolent despot, Hercule Poirot, who to this day keeps a firm grasp on the affection of countless subjects, made his debut as a fully formed foreign eccentric on page 34 of his creator's first book, *The Mysterious Affair at Styles*. On page 35 Cynthia Murdoch of Styles Court made a pioneer English attempt to describe him. 'He's a dear little man,' she said.

Her remark was to stand the test of time wonderfully well, though not everyone who was to meet Poirot over the next six decades – especially not those attempting to cover up crimes – would agree with her. 'You unutterable little jackanapes of a foreigner!' more than one was to cry, purple with rage. Poirot himself would have been annoyed if he had heard Cynthia's remark. 'My name is Hercule Poirot,' he was apt to say to those not appropriately impressed, 'and I am probably the greatest detective in the world.'

A number of Christie scholars have debated his origins. The most important clues, of course, have been provided by Agatha Christie herself. In 1916, in her twenty-sixth year, she set herself the task of writing a detective novel:

> Who could I have as a detective? I reviewed such detectives as I had met and admired in books. There was Sherlock Holmes, the one and only – I should never be able to emulate *him*. There was Arsène Lupin – was he a criminal or a detective? Anyway, not my kind. There was the young journalist Rouletabille in *The Mystery of the Yellow Room* – that was the *sort* of person whom I would like to invent . . . then I remembered our Belgian refugees. We had quite a colony of refugees living in the parish of Tor . . . Why not make my detective a Belgian? I thought. There were all types of refugees. How about a refugee police officer? A retired police officer. Not too young a one . . .
>
> Anyway, I settled on a Belgian detective. I allowed him slowly to grow into his part. He should have been an inspector, so that he would have a certain knowledge of crime. He would be meticulous, very tidy . . . always arranging things, liking things in pairs, liking things square instead of round. And he should be very brainy – he should have little grey cells of the mind – that was a good phrase: I must remember that – yes, he would have little grey cells.

Other possible predecessors and contemporaries have been suggested: G. K. Chesterton's Hercule Flambeau, Robert Barr's Eugène Valmont, A. E. W. Mason's Inspector Hanaud, Marie Belloc Lowndes's Hercules Popeau, and inevitably – despite Agatha Christie's disclaimer – Sherlock Holmes.

Like Holmes, Poirot was vain, brilliant, and a bachelor; like Holmes he possessed, in Arthur Hastings, a faithful

Watson; and, as readers will discover, there occur from time to time in the Poirot canon situations and frames of mind distinctly Holmesian. 'Ah, well,' as Poirot himself said complacently in *Cards on the Table*, 'I am not above stealing the tricks of others.' *He* knew perfectly well who he was. He was the one and only, the unique Hercule Poirot. If *he* had been asked about origins, I imagine him stroking his moustaches, his eyes as green as a cat's. 'Once upon a time,' he might have replied, with an imperious wave of his hand, 'there was born in the kingdom of Belgium a baby with an egg-shaped head . . .'

The kingdom of Belgium was – and still is – a neat, cautious, Catholic country that knows what it's about. Family businesses flourish. Education and the arts are taken seriously and so is food. Its restaurants are well known to gourmets and its pastry chefs are famous.

Its capital, Brussels – the city where Poirot was probably born, and certainly flourished for many years – possesses what is probably the most beautiful and sociable square in Europe, the *Grand Place*. Here, high atop the magnificent Hôtel de Ville, a gilded figure of St Michael watches over the city. It is perfectly possible that, once upon a time, St Michael watched a procession of Poirots taking a new baby to church to be christened.

When was Hercule Poirot born? In what he himself would have called 'supreme exercises of imagination', a number of serious attempts have been made to pinpoint one improbable year or another. Usually these calculations depend on a remark of Poirot's in *Three Act Tragedy* that he was 'due' to retire from the Belgian Police Force at the time of the outbreak of the First World War. Making an undocumented guess at a retirement age of sixty to sixty-five years, the conclusion has then been reached that he was born between 1849 and 1854.[1]

Tempting as it is to reconstruct a chronological Poirot in this matter of age – particularly as he was still flourishing in the early 1970s – I suspect that Agatha Christie, and Poirot himself, would have been amused by all this arithmetic. In context, Poirot seems to be a man in his late fifties or early sixties when he arrives in England and somewhere in his mid-eighties in *Curtain*, his last case. That close to sixty years of elegant ageing elapsed between, with never a diminution of his grey cells, was a *tour de force* for his adroit creator and one of Poirot's great charms. 'Men have as many years as they feel,' says an Italian proverb. In this matter of years, and of his age at any particular time, Poirot was always extremely – and wisely – reticent.

In *The Labours of Hercules* Dr Burton, a Fellow of All Souls College, ruminated on Hercule Poirot's first name. 'Hardly a *Christian* name,' he pointed out. 'Definitely pagan. But why? That's what I want to know. Father's fancy? Mother's whim?' Whether moved by fancy or whim, the Poirots showed no timidity. In an inspired moment they delved into Greek mythology and named their son after Hercules the Strong, the mightiest of the ancient heroes. Poirot himself loved his name; it was to prove a glorious compensation for his diminutive size. 'It is the name of one of the great ones of this world,' he boasted in *The Mystery of the Blue Train*.[2]

All his life Poirot preferred privacy and was particularly unforthcoming about his earlier (and long) life in Belgium. References to his past are rare, but in *Three Act Tragedy* we are permitted an insight into his childhood: 'See you, as a boy I was poor. There were many of us. We had to get on in the world.' One glimpses the Poirots again, hard-working and close-knit, in his lifelong devotion to The Family. 'I am very strong on the family life, as you know,' he declared to Hastings on one occasion, and 'Family strength is a marvellous thing,' he said on another.

Papa Poirot is scarcely mentioned. All evidence suggests that the mother was the strong one in this family. 'Madam, we, in our country, have a great tenderness, a great respect for the mother. The *mère de famille*, she is everything!' was how he introduced himself to a matron in 'The King of Clubs'; and 'I comprehend the mother's heart. No one comprehends it better than I, Hercule Poirot,' he told the Dowager Duchess of Merton in *Lord Edgware Dies*. Throughout his life he was to stand in awe of mothers. 'Mothers, Madame, are particularly ruthless when their children are in danger,' he said to a somewhat enigmatic one in *Death on the Nile*. Perhaps Madame Poirot had cause to be formidable? One imagines her determined and orderly, keeping strict accounts, supervising lessons, fighting against considerable odds to bring her children up to be good little *bourgeois*, and insisting, in their small quarters, that everyone have good manners and be very neat. Is it Madame Poirot we are seeing, shepherding her large flock to church, in Poirot's recollection of how women looked in his youth: '. . . a coiffure high and rigid – so – and the hat attached with many hatpins – *là – là – là et là*.'

But life was not all obedience and hard work. Madame Poirot's children had some good times as well. '*Les Feux d'Artifices*, the Party, the Games with balls,' recalled Poirot in *Peril at End House*. Little Hercule must have been especially enthralled with 'the conjurer, the man who deceives the eye, however carefully it watches'. And they all must have had a splendid time at the *Ommegang*, the great holiday in July when the *Grand Place* is thronged with merrymakers. Like most Europeans, however, Poirot regarded childhood as not a particularly desirable state, but as something to be got over with as quickly as possible. In *Mrs McGinty's Dead*, listening to Superintendent Spence dwell in nostalgic detail on the pleasure of childhood:

> Poirot waited politely. This was one of the moments when, even after half a lifetime in the country, he found the English incomprehensible. He himself had played at *Cache Cache* in his childhood, but he felt no desire to talk about it or even think about it.

What of his brothers and sisters? 'There were many of us,' he told Mr Satterthwaite, but there is a mention of only one of them in all the Poirot literature, and it is a mention that is quickly erased. In the original version of 'The Chocolate Box', a short story that recalls his earlier days in Belgium, Poirot says:

> 'I was informed that a young lady was demanding me. Thinking that it was, perhaps, my little sister Yvonne, I prayed my landlady to make her mount.'[3]

Later versions of this story omit this reference to Yvonne, but it does provide an affectionate glimpse of Poirot as an older brother, a glimpse reflected in an avuncular way a generation later in *Cards on the Table* when Poirot says to a young woman:

> 'It is, you understand, that Christmas is coming on. I have to buy presents for many nieces and grand-nieces.'

One has to be a bit wary about this mention of nieces and grand-nieces, however, as Poirot, who practically never mentioned his real family, was apt to invent imaginary relatives to suit his purposes. The most outrageous example of this is the appearance among the *dramatis personae* of *The Big Four* of a twin brother, Achille. When first told of this hitherto unsuspected twin, Hastings was understandably surprised. 'What does he do?' he demanded, 'putting aside a half-formed wonder as to the character and disposition of the late Madame Poirot, and her classical taste in Christian names.' Replied Poirot, smoothly:

> 'He does nothing. He is, as I tell, of a singularly indolent disposition. But his abilities are hardly less than my own – which is saying a great deal.'
>
> 'Is he like you to look at?'
>
> 'Not unlike. But not nearly so handsome. And wears no moustaches.'[4]

In *The Murder of Roger Ackroyd* Poirot invented a nephew to extract information from that indomitable purveyor of village news, Miss Caroline Sheppard. 'I never knew that Poirot had an imbecile nephew?' said her brother, Dr Sheppard.

> 'Didn't you? Oh, he told me all about it. Poor lad. It's a great grief to all the family. They've kept him at home so far, but it's getting to such a pitch that they're afraid he'll have to go into some kind of institution.'
>
> 'I suppose you know pretty well everything there is to know about Poirot's family by this time,' I said, exasperated.
>
> 'Pretty well,' said Caroline complacently. 'It's a great relief to people to be able to tell all their troubles to some one.'

In *Dumb Witness*, to Hastings's amusement, Poirot produced three more unfortunate relatives: an invalid uncle, a cousin with jaundice, and an ailing but belligerent mother:

> This time he had an aged mother for whom he was anxious to find a sympathetic hospital nurse.
>
> 'You comprehend – I am going to speak to you quite frankly. My mother, she is difficult. We have had some excellent nurses, young women, fully competent but the very fact that they are young has been against them. My mother dislikes young women, she insults them, she is rude and fractious, she fights against open windows and modern hygiene. It is very difficult.'

There may, of course, have been germs of truth in some of these confidences, but one thing we can be sure of is that Poirot once had a grandfather who possessed 'a large turnip of a watch' (Hastings called it 'a large grotesque turnip of a watch') and that Poirot fell heir to it. 'Take my watch in your hand – with care,' he once instructed. 'It is a family heirloom!'

As a young child, Poirot, a good little Catholic, was 'educated by the nuns'. There is an evocative scene in 'The Apples of the Hesperides' when, working on a case in Ireland, he heard the tolling of a convent bell. At once he was transported back in time: 'He understood that bell. It was a sound he had been familiar with from early youth.' He may have heard it with mixed feelings. In *Five Little Pigs* there is a clue that his convent school had its share of dragons. In meeting 'the shrewd, penetrating glance' of a retired governess, Poirot 'once again felt the years falling away and himself a meek and apprehensive little boy'.

As to his later education – and despite Dr Burton's

suspicions that he was never properly taught the classics – Poirot appears to have undergone a thorough and conventional schooling including the study of English, German and Italian in addition, of course, to the two languages of Belgium, French and Flemish. 'Alas, there is no proper education nowadays,' he lamented in *After the Funeral*. 'Apparently one learns nothing but economics – and how to set Intelligence Tests!'

It is not easy to imagine Poirot as a youth, his moustache in mere infancy, but bits and pieces emerge in the kindness he later showed to injudicious and awkward young men. 'I cannot overcome my shyness. I say always the wrong thing. I upset water jugs,' confessed one of them in *Murder in Mesopotamia*. '"We all do these things when we are young," said Poirot, smiling. "The poise, the *savoir faire*, it comes later"'; and 'It is the time for follies, when one is young,' he said encouragingly to another in 'Christmas Adventure'.[5]

An endearing glimpse of Poirot himself as a youth is provided in *Evil Under the Sun*:

> 'When I was young (and that, Mademoiselle, is indeed a long time ago) there was a game entitled "*If not yourself, who would you be?*" One wrote the answer in young ladies' albums. They had gold edges and were bound in blue leather.'

From an early age Poirot knew exactly who he would be:

> 'To most of us the test comes early in life. A man is confronted quite soon with the necessity to stand on his own feet, to face dangers and difficulties and to take his own line of dealing with them.'

And here we have it, the surprising lure to this tidy and

diminutive young man of a life of dangers and difficulties. 'I entered the police force,' he told Mr Satterthwaite.[6]

In police circles, in Poirot's day, Belgium, which claimed to have an almost perfect statute book, was considered one of the least policed countries in Europe, so law-abiding were her citizens. Nevertheless, Poirot – who quickly became attached to the judicial police whose duties were to investigate crimes and apprehend offenders – had at least one combative moment. A reminiscence in *Curtain* recalls him in a startling role – Poirot, the Sharpshooter:

> 'As a young man in the Belgian police force I shot down a desperate criminal who sat on a roof and fired at people below.'

In a few laconic sentences, Poirot, many years later, summed up perhaps forty to forty-five years he spent with the Belgian police:

> 'I worked hard. Slowly I rose in that force. I began to make a name for myself. I made a name for myself. I began to acquire an international reputation.'

Poirot's career was brilliant. In time he became head of the force. As Hastings described him in *The Mysterious Affair at Styles*:

> . . . this quaint dandified little man . . . had been in his time one of the most celebrated members of the Belgian police. As a detective, his *flair* had been extraordinary, and he had achieved triumphs by unravelling some of the most baffling cases of the day.

In his English life Poirot occasionally spoke of these Belgian days, and when he did it was almost always of the one case in which he had been utterly fooled.

This dreadful experience was recounted one stormy night as Poirot and Hastings traded confidences before the fire ('Outside, the wind howled malevolently, and the rain beat against the windows in great gusts'). 'You ask me if I have ever made the complete ass of myself, as you say over here?' said Poirot, and there followed the story of 'The Chocolate Box',[7] a case of a political murder in Brussels in which, outfoxed by a most unlikely killer, he had completely misread the evidence and nearly arrested the wrong person. '*Sapristi*! It does not bear thinking of!' he cried (but what a consolation for Hastings, one can't help thinking).

Another case Poirot recalled from time to time – 'one of my early successes' – was the affair of the soap manufacturer of Liège, a man of porcine appearance who was found guilty of poisoning his wife in order to marry his secretary. In 'The Nemean Lion', while gazing upon 'the swelling jowl, the small pig eyes, the bulbous nose, and the close-lipped mouth' of his client, Sir Joseph Hoggin, 'a memory stirred dimly. A long time ago . . . in Belgium . . . something, surely, to do with *soap* . . .' On a hunch that his client was up to no good, Poirot immediately recounted the story of The Soapmaker of Liège to Sir Joseph, who went quite pale. Before long his wife, Lady Hoggin, was saying to her husband: 'Funny, this tonic tastes quite different. It hasn't got that bitter taste any more. I wonder why?' Poirot was especially proud of this case. 'Prevention, always, is better than cure,' he said of it in *Hickory Dickory Dock*.

Two collaborations with the British police in these earlier days (Poirot spoke a tolerable, if mannered, English) were to have important consequences as it was through them that he met the ebullient Inspector Jimmy Japp of Scotland Yard. In 1916, in *The Mysterious Affair at Styles* – Poirot's first case as a private detective in England – he encountered Japp again:

> 'I fear you do not remember me, Inspector Japp.'
>
> 'Why, if it isn't Mr Poirot!' cried the Inspector. He turned to the other man. 'You've heard me speak of Mr Poirot? It was in 1904 he and I worked together – the Abercrombie forgery case – you remember, he was run down in Brussels. Ah, those were great days, moosier. Then, do you remember "Baron" Altara? There was a pretty rogue for you! He eluded the clutches of half the police in Europe. But we nailed him in Antwerp – thanks to Mr Poirot here.'

After this, Japp took Poirot under his wing – or was it the other way around? No matter, in England their guarded friendship would flourish for years.

In the long run, the most significant link Poirot forged with England in his Belgian days was the assistance he gave to Arthur Hastings, a young employee of Lloyd's. The nature of the business that brought Hastings from London to Brussels is not recorded, but through it he met Poirot and fell hopelessly under his spell. Hastings was ripe for this. 'Well, I've always had a secret hankering to be a detective!' he confessed to a new friend in *The Mysterious Affair at Styles*.

> 'The real thing – Scotland Yard? Or Sherlock Holmes?'
>
> 'Oh, Sherlock Holmes by all means. But really, seriously, I am awfully drawn to it.'

Hastings came back from Belgium inspired and reciting, at every opportunity, 'the various exploits and triumphs of Hercule Poirot'. That in a few years he would be permitted to work under the tutelage of this great man would have been, at that time, the stuff of his wildest dreams.

As we have seen, Poirot was due to retire in about 1914. Perhaps he had already begun to plan a quiet new life amidst '*les dunes impeccables*' of Knocke-sur-Mer? In August of 1914, however, catastrophe struck with the invasion of neutral Belgium by Germany. The Great War had begun.

The years of German occupation were a period of great suffering for Belgium. Under a German governor, many Belgians who refused to collaborate were executed or deported. In defiance workers withdrew their services, universities voluntarily closed, and newspapers ceased publication. A British heroine, Edith Cavell, the Matron of the Belgian School of Nursing, was shot for aiding escaped Allied soldiers. Countless patriots went underground.

Somewhere in this resistance, we may be sure, was Poirot. As chief of a police force that declined to co-operate, he would have been a prime target for imprisonment by *les Bosches* – or worse, for under the occupation the penalty for those in the Belgian intelligence service was death. For almost two years Poirot dropped from sight. Evidence of his importance to the resistance surfaced towards the end of the war in the case of 'The Kidnapped Prime Minister', a commission which came from the highest levels of the British Government. 'What made you come to me?' he asked a delegation from the War Cabinet. 'I am unknown, obscure in this great London of yours.' From the reply it is clear that it had been

King Albert himself, the Belgians' monarch in exile, who had suggested his small compatriot as the one person in England capable of wresting a missing prime minister from the enemy.

In the spring of 1916 the Germans must have been closing in on Poirot. Badly wounded, he was smuggled out of Belgium into France. Years later, in *Murder on the Orient Express*, he reminded a French General of the debt he owed him:

> 'But indeed, do I not remember that once you saved my life?' And then the General had made another fitting reply to that, disclaiming any merit for that past service; and with more mention of France, of Belgium, of glory, of honour and of such kindred things they had embraced each other heartily.

From France Poirot came, 'a sad and weary refugee to England'.

From the outset of the war the English had opened their hearts and homes to Belgian refugees. 'REMEMBER BELGIUM', admonished enlistment posters, and '*Vivent les braves Belges!*' was the cry, even some seven years later, of the young people in 'Christmas Adventure'. Hard-working officials toiled to place these bewildered exiles with appropriate benefactors. Where, they must have wondered, should they send this funny little policeman? Perhaps to Mrs Inglethorp?

Emily Inglethorp, the autocratic mistress of Styles Court in the pretty Essex village of Styles St Mary, had already established a colony of six Belgians in a small cottage called Leastways, not far from the park gates. In the early summer of 1916 her seventh refugee limped down from a train at the village station.

'A kind lady gave me hospitality,' said Poirot of Mrs Inglethorp. 'We Belgians will always remember her with gratitude.' At Leastways he was given an upstairs room and there he seems to have spent most of his days sitting by a window overlooking the village street, smoking an occasional Russian cigarette, and pondering his fate. 'You may speak for yourself, Hastings,' said Poirot in *Curtain*. 'For me, my arrival at Styles St Mary was a sad and painful time. I was a refugee, wounded, exiled from home and country, existing by charity in a foreign land.'

What was he to do now, the famous Hercule Poirot, suddenly without aim and far from young? Time must have passed very slowly in this quiet sanctuary 'in the midst of green fields and country lanes'.

I am sure that, as an occasional diversion, Poirot and his compatriots were hospitably summoned to Styles Court – Styles, as the family called it – to have tea with Mrs Inglethorp and her *ménage*. At Mrs Inglethorp's side would have been her new husband, her junior by twenty years, the black-bearded Alfred Inglethorp (the 'fortune hunter', her bitter family called him). The refugees would have been introduced as well to Mrs Inglethorp's two stepsons from an earlier marriage, John Cavendish, who played at being a country squire, and Lawrence, who published 'rotten verses in fancy bindings'. And they would have met Mary, John Cavendish's stormy-eyed wife, and plucky Cynthia Murdoch, another of Mrs Inglethorp's protégées.

'You've been entertaining a celebrity unawares,' Hastings was to tell them later, and it is interesting to imagine Poirot observing this promising group as he politely sipped a cup of the dreaded English tea. Perhaps, for the first time since coming to England, a gleam of professional interest appeared in those inquiring green eyes?

Notes

1 For reasons not explained, some researchers and obituaries have taken a mention in *The Mysterious Affair at Styles* that Poirot and Inspector Japp of Scotland Yard first met in Brussels in 1904, while working on the Abercrombie Forgery Case, as the year of Poirot's retirement and have concluded that he was born between 1839 and 1844. Assumptions have then been made that he worked as a private detective in Belgium or France between 1904 and 1914.

Adding to the confusion, a charming but suspect foreword to *Hercule Poirot: Master Detective*, an omnibus collection published in 1936, has Poirot stating: 'I began work as a member of the detective force in Brussels on the Abercrombie Forgery Case in 1904.' As we know Poirot joined the Belgian police force as a young man, this red herring would have us believe he was born about 1884 and arrived in England at about the age of thirty-two.

2 His family name was to cause difficulties later on. Pwarrit, Porritt, Peerer, Porrott and Prott were some of the ways the English attempted to pronounce it. On three different occasions, in the interests of subterfuge, Poirot himself garbled his name and gave it as Poirier, Pontarlier and Parotti.

3 First published as 'The Clue of the Chocolate Box' in *The Sketch*, 23 May 1923.

4 Some prefer to believe that a triple bluff was played in *The Big Four* and that Achille really did exist, despite Poirot's assurances that 'Brother Achille has gone home again – to the land of myths.'

5 This quotation is from 'Christmas Adventure', the first version of 'The Adventure of the Christmas Pudding'.

6 In one of his last cases, *Hallowe'en Party*, Poirot expressed a slight change of mind: 'There were times when he almost regretted that he had not taken to the study of theology,

instead of going into the police force in his early days. The number of angels who could dance on the point of a needle; it would be interesting to feel that that mattered and to argue passionately on the point with one's colleagues.'

7 Also published under the titles 'The Clue of the Chocolate Box' and 'The Time Hercule Poirot Failed'. There is some confusion as to when this case actually occurred. In *Cards on the Table*, set in 1937, Poirot spoke of it as having happened 'twenty-eight years ago', which places it in 1909, but in *Peril at End House* he referred to it as 'a bad failure in Belgium in 1893'.

2

The English Debut

'He stepped forward, beaming'.

—'The Affair at the Victory Ball'

Towards five o'clock on the afternoon of 17 July 1916, an incongruous figure advanced steadily upon the post office of the village of Styles St Mary:

> . . . an extraordinary looking little man. He was hardly more than five feet, four inches, but carried himself with great dignity. His head was exactly the shape of an egg . . . His moustache was very stiff and military. The neatness of his attire was almost incredible.

It was Poirot, limping gallantly and no doubt bored to tears. On that fateful afternoon, however, deliverance from *ennui* was at hand, for out of the post office, and straight into Poirot, there catapulted a large boyish man. As Hastings was later to write:

> I drew aside and apologized, when suddenly, with a loud exclamation, he clasped me in his arms and kissed me warmly. '*Mon ami* Hastings!' he cried. 'It is indeed *mon ami* Hastings!'

The surprise and excitement of Captain Arthur Hastings at this chance meeting equalled Poirot's. Had he not, just a few days before, described this very gnome to Mary Cavendish?

> 'I came across a man in Belgium once, a very famous detective, and he quite inflamed me. He was a marvellous little fellow. He used to say that all good detective work was a mere matter of method . . . He was a funny little man, a great dandy, but wonderfully clever.'

After further exclamations and explanations, and after promising to visit Poirot at the refugees' cottage, Hastings returned to Styles, where he had recently arrived to stay with the Cavendishes during the last of his convalescence from a war injury. But what a momentous encounter occurred on that warm sleepy day! No doubt the post office of Styles St Mary now bears a plaque commemorating the genesis of Poirot's English career? For early the next morning the household at Styles was awakened by agonized sounds coming from Mrs Inglethorp's bedroom. Someone had poisoned her with strychnine.

'I am going to ask you something,' said Hastings to his old friend, John Cavendish, within an hour of his stepmother's death. 'You remember my speaking of my friend Poirot? The Belgian who is here? He has been a most famous detective . . . I want you to let me call him in – to investigate this matter.' So began an illustrious association that was to span almost sixty years, and so began that celebrated landmark of detective fiction, *The Mysterious Affair at Styles.*

Styles!

'We will proceed to the château,' said Poirot, when summoned, 'and study matters on the spot.' How many millions have since gazed upon the historic plan of the eleven bedrooms and the one bathroom of Styles Court drawn by Arthur Hastings in 1916?[1]

It was a household at war. Petrol was rationed. Supper was at half-past seven ('We have given up late dinner for some time now'). Every scrap of paper was saved and sent away in sacks. Only three gardeners were left (one of them 'a new-fashioned woman gardener in breeches and such-like'). John Cavendish helped with the farms and drilled with the volunteers. Mary Cavendish was up and dressed in her white land smock every morning at five. Cynthia Murdoch worked in the dispensary of the nearby Red Cross Hospital. The formidable Mrs Inglethorp continually presided at patriotic events. A German spy (soon to be unmasked) dropped by from time to time. And, nearby, Leastways Cottage sheltered seven refugees, 'them Belgies'.

'WEALTHY LADY POISONED', trumpeted the newspapers, and Styles was under siege. At the inquest held a few days later at the Stylites Arms, Poirot recognized an old colleague and nudged Hastings. 'Do you know who

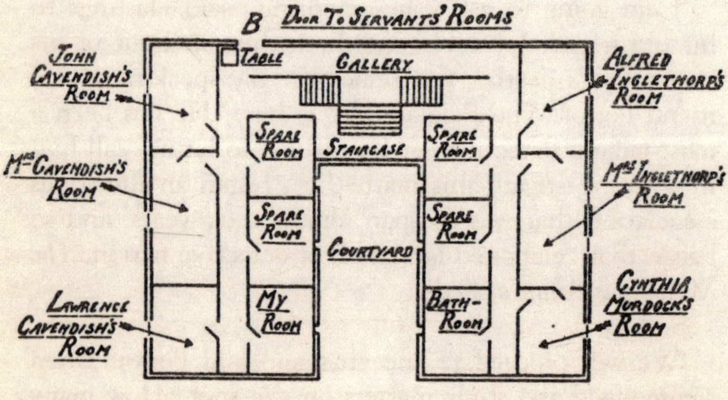

that little man is?' he asked, indicating someone 'sharp, dark, ferret-faced' near the door. Hastings shook his head. 'That is Inspector James Japp of Scotland Yard,' replied Poirot. 'Jimmy Japp.'

Thus, in *The Mysterious Affair at Styles*, published in 1920, are to be found the archetypal ingredients of many a future adventure – a wilful murder committed amid pleasant surroundings, and a solution at length achieved by a small foreign man with an egg-shaped head. Helping and hindering will be the bluff and energetic Inspector James Japp of Scotland Yard and, faithfully recording it all for posterity, the devoted Arthur Hastings, ever bewildered, ever admiring. It was to prove a great run. 'Ah!' Hastings was to write many, many years later, 'if this could have been that day in 1916 when I first travelled to Styles . . .'

The Styles mystery and the subsequent murder trial at the Old Bailey occupied everyone concerned for several months. Wrote Hastings:

> September found us all in London. Mary took a house in Kensington, Poirot being included in the family party.
>
> I myself had been given a job at the War Office, so was able to see them continually.

It was probably while staying with the Cavendishes that Poirot, no longer limping, began looking for a more permanent home. A later story, 'The Lemesurier Inheritance', indicates that at about this time Poirot was asked to undertake a small matter for the War Office. Perhaps he took this as a sign? Why return to the rural obscurity of Styles St Mary? As he later told Mr Satterthwaite, the Styles Affair had given him fresh confidence:

'I found that I was not yet finished. No, indeed, my powers were stronger than ever. Then began my second career – that of a private inquiry agent in England.'

Poirot's new enterprise was no doubt launched by the ordering of appropriate business cards and a search for suitable quarters. And, for guidance through the thickets of English customs and manners, who could be better than Arthur Hastings, now invalided out of the army and assigned a London job at recruiting? Firmly bonded to Poirot by the Styles Affair, and still hoping to become a detective himself, Hastings stuck to Poirot like glue.

In time Poirot would become the most fashionable detective in London and would live in considerable style, but at the outset he took modest rooms, often shared by Hastings, and endured certain privations:

> Poirot had just finished carefully straightening the cups and saucers which our landlady was in the habit of throwing, rather than placing, on the table. He had also breathed heavily on the metal teapot, and polished it with a silk handkerchief.

In these surroundings Poirot commenced his practice as a private detective, and Hastings began to look forward to each evening's account of the cases on hand. Several bread-and-butter years passed pleasantly enough and then, at last, Poirot received a commission of major consequence. As Hastings described it, he had just settled down one evening to listen to developments in the current investigation, a charlady's missing husband ('A difficult affair, needing the tact'), when:

... the landlady thrust her head round the door and informed him there were two gentlemen below who wanted to see him.

'They won't give their names, Sir, but they say as it's very important.'

'Let them mount,' said Poirot ...

In a few minutes the two visitors were ushered in, and my heart gave a leap as in the foremost I recognized no less a personage than Lord Estair, Leader of the House of Commons; whilst his companion, Mr Bernard Dodge, was also a member of the War Cabinet, and, as I knew, a close personal friend of the Prime Minister.

Clients worthy of Poirot's mettle at last! And what a case they brought to his sitting-room – the disappearance of the Prime Minister on the eve of the approaching Allied Conference at Versailles. Said a grave Lord Estair:

'We sought you out on the express recommendation and wish of a very great man of your own country.'

'*Comment*? My old friend the *Préfet* – ?'

Lord Estair shook his head.

'One higher than the *Préfet*. One whose word was once law in Belgium – and shall be again! That England has sworn!'

Poirot's hand flew swiftly to a dramatic salute.

'Amen to that!'

In the melodramatic episode that followed, 'The Kidnapped Prime Minister', which, one wonders, was sweeter for Poirot – foiling a desperate set of German agents, or succeeding where the French police and Detective Inspector Japp had failed? Wrote Hastings of this affair, his eye already on posterity:

'I feel it is only just that England should know the debt it owes to my quaint little friend, whose marvellous brain so ably averted a great catastrophe.'

Whether the charlady's husband was ever found is not recorded.

Soon after this *coup* there occurred a case that Hastings grandly and prematurely called 'the ultimate problem brought to Poirot to solve'. This harked back to 1916 when Hastings had renewed his acquaintance with Captain Vincent Lemesurier, a fellow officer from an old Northumberland family. Remembering her husband's account of his introduction to Poirot two years before, Mrs Lemesurier, a troubled and determined mother, sought his assistance in exorcizing the family's medieval curse. Were all first-born Lemesurier sons doomed to die before inheriting the estate? In the short story, 'The Lemesurier Inheritance', Poirot, at work like 'an intelligent terrier', proved that they need not.

In the spring of 1919, as England celebrated the end of the Great War, young Viscount Cronshaw was stabbed to death at a grand victory ball. 'Every twopenny-halfpenny hop calls itself that nowadays, but this was the real thing, held at the Colossus Hall, and all London at it,' reported Japp, dropping by Poirot's rooms to invite him to lend a hand in tracking the Viscount's murderer – or, as Hastings observed, 'seeking favours under the guise of conferring them!' Poirot had 'a good opinion of Japp's abilities, though deploring his lamentable lack of method' and, probably realizing how much Japp must have smarted over the case of the kidnapped prime minister, he consented to join in the hunt. In 'The Affair at the Victory Ball' he cracked open a sensational cocaine case involving such Bright Young Things as Miss Coco Courtenay and the Honourable Eustace Beltane. '*Une belle affaire*!' Poirot later pronounced it, celebrating at a '*recherché* little supper'.

With these four cases – the unmasking of a country house murderer, the rescue of a prime minister, the laying of a family ghost, and the solving of a Mayfair stabbing – Poirot's credentials as a private detective of brilliance and discretion were assured. Furthermore, he had found a new home and a new purpose. For the next half century his energies would be almost entirely devoted to the remarkable crimes of the bloodthirsty English.

Notes

1 Even though Hastings was rapidly falling in love with Cynthia Murdoch, he misspelled her name on the plan.

3

The 1920s

'This street, it is not aristocratic, *mon ami*! In it there is no fashionable doctor, no fashionable dentist – still less is there a fashionable milliner! But there *is* a fashionable detective. *Oui*, my friend, it is true – I am become the mode, the *dernier cri!*'

—Hercule Poirot,
'The Adventure of "The Western Star"'

The Great War over, the 1920s were years of economic and social upheaval and an uncertain but flourishing time for the middle and upper classes of England. Poirot, devoting himself to their expensive and interesting crimes, flourished along with them. His moustache, his famous hallmark, reflected it all. Described in the earlier years as 'stiff' and 'military', it waxed luxurious as the decade progressed.

At some time in the early 1920s Poirot and Hastings – who had acquired a position as 'a sort of private secretary . . . to an M.P.' – became the tenants of a nicer landlady, Mrs Pearson of 14 Farraway Street, and to their sitting-room came a seemingly endless stream of troubled clients. There were housewives, for example ('Private – that's what I want. I don't want any talk or fuss, or things in the papers'). There was Royalty ('He was a strange-looking youth, tall, eager, with a weak chin, the famous Mauranberg mouth, and the dark fiery eyes of the fanatic'). There were film stars ('Lord Cronshaw was telling me last night how wonderfully you cleared up the mystery of his nephew's death'). There were ladies in distress ('From the costly simplicity of her attire, I deducted at once that she belonged to the upper strata of society'). There were men on the run ('Poirot hurried to his side . . . "Brandy – quickly"'). To Hastings's delight, there was hardly a dull moment.

And if clients couldn't, or wouldn't, come to Poirot, he would go to them, usually accompanied by Hastings, seemingly unconstrained by his job – to the superb Park Lane house of an American magnate, for example ('Poirot picked up a pin from the carpet, and frowned at it severely'); to a country house drawing-room at the moment of a midnight robbery ('The women were in becoming négligées'); to old-fashioned gardens where 'the smell of stocks and mignonette came sweetly wafted on the evening breeze'; to an opium den in Limehouse ('Then there came to us the proprietor, a Chinaman with a face of evil smiles'); to luncheons of steak and kidney pudding at the Cheshire Cheese; to clandestine laboratories ('I believe that she has, to a certain extent, succeeded in liberating atomic energy and harnessing it to her purpose'); to villas in the suburbs ('The place was somewhat overloaded with gimcrack ornaments, and a good many family portraits of surpassing ugliness adorned the walls').

Most of the accounts of Poirot's adventures in the early 1920s are preserved in the writings of his devoted colleague and scribe, Arthur Hastings, whose usual mode was the short story. Taken collectively, these recall exhilarating days.[1]

'The Disappearance of Mr Davenheim'[2] opens with Inspector Japp, by now something of a constant in Poirot's life, dropping by for tea. For Poirot and Hastings it was still the days of the untidy landlady and the metal teapot, but these trials were soon forgotten with Japp's news of the disappearance of a famous financier. After a lively discussion on rival methods, Poirot wagered Japp five pounds that, without leaving his chair and given the same information as Scotland Yard, he could retrieve Mr Davenheim within a week.

Five days later, with their inevitable winnings, Poirot and Hastings fled their landlady and took Japp out to dinner. But had he learned his lesson? The next case, the murder of a millionaire's daughter in 'The Plymouth Express',[3] was later used by Poirot in a tutorial session with Hastings:

> 'Remember the Plymouth Express mystery. The great Japp departed to make a survey of the railway line. When he returned, I, without having moved from my apartments, was able to tell him exactly what he had found.'

Poirot was probably apt to cite 'The Adventure of the Cheap Flat', which turned into a case of international proportions, as another salutary lesson: never neglect the trivial. How, for example, in overcrowded post-war London, had the young Robinsons managed to rent a handsome Knightsbridge flat for only eighty pounds a year? When put to Poirot by Hastings as a mock challenge, the little detective figuratively sniffed the air:

> 'It is as well, *mon ami*, that we have no affairs of moment on hand. We can devote ourselves wholly to the present investigation.'
>
> 'What investigation are you talking about?'
>
> 'The remarkable cheapness of your friend, Mrs Robinson's, new flat.'

Another exciting spy story in those 'difficult days of reconstruction' is told in 'The Submarine Plans'.[4] In this case Poirot was summoned by the Minister of Defence on a matter of national emergency, the disappearance of the new Z type submarine plans. 'I remember only too well what you did for us during the war, when the Prime Minister was kidnapped,' said the shaken Minister to Poirot. 'Your masterly deductions – and may I add your discretion – saved the situation.' In Hastings's opinion, Poirot treated this matter of the Z type submarines far too lightly, but 'One thing is quite certain,' he recorded with satisfaction. 'On the day when Lord Alloway became Prime Minister, a cheque and a signed photograph arrived.'

It must be admitted that momentous cases such as this tended to go to Poirot's head. 'You have a client,' announced Hastings in 'The Adventure of the Clapham Cook'.[5] 'Unless the affair is one of national importance, I touch it not,' declared Poirot. He reconsidered, however, when faced with an intimidating Mrs Todd, whose prized cook had disappeared. 'It's all this wicked dole,' said Mrs Todd. 'Putting ideas into servants' heads, wanting to be typists and what nots.' A chastened Poirot decided that Mrs Todd's cook *was* a matter of national importance, after all, though privately he cautioned Hastings: 'Never, *never*, must our friend Inspector Japp get to hear of this!'

Hard on the heels of Mrs Todd came Mrs Pengelley of Polgarwith to confide to Poirot her suspicions that she was being gradually poisoned by her husband.

> 'I don't intend to let him have it all his own way. Women aren't the downtrodden slaves they were in the old days, M. Poirot.'
>
> 'I congratulate you on your independent spirit, Madame

. . . I have nothing of great moment on hand. I can devote myself to your little affair.'

But in 'The Cornish Mystery' this 'little affair' soon got out of hand. On the very next day Poirot found himself investigating Mrs Pengelley's death. It was a sad experience for this kind and protective man. 'May the good God forgive me, but I never believed anything would happen at all,' he cried to Hastings.

'The Cornish Mystery' is a good example of Poirot afield. He and Hastings were forever snatching up timetables to find the best trains and reconnoitring country inns ('a night of horror upon one of your English provincial beds, *mon ami*'). In 'The Tragedy at Marsdon Manor' Poirot was commissioned by an insurance company to investigate a misadventure in Essex. Was Mr Maltravers's sudden death while shooting rooks entirely due to natural causes?

In 'The Mystery of Hunter's Lodge' Hastings, attempting an investigation on his own, accompanied a distraught Hon. Roger Havering to a remote shooting-box on the Derbyshire moors in response to a telegram from his wife:

'Come at once uncle Harrington murdered last night bring good detective if you can but do come – Zoe.'

Left behind in London in the grip of 'flu, Poirot kept relentlessly in touch:

'. . . wire me description of housekeeper and what clothes she wore this morning same of Mrs Havering do not waste time taking photographs of interiors they are underexposed and not in the least artistic.'

And so on.

A village inn could be a trial, but nothing, in Poirot's opinion, could equal the sufferings of a voyage at sea. Just such a martyrdom is described in 'The Adventure of the Egyptian Tomb', in which members of an archaeological team had met mysterious deaths within a month of uncovering the tomb of the shadowy King Men-her-Ra. In the aftermath of these tragedies, Poirot was commissioned by Lady Willard, widow of the expedition's leader, to travel to Egypt to investigate.

Could the curse of Men-her-Ra have been at work? 'You must not underrate the force of superstition,' said Poirot to Hastings, 'But oh . . . the sea! The hateful sea!' The agony of a few days' voyage from Marseilles to Alexandria, with a camel ride at the end of it, called forth 'shrieks, gesticulations and invocations to the Virgin Mary and every Saint in the calendar.'

Despite these anxieties about travel, Hastings persuaded Poirot to go on holiday from time to time, but these expeditions seldom provided an escape from crime. A relaxing weekend at a comfortable hotel in Brighton, for example, turned into an energetic hunt for a glamorous pearl necklace ('The Jewel Robbery at the Grand Metropolitan'[6]); a week's holiday in Devon became a search for a collection of stolen miniatures ('Double Sin'[7]); and a quiet weekend arranged by a surprisingly solicitous Inspector Japp at a delightful country inn ('Nobody knows us, and we know nobody . . . That's the idea') saw Sunday breakfast abandoned at the stirring summons of the local constable: 'Gentleman up at Leigh Hall – shot himself – through the head' ('The Market Basing Mystery').

By now Poirot was much in vogue, his discreet services increasingly in demand by the aristocracy (particularly members of tottering European dynasties), by London high society, and by imitators and hangers-on in the *demimonde*. Adventures in these elegant, sometimes dangerous worlds were of great satisfaction to a detective invincibly bourgeois. Of course the companionship of Hastings, admiringly agog and breathing heavily, added pleasure to the chase.

In 'The King of Clubs',[8] a particularly complex case, Poirot was retained by Prince Paul of Maurania who trembled to know the truth: could the recent murder of a notorious blackmailer have possibly been committed by the Prince's fiancée, the dancer Valerie Saintclair? Surprisingly, this commission led Poirot and Hastings to a suburban drawing-room to interview a solid English family, the Oglanders, about certain events that had occurred on the night of the murder.

'I think that Miss Oglander made a mistake in going one no trump. She should have gone three spades,' murmured Poirot to an exasperated Hastings, who was expecting more impressive sleights of hand. In future cases, to remind Hastings of the importance of trivia, Poirot was apt to admonish: 'Remember the case of the dancer, Valerie Saintclair.'

Poirot was, of course, *always* lecturing Hastings. 'We all have the little grey cells. And so few of us know how to use them,' he exclaimed in 'The Adventure of the Italian Nobleman', patiently taking his Watson step by step through the maze that would eventually explain the bashing in of Count Foscatini's head.

In 'The Double Clue',[9] an important case in Poirot's personal life, his client was Mr Marcus Hardman, a mildly rich collector ('Old lace, old fans, antique jewellery – nothing crude or modern for Marcus Hardman'). In great distress, he sought out Poirot. Which of his beloved guests, Mr Hardman beseeched Poirot to discover, had stolen a collection of medieval jewels at yesterday's little tea party? Very soothingly, and with great tact, Poirot arranged the jewels' return. In doing so he lost his heart to the dashing and daring Countess Rossakoff, a Russian *émigrée* of the old regime. 'A remarkable woman,' sighed Poirot to Hastings. 'I have a feeling, my friend – a very decided feeling – I shall meet her again.'

'A pleasing little problem, obscure and charming' was, in Poirot's opinion, 'The Adventure of Johnnie Waverly',[10] a case which saw a happy ending to the kidnapping of a three-year-old son and heir. But shortly thereafter Hastings failed to share Poirot's satisfaction in another undertaking, 'The Case of the Missing Will', which brought to their sitting-room a 'so-called New Woman', a species the hopelessly sexist Hastings viewed with great suspicion. Miss Violet Marsh was a young scientist and the heir to the estate of her recently deceased uncle, a man unalterably opposed to the higher education of women. Challenged from beyond the grave to find her hidden inheritance within a year, Miss Marsh cleverly hired Poirot to find it for her. Hastings thought this all rather unfair.

> 'But no, Hastings. It is *your* wits that go astray. Miss Marsh proved the astuteness of her wits and the value of the higher education for women by at once putting the matter in *my* hands. Always employ the expert. She has amply proved her right to the money.'

We next find Hastings brooding over his chronic overdraft at the bank, and toying with the dubious charm of The Porcupine Oilfields whose prospectus predicted dividends of 100%. This prompted the prudent Poirot to recall a cautionary tale of an expensive fleecing, 'The Lost Mine'. As if to reinforce this lesson, they were both soon involved in solving a scandal that rocked the London and Scottish Bank, 'The Million Dollar Bond Robbery'.[11]

Towards the end of this hectic period there came an unexpected lull, a dearth of interesting cases. To cheer Poirot up, Hastings resorted to Watson's methods and read aloud from the morning paper:

> 'Here's an Englishman mysteriously done to death in Holland . . .'
>
> 'They always say that – and later they find that he ate the tinned fish and that his death is perfectly natural.'
>
> 'Well, if you're determined to grouse!'

At that moment a beautiful young lady, heavily veiled, was ushered in. She was, she explained, 'in a soft musical voice', being shamefully blackmailed by a brute.

'The dirty swine!' cried Hastings.

'Have faith in Papa Poirot, said Poirot reassuringly, and within a day, using tactics that shook Hastings, he had the problem of 'The Veiled Lady'[12] solved.

In 'The Adventure of the "Western Star"' two very different ladies coincidentally consulted Poirot on the same delicate matter – Mary Marvell, the well-known film star, referred by a friend from 'The Affair at the Victory Ball', and Lady Yardly, of an impoverished old country family, sent by Mary Cavendish of *The Mysterious Affair at Styles*. There followed an energetic tale of feudal estates, sinister Chinamen, and legendary temple diamonds.

Murder on the Links, published in 1923, was the second full-length book devoted to Poirot. Its title tends to conjure up summer days somewhere in the British Isles but, set in a fashionable villa in northern France, it is one of Poirot's Continental mysteries and very dramatic it is.

Early in this adventure we find Poirot and Hastings at breakfast. Once again Poirot was in a fret:

> 'The cases I have been employed upon lately were *banal* to the last degree. In verity I am reduced to recovering lost lap-dogs for fashionable ladies! The last problem that presented any interest was that intricate affair of the Yardly diamond, and that was – how many months ago, my friend?'
>
> He shook his head despondently.
>
> 'Cheer up, Poirot, the luck will change. Open your letters. For all you know, there may be a great case looming on the horizon.'

For once Hastings was correct. In the morning post came a letter from France from Paul Renauld, a well-known South American millionaire. 'For God's sake, come!' it pleaded. 'I go in daily fear of my life . . . I will send a car to meet you at Calais . . . I shall be content for you to name your own fee . . .' and so on.

'The Continental express leaves Victoria at 11 o'clock,' cried Poirot, and by the afternoon they were face to face with an imposing *sergent de ville* at the gate of the Villa Geneviève.

'M. Renauld was murdered this morning,' announced *le sergent*.

'I have a feeling,' said Poirot, 'that this is going to be a big affair – a long, troublesome problem that will not be easy to work out.' Adding zest to the case was the war instantly declared between M. Poirot and M. Giraud of the Paris *Sûreté*.

'I know you by name, M. Poirot,' said Giraud, 'you cut quite a figure in the old days, didn't you? But methods are very different now.'

'The human foxhound!' Poirot called Giraud, who spent most of his time crawling on hands and knees in search of significant footprints, cigarette stubs and unlighted matches, tactics that Poirot professed to deplore. For his part Giraud referred to Poirot as the 'old fossil'.

So heated did the rivalry at the villa Geneviève become that Poirot wagered Giraud 500 francs he would find the murderer first. 'I have no wish to take your money from you,' sneered Giraud. The end of the affair saw Giraud back in Paris with 'a *crise* of the nerves', and Poirot back in London with a splendid model of a foxhound costing 500 francs and no doubt exhibited to Inspector Japp of Scotland Yard at the first possible moment.

Murder on the Links did more than dispel Poirot's immediate boredom – it changed his life profoundly, for it was during this adventure that Hastings fell in love with a most unlikely person, Dulcie Duveen.

Now Hastings was forever falling in love, but until he met Dulcie he had always fallen in love with young women from very proper backgrounds. As he himself wrote:

> I am old-fashioned. A woman, I consider, should be womanly. I have no patience with the modern neurotic girl who dances from morning to night, smokes like a chimney, and uses language which would make a Billingsgate fishwoman blush!

Who, then, could have imagined Arthur Hastings seriously proposing marriage to an impudent young woman with an explicit vocabulary who had earned her living since the age of six as a dancer and an acrobat? And who could have imagined the nimble-witted and passionate Dulcie (or Cinderella, as she liked to be called) deciding to marry Hastings? 'She looked over her shoulder. A dimple appeared in each cheek. She was like a lovely picture by Greuze,' wrote the smitten Hastings. 'I knew you weren't such a mutt as you looked,' declared Cinderella. While Giraud hunted footprints and matches, and Poirot reviewed his grey cells, Hastings and Cinderella were falling in love.

How did Poirot take all this? In principle, in the matter of marriages, he took a dim view of the way *les Anglais* conducted themselves: 'No method – absolutely none whatever. They leave all to chance!' And in the matter of marriage and Hastings in particular – up to now but a theoretical possibility – had he not said, 'Some day, if you permit, I will arrange you a marriage of great suitability'? And here was Hastings, his ever present student and friend, contemplating marriage to an acrobat and talking of emigration to the Argentine.

In justice it must be said that Poirot initially took all this very well. He generously put his friend's happiness before his own in reuniting the lovers at the dénouement of *Murder on the Links*, even though Hastings's declaration, 'in future I must take my own line', must have come as a shock. Perhaps Poirot did not believe him? Perhaps he expected this infatuation, like the others, would come to nothing?

But it did come to something, and in the latter part of 1923 there must have been a great packing of valises and trunks at 14 Farraway Street, and Mrs Pearson must have wrung her hands at the loss of such a good tenant, as Hastings departed for marriage and a ranch in the Argentine.

Before these unsettling events occurred, were there long discussions over *tisanes* and whiskies and sodas in the joint sitting-room? Or did Hastings leave quite suddenly? Whatever the circumstances, it was a decidedly forlorn

Poirot, mourning his friend who 'has gone away across the sea to the South America', whom the Endicott family invited to the country in the short story 'The Adventure of the Christmas Pudding'.[13]

'You are not like me, old and alone,' lamented Poirot at the Endicotts' Christmas, but he soon cheered up under the influence of crackling logs and snowmen, and honoured the occasion by donning a red waistcoat and treating the household to the capture of a pair of criminals about to make off with a famous jewel.

And what of Hastings? Fear not that he was forever lost to Poirot in 'the free and easy life of the South American continent', for on a morning a year and a half later we find him at the rail of a ship approaching the cliffs of Dover:

> I had landed in France two days before, transacted some necessary business, and was now *en route* for London. I should be there some months – time enough to look up old friends, and one old friend in particular. A little man with an egg-shaped head and green eyes – Hercule Poirot! I proposed to take him completely by surprise.

Poirot was indeed surprised as, in the interests of an enormous commission, he was busy packing for a dreaded sea voyage to Rio. Tearful embraces concluded, he explained to Hastings:

> 'And there was a second attraction – *you*, my friend. For this last year and a half I have been a very lonely old man. I thought to myself, why not? I am beginning to weary of this unending solving of foolish problems. I have achieved sufficient fame. Let me take this money and settle down somewhere near my old friend.'

How these two might have resolved all this we shall never know, as fate immediately intervened to plunge them into the all-consuming case of *The Big Four*.[14] To meet this challenge, Poirot unpacked his enormous trunk and Hastings moved his luggage to Farraway Street. It was just like old times.

An earlier case, 'The Veiled Lady', had found Hastings musing on Poirot's vanity:

> He always imagines that the whole world is thinking and talking of Hercule Poirot . . . but I could hardly believe that his existence struck terror into the criminal world.

The Big Four proved Hastings wrong. In it Poirot found himself the chief adversary of an international conspiracy of four master criminals out 'to destroy the existing social order'. This struggle became a duel to the death, an epic that saw such excitements as Poirot sacrificing his moustache to foil the enemy, Hastings sacrificing himself to save Poirot, the reappearance of the dashing Countess Rossakoff (Poirot's 'woman in a thousand'), and a premature funeral for Poirot at which he was mourned and buried. 'World-wide unrest, the labour troubles which beset every nation, and the revolutions that break out in some' loomed in the background.

While locked in combat with the Titans, Poirot 'abandoned his private practice almost entirely', and Hastings's 'business complications', his reason for coming to England, fell by the way. 'Little Cinderella as you call her, what does she say?' asked Poirot uneasily after six months of the campaign had passed with no end in sight. Replied Hastings: 'I haven't gone into details, of course, but she understands.'

In the end it took Poirot and Hastings the better part

of a year to save the world from anarchy. 'The great case of my life,' Poirot called it. 'Anything else will seem tame after this.'[15]

Hastings, sailing away to Buenos Aires, no doubt thought so too. And, in the wake of *The Big Four* and Hasting's second departure, Poirot made an extraordinary decision – he would leave Farraway Street, retire to the country, and devote the rest of his life to the scientific cultivation of vegetable marrows.

We now come to one of the strangest periods in Poirot's life – a year of seclusion in the quiet village of King's Abbot, a seclusion so complete as to drive the village Intelligence Corps, led by his neighbour, Miss Caroline Sheppard, close to despair. Who was he? Where had he come from? Why was he there? 'Someone very like Caroline must have invented the questions on passports,' observed Miss Sheppard's brother. 'The one thing we do know about him is that he is interested in the growing of vegetable marrows.'

Vegetable marrows? Poirot? Had he gone quite mad? Was he pining for Hastings? Or the audacious Countess Rossakoff? Or both? Was a year spent virtually alone in a neat walled garden and an overheated sitting-room in King's Abbot Poirot's tidy version of a nervous breakdown? It is true that he was now comfortably off, his reputation assured by the recent publication of Hastings's memoirs, but this period of self-imposed exile, with only the marrows and an ancient Breton housekeeper for company, was a curious episode indeed. Fortunately, one afternoon something snapped. In anger he threw his most impressive vegetable marrow over the garden wall (it landed with 'a repellent squelch') and re-entered the world. King's Abbot, on the very day that Roger Ackroyd was murdered, was at last permitted to know that in its midst dwelt the most eminent detective in Europe.

The Murder of Roger Ackroyd, published in 1926, is a Big House Mystery, and the man who by his own death inadvertently rescued Poirot from the marrows was a selfmade country squire, described by Dr James Sheppard, the narrator of this famous affair, as 'the life and soul of our peaceful village'. Roger Ackroyd stabbed to death in his comfortable study was a Big Case, not only for Poirot but also for the history of detective fiction. It invariably leaves its readers shaken, and it certainly shook King's Abbot.

Poirot's attempts at retirement now took a different form. The old housekeeper in the huge Breton hat was returned to her homeland and we hear no more of King's Abbot. Rustication behind him, Poirot embarked on a life on the Riviera:

> 'I take it, M. Poirot, that you no longer exercise your profession?'
>
> 'That is so, Monsieur. I enjoy the world.'

And so he did, and could be seen on many a fine day in Nice setting forth from his hotel in a white duck suit with a camellia in his buttonhole to lunch on *fillet de sole à la Jeanette*.

The Mystery of the Blue Train, published in 1928, demonstrates, however, that Poirot's retirement had not quite taken. The robbing and strangling of a beautiful heiress, Ruth Kettering, in a sleeping compartment of the Riviera-bound Blue Train, the request of her wealthy father that Poirot find her murderer, and the flattering gratitude of the French police at even a hint that the great detective might take an interest in the affair, soon had Poirot back in harness.

A major event in *The Mystery of the Blue Train*, and an indication of Poirot's new style, was his acquisition of an English valet, the wooden-faced George. From this time on Poirot no longer had to concern himself with the removal of grease spots and the brewing of hot chocolate, or depend for an audience on friends who might disappear to South America. For the rest of his long, long life he could depend on the faithful George.

> 'You have a wide experience, Georges,' murmured Poirot. 'I often wonder having lived so exclusively with titled families that you demean yourself by coming as a valet to me. I put it down to love of excitement on your part.'
>
> 'Not exactly, sir,' said George, 'I happened to see in *Society Snippets* that you had been received at Buckingham Palace. That was just when I was looking for a new situation. His Majesty, so it said, had been most gracious and friendly and thought very highly of your abilities.'[16]

Poirot's retirement to the Riviera was even briefer than his retirement to King's Abbot. By 1929 he was back in London, though tentatively at first, on a case requiring temporary accommodation and an assumed name.

'I take the flat in the name of Mr O'Connor,' he announced to a neighbour startled at encountering 'a little man with a very fierce moustache and an egg-shaped head', and added, unnecessarily, 'But I am not an Irishman.' As it happened, his neighbour and her friends had just had the bad luck to discover a body. Resplendent in a handsome dressing-gown and embroidered slippers, Poirot, in 'The Third Floor Flat',[17] had the mystery solved within a couple of hours.

In 'The Under Dog' Poirot was firmly back in business ('at this present time I have many cases of moment on hand') and settled in a flat with George in attendance. From there he was summoned to the country by a recent widow, Lady Astwell, who, against all evidence, was convinced that her husband had been murdered by his inoffensive secretary. To uncover the truth Poirot subjected a large household to a reign of terror:

> 'For two weeks now I have played the comedy, I have showed you the net closing slowly around you. The fingerprints, footprints, the search of your room with the things artistically replaced. I have struck terror into you with all of this; you have lain awake at night fearing and wondering; did you have a fingerprint in the room or a footprint somewhere?'

A strange little story is 'Wasps' Nest'[18] in which Poirot took as his mission the solution of a murder before it even occurred. The setting is charming:

> John Harrison loved his garden, and it had never looked better than it did on this August evening, summery and languorous. The rambler roses were still beautiful; sweet peas scented the air

Two months later the stock markets crashed around the world. We can be sure, however, that Poirot, that canny practitioner of Flemish thrift, continued to sip his *tisanes* with equanimity. By the end of the 1920s he was a very rich man and remained so for the rest of his life. 'I like not the sensational. For me the safe, the prudent investment . . . what you call the gilded edge.'

Notes

1 Later collected into books, sometimes with minor changes, many of these stories first appeared in magazines such as *The Sketch* (1923) and *Blue Book* (1923–25).

2 Also published under the title 'Mr Davenby Disappears'.

3 Also published under the title 'The Mystery of the Plymouth Express'.

4 A much expanded version of this story was published in 1937 under the title 'The Incredible Theft'.

5 Also published under the title 'The Mystery of the Clapham Cook'.

6 Also published under the title 'The Curious Disappearance of the Opalsen Pearls'.

7 Also published under the title 'By Road or Rail'.

8 Also published under the title 'The Adventure of the King of Clubs'.

9 Also published under the title 'The Dubious Clue'.

10 Also published under the title 'The Kidnapping of Johnnie Waverly'.

11 Also published under the title 'The Million Dollar Bank Robbery'.

12 Also published under the title 'The Case of the Veiled Lady'.

13 The history of this delectable story is complicated. The first version appeared in *The Sketch*, 12 December 1923, and made other appearances under the title 'Christmas Adventure'. In 1960 a much expanded and updated version, set in the 1950s, appeared under two titles: 'The Adventure of the Christmas Pudding' and 'The Theft of the Royal Ruby'.

14 Though first published as a book in 1927, *The Big Four* is a somewhat expanded collection of twelve stories which appeared serially in *The Sketch* in 1924.

15 In 1929, in *Partners in Crime*, Tommy and Tuppence Beresford, actors in another corner of the Christie arena,

parodied the exploits of Poirot and Hastings in *The Big Four* in their adventure 'The Man Who was No. 16'.

16 Presumably in defending the existing social order against the Big Four. It was probably at this time, for his share in the victory, that Hastings received an OBE. We are never told what Poirot thought of *that*.

17 Also published under the title 'In the Third Floor Flat'.

18 Also published under the title 'The Worst of All'.

4

The 1930s

'Monsieur Poirot here,' said Japp. 'Quite a good advertisement for a hair tonic, he'd be. Face fungus sprouting finer than ever. Coming out into the limelight, too, in his old age. Mixed up in all the celebrated cases of the day. Train mysteries, air mysteries, high society deaths – oh, he's here, there and everywhere.'

—The ABC Murders

For many the 1930s were disturbing years. Even among Poirot's clients it was understood that most people were not as well off as before. Complained Elinor Carlisle in *Sad Cypress*: 'Everything costs so much – clothes and one's face – and just silly things like movies and cocktails – and even gramophone records!' Some people actually became *poor*. 'Darling,' confided the Hon. Joanna South-wood in *Death on the Nile*,

> 'if any misfortunes happen to my friends I always drop them at once! It sounds heartless, but it saves such a lot of trouble later! They always want to borrow money off you, or else they start a dressmaking business and you have to get the most terrible clothes from them. Or they paint lampshades, or do Batik scarves.'

In Poirot's world the uncertain political times – the 'question' of India, the 'troubles' in China, agitation against the Establishment, 'Bolshies, Reds, all that sort of thing' – were spoken of over cocktails and at tea. Towards the end of the decade a Europe under the shadow of war brought talk of armaments, the race for Supremacy in the Air, Hitler and Mussolini, the Spanish Civil War, 'days of crisis'.

In Chelsea flats Poirot was apt to encounter chairs made of webbing and chromium, and in country drawing-rooms even elderly hostesses made concessions to 'modernity' by allowing guests to smoke. Egypt in winter was expensive, Majorca was cheap, and 'Paris doesn't cut any ice nowadays. It's London and New York that count,' cried Jane Wilkinson in *Lord Edgware Dies*. Bottles of mouthwash could turn out to hold liquor instead, and gold-topped perfume bottles might hide cocaine. People now flew regularly across the Channel, and in one of Poirot's cases air travel made possible the appearance of a surprise witness from New Zealand.

In the younger generation people of fads and crazes might aspire to be 'all S.A. and IT', and in the older – like the Misses Tripp in *Dumb Witness* – to be 'vegetarians, theosophists, British Israelites, Christian Scientists, spiritualists and enthusiastic amateur photographers'. Dinner parties might conclude with dancing to phonograph records, or with poker or bridge – in *Cards on the Table* Mrs Lorrimer declared: 'I simply will *not* go out to dinner now if there's no bridge afterwards!' – or with earnest conversations, as deplored in *One, Two, Buckle My Shoe*:

> 'Jane has changed a lot lately. Where does she get all these ideas?'
>
> 'Take no notice of what Jane says,' said Mrs Olivera.

'Jane's a very silly girl. You know what girls are – they go to these queer parties in studios where the young men have funny ties and they come home and talk a lot of nonsense.'

Fashion in clothes was a subject dear to Poirot's heart, and in the 1930s he often found reason to regard his immediate world with satisfaction. 'She really is a lovely girl,' said Hastings of Thora Grey in *The ABC Murders*. 'And wears very lovely clothes,' mused Poirot. 'That crêpe moracain and the silky fox collar – *dernier cri*!'. In *Murder on the Orient Express* he gazed with delight upon the Countess Andrenyi dressed in 'a tight-fitting little black coat and skirt, white satin blouse, small chic black toque perched at the fashionable outrageous angle'. To match, there were plenty of sleek-headed men in well tailored clothes, though most of Poirot's English circle tended to look askance at men (including Poirot) who paid too much attention to their appearance. 'He was too well dressed – he wore his hair too long – and he smelt of scent,' said Major Despard disparagingly of a murder victim in *Cards on the Table*.

The 1930s found Hercule Poirot at the height of his powers. For him it was to prove a decade of triumphs, *la crème de la crème*.

In *Black Coffee*,[1] a play first staged in 1930, Poirot rescued for England a formula for the disintegration of atoms. This coup, and the solution to the after-dinner death of a brilliant scientist, Sir Claud Amory, was but the work of a few hours with the assistance of Hastings – presumably back on another business trip – and an enthusiastic Inspector Japp.

On his own once more, Poirot travelled to Lytcham

Close, 'one of the most famous old houses in England', at the summons of the eccentric Hubert Lytcham Roche, a man of ungovernable temper and a fanatic for punctuality. As not infrequently occurred in Poirot's cases, his announced arrival was slightly preceded by his client's untimely death. For the first and last time, in 'The Second Gong',[2] Hubert Lytcham Roche was late for dinner.

Fourteen full-length books are devoted to Poirot's exploits in the 1930s, and the first two of these – *Peril at End House*, published in 1932, and *Lord Edgware Dies*,[3] published in 1933 – find Arthur Hastings at his side. As a sort of appetizer to these major cases, Hastings first enjoyed collaborating in a shorter one, 'The Mystery of the Baghdad Chest',[4] a macabre society murder which Poirot pronounced 'an artistic masterpiece!' On the perpetrator he bestowed the greatest of compliments:

> 'It goes to my heart to hang a man like that. I may be a genius myself, but I am capable of recognizing genius in other people. A perfect murder, *mon ami*. I, Hercule Poirot, say to you. A perfect murder.
>
> *Epatant!*'

Welcome as he was to Poirot, Hastings-watchers may find his frequent returns to England rather disconcerting. Wasn't all that sailing back and forth terribly expensive? Could the ranch afford it? Didn't Cinderella mind? One imagines her standing on the verandah gazing across the pampas, the *cicharra* singing, as Arthur and his steamer trunk depart once again for England. From scattered references one rather imagines her waving cheerfully. '*Tiens!*' as Poirot was apt to say about mysteries. '*C'est curieux, n'est-ce pas?*'

Presumably Hastings sent Cinderella several postcards from the Majestic Hotel in St Loo, the 'Queen of the Watering Places' on the Cornish coast, where he and Poirot spent an unexpectedly eventful holiday in *Peril at End House*. Once again Poirot was in one of his retirement fits. Flattering appeals for help from the Home Secretary left him unmoved ('I have retired! It is finished!'), but how could he resist intervening when only he could see that someone in St Loo was determined to murder a very independent young thing, Miss Nick Buckley?

Peril at End House was a slippery case. Unchaperoned young women partying and weekending and wearing watches filled with cocaine dumbfounded poor Hastings, but Poirot – who tended to be at his most avuncular at the seaside – took everything in his stride:

> 'My friend Hastings is shocked,' remarked Poirot. 'You must be more careful, Mademoiselle. He is out of date, you comprehend. He has just returned from those great clear open spaces, etc., and he has yet to learn the language of nowadays.'

Poirot, with Hastings in tow, was soon back in London and accepting commissions from wealthy clients. In *Lord Edgware Dies* some of these clients' requests were outside Poirot's usual *genre*. He reluctantly acceded to Lady Edgware's request that he ask her husband to give her a divorce ('Of course if we were only in Chicago,' she exclaimed, 'I could get him bumped off quite easily'), but drew the line at accepting an overlapping commission from Lady Edgware's next prospective mother-in-law, the Dowager Duchess of Merton, to stop Lady Edgware from marrying her son. The two men in question were a very rum lot in Hastings's opinion. Lord Edgware was secretive, sneering, and had most peculiar tastes in art and literature, while the Duke of Merton, 'A young man of monkish tendencies, a violent Anglo-Catholic . . . was supposed to care nothing for women.'

Poirot was preparing to cut and run on all this when the sensation of Lord Edgware's murder broke upon London. There he lay in his handsome library, stabbed in the back of the neck, a challenge for Inspector Japp of Scotland Yard. But could Poirot, whose mind should have been elsewhere – the strange disappearance of an ambassador's boots, for example – leave well enough alone? 'To say I have the head of a pig is not pretty,' Poirot exclaimed indignantly to Japp as he clambered aboard the case. Within a day or two of Poirot's inspired solving of the Edgware affair, Hastings was 'suddenly recalled to the Argentine' and Poirot resumed his distinguished life as a consultant on matters of the greatest importance. 'I belong to the world,' he declared loftily, and we find him next journeying in the Middle East after 'disentangling some military scandal in Syria'. On his way to Baghdad a diversionary case, '*a fantastic crime*', plucked him from his course.

The narrator of *Murder in Mesopotamia*[5] is Amy Leatheran, 'a woman of thirty-five of erect, confident bearing', temporarily employed as a nurse to Louise Leidner, the beautiful but overweight wife of the leader of the University of Pittstown's expedition to Iraq. In what Nurse Leatheran was to call 'the Tell Yarimjah business', her assignment placed her in the compound of an archaeological team, a tense group of people that Poirot was to label 'Mrs Leidner's entourage'.

Mrs Leidner's murder – predicted by herself – confounded the local authorities and brought Hercule Poirot jolting down the dusty track to Tell Yarimjah. Amy Leatheran described her first sight of him:

> I don't know what I'd imagined – something rather like Sherlock Holmes – long and lean with a keen, clever face. Of course, I knew he was a foreigner, but I hadn't expected him to be *quite* as foreign as he was, if you know what I mean.
>
> When you saw him you just wanted to laugh! He was like something on the stage or at the pictures. To begin with, he wasn't above five foot five, I should think – an odd plump little man, quite old, with an enormous moustache, and a head like an egg. He looked like a hairdresser in a comic play!
>
> And this was the man who was going to find out who killed Mrs Leidner!

Some years later Nurse Leatheran neatly settled her starched cuffs and wrote an excellent account of how Poirot solved the murder. As she neared her conclusion she observed laconically: 'M. Poirot went back to Syria and about a week later he went home on the Orient Express and got himself mixed up in another murder.'

At the outset of this next adventure we glimpse Poirot, 'of whom nothing was visible but a pink-tipped nose and the two points of an upward-curled moustache', in danger of freezing to death on a winter morning on the platform of a Syrian railway station. Just behind him lay The Syrian Army Case ('"You have saved us, *mon cher*," said the General emotionally . . . "You have saved the honour of the French Army"') and the *crime passionnel* of the Mesopotamian Murder Case. Just ahead a telegram awaited him in Stamboul recalling him to England on important business. And just beyond that, all unforeseen as he stamped his galoshes on the railway platform, lay an immobilization in snowdrifts aboard the most fabled train in detective literature.

Murder on the Orient Express[6], published in 1934, was a lovely romp for Poirot – no outside interferences, no police, no need to rush elsewhere, and all set amidst the most comfortable of surroundings with excellent food and absorbing witnesses at hand. In this agreeable milieu Poirot solved one of his most famous cases, the stabbing in the next compartment of a notorious criminal recently acquitted in the United States of the kidnapping and death of little Daisy Armstrong, the child of famous parents. How grateful was the *Compagnie Internationale des Wagons Lits* to Poirot for rescuing it from a potential embarrassment! And how grateful was Poirot for his snowbound diversion: 'I was reflecting . . . that many hours of boredom lay ahead whilst we are stuck here.'

Three Act Tragedy,[7] published in 1934, was a very sociable case. With an eye to the audience its cast busied itself with all sorts of camaraderie and hospitality (even Poirot rose to the occasion and gave a sherry party), while the nicotine which in turn dispatched three victims was neatly administered in an excellent martini, a glass of port, and a box of chocolates.

Tiens! Though pretending yet again to be semi-retired, how could Poirot resist rushing home from the Riviera when he heard all this? In this case, however, Poirot was at times gently upstaged by another small elderly man, Mr Satterthwaite:[8]

> A dried-up little pipkin of a man, Mr Satterthwaite, a patron of art and the drama, a determined but pleasant

snob, always included in the more important house parties and social functions – the words 'and Mr Satterthwaite' appeared invariably at the tail of a list of guests. Withal, a man of considerable intelligence and a very shrewd observer of people and things.

Poirot came to have a high regard for Mr Satterthwaite's acute observation of the social scene, but in the end, the murderer in *Three Act Tragedy* unmasked, he insisted on having the last word. Said Mr Satterthwaite:

'My goodness . . . I've only just realized it! That rascal, with his poisoned cocktail! Anyone might have drunk it! It might have been me!'

'There is an even more terrible possibility that you have not considered,' said Poirot.

'Eh?'

'It might have been *me*'.

'If anyone had told me a week ago,' said Inspector Japp, in September of 1934, 'that I should be investigating a crime where a woman was killed with a poisoned dart with snake venom on it – well, I'd have laughed in his face!' Poor Japp! He had come in all innocence to Croydon Aerodrome on the off-chance of catching a smuggler and had found himself confronted with the airliner 'Prometheus' just landed from Paris with the body of a French passenger murdered *en route*. Also on board, as a further annoyance, was an airsick Hercule Poirot who, although claiming to be the greatest detective in the world, had slept through the whole thing. 'Luckily,' said Japp, breathing heavily, 'it's one of those semiforeign cases.'

But who could the murderer be? wondered Japp, Poirot,

and M. Fournier of the French Sûreté as they pondered the list of passengers. Could it be the chatty English mystery writer, whose most recent whodunit, *The Clue of the Scarlet Petal,* hinged on poisoned darts? Could it be Japp's favourite suspects, two seedy-looking Frenchmen? ('What you say is possible, certainly,' murmured Poirot tactfully, 'but as regards some of your points, you are in error, my friend. Those two men are not toughs or cutthroats, as you suggest. They are, on the contrary, two distinguished and learned archaeologists.') Could it be – as initially decided by a xenophobic coroner's jury – Hercule Poirot? ('The coroner frowned. "Nonsense, I can't accept this verdict."') And so on. There was no doubt that a very clever murder had been committed in mid air. 'Our Irish stew' was one more of the things Japp called *Death in the Clouds,*[9] published in 1935. Poirot, once he had recovered from his airsickness, had a splendid time solving it.

A short story which first appeared in 1935 is 'How Does Your Garden Grow?', in which Miss Amelia Barrowby of Charman's Green in Buckinghamshire wrote to request a consultation with Poirot, on 'a very delicate family matter', just before succumbing to strychnine poisoning. Besides the mystery of Miss Barrowby's sad death, this story is memorable as landmark evidence of Poirot's mounting press of business, for in it we are introduced for the first time to a very formidable person, Miss Lemon, who rejoices for the rest of this saga in the title of Confidential Secretary to Hercule Poirot.[10] Like George the valet, Felicity Lemon fully met all her employer's fanatical specifications for neatness and order ('Her real passion in life was the perfection of a filing system beside which all other filing systems should sink into oblivion') and, like

George, while overlooked in the excitement of a number of cases, she served faithfully in the background for many more years.

Back from Argentina in June of 1935 came Arthur Hastings to find Poirot established in Whitehaven Mansions, 'an outstanding building of modern flats'. Taking stock, the two men immediately began talking about each other's hair. Inspector Japp, dropping by, had something to add. 'Just a little bit thin on top, eh?' he remarked tactlessly to Hastings, and Poirot made things even worse:

> 'You know, Hastings, there is a little device – my hairdresser is a man of great ingenuity – one attaches it to the scalp and brushes one's own hair over it – it is not a wig, you comprehend – but – '
>
> 'Poirot,' I roared. 'Once and for all I will have nothing to do with the beastly inventions of your confounded hairdresser'

and added, testily, that Japp – for whom Hastings had never had much affection – was 'getting as grey as a badger' and looking much older.

Poirot, of course, was secure with his hairdresser and a black bottle of REVIVIT.

But more important matters were soon at hand – the extraordinarily senseless serial murders recounted in *The ABC Murders*, published in 1936. Poirot had been hoping for just such a case to enliven Hastings's visit:

> 'As soon as I heard you were coming over I said to myself: Something will arise. As in former days we will hunt together, we two. But if so it must be no common

> affair. It must be something' – he waved his hands excitedly – 'something *recherché* – delicate – *fine* . . .' He gave the last untranslatable word its full flavour.
>
> 'Upon my word, Poirot,' I said. 'Any one would think you were ordering a dinner at the Ritz.'

The puzzle of the ABC killings, in which the date and whereabouts of each murder was ghoulishly announced to Poirot before it was committed, made for an exciting summer. For Poirot it was an interesting departure from his usual type of case, the *crime intime*: 'Here, for the first time in our association, it is cold-blooded, impersonal murder. Murder from the *outside*.' For Hastings it was, no doubt, a welcome change from worrying about the ranch. What a splendid return! What a 'cream of crime'! Who cared, after all, if one was going a trifle bald?

The ABC murderer was caught in November, just one month short of Hastings's return to Argentina, and in June of the following year we find him back again enjoying 'the roar of London' from Poirot's sitting-room window and making notes for the narration of a new case:

> But though Miss Arundell's death surprised no one, something else did. The provisions of her will gave rise to varying emotions, astonishment, pleasurable excitement, deep condemnation, fury, despair, anger and general gossip. For weeks and even months Market Basing was to talk of nothing else!

Thus began *Dumb Witness*,[11] published in 1937, in which Poirot, to Hastings's horror, told many lies to find the killer of Miss Emily Arundell, an upright and shrewd Victorian, whose death would never have been investigated had she not, in a fatally delayed letter, asked Poirot to undertake unspecified investigations on her behalf.[12]

In Market Basing, Hastings was very drawn to the late Miss Arundell's household. Of her drawing-room he wrote:

> A faint fragrance of pot-pourri hung about it. The chintzes were worn, their pattern faded garlands of roses. On the walls were prints and water-colour drawings. There was a good deal of china – fragile shepherds and shepherdesses. There were cushions worked in crewel stitch. There were faded photographs in handsome silver frames. There were many inlaid workboxes and tea caddies. Most fascinating of all to me were two exquisitely cut tissue-paper ladies under glass stands. One with a spinning-wheel, one with a cat on her knee.

He was also very taken with her amiable wire-haired terrier, Bob. In the end the orphaned dog was given to Poirot but Hastings quickly claimed him as a spoil of war. 'My word, Poirot, it's good to have a dog again,' he said, and off he went, back to Argentina. This time, for whatever reasons and however homesick, Hastings did not return to England for many years.

It was probably in this same year that the three cases recorded in the short stories 'Problem at Sea', 'Triangle at Rhodes', and 'Murder in the Mews' occurred.[13]. In all three of these, as so often happened to Poirot, his presence at or near scenes of murder was a direct result of futile attempts to take restful holidays or lead a calm social life.

In 'Problem at Sea'[14] his determination to escape was clearly a case of masochism:

> 'Are you enjoying this trip, M. Poirot?'
>
> 'Frankly, no. It was an imbecility to allow myself to be persuaded to come. I detest *la mer*. Never does it remain tranquil – no, not for a little minute.'

Before long, however, Poirot was enjoying himself very much as he graphically explained to a captive audience in the main lounge just how it was that disagreeable Mrs Clapperton came to be murdered in her locked cabin while the ship was docked in Alexandria.[15]

Surely, though, in 'Triangle at Rhodes', one could expect a little peace in the kind October sun? But even here, uneasily surveying the emotions surging just below the surface at his quiet hotel, 'M. Poirot perceived the inevitable shaping of events to come' – the duty to solve, while on holiday, a *crime passionnel*.

And could any meal with Inspector Japp – like one on a Guy Fawkes night for example – *not* lead to a murder investigation?

> Turning off the main road, the two men passed into the comparative quiet of a mews. They had been dining together and were now taking a short cut to Hercule Poirot's flat.
>
> As they walked along the sound of squibs was still heard periodically. An occasional shower of golden rain illuminated the sky.
>
> 'Good night for a murder,' remarked Japp with professional interest. 'Nobody would hear a shot, for instance, on a night like this.'

How true! Nor was Japp alone in such thoughts, as subsequent events in 'Murder in the Mews' proved.

* * *

Poirot had murmured in *The ABC Murders*:

> 'Supposing that four people sit down to play bridge and one, the odd man out, sits in a chair by the fire. At the end of the evening the man by the fire is found dead. One of the four; while he is dummy, has gone over and killed him, and, intent on the play of the hand, the other three have not noticed. Ah, there would be a crime for you! *Which of the four was it?*'

Just such a closed circle puzzle is set in *Cards on the Table*, published in 1936,[16] in which a diabolical host, the fashionable Mr Shaitana, who 'existed richly and beautifully in a super flat in Park Lane', invited to dinner four people he was convinced were secret murderers, and four others well known for detection: the celebrated Hercule Poirot, the venerable Superintendent Battle of Scotland Yard, the popular detective fiction writer, Ariadne Oliver, and a distinguished veteran of the Secret Service, Colonel Race.[17] After dinner Mr Shaitana arranged two tables of bridge. The four famous sleuths were sent to the smoking room:

> 'Five diamonds. Game and rubber,' said Colonel Race. 'Good for you, partner,' he said to Poirot. 'I didn't think you'd do it. Lucky they didn't lead a spade.'
>
> 'Wouldn't have made much difference, I expect,' said Superintendent Battle, a man of gentle magnanimity.
>
> He had called spades. His partner, Mrs Oliver, had had a spade, but 'something had told her' to lead a club – with disastrous results.

Meanwhile in the drawing-room, alone with his four suspected murderers, something much more disastrous was happening to Mr Shaitana. While seated by the fire he was deftly slain with a jewelled stiletto. *Which of the four did it?*

With only the bridge scores as a tangible clue, with three fine collaborators in Superintendent Battle, Mrs Oliver and Colonel Race, and with the removal, by Mr Shaitana's untimely death, of 'the only moustache in London, perhaps, that could compete with that of M. Hercule Poirot', it is no wonder that Agatha Christie observed, in a foreword to *Cards on the Table*, that this was one of Poirot's favourite cases.

A year later, far from Mr Shaitana's drawing-room, Poirot encountered Colonel Race again on a steamer on the Nile. Poirot was once more in pursuit of a holiday. ('This winter I shall visit Egypt, I think . . . One will escape from the fogs, the greyness, the monotony of the constantly falling rain'), and Colonel Race, a man 'usually to be found in one of the outposts of Empire where trouble is brewing', was in pursuit of a political agitator; but these goals were forgotten in the excitement of three murders committed in quick succession as the *Karnak* churned toward the Second Cataract.

'A journey on a swift-moving river, between dangerous rocks, and heading for who knows what currents of disaster . . .' Thus did Hercule Poirot predict the course of events in one of his most famous cases, *Death on the Nile*,[18] published in 1937. At first acquaintance the passengers on the *Karnak* seemed a pleasant enough lot – Poirot certainly enjoyed the company of Mrs Allerton, for example, 'one of the most charming people I had ever met' – but as he and Colonel Race pursued their murder investigations some very nasty secrets came to light. 'So many conflicting hates and jealousies and envies and meannesses. It is like a cloud of flies, buzzing, buzzing . . .'

* * *

Poirot's next case, *Appointment with Death*, unfolded in Palestine and Jordan. As it follows on the heels of *Death on the Nile*, it is fair to assume that both cases occurred on the same eventful holiday, and that Poirot proceeded from the *Karnak* on the Nile to the Solomon Hotel in Jerusalem and thence to Amman. With him he brought a letter of introduction from Colonel Race to Colonel Carbury, an administrative 'power' in Transjordania. Raising his eyes from Race's letter, Colonel Carbury, a devotee of detective fiction, smiled hopefully upon his guest:

> 'Tell me, d'you ever find your own special job has a way of following you around?'
>
> '*Pardon?*'
>
> 'Well – to put it plainly – do you come to places expecting a holiday from crime – and find instead bodies cropping up?'
>
> 'It has happened, yes – more than once.'
>
> 'H'm,' said Colonel Carbury, and looked particularly abstracted.
>
> Then he roused himself with a jerk.
>
> 'Got a body now I'm not very happy about,' he said.

The body was that of an American tourist, the autocratic Mrs Boynton – 'a distorted old Buddha – a gross spider in the centre of a web!' – whose life had been universally pronounced as ruinous to all around her, and whose sudden death, while surrounded by her family in a tourist encampment at Petra, now raised a most disagreeable question: had someone slain the dragon?

In the course of his investigations Poirot enjoyed fulfilling Colonel Carbury's every expectation of how a detective should behave:

'You desire to know, do you not, Colonel Carbury, *who killed Mrs Boynton*? (That is, if she was killed and did not die a natural death.) Exactly *how* and *when* she was killed – and, in fact, the whole truth of the matter?'

'I should like to know that, yes.' Carbury spoke unemotionally.

Hercule Poirot said slowly:

'I see no reason why you should not know it!'

And promising a solution within twenty-four hours, Poirot commenced to unravel the tangled web at Petra, thereby encountering a *ménage* of tourists who, when their minds were not on Mrs Boynton's death, tended to discuss questions of the day: the League of Nations, the enmity of the Arabs toward the Jews, the menace of white slavers and drug dealers, and the benefits or otherwise of psychotherapy.

But Colonel Carbury was only concerned with the whodunit writing itself before his very eyes:

'I suppose you couldn't do the things the detective does in books? Write a list of significant facts – things that don't seem to mean anything but are really frightfully important – that sort of thing?'

'Ah,' said Poirot kindly. 'You like that kind of detective story! But certainly, I will do it for you with pleasure.'

He drew a sheet of paper towards him and wrote quickly and neatly: SIGNIFICANT POINTS.

In one respect *Hercule Poirot's Christmas*,[19] published in 1938, is reminiscent of 'The Adventure of the Christmas Pudding' of the early 1920s – the outset of each case finds Poirot ill at ease with country Christmas cheer and gazing gloomily upon a blazing Yuletide fire. In 'The Adventure of the Christmas Pudding' he had been in mourning for a Hastings departed to the Argentine. In *Hercule Poirot's Christmas*, in the home of Colonel Johnson, the Chief Constable of Middleshire and a friend from the *Three Act Tragedy* case, his secret lamentations were all for his neck. In the absence of central heating it was, he felt sure, dreadfully at risk from cold draughts.

Inevitably, an alarming distraction soon came to hand. 'Damn it all!' cried the Chief Constable. 'Case of murder! On Christmas Eve too!' This led to Poirot's posthumous introduction to a neighbouring millionaire, the tyrannical Simon Lee, whose neck – cut neatly through the jugular vein – had suffered a far greater misfortune than Poirot's that Christmas Eve.

The surviving members of the Lee family, as described by Colonel Johnson, were of a mode familiar to Poirot from many an earlier case:

> 'All the same, it's incredible, you know. Here's a particularly crude and brutal murder – and whom have we as suspects? Alfred Lee and his wife – both charming, well-bred, quiet people. George Lee, who's a member of parliament and the essence of respectability. His wife? She's just an ordinary modern lovely. David Lee seems a gentle creature and we've got his brother Harry's word for it that he can't stand the sight of blood. His wife seems a nice, sensible woman – quite commonplace. Remains the Spanish niece and the man from South Africa.'

Well, there they all were. As Poirot commented, as he set to work, on Christmas Eve there is apt to be 'a great amount of *strain*' in families.

Two cases of this busy period, described in the short stories

'Yellow Iris' and 'The Dream', took place in London and mercifully required no more than the summoning of taxis to bring Poirot to the scenes of impending crimes.

Nevertheless, the affair of the 'Yellow Iris' did tear him away, on a chilly night, from the contemplation of his beloved electric radiator to the far less certain pleasures of a champagne supper at a fashionable restaurant. Here – according to an anonymous phonecall – someone at a table decorated with yellow irises was in danger of being murdered. Dutifully insinuating himself into this lively scene, Poirot encountered hazards of his own. Seated beside a well-known South American dancer, he murmured:

> 'Señora, as the evening advances I become more brave. If you would dance with me now – '
>
> 'Oh, yes, indeed. You are – you are ze cat's whiskers, M. Poirot. I inseest on dancing with you.'
>
> 'You are too kind, Señora.'

Altogether it turned out to be a tense evening. So quickly and cleverly did Poirot foil a murderer, however, that his *amour propre* returned in a rush:

> 'Señora, as the evening advances I become more brave. If you would dance with me now – '
>
> 'Oh, yes, indeed. You are – you are ze cat's whiskers, M. Poirot. I inseest on dancing with you.'
>
> 'You are too kind, Señora.'

Poirot found events in 'The Dream' far less exciting. In this case a summons for help took him to the somewhat *déclassé* mansion of a reclusive millionaire, Benedict Farley, a man constantly tormented by a dream that at exactly twenty-eight minutes past three he will shoot himself.

Poirot firmly declined the case ('For that, Monsieur Farley, I should recommend Napoleon's *Book of Dreams* – or the latest practising psychologist from Harley Street'), but within a week Farley's dream had come true, and Poirot was summoned again. Gathered together were Farley's widow, his daughter, his secretary, his doctor and a police inspector. Poirot heard out their stories, sat back, and inquired:

> 'One more question, Mrs Farley. Had your husband good sight?'
>
> 'No. Not without his glasses.'
>
> 'He was very short-sighted?'
>
> 'Oh, yes, he was quite helpless without his spectacles.'
>
> 'He had several pairs of glasses?'
>
> 'Yes.'
>
> 'Ah,' said Poirot. He leaned back. 'I think that that concludes the case . . .'
>
> There was silence in the room. They were looking at the little man who sat there complacently stroking his moustache.

It is clear from a number of contemporary references that Poirot's next investigation, *One, Two, Buckle My Shoe*,[20] published in 1940, takes place in the first half of the catastrophic year of 1939. Hints of dangers in Europe – Communists and Fascists, arms dealers and assassins, spies and counter-spies – surface like piranha throughout this complex affair. As for England, there is much talk of preserving a solvent economy and conservative values at all costs, the Prime Minister is shot at, and the Imperial Shirts 'march with banners and have a ridiculous salute'.

Disturbing as all this was, at the outset of the case Poirot was preoccupied with anxieties of his own:

There are certain humilating moments in the lives of the greatest of men. It has been said that no man is a hero to his valet. To that may be added that few men are heroes to themselves at the moment of visiting their dentist.

Hercule Poirot was morbidly conscious of this fact.

He was a man who was accustomed to have a good opinion of himself. He was Hercule Poirot, superior in most ways to other men. But in this moment he was unable to feel superior in any way whatever. His morale was down to zero. He was just that ordinary, that craven figure, a man afraid of the dentist's chair.

'It is a beautiful thought,' said a deliriously happy Poirot half an hour later to a taxi driver, 'that I have been to the dentist and I need not go again for six months.' But even as he was digesting a celebratory lunch, George handed him the telephone: 'It's Chief Inspector Japp, sir.' Astonishingly, within an hour of Poirot's departure, Mr Morley, his chatty and inoffensive dentist, had committed suicide.

Or was it murder? Or espionage? Or a monstrous double bluff of which poor Mr Morley was but an accidental victim? Steadily gathering victims, and paced by a familiar nursery rhyme, the case advanced like a juggernaut. Who was he really up against, Poirot began to wonder. Was he trying to avenge his dentist? Or was he, in fact, trying to save England? When Japp was called off the case by the highest authority, Poirot soldiered on alone:

George entered the room with his usual noiseless tread. He set down on a little table a steaming pot of chocolate and some sugar biscuits.

'Will there be anything else, sir?'

'I am in great perplexity of mind, George.'

'Indeed, sir? I am sorry to hear it.'

Hercule Poirot poured himself out some chocolate and stirred it thoughtfully.

When the case was all over, Poirot found himself exhausted. 'Is it possible,' he said to himself with astonishment, 'that I am growing old?'

The murder in Poirot's last case of the 1930s occurred on 27 July 1939, and his investigation of it is superbly recounted in *Sad Cypress*, published in 1940. It is a story of letters and wills, love and greed.

The centrepiece of *Sad Cypress* is the trial for murder of a young woman, Elinor Carlisle. Caught in a love triangle, her rival poisoned, the evidence against her is overwhelming. When all appears lost, a friend and would-be lover calls in Poirot.

It was a most tactful and beguiling Poirot, looking 'very Londonified' and 'wearing patent leather shoes', who descended upon the village of Maidensford to interview a majestic housekeeper, a lovelorn garage mechanic, and a confused under-gardener. The re-examination of old evidence over many cups of tea became, at times, a game of cat and mouse. To win the confidence of the housekeeper, for example ('for Mrs Bishop, a lady of conservative habits and views, strongly disapproved of foreigners'), Poirot had to play a trump card:

> He recounted with naïve pride a recent visit of his to Sandringham. He spoke with admiration of the graciousness and delightful simplicity and kindness of Royalty.
>
> Mrs Bishop, who followed daily in the court circular the exact movements of Royalty, was overborne. After all, if They had sent for Mr Poirot . . . Well, naturally, that made All the Difference. Foreigner or no foreigner,

who was she, Emma Bishop, to hold back where Royalty had led the way?

Notes

1 *Black Coffee* stands on its own as the only Poirot play not based on a previously published work.

2 An expanded version of this story, with a changed ending, was published in 1937 under the title 'Dead Man's Mirror'.

3 Also published under the title *Thirteen at Dinner*.

4 An expanded version of this story was published in 1960 under the title 'The Mystery of the Spanish Chest'.

5 Though published in 1936, the Foreword to *Murder in Mesopotamia* states: 'The events chronicled in this narrative took place some four years ago.'

6 Also published under the title *Murder in the Calais Coach*.

7 Also published under the title *Murder in Three Acts*.

8 In the 1920s, and always to his great astonishment, Mr Satterthwaite had been the associate of another of Agatha Christie's detectives, the mysterious Harley Quin.

9 Also published under the title *Death in the Air*.

10 Before coming to work for Poirot, Miss Lemon served as secretary to yet another of Agatha Christie's detectives, Parker Pyne.

11 Also published under the title *Poirot Loses a Client*.

12 Though a much longer case, Miss Arundell's posthumous summoning of Poirot is reminiscent of Miss Barrowby's in 'How Does Your Garden Grow?'.

13 Two others published during this period, 'The Incredible Theft' and 'Dead Man's Mirror', are expanded versions of 'The Submarine Plans' and 'The Second Gong'.

14 Also published, sometimes in slightly differing versions, under the titles 'Crime in Cabin 66', 'The Mystery of the Crime in Cabin 66', and 'Poirot and the Crime in Cabin 66'.

15 During this voyage a fellow passenger asked Poirot if he had ever been to Egypt. 'Never, Mademoiselle,' he replied, completely forgetting 'The Adventure of The Egyptian Tomb' of the 1920s, a remarkable lapse of Poirot's famous memory that I can only ascribe to seasickness.

16 Although *Cards on the Table* was published in 1936, a sobering remark by one of its characters – 'Even if somebody did push their great-aunt down the stairs in 1912, it won't be much use to us in 1937' – places events of this case in the following year.

17 Like Poirot himself, Superintendent Battle, Ariadne Oliver and Colonel Race each has his or her own separate sphere in Christie literature. To bring the four of them together at his dinner table was certainly a triumph for Mr Shaitana.

18 This book should not be confused with a Parker Pyne short story of the same title.

19 Also published under the titles *Murder for Christmas* and *A Holiday for Murder*.

20 Also published under the titles *The Patriotic Murders* and *An Overdose of Death*.

5

The 1940s

'And someone who solves crimes is coming to lunch tomorrow.'

—Midge Hardcastle, The Hollow

A charming book that spans Poirot's life from late 1939 to late 1940 is *The Labours of Hercules*, published in 1947.[1] This cycle of adventures was launched by the visit of an old friend:

Hercule Poirot's flat was essentially modern in its furnishings. It gleamed with chromium. Its easy chairs, though comfortably padded, were square and uncompromising in outline.

On one of these chairs sat Hercule Poirot, neatly – in the middle of the chair. Opposite him, in another chair, sat Dr Burton, Fellow of All Souls, sipping appreciatively at a glass of Poirot's Château Mouton Rothschild. There was no neatness about Dr Burton. He was plump, untidy and beneath his thatch of white hair beamed a rubicund and benign countenance. He had a deep wheezy chuckle and the habit of covering himself and everything round him with tobacco ash. In vain did Poirot surround him with ash trays.

> Dr Burton was asking a question.
>
> 'Tell me,' he said. 'Why Hercule?'
>
> 'You mean, my Christian name?'
>
> 'Hardly a *Christian* name,' the other demurred.

Warmed by the Château Mouton Rothschild, Dr Burton then launched into a short lecture on Greek mythology and, in particular, on Poirot's epic namesake and his twelve famous labours. At first Poirot chose to be unimpressed: 'Take this – Hercules – this hero! Hero indeed? What was he but a large muscular creature of low intelligence and criminal tendencies!' But further research in the calf-bound classical dictionaries obediently provided by Miss Lemon inspired Poirot – once again in a retirement mode – to a grand scheme.

Why not bow out dramatically from his life as a detective by modelling himself on the Hercules of old?

> In the period before his final retirement he would accept twelve cases, no more, no less. And those twelve cases should be selected with special reference to the twelve labours of ancient Hercules. Yes, that would not only be amusing, it would be artistic, it would be *spiritual*.

With this lofty resolve, Poirot sat back confidently in expectation of a case to match Hercules's first Labour, the capture of the Nemean Lion.

> Naturally he did not expect a case to present itself actually involving a flesh and blood lion. It would be too much of a coincidence should he be approached by the Directors of the Zoological Gardens to solve a problem for them involving a real lion.
>
> No, here symbolism must be involved. The first case

> must concern some celebrated public figure, it must be sensational and of the first importance! Some master criminal – or, alternatively, someone who was a lion in the public eye. Some well-known writer, or politician, or painter – or even royalty?

But the lion, when he made his appearance, was none of these. He was small and snuffly, his name was Shan Tung, and he was a Pekinese dog. Over the years Poirot had resented being consulted about kidnapped lap-dogs, but in the story of 'The Nemean Lion'[2] he unerringly perceived a splendid case of mythology in the making.

In ancient Greece many would-be heroes attempted to slay the nine-headed Hydra, but only Hercules proved equal to the task. In the case of 'The Lernean Hydra',[3] when appealed to by a country doctor whose village was rife with rumours that he had poisoned his wife, Poirot knew at once he had found his second Labour:

> 'We are going into the country, Georges,' said Hercule Poirot to his valet.
>
> 'Indeed, sir?' said the imperturbable George.
>
> 'And the purpose of our journey is to destroy a monster with nine heads.'
>
> 'Really, sir? Something after the style of the Loch Ness Monster?'
>
> 'Less tangible than that. I did not refer to a flesh and blood animal, Georges.'

Together, in Market Loughborough, Poirot and George beheaded the monster.

In legendary times Hercules pursued a gold-horned hind

across a magic landscape for a year before capturing her, and in the story 'The Arcadian Deer'[4] Poirot, his usually prudent namesake, spent more time and money than he could ever have imagined, and with no fee in sight, to find the lost sweetheart of a village mechanic – but then Poirot always was a romantic and matchmaker at heart.

The end of the third Labour found Poirot in Switzerland, where he decided to remain for a short holiday in the Alps. It was in snow and mountains such as these that an earlier Hercules had tracked the fabled boar of Erymanthia. None of the dangers he encountered, however, was greater than those faced by a Poirot coaxed into aiding the Swiss Police in the capture of a vicious master criminal, Marrascaud.

> Hercule Poirot sighed. To hunt down a ruthless killer was not his idea of a pleasant holiday. Brain work from an armchair, he reflected, was more in his line. Not to ensnare a wild boar upon a mountainside.

But there it was, the fourth Labour, and in 'The Erymanthian Boar'[5] Poirot, marooned with the killer and his gang in a most disorganized hotel, displayed bravery, wit, and a hitherto unsuspected skill:

> Monsieur Lementeuil, Commissaire of Police, seized Poirot by both hands.
>
> 'Ah, my friend, with what emotion I greet you! What stupendous events – what emotions you have passed through! And we below, our anxiety, our fears – knowing nothing – fearing everything. No wireless – no means of communication. To heliograph, that was indeed a stroke of genius on your part.'
>
> 'No, no.' Poirot endeavoured to look modest.

Like the Hercules of old, Poirot, in the affair of 'The Augean Stables', undertook to clean up an awful mess. Summoned to meet with a pompous home secretary and an admirable new prime minister, he was told:

> 'The situation is an extremely delicate one, M. Poirot.'
>
> A faint smile flitted across Hercule Poirot's lips. He almost replied, *It always is!*
>
> Instead, he composed his face and put on what might be described as a bedside manner of extreme discretion.
>
> Sir George Conway proceeded weightily. Phrases fell easily from his lips – the extreme delicacy of the Government's position – the interests of the public – the solidarity of the party – the necessity of presenting a united front – the power of the press – the welfare of the country . . .

In short, Poirot was being asked to hush up a terrible political scandal. Whether the best interests of the country were served in the long run by Poirot's cunning is another matter, but it is a fact that his brilliant counter-offensive against the gossip-mongering *X-Ray News* soon had the government smelling like a rose.[6]

Shortly thereafter – perhaps spending some of the handsome fee the Government undoubtedly paid him for its rescue – Poirot attempted yet another holiday in an out-of-the-way hotel in the tiny Balkan state of Herzoslavakia. With Greece not far away, he must surely have pondered on his inevitable sixth Labour. Could anything possibly resembling the frightful iron-beaked vultures of Stymphalus be lurking amid these tidy pine woods and pretty lakes? But birds of prey in the form of blackmailers were indeed about, and in the case of 'The Stymphalean

Birds'[7] Poirot kindly rescued their victim – a decent young Englishman – between afternoon tea on the terrace and breakfast next morning. 'I strive only to follow the example of my great predecessor, Hercules,' he murmured.

The case of 'The Cretan Bull'[8] was also concerned with the fate of a decent young Englishman.

In ancient times, moved by Pasiphae's sorrow, Hercules set free her beloved Cretan Bull. Poirot's seventh task began with a visit from a distraught new client. Always one to put considerable store in first impressions,

> Hercule Poirot looked thoughtfully at his visitor.
>
> He saw a pale face with a determined-looking chin, eyes that were more grey than blue, and hair that was of that real blue-black shade so seldom seen – the hyacinthine locks of ancient Greece.
>
> He noted the well-cut but also well-worn country tweeds, the shabby handbag, and the unconscious arrogance of manner that lay behind the girl's obvious nervousness. He thought to himself:
>
> *Ah, yes, she is 'the County' – but no money! And it must be something quite out of the way that would bring her to me.*

It was indeed something quite out of the way – the plight of her impressive fiancé ('Tall, magnificently proportioned, with a terrific chest and shoulders, and a tawny head of hair. There was a tremendous air of strength and virility about him') who had apparently fallen heir to a most alarming insanity, the nocturnal murdering of cats, parrots and sheep. In this Labour Poirot had to unravel a sorry tangle of family secrets before the adored young bull could be set free.

* * *

In 'The Horses of Diomedes',[9] events took Poirot to Mertonshire:

> Mertonshire is a reasonable distance from London. It has hunting, shooting, and fishing, it has several very picturesque but slightly self-conscious villages, it has a good system of railways and a new arterial road facilities motoring to and from the metropolis. Servants object to it less than they do to other, more rural, portions of the British Isles. As a result, it is practically impossible to live in Mertonshire unless you have an income that runs into four figures, and what with income tax and one thing and another, five figures is better.

There, on the trail of a cocaine ring, Poirot found occasion to call on a shrewd observer, old Lady Carmichael:

> 'You're up to something, Hercule Poirot.'
>
> 'Are you acquainted with the classics, Madame?'
>
> 'What have the classics got to do with it?'
>
> 'They have this to do with it. I emulate my great predecessor Hercules. One of the Labours of Hercules was the taming of the wild horses of Diomedes.'
>
> 'Don't tell me you came down here to train horses – at your age – and always wearing patent leather shoes! You don't look to me as though you'd ever been on a horse in your life!'
>
> 'The horses, Madame, are symbolic. They were wild horses who ate human flesh.'

In the unlikely pastures of upmarket Mertonshire, Poirot soon rounded up the wild horses of Diomedes.

Flemish though he was, Rubens was not an artist Poirot

particularly admired, so it was rather a bore for him to be asked to recover a friend's treasured painting stolen from an exhibition at Simpson's Galleries. In tracking the painting to the Continent, however, Poirot managed to combine this quest with a much more interesting search (suggested by Japp) for an English schoolgirl missing somewhere in France. Retrieving both the painting and the schoolgirl in 'The Girdle of Hyppolita',[10] his ninth Labour, Poirot was rewarded by torrents of gratitude and a deluge of 'young, vigorous femininity' – twenty-five schoolgirls demanding: 'M. Poirot, will you write your name in my autograph book?' No doubt, as well, they all had a good giggle over Rubens's voluptuous painting of Queen Hyppolita presenting her girdle to Hercules.

'The Flock of Geryon'[11] found Poirot emulating his great predecessor's tenth Labour, the rescue of a herd of cattle from the triple-bodied monster, Geryon. The flock Poirot set out to rescue were victims of a bogus charismatic cult and were being fleeced, by injections of *cannabis indica*, into handing over money to its handsome leader, 'The Great Shepherd'. In a pleasant field in Devon Poirot managed to defeat this monster in sheep's clothing and solve a number of hitherto unsuspected murders. 'You might start a new religion yourself,' said Japp, 'with the creed: 'There is no one as clever as Hercule Poirot, Amen, D.C. Repeat ad lib?!"'

As his eleventh Labour Hercules carried away the golden apples guarded by the Hesperides, the 'daughters of the evening star', who dwelt in the mysterious west. As his eleventh task Poirot accepted a commission to find a Renaissance treasure of the Borgias, a goblet embellished with a jewelled serpent and emerald apples. His search, a long one, took him to the west of Ireland, the legendary end of the world. Disconcerted at first by a landscape where 'the Romans had never marched, tramp, tramp, tramp; had never fortified a camp; had never built a well-ordered, sensible, useful road', Poirot, in 'The Apples of the Hesperides',[12] was moved to rhapsody:

> 'Let me describe for you the place where I found it – the Garden of Peace, looking out over the Western Sea toward a forgotten Paradise of Youth and Eternal Beauty.'

'The Capture of Cerberus'[13] – in mythical times the vanquishing of the many-headed dog who guarded the gate of the underworld – relates the most poignant of Poirot's Labours.

One early evening, while travelling on the London Underground, Poirot heard his name called from an opposite escalator. Before his astonished eyes there passed before him:

> . . . a visitation from the past. A woman of full and flamboyant form; her luxuriant henna-red hair crowned with a small plastron of straw to which was attached a positive platoon of brilliantly feathered little birds. Exotic-looking furs dripped from her shoulders.

It was his darling Countess Vera Rossakoff, whom he had not seen for well over twenty years.

Twisting himself sideways, leaning over the balustrade, Poirot cried despairingly:

'*Chère Madame* – where then can I find you?'

Her reply came to him faintly from the depths. It

was unexpected, yet seemed at the moment strangely apposite.

'*In Hell.*'

What could she mean? Next morning Poirot consulted the font of all knowledge:

> 'Miss Lemon, may I ask you a question?'
>
> 'Of course, M. Poirot.' Miss Lemon took her fingers off the typewriter keys and waited attentively.
>
> 'If a friend asked you to meet her – or him – in Hell, what would you do?'
>
> Miss Lemon, as usual, did not pause. She knew, as the saying goes, all the answers.
>
> 'It would be advisable, I think, to ring up for a table,' she said.

And so followed an emotional adventure in which Poirot ensconced himself night after night at a small table in *Hell*, a trendy nightclub presided over by the incorrigible Countess. A suspicion soon dawned on him, however – a suspicion confirmed by Japp – that the Countess and her spectacular *Hell* were being used as a front for a narcotics ring. 'I entertain for you much affection,' he said as he saved the Countess in the nick of time from a police raid. 'And I do not want to see you in what is called the jam.'

'Ah, but you are wonderful – *wonderful*,' she cried, embracing Poirot. 'Lipstick and mascara ornamented his face in a fantastic medley.'

'Good gracious,' murmured Miss Lemon. 'I wonder . . . Really – at *his* age! . . . Surely not . . .'

Thus ended the Labours of Hercules.[14]

It must now be recalled that at the outset of his self-imposed Labours Poirot had once more vowed to retire.

He had even gone so far as to confide in the horrified Dr Burton a reawakened interest in the cultivation of vegetable marrows. He would take only twelve cases more, he had said, 'no more, no less'. The addict of anything will instantly recognize the danger signals in this remark, and will not be surprised to find Poirot's career continuing – admittedly in a semi-retired mode – for decades to come. As he himself had said to Hastings in *The ABC Murders*:

> 'I know very well what you will say – I am like the Prima Donna who makes positively the farewell performance! That farewell performance, it repeats itself an indefinite number of times! Each time I say: This is the end. But no, something else arises! And I will admit it, my friend, the retirement I care for it not at all. If the little grey cells are not exercised, they grow the rust.'

As competently as ever, the virtuoso performances continued. Indeed, the cases of the 1940s were to be some of the most interesting Poirot ever undertook.

But where in this decade, one may very well ask, is Poirot and the Second World War? There had, after all, been forebodings of events to come in several of the cases of the late 1930s.

'Very fine man, King Leopold, so I've always heard,' Mr Morley, the doomed dentist in *One, Two, Buckle My Shoe*, had remarked to his quivering patient. The alarming events of 1940 – particularly the invasion of Belgium and its betrayal by her king – must have come as a shock to Poirot and revived vivid memories of his own plight in the earlier war. However, as is the case with Miss Marple in wartime,[15] we are told practically nothing of Poirot's activities. In *Taken at the Flood*, set in

1946, we are allowed a glimpse backward to an evening Poirot spent in the autumn of 1944 at a venerable club where 'the fact that an Air Raid was in progress made no difference to normal procedure', and in *Dead Man's Folly*, published in 1956, Poirot recalled another occasion when bombs were falling and he was more preoccupied with pain from a corn on his little toe than with thoughts of death, but, apart from fragments such as these, a curtain of silence temporarily falls on anything to do with the times. Is this a coincidence, one wonders? It is hard to believe that Poirot, the last hope of British cabinets over the years, and a tidy spider who always kept carefully intact his police and political connections with the Continent, would be allowed to remain – or allow himself to remain – tamely on the sidelines.[16]

However, whether as a smokescreen or not, Poirot remained in his flat in London and continued accepting cases. Those recorded for posterity have nothing to do with the war.

The classic, *Evil Under the Sun*, published in 1941, is, in Poirot's words, 'like a mosaic – many colours and patterns – and every strange-shaped little piece must be fitted into its own place'. Its setting was the Jolly Roger, a pleasant hotel presiding over a small island tucked into the coast of Devon. In the August in which the events of *Evil Under the Sun* occurred:

> There was one very important person (in his own estimation at least) staying at the Jolly Roger. Hercule Poirot, resplendent in a white duck suit, with a Panama hat tilted over his eyes, his moustaches magnificently befurled, lay back in an improved type of deck-chair and surveyed the bathing beach.

Every day, on this beach, Poirot's fellow guests happily sunbathed in various states of undress. This agreeable scene was soon disrupted, and the social structure at the Jolly Roger rent, by the arrival of a guest more spectacular than all the others:

> It would seem that she was too used to the invariable effect her presence produced. She was tall and slender. She wore a simple backless white bathing dress and every inch of her exposed body was tanned a beautiful even shade of bronze. She was as perfect as a statue.

'Our Vamp', as the more unappreciative guests came to call her, brought with her a number of surprising past associations and an unsettling little plot of her own in progress. In due course all these had to be sorted out by Poirot when someone strangled the Vamp – as she sunbathed, of course.

The short story, 'Four-and-Twenty Blackbirds',[17] is a feast of plain English fare. The case began at the Gallant Endeavour Restaurant in Chelsea with a waitress, Molly, expressing amazement at the sudden change in the habits of an old customer, Mr Gascoigne:

> 'I dare say you gentlemen will laugh at me,' Molly flushed up, 'but when a gentleman has been here for ten years, you get to know his likes and dislikes. He never could bear suet pudding or blackberries and I've never known him take thick soup – but on that Monday night he ordered thick tomato soup, beefsteak and kidney pudding and blackberry tart! Seemed as though he just didn't notice *what* he ordered!'

'Do you know,' said Poirot (letting his French idiom slip a bit while eating turkey stuffed with chestnuts), 'I find that extraordinarily interesting.'

'The trouble with you is that you've started going to look for crime – instead of waiting for crime to come for you,' said his friend, Mr Bonnington. He was quite right, as Poirot's relentless pursuit of the mystery of Mr Gascoigne's dinner demonstrates.

Poirot's client in *Five Little Pigs*,[18] published in 1942, was from Canada:

> There had been nothing distinctive in the letter she had written. It had been a mere request for an appointment, with no hint of what lay behind that request. It had been brief and businesslike. Only the firmness of the handwriting had indicated that Carla Lemarchant was a young woman.

This determined young woman had come to England to re-investigate a dreadful murder. Sixteen years before, her father, a brilliant artist, had died from hemlock poisoning. Her mother, tried and convicted for murder, had died after a year in prison. A letter to her daughter, held in trust until her twenty-first birthday, protested her innocence.

'I've heard about you,' Carla said to Poirot:

> 'The things you've done. The *way* you have done them. It's psychology that interests you, isn't it? Well, that doesn't change with time. The tangible things are gone – the cigarette end and the footprints and the bent blades of grass. You can't look for those any more. But you can go over all the facts of the case, and perhaps talk to the people who were there at the time – they're all alive still

– and then – and then, as you said just now, you can lie back in your chair and *think*. *And you'll know what really happened . . .*'

Hercule Poirot rose to his feet. One hand caressed his moustache. He said, 'Mademoiselle, I am honoured! I will justify your faith in me. I will investigate your case of murder. I will search back into the events of sixteen years ago and I will find out the truth.'

Finding that truth was no easy matter. It was difficult enough to sort out events of a September morning sixteen years before, but even more difficult was the reinterpreting of these events to arrive at a new conclusion.

This puzzle saw Poirot out of his armchair and working hard. Once old newspaper files had been read, and lawyers and police in retirement duly interviewed ('Oh, damn it all, man . . . It's all over and done with years ago. Of course she did it'), there remained for Poirot five witnesses to the circumstances surrounding the crime:

A jingle ran through Poirot's head. He repressed it. He must *not* always be thinking of nursery rhymes. It seemed an obsession with him lately. And yet the jingle persisted:

'*This little pig went to market, this little pig stayed at home . . .*'

The meat of this case – one of Poirot's best – is the sum of the different accounts he extracted from the five witnesses of what each had seen and heard – or said they had seen and heard – on the day of the long-ago murder.

In the words of an elderly solicitor's clerk consulted by Poirot in the course of his investigation:

'That hemlock didn't get into Mr Crale's beer by accident. It was put there. And if Mrs Crale didn't put it there, who did?'

A problem solved with much dispatch in 'Poirot and the Regatta Mystery',[19] a short story first published in 1943, was the disappearance before all eyes of a famous diamond, 'The Morning Star', at a yachting party in Dartmouth Harbour. In the wake of this awkward evening, the guest most suspected sought out Poirot in London. Carefully noting all the facts his client could supply, Poirot wished him a good morning.

'Will you call again in three days' time? I think the whole thing will be quite satisfactorily cleared up by then.'

'Are you joking, M. Poirot?'

'I never joke on professional matters,' said Poirot with dignity. 'This matter is serious. Shall we say Friday at 11.30?'

A splendid weekend book, *The Hollow*,[20] published in 1946, is presided over by an unforgettable hostess, Lucy Angkatell. In the words of her husband, Sir Henry Angkatell, a retired administrator and diplomat:

'She gets away with things. She always has.' He smiled. 'She's flouted the traditions of Government House – she's played merry hell with precedence at dinner parties (and that, Midge, is a black crime!). She's put deadly enemies next to each other at the dinner table, and run riot over the Colour question! And instead of raising one big almighty row and setting everyone at loggerheads and bringing disgrace on the British Raj – I'm damned if she hasn't got away with it!'

But in *The Hollow*, in inviting for the weekend a group of friends and cousins already much entangled by loves and hates, even Lady Angkatell began to suspect she had gone a bridge too far.

> 'I've asked the crime man to lunch on Sunday. It will make a distraction, don't you think so?'
>
> 'Crime man?'
>
> 'Like an egg,' said Lady Angkatell. 'He was in Baghdad, solving something, when Henry was High Commissioner. Or perhaps it was afterwards? We had him to lunch with some other duty people. He had on a white duck suit, I remember, and a pink flower in his buttonhole, and black patent leather shoes. I don't remember much about it because I never think it's very interesting who killed who. I mean once they are dead it doesn't seem to matter why, and to make a fuss about it all seems so silly . . .'
>
> 'But have you any crimes down here, Lucy?'
>
> 'Oh no, darling. He's in one of those funny new cottages – you know, beams that bump your head and a lot of very good plumbing and quite the wrong kind of garden. London people like that sort of thing.'

So it was that on a fine September Sunday Poirot carefully latched behind him the gate of 'Resthaven', his new weekend cottage, and embarked on a second luncheon with the Angkatells.

Upon arrival, and ushered to the swimming pool pavilion for a drink before lunch, he was not amused. 'The passion of the English for sitting outdoors irritated Hercule Poirot'; and worse was to come, for as he emerged upon the scene a tiresome game appeared ready to begin:

He was annoyed and he was bored – oh! how he was bored! Death was not, to him, amusing. And here they had arranged for him, by way of a joke, a set piece.

For what he was looking at was a highly artificial murder scene. By the side of the pool was the body, artistically arranged with an outflung arm and even some red paint dripping gently over the edge of the concrete into the pool. It was a spectacular body, that of a handsome fair-haired man. Standing over the body, revolver in hand, was a woman, a short, powerfully built, middle-aged woman with a curiously blank expression.

Alas, this was no game – the case that followed was one of the most perplexing of Poirot's career. For her part, Lady Angkatell rose to the occasion:

'Of course, say what you like, a murder is an awkward thing – it upsets the servants and puts the general routine out – we were having ducks for lunch – fortunately they are quite nice eaten cold.'

And her servants backed her up magnificently. Said her butler, Gudgeon, when questioned by a police inspector about a revolver found lying on the hall table:

'I don't think it is loaded, sir. None of Sir Henry's collection is kept loaded. And as for fingerprints, I polished it over with my handkerchief before replacing it, sir, so there will only be my fingerprints on it.'

'Why did you do that?' asked Grange sharply.

But Gudgeon's apologetic smile did not waver.

'I fancied it might be dusty, sir.'

Once the war was over, people in Poirot's circle began talking about its effects. The time and setting of *Taken at the Flood*,[21] published in 1948, is the late spring of 1946 in a village off the beaten track:

> Warmsley Vale, tucked away amongst wooded hills . . . is in essence a microscopic old-fashioned market town now degenerated into a village. It has a main street of Georgian houses, several pubs, a few unfashionable shops and a general air of being a hundred and fifty instead of twenty-eight miles from London.

Here, with peace at last, the various households of the kindly and prosperous Cloade family were attempting to put their lives together again. Their houses needed repair, their servants had long disappeared, their incomes were being eroded by taxation, and life altogether – especially for the women – continued to be an unending treadmill of queues, shortages and ration coupons.

Adding to all this was another cross the Cloades had to bear. Trained for years to look to Gordon Cloade, the wealthy bachelor head of the family, for financial support, an air raid in the last year of the war had not only removed him from the scene but had left his immense fortune in the hands of his young and unsuitable new wife. Bewildered, impoverished and angry, the proud Cloades licked their wounds and wondered – aloud to each other, and secretly to themselves – what to do next.

Perched in his flat in London, Poirot had been hearing for some time of trouble brewing in Warmsley Vale. Indeed, one of the more scatty members of the family had already attempted to hire him to find evidence to disinherit Gordon Cloade's bride:

> 'M. Poirot,' she said, 'I have come to you under spirit guidance.'

Poirot blinked slightly.

'Indeed, Madame. Perhaps you will take a seat and tell me – '

He got no further.

'Both ways, M. Poirot. With the automatic writing and with the ouija board. It was the night before last. Madame Elvary (a wonderful woman she is) and I were using the board. We got the same initials repeatedly H.P. H.P. H.P. . . . I racked my brains thinking of someone with those initials – I knew it must connect up with the last séance – really a most poignant one, but it was some time before I got it. And then I bought a copy of *Picture Post* (spirit guidance again, you see, because usually I buy the *New Statesman*) and there you were – a picture of you, and described, and an account of what you had done. It is wonderful, don't you think, M. Poirot, how everything has a purpose? Clearly, you are the person appointed by the Guides to elucidate this matter.'

Poirot firmly declined the commission – 'My fees,' he said, to induce discouragement, 'are very expensive. I may say enormously expensive!' – but he kept his eye on the newspapers and, when a report of an unexplained death in Warmsley Vale appeared, and yet another Cloade sought his aid, the urge to be at the scene proved irresistible:

'Come on, Lynn. We must get going. I expect M. Poirot wants to get back to town.'

Poirot said smilingly:

'But I am not going back to town.'

'What?'

Rowley stopped dead, giving a queer wooden effect.

'I am staying here, at the Stag, for a short while.'

'But – but why?'

'*C'est un beau paysage*,' Poirot said placidly.

Rowley said uncertainly, 'Yes, of course . . . But aren't you – well, I mean, busy?'

'I have made my economies,' said Poirot, smiling. 'I do not need to occupy myself unduly. No, I can enjoy my leisure, and spend my time where the fancy takes me.'

NOTES

1 The twelve short stories that constitute *The Labours of Hercules* were first published separately in British and American magazines between November 1939 and September 1940. Some slight changes in text occurred in the stories' final forms.

2 Also published under the title 'The Case of the Kidnapped Pekinese'.

3 Also published under the title 'The Invisible Enemy'.

4 Also published under the title 'The Vanishing Lady'.

5 Also published under the title 'Murder Mountain'.

6 'Who's the Home Secretary's little pet? You are. Who's got half the Cabinet in his pocket? You have. Hushing up their scandals for them . . . Sometimes, Poirot, I think you haven't any scruples at all!' Scolded Inspector Japp in *One, Two, Buckle My Shoe*. The fact that he knew about the Augean Stables case before it apparently happened is one of the quirks of Poirot chronology.

7 Also published under the titles 'The Birds of Ill Omen' and 'Vulture Women'.

8 Also published under the title 'Midnight Madness'.

9 Also published under the title 'The Case of the Drug Peddler'.

10 Also published under the titles 'The Girdle of Hippolyte' and 'The Disappearance of Winnie King'.

11 Also published under the title 'Weird Monster'.

12 Also published under the title 'The Poison Cup'.

13 Also published under the title 'Meet Me in Hell'.

14 In *Agatha Christie: A Biography*, Janet Morgan cites Christie's annoyance with the dust-jacket proposed by her publisher for *The Labours of Hercules*: 'It suggests Poirot going naked to the bath!!! All sorts of obscene suggestions are being made by my family. I have, I hope, been tactful but firm. Put statuary on the cover but make it clear it is statuary – not Poirot gone peculiar in Hyde Park!!!'

15 See *Agatha Christie's Miss Marple* by Anne Hart.

16 In *Third Girl*, published in 1966, Poirot concocted an elaborate reminiscence to win the confidence of Sir Roderick Horsefield, who had played a vital role in weapons development but whose memory was now slipping fast. 'We have to go back so far as the last war. It was, I think, in Normandy the last time,' Poirot told him. 'What decisions we had to take! And what difficulties we had with security.' Was Poirot speaking entirely from imagination?

17 First published in 1941 under the title 'Poirot and the Regular Customer'.

18 Also published under the title 'Murder in Retrospect'.

19 Also published under the title 'The Regatta Mystery', this is a surprising first cousin of an earlier short story, also entitled 'The Regatta Mystery', in which Parker Pyne solved an identical case.

20 Also published under the title *Murder After Hours*.

21 Also published under the title *There is a Tide . . .*

6

The Last Three Decades

> He was the great, the unique Hercule Poirot, but he was also a very old man and his shoes were tight.
>
> —Mrs McGinty's Dead

The six years that passed between the setting in 1946 of *Taken at the Flood* and the publication in 1952 of *Mrs McGinty's Dead* are evidence of Poirot's continuing drift – at least as far as murder cases were concerned – into semi-retirement. Miss Lemon might work away as furiously as ever in her little room, but if all she had to type were reports on delicate missions for oil companies, and if Inspector Japp, his old companion in arms, would insist on retiring, life could seem very dull at times to Hercule Poirot. 'I have leisure – too much leisure,' he complained:

> 'The retired financier takes up golf, the little merchant puts bulbs in his garden, me, I eat. But there it is, I come round to it again. *One can only eat three times a day*. And in between are the gaps.'

Which is why, in *Mrs McGinty's Dead*,[1] Poirot seized the opportunity to investigate a most unlikely case, the murder of a charwoman.

It all began with a visit from Superintendent Spence of the Kilchester Police, a friend from *Taken at the Flood*. Sipping a beer thoughtfully provided by George, the Superintendent confided his unease over a recent case – the death of an old woman in the village of Broadhinny. All evidence of the murder had pointed towards Mrs McGinty's unprepossessing lodger, a man named James Bentley. Duly arrested, Bentley had been brought to trial:

> 'The case came on at the Assizes. Yesterday. Open and shut case. The jury were only out twenty minutes this morning. Verdict: Guilty. Condemned to death.'
>
> Poirot nodded.
>
> 'And then, after the verdict, you got in a train and came to London and came here to see me. Why?'
>
> Superintendent Spence was looking into his beer glass. He ran his finger slowly round and round the rim.
>
> 'Because,' he said, 'I don't think he did it . . .'

'Supposing,' queried Poirot, 'that after all, he did kill her?'

'In that case I'd be only too thankful to be convinced of it,' replied Spence. Poirot gazed upon him with affection. This was far more interesting than oil companies. '*Voilà*, everything is settled,' he declared. 'I precipitate myself upon the business.'

Bored he admittedly may have been, but it says much for Poirot, who could, after all, have remained in his comfortable flat in London ministered to by George and Miss Lemon, that he took up the cold scent of this obscure and profitless case and pursued it as vigorously as if he had been a far younger detective with everything to prove. Moreover, in Broadhinny Poirot emerged upon a postwar landscape of great discomfort – a village of housing shortages and suspicious newcomers, set upon a tortuously long hill. Up and down this hill Poirot trudged in his tight patent leather shoes. Who was this funny little foreign man? And why was he asking all these questions about a murder already solved? As for the victim, Mrs McGinty, the village's sole regret seemed to be that her violent death had deprived Broadhinny of its one reliable char.

To complete this gloomy scene, the only place to stay in the village was Long Meadows, a beautiful but decrepit country house whose likeable owners, the Summerhayes, gamely tried to make ends meet by taking in paying guests. Of their misguided efforts Poirot could only say:

> 'The cooking of Madame Summerhayes, it is beyond description. It is not cooking at all. And the draughts, the cold winds, the upset stomachs of the cats, the long hairs of the dogs, the broken legs of the chairs, the terrible, terrible bed in which I sleep' – he shut his eyes in remembrance of agonies – 'the tepid water in the bathroom, the holes in the stair carpet, and the coffee – words cannot describe to you the fluid which they serve to you as coffee.'

In all this there was one consolation for Poirot, the visit to Broadhinny at the same time as himself of the famous mystery writer, Ariadne Oliver. Some fifteen years before, her enthusiastic presence had greatly enlivened events in *Cards on the Table*:

> Mrs Ariadne Oliver was extremly well known as one of the foremost writers of detective and other sensational stories. She wrote chatty (if not particularly grammatical)

articles on *The Tendency of the Criminal; Famous Crimes Passionnels; Murder for Love v. Murder for Gain.* She was also a hotheaded feminist, and when any murder of importance was occupying space in the Press there was sure to be an interview with Mrs Oliver, and it was mentioned that Mrs Oliver had said, 'Now if a *woman* were the head of Scotland Yard!' She was an earnest believer in woman's intuition.

For the rest she was an agreeable woman of middle age, handsome in a rather untidy fashion with fine eyes, substantial shoulders and a large quantity of rebellious grey hair with which she was continually experimenting.

Upon reacquaintance, Mrs Oliver proved as entertaining and helpful as ever. To her a depressed Poirot explained his case:

'An elderly charwoman who was robbed and murdered five months ago. You may have read about it. Mrs McGinty. A young man was convicted and sentenced to death – '

'And he didn't do it, but you know who did, and you're going to prove it,' said Mrs Oliver rapidly. 'Splendid.'

'You go too fast,' said Poirot with a sigh. 'I do not yet know who did it – and from there it will be a long way to prove it.'

'Men are so slow,' said Mrs Oliver disparagingly. 'I'll soon tell you who did it. Someone down here, I suppose? Give me a day or two to look round, and I'll spot the murderer.'

It took more than a day or two, and several disconcerting incidents (Mrs Oliver was to be first on the scene of a second murder, and someone would attempt to push Poirot under a train) but in the end, amid great excitement, the real murderer of Mrs McGinty was unmasked.

'And,' said Poirot as he prepared for his return to the comforts of Whitehaven Mansions, 'I have given Mrs Summerhayes a cookery book and I have also taught her personally how to make an omelette.'

The following year, in *After the Funeral*,[2] Poirot was persuaded to take on a major case by an old friend, Mr Entwhistle, the shrewd senior partner of an eminent legal firm.

They dined first, before coming to business:

> The efficient George materialized with some *Pâté de Foie Gras* accompanied by hot toast in a napkin.
>
> 'We will have our *Pâté* by the fire,' said Poirot. 'Afterwards we will move to the table.'
>
> It was an hour and a half later that Mr Entwhistle stretched himself comfortably out in his chair and sighed a contented sigh.
>
> 'You certainly know how to do yourself well, Poirot. Trust a Frenchman.'
>
> 'I am a Belgian. But the rest of your remark applies. At my age the chief pleasure, almost the *only* pleasure that still remains, is the pleasure of the table. Mercifully I have an excellent stomach.'
>
> 'Ah,' murmured Mr Entwhistle.
>
> They had dined off a *Sole Véronique*, followed by *Escalope de Veau Milanaise*, proceeding to *Poire Flambée* with ice cream.

The replete Mr Entwhistle then made his request. 'I know you don't take cases any more, but I ask you to take this one,' he said, and plunged into a description of the very sort of problem Poirot had so enjoyed in the past – the death of a patriarch in a fine old country house, followed by violent events in the family circle.

In coming to grips with the mysteries of Enderby Hall and the various branches of the Abernethie family, Poirot resorted to the talents of the remarkable Mr Goby, a private investigator he employed increasingly as the years went by. He had first come across Mr Goby twenty-five years before in *The Mystery of the Blue Train*. At that time it had been said: 'Give him twenty-four hours and he would lay the private life of the Archbishop of Canterbury bare for you', and in the intervening years nothing had changed:

> At the flick of Mr Goby's double-jointed thumb, hundreds of patient questioning plodding men and women, old and young, of all apparent stations in life, were despatched to question, and probe, and achieve results.

For his part, Poirot insinuated himself into Enderby Hall under the guise of a United Nations official:

> 'I intend,' added Hercule Poirot, 'to purchase a country mansion for foreign refugees. I represent U.N.A.R.C.O.'
> 'And what's U.N.A.R.C.O.?'
> 'United Nations Aid for Refugee Centres Old Age.'

To Timothy Abernethie, a choleric member of the older generation, it was perfectly clear who was responsible for all these murders and changes:

> 'It all began with that damned Labour Government,' said Timothy. 'Sending the whole Country to blazes. And the Government we've got now is no better. Mealy-

mouthed milk-and-water socialists! Look at the state *we're* in! Can't get a decent gardener, can't get servants – poor Maude here has to work herself to a shadow messing about in the kitchen – (by the way I think a custard pudding would go well with the sole tonight my dear – and perhaps a little clear soup first?)'

An incredible event heralded Poirot's next recorded case. One morning at Whitehaven Mansions Miss Lemon, his secretary, made three mistakes while typing a perfectly straightforward letter. 'This was one of the things that could not happen – but it had happened!' So began *Hickory Dickory Dock*,[3] published in 1955.

Said the horrified Miss Lemon:

'I can't think how – at least, I can. It's because of my sister.'

'Your sister?'

Another shock. Poirot had never conceived of Miss Lemon's having a sister. Or, for that matter, having a father, mother or even grandparents. Miss Lemon, somehow, was so completely machine-made – a precision instrument, so to speak – that to think of her having affections, or anxieties, or family worries, seemed quite ludicrous.

Encouraged by sympathetic nods and helpful clucking noises, Miss Lemon became a mere mortal and found herself confiding her worries to Hercule Poirot. Her widowed sister, she explained, held the post of Matron in a hostel for students, and in this hostel all sorts of things had mysteriously disappeared.

Hercule Poirot was silent for a minute and a half.

Did he wish to embroil himself in the troubles of

Miss Lemon's sister and the passions and grievances of a polyglot hostel? But it was very annoying and inconvenient to have Miss Lemon making mistakes in typing his letters. He told himself that *if* he were to embroil himself in the matter, that would be the reason. He did not admit to himself that he had been rather bored of late and that the very triviality of the business attracted him.

The very next day George was instructed to provide sandwiches and crumpets (square crumpets). Miss Lemon's sister arrived for tea, and Poirot found himself gazing upon the following list:

Evening shoe (one of a new pair)
Bracelet (costume jewellery)
Diamond ring (found in plate of soup)
Powder compact
Lipstick
Stethoscope
Earrings
Cigarette lighter
Old flannel trousers
Electric light bulbs
Box of chocolates
Silk scarf (found cut to pieces)
Rucksack (ditto)
Boracic powder
Bath salts
Cookery book

All these had gone missing. Entranced, Poirot quivered like a retriever. 'I congratulate you,' he said to Mrs

Hubbard, 'on having such a unique and beautiful problem,' and he plunged with gusto into a milieu of students, rucksacks and spaghetti and a case which, before it was over, was to see as many murders as the typing errors committed by Miss Lemon.

A country fête is chronicled in *Dead Man's Folly*, published in 1956, and anyone who happened to be present on that spectacular afternoon must have talked about it for years.

For just half-a-crown this is what one got: the opening of the fête at two-thirty by a minor film star, the enticements of the fête itself, the right to roam at will through the grounds of Sir George Stubbs's beautiful estate, the opportunity to take part in a murder hunt organized by the famous crime writer Ariadne Oliver, the possibility of being presented with a prize by the celebrated detective Hercule Poirot ('Who is Hercule Poirot?' asked one or two of the younger generation), and – and this is the awful part – the sight of the police arriving in the late afternoon to investigate a genuine murder in the boat-house.

What an afternoon! And, to add to it, Lady Stubbs, last seen wearing a coolie hat, and masses of diamonds, had completely disappeared.

Hercule Poirot finally caught the murderer, of course, and when he did he looked just like a cat that has lapped up a saucer of cream.

> 'Actually,' said Mrs Oliver, 'I'm thinking of turning it into a book. It would be a pity to waste it.'

In *Cat Among the Pigeons*, published in 1959, a most unlikely client turned up:

George, Hercule Poirot's immaculate valet and manservant, opened the door and contemplated with some surprise a schoolgirl with a rather dirty face.

'Can I see M. Hercule Poirot, please?'

George took just a shade longer than usual to reply. He found the caller unexpected.

'M. Poirot does not see anyone without an appointment,' he said.

'I'm afraid I haven't time to wait for that. I really must see him now. It is very urgent. It's about some murders and a robbery and things like that.'

'I will ascertain,' said George, 'if M. Poirot will see you.'

A few minutes later Julia Upjohn, seated in a very square armchair in a very tidy sitting-room, gazed expectantly upon a small elderly man with a kind expression and suspiciously black hair.

'You bewilder me,' said Poirot. 'Where have all these exciting happenings taken place?'

'At my school – Meadowbank.'

Ah, Julia's school! Who could have imagined that Meadowbank, one of the most famous girls' schools in England, would ever find itself in such terror and disorder – two of its mistresses murdered, a student princess kidnapped, and pupils evaporating as fast as their parents could send chauffeurs to fetch them?

When Poirot appeared on the scene, Julia in tow, there gracefully occurred the usual capitulation of the local police:

'The idea is,' said the Chief Constable, 'that we try to pool our ideas and information. We are very glad to have you with us, M. Poirot,' he added. 'Inspector Kelsey remembers you well.'

In this case, besides working with the police, Poirot found himself in touch with two grey eminences – the fat and apparently ever sleepy Colonel Pikeaway, who ran a very secret service operation out of a hideaway in Bloomsbury, and Mr Robinson, who ran 'a network all over the globe. We are, how shall I put it, the arrangers behind the scenes.'[4]

In the course of a high-powered race to solve the mysteries of Meadowbank School, Poirot did not lose his sense of perspective. When told by Julia that she had learned of his fame while visiting a friend of her mother's in the village of Broadhinny, Poirot's mind flew back to his sufferings at the Long Meadows guest home in *Mrs McGinty's Dead*:

> 'And the food? Did you enjoy the food?'
>
> 'Well, it was a bit peculiar sometimes,' Julia admitted.
>
> 'Peculiar, yes, indeed.'
>
> 'But Aunt Maureen makes smashing omelettes.'
>
> 'She makes smashing omelettes.' Poirot's voice was happy.
>
> He sighed.
>
> 'Then Hercule Poirot has not lived in vain,' he said. 'It was *I* who taught your Aunt Maureen to make an omelette.'

Cat Among the Pigeons, Poirot's last case of the 1950s,[5] found him briskly at work and seemingly oblivious to old age, but *The Clocks*, published in 1963, presents a different picture.

In a prim Victorian crescent in a seaside town, Colin

Lamb, a young undercover agent, stumbles on a murder. Discussing the case with Detective Inspector Hardcastle of the Crowdean Police, Colin suggests consulting a specialist:

> 'A private detective – a friend of my dad's – and a friend of mine. This fantastic business of yours will be just down his street. He'll love it – it will cheer him up. I've an idea he needs cheering up.'
>
> 'What's his name?'
>
> 'Hercule Poirot.'
>
> 'I've heard of him. I thought he was dead.'
>
> 'He's not dead. But I have a feeling he's bored. That's worse.'[6]

Before ushering Colin into Poirot's sitting-room, George murmured discreetly into his ear, 'I think, sir, that sometimes he gets a little depressed' – and it was indeed a bit sad to find the great Hercule Poirot whiling away his time reading detective novels:

> 'Then we will take the *Adventures of Arsène Lupin*,' Poirot went on. 'How fantastic; how unreal. And yet what vitality there is in them, what vigour, what life! They are preposterous, but they have panache. There is humour, too.'
>
> He laid down the *Adventures of Arsène Lupin* and picked up another book. 'And here is *The Mystery of the Yellow Room*. That – ah, that is really a classic! I approve of it from start to finish. Such a logical approach!'

But oh for a real problem!

He sighed. 'But problems, *mon cher*, are not so easy to come by. It is true that last Thursday one presented itself to me. The unwarranted appearance of three pieces of dried orange peel in my umbrella stand. How did they come there? How *could* they have come there? I do not eat oranges myself. Georges would never put old pieces of orange peel in the umbrella stand. Nor is a visitor likely to bring with him three pieces of orange peel. Yes, it was quite a problem.'

'And you solved it?'

'I solved it,' said Poirot.

He spoke with more melancholy than pride.

'It was not in the end very interesting.'

It was clearly time for a more substantial case. Recounting the strange events at Wilbraham Crescent – the discovery of an unknown man stabbed to death in a sitting-room mysteriously filled with clocks – Colin demanded a solution. 'I've given you the facts,' he said to Poirot, 'and now I want the answer.'

'Just like that, *hein*?' said Poirot and in due course, patiently peeling away the 'fantastic trappings' of the crime, he found it. Everyone was delighted.

It is an interesting and endearing fact about the elderly Poirot that while people like George and Colin Lamb were being kind and concerned and a bit condescending about his lack of anything more to do than read old whodunits, Poirot was, in fact, researching and writing a very solid book. On the first page of *Third Girl*, published in 1966, we are treated to a picture of satisfaction in a job well done:

He had finished his *Magnum Opus*, an analysis of great writers of detective fiction. He had dared to speak scathingly of Edgar Allan Poe, he had complained of the lack of method or order in the romantic outpourings of Wilkie Collins, had lauded to the skies two American authors who were practically unknown, and had in various other ways given honour where honour was due and sternly withheld it where he considered it was not. He had seen the volume through the press, had looked upon the results and, apart from a really incredible number of printer's errors, pronounced that it was good. He had enjoyed this literary achievement and enjoyed snorting with disgust as he flung a book across the floor (though always remembering to rise, pick it up and dispose of it tidily in the waste-paper basket) and had enjoyed appreciatively nodding his head on the rare occasions when such approval was justified.

But on the heels of this accomplishment there came a painful blow to Poirot's pride – a would-be client who changed her mind about consulting him on a murder she *might* have committed.

His visitor was a girl of perhaps twenty-odd. Long straggly hair of indeterminate colour strayed over her shoulders. Her eyes, which were large, bore a vacant expression and were of a greenish blue. She wore what were presumably the chosen clothes of her generation. Black high leather boots, white open-work woollen stockings of doubtful cleanliness, a skimpy skirt, and a long and sloppy pullover of heavy wool.

She and Poirot looked at each other. '*You're too old*,' she said, 'I'm really very sorry.' Nameless and distraught, she blundered away.

It took a large cup of chocolate topped with whipped cream before Mrs Oliver, to whom Poirot rushed for comfort, could calm him. 'You do not understand,' he cried, when she urged him to forget his strange caller. 'I am worried about this girl. She came to me for *help*.'

To lighten his misery they set out to find Poirot's visitor. Early in their investigation Mrs Oliver deduced that she was a Third Girl. Poirot had never heard the term before.

> 'Good gracious, don't you know what a third girl is? Don't you read *The Times*' . . .
>
> She went to a side table and snatched up *The Times*, turned the pages over and brought it to him. 'Here you are – look. 'THIRD GIRL *for comfortable second floor flat, own room, central heating, Earl's Court.*' '*Third girl wanted to share flat, 5gns. week own room.*' . . . It's the way girls like living now. Better than P.G.s or a hostel. The main girl takes a furnished flat, and then shares out the rent. Second girl is usually a friend. Then they find a third girl by advertising if they don't know one.'

In searching for their third girl, and in tracking her difficulties, Hercule Poirot and Ariadne Oliver encountered the swinging London of the Sixties. Poirot had observed the mores of the young in the late 1950s – Teddy Boys, coffee bars, stereos, tight blue jeans, fishermen's jerseys and so on – but now the youth revolution burst upon him in full flower. 'Long-haired young fellows, beatniks, Beatles, all sorts of names they've got,' complained one of his contemporaries:

> 'They probably look like mods or rockers or beatniks or whatever they call these chaps nowadays with the long

hair and the dirty nails. I've seen more than one of them prowling about. One doesn't like to say 'Who the devil are you?' You never know which sex they are, which is embarrassing. The place crawls with them. I suppose they're Norma's friends. Wouldn't have been allowed in the old days. But you turn them out of the house, and then you find out it's Viscount Endersleigh or Lady Charlotte Marjoribanks. Don't know where you are nowadays.'

It was all very confusing. At times in *Third Girl* – despite once again hiring the formidable talents of Mr Goby and receiving behind-the-scenes help from Scotland Yard – Poirot wondered if he and Mrs Oliver would ever manage to solve this case. Mrs Oliver was coshed on the head in an alley near the King's Road, and Poirot was reduced to the depths of despair ('Perhaps I *am* too old . . . What *do* I know?'), but in the end they overcame.

Hallowe'en Party, published in 1969, saw the collaboration once again of Poirot, Mrs Oliver and Superintendent Spence, the trio who had worked together so winningly in *Mrs McGinty's Dead*.

In the latter years of Poirot's life the ever-enthusiastic Ariadne Oliver became something of a constant. 'Hercule Poirot speaks' was one of the grandiloquent ways in which he answered the phone, and increasingly the voice on the other end tended to be Mrs Oliver's – 'a magnificent booming contralto which caused Poirot hastily to shift the receiver a couple of inches further from his ear'. 'That's wonderful,' she might begin, all out of breath. 'I wanted to get hold of you urgently – absolutely urgently,' for Mrs Oliver not only constantly invented murders in the course of writing detective novels, but she had, as well, the habit of encountering them first-hand in her own gloriously disorganized life.

Superintendent Spence, Poirot's other great ally in old age, was by now retired, but in his day he had been a police officer of high rank and reputation. He and Poirot held each other in great esteem, and in several of Poirot's later cases Spence's well maintained contacts with Scotland Yard and local police forces proved invaluable.

In *Hallowe'en Party* Ariadne Oliver, while visiting a friend in the town of Woodleigh Common, had the misfortune to be present at a children's party at which an appalling murder was committed – the drowning of a thirteen-year-old girl in a galvanized water bucket as she knelt to bob for apples.

Poor Mrs Oliver! With her, apples were almost a motif:

> She was either eating an apple or had been eating an apple – witness an apple core nestling on her broad chest – or was carrying a bag of apples.

But never again. 'I hate apples,' she announced to Poirot when she burst upon him with news of this murder. 'I never want to see an apple again . . .' It was now his turn to be soothing: 'He stretched out a hand and filled a small glass with cognac. "Drink this," he said. "It will do you good,"' and as soon as Mrs Oliver had recovered a bit, and Poirot had recalled that Superintendent Spence lived in Woodleigh Common, their course was set. In their subsequent investigation the police co-operated beautifully, of course.

A dreamy quality, a gradual slowing of pace, are often present in Poirot's last cases, and nowhere are these more evident than in this narrative set in an early November. 'We are up against ruthlessness, quick reactions, greed pushed beyond an expectable human limit,' said Poirot, but in vanquishing these dragons he often paused to contemplate other things: the artifacts of old rituals, the secret lives of children, the stirrings of leaves and shadows in an enchanted garden.

The case of *Elephants Can Remember*, published in 1972, began with Ariadne Oliver's reluctant attendance at a literary luncheon. In the course of it she was trapped over coffee by what Poirot was apt to call *une femme formidable*:

> 'You'll be very surprised, really, at what I'm going to say,' said Mrs Burton-Cox. 'But I have felt, from reading your books, how sympathetic you are, how much you understand of human nature. And I feel that if there is anyone who can give me an answer to the question I want to ask, you will be the one to do so.'

Her question was about a young woman, Celia Ravenscroft, a god-daughter of Mrs Oliver's, whom Mrs Burton-Cox's only son hoped to marry. 'Mrs Burton-Cox leaned forward and breathed hard . . . 'Did her mother kill her father or was it the father who killed the mother?' she asked.'

> And really, thought Mrs Oliver, wishing she was brave enough to say it, how on earth *you* have the impertinence to ask me such a thing, I don't know.

Neither did she know the answer to the question. She remembered Celia as a baby ('and had found a very nice Queen Anne silver strainer as a christening present. Very nice. Do nicely for straining milk and would also be the sort of thing a god-daughter could always sell for a nice little sum if she wanted ready money at any time'), and she remembered the dreadful news of Celia's parents' deaths – both found shot at the top of a cliff – but beyond this she knew nothing. As 'Mrs Burton-Cox dipped a lump of sugar in her coffee and crunched it in a rather carnivorous way, as though it was a bone', Mrs Oliver was seized with sudden concern for her mislaid god-daughter and, it must be admitted, rampant curiosity. Which of Celia's parents *had* killed the other?

As always in such quandaries, she sought out Poirot:

> 'I expect I'm mad,' said Mrs Oliver sadly. She brushed her hands through her hair again so that she looked like the old picture books of Struwwelpeter. 'I was just thinking of starting a story about a golden retriever. But it wasn't going well. I couldn't get started, if you know what I mean.'

'All right, abandon the golden retriever,' replied Poirot, who had scented something far more interesting. Their new case had begun.

It was, of course, a trip to the past to reconstruct and re-interpret old motives and events. First Mrs Oliver had to retrieve her god-daughter ('And – very modern, you know. Goes about with long-haired people in queer clothes. I don't think she takes drugs'). Next, a consultation had to be arranged:

> 'This is Monsieur Hercule Poirot. He has special genius in finding out things.'
>
> 'Oh,' said Celia.
>
> She looked very doubtfully at the egg-shaped head, the monstrous moustaches and the small stature. 'I think,' she said rather doubtfully, 'that I have heard of him.'

> Hercule Poirot stopped himself with a slight effort from saying firmly, 'Most people have heard of me.' It was not quite as true as it used to be, because many people who had heard of Hercule Poirot and known him were now reposing with suitable memorial stones over them in churchyards.

Then serious sleuthing began. In the course of it Poirot even flew to Geneva to interview a retired governess, but mainly he relied on that splendid network of his old age: Superintendent Spence – who produced the very police officer who had once been in charge of the case – and that 'great purveyor of information', the enigmatic Mr Goby:

> Mr Goby came into the room and sat, as indicated by Poirot, in his usual chair. He glanced around him before choosing what particular piece of furniture or part of the room he was about to address. He settled, as often before, for the electric fire, not turned on at this time of the year. Mr Goby had never been known to address the human being he was working for directly. He selected always the cornice, a radiator, a television set, a clock, sometimes a carpet or a mat. Out of a briefcase he took a few papers.
>
> 'Well,' said Hercule Poirot, 'you have something for me?'
>
> 'I have collected various details,' said Mr Goby.

Elephants Can Remember was Poirot's penultimate case. Had he discovered, in his awful *tisanes* and *sirops*, the secret of eternal life? Sadly, as we shall see in *Curtain*, his last case, he was to meet an end common to all, but before taking again the road to Styles, there is still much to learn about Hercule Poirot.

NOTES

1 Also published under the title *Blood Will Tell.*

2 Also published under the title *Funerals are Fatal.*

3 Also published under the title *Hickory Dickory Death.*

4 While this is Poirot's only recorded contact with The Arrangers, Mr Robinson and his syndicate appeared in several other Christie novels.

5 Though set in the 1950s, the lively short story 'The Adventure of the Christmas Pudding' (also published under the title 'The Theft of the Royal Ruby') is an expanded version of the 'Christmas Adventure' of the 1920s. Also set in the 1950s, 'The Mystery of the Spanish Chest' is an expanded version of 'The Mystery of the Baghdad Chest' of the 1930s.

6 It is likely that Colin Lamb, who operated under an assumed name, was the son of Superintendent Battle, Poirot's old friend from *Cards on the Table.*

7

The Complete Poirot

'You're unique. Once seen, never forgotten.'
—Inspector Japp, Peril At End House

Any number of artists have taken a turn at depicting Hercule Poirot. The most memorable examples appeared with the early short stories in magazines of the 1920s. A familial resemblance of moustaches and a foreign dandified look links these illustrations but there are also great differences. Here he is elderly and almost bald, there he is middle-aged and well-thatched. Here he is lean and dangerous in a lounge suit, there he is rotund and comic in tails.

The most famous of these illustrations is W. Smithson Broadhead's portrait of Poirot which appeared in *The Sketch* of 21 March 1923. In it a small sturdy Poirot stands in a haughty pose, his left hand leaning on stick, his right hand holding a top hat and gloves. He is wearing impeccably formal clothes and on his feet are pointed black shoes and gleaming white spats. His head is tilted to one side and on his face – moustaches curling upwards, eyebrows raised – is a disdainful expression in the Versailles mode. *C'est moi*! It was 'not unlike my idea of him', wrote Agatha Christie in her autobiography, 'though he was depicted as a little smarter and more aristocratic than I had envisaged him.' With those in the role of Poirot on stage and screen she was not so happy. 'It always seemed strange to me,' she observed, 'that whoever plays Poirot is always an outsize man'; and she wrote him out of several adaptations of books to the stage rather than see him miscast.[1]

Poirot himself had a very clear idea of his appearance and spent an inordinate amount of time maintaining it. He had only to look in a mirror (and he often did) to see, as in *The Labours of Hercules*, 'a small compact figure attired in correct urban wear with a moustache . . . magnificent yet sophisticated'. This accords well with many descriptions of him over the years. Here is a typical one from *Third Girl*, one of his last cases. It could as easily have been from his first:

> A moment or two later Claudia Reece-Holland returned ushering with her a small man with an egg-shaped head, large moustaches, pointed patent leather shoes and a general air of complacency . . .

There is no doubt, however, that to English eyes Poirot looked odd. 'It was an unfortunate circumstance,' wrote Hastings in *The ABC Murders*, 'that the first time people saw my friend they were always disposed to consider him a joke of the first order.' 'A ridiculous-looking little man,' thought Mary Debenham in *Murder on the Orient Express*. 'The sort of little man one could never take seriously.' People often mistook him for a hairdresser or a piano tuner.

He was five feet, four inches tall and 'delicately plump' with a stomach 'pleasantly rounded'. His feet were small and he had 'tiny, fastidiously groomed hands' with 'short stubby' fingers. His head, as was so often remarked, was egg-shaped, and his eyes, 'bright, inquiring, roguish', were a 'queer catlike green'. His Gallic eyebrows were expressive and on occasion 'climbed slowly up his forehead until they nearly disappeared into his hair'.

Throughout his long life his straight hair remained a glossy black. We have already heard him recommending his ingenious hairdresser to a horrified Hastings, and, as a back-up, he kept in his bedroom a bottle of REVIVIT:

> REVIVIT – *To bring back the natural tone of the hair.* REVIVIT *is* NOT *a dye. In five shades, Ash, Chestnut, Titian, Brown, Black.*

Is there a single word to do justice to Poirot's famous moustaches, which pointed to the skies with such flamboyant *élan*? 'Gigantic', 'luxurious', 'immense', 'amazing', 'magnificent', are but a few of the adjectives that attempted it. 'In England,' he once said, 'the cult of the moustache is lamentably neglected'; and he tended his moustaches, which were as suspiciously black as his hair, with tiny combs, a variety of pomades, and curling tongs which he heated over a small spirit stove.

One of the reasons Poirot disliked travel – especially in warm climates – was that the 'ferocious' points of his moustaches were apt to go limp, and one of the greatest sacrifices he ever made was to temporarily shave his moustaches off to outwit the Big Four. A prospect even more appalling was suggested by Hastings in *The ABC Murders*:

> 'I suppose next time I come home I shall find you wearing false moustaches – or are you doing so now?'
>
> Poirot winced. His moustaches had always been his

sensitive point. He was inordinately proud of them. My words touched him on the raw.

'No, no, indeed, *mon ami*. That day, I pray the good God, is still far off. The false moustaches! *Quelle horreur*!'

Poirot was also a fanatic in the matter of clothes. 'Madame, I like to look *soigné* in my appearance,' he told Ariadne Oliver in *Hallowe'en Party*. Wrote Hastings in 'The Mystery of the Baghdad Chest':

> To see Poirot at a party was a great sight. His faultless evening clothes, the exquisite set of his white tie, the exact symmetry of his hair parting, the sheen of pomade on his hair, and the tortured splendour of his famous moustaches – all combined to paint the perfect picture of an inveterate dandy.

As to his daytime attire, there are mentions of grey or brown suits and waistcoats. In pre-war years he was apt to be more formally dressed, as in *The Labours of Hercules*:

> Dr Burton's eyes swept over Hercule Poirot, over his small neat person attired in striped trousers, correct black jacket, and natty bow tie, swept up from his patent leather shoes to his egg-shaped head and the immense moustache that adorned his upper lip.

When anywhere near the Mediterranean Poirot liked his clothes to be white – a white duck suit for the Riviera, for example, white flannels for Rhodes, and white silk for Egypt. A black bow tie, a pink shirt, and a flower in his buttonhole typically completed the dazzling effect.

Why the elegant cut of these clothes was not hopelessly

marred by all Poirot carried in his pockets is a mystery in itself. He seemed never to be without a small comb, a mirror, a clothes brush, a large silk handkerchief, a pocket case or wallet, a card case, a tiny notebook with a pencil in the loop, a cigarette case, a pocket almanac, a safety pin, and, of course, his turnip-shaped watch (in later years this was put away and replaced by a neat wrist-watch). From time to time – and despite his criticisms of Holmesian methods of detection – he also produced from his pockets a folding measure, a pocket lens, a pocket microscope, tweezers, small forceps, an electric torch, an empty matchbox, an empty test tube, a thumbograph album for fingerprinting, a small flask of brandy, a bottle of turpentine and a sponge, and a set of burglary tools. On one occasion, in his duel to the death with the Big Four, he carried a small automatic pistol, and in *Murder in Mesopotamia*, behind the lapel of his coat, he secreted 'a long sharp darning needle with a blob of sealing wax making it into a pin'.

Out of doors Poirot always wore a hat – a top hat for evenings, a grey Homburg or black bowler by day, and a Panama in warm climates. In *Death on the Nile* he wore a white toupee on one occasion and, on another, carried 'a highly ornamental fly whisk with a sham amber handle'. When in an officious mood he carried a small dispatch-case and when in a sociable one something to swing with a jaunty air. Sometimes he carried a cane, but more often it was an ornate walking stick with an embossed gold handle, the very thing to make a bluff Englishman, like Commander Challenger in *Peril at End House*, wince. In his jewel case were to be found a gold scarf pin and pearl studs and, on his feet, pointed black patent leather shoes.

Oh those cruel shoes of Poirot! 'A nice pair of brogues?'

George respectfully suggested from time to time. On one occasion, when holidaying in Devon, Poirot recklessly wore a pair of white suede shoes, but for most of his life nothing could part him from his black patent leather shoes. 'Take your shoes off,' Mrs Oliver suggested in *Hallowe'en Party* when Poirot complained of his painful feet:

> 'No, no, I could not do that.' Poirot sounded shocked at the possibility.
>
> 'Well, we're old friends together,' said Mrs Oliver . . . 'You know, if you'll excuse my saying so, you oughtn't to wear patent leather shoes in the country. Why don't you get yourself a nice pair of suede shoes? Or the things all the hippy-looking boys wear nowadays? You know, the sort of shoes that slip on, and you never have to clean . . .'
>
> 'I would not care for that at all,' said Poirot severely. 'No indeed!'

Poirot took the outdoors very seriously – especially the English outdoors – and in his wardrobe hung several mackintoshes and a large collection of overcoats: thin ones, heavy ones, and, when he became rich, fur-lined ones. With them he wore silk scarves in warm weather and woolly waistcoats and mufflers in cool. In temperatures below freezing he could be found in *several* coats and mufflers. He wore galoshes at the slightest hint of rain and had gloves for every occasion. Oddly, he never seems to have carried an umbrella.

When he took off his clothes and his painful shoes Poirot donned a 'resplendent' dressing-gown and embroidered slippers. In *After the Funeral*, Lanscombe, the butler at Enderby Hall:

> looked disapprovingly at Hercule Poirot's back as the latter climbed the stairs. Poirot was attired in an exotic silk dressing gown with a pattern of triangles and squares.

In bed Poirot wore the fashions of two eras. When he turned out the light in 'The Adventure of the Christmas Pudding'[2] he was arrayed in pyjamas *and* a nightcap.

'The neatness of his attire was almost incredible,' wrote Hastings. 'I believe a speck of dust would have caused him more pain than a bullet wound.' Very occasionally Poirot went against his better judgement and allowed himself, in the interests of a case, to be untidy. In 'The Veiled Lady', for instance, to Hastings's amazement, he groped through a Wimbledon coal-bin, and in 'The Lost Mine' he was persuaded to make a dishevelled appearance in an opium den, but such exceptions only proved the rule – there was no peace of mind for Poirot unless he was faultlessly dressed.

Maintaining these impeccable standards consumed most of Poirot's spare time for years. By day his clothes brush 'waged an unceasing war on the dust which accumulated on his dark apparel', and in the evenings the smell of benzene hung in the air. When summer came his winter clothes had to be laid away in 'the powder of Keatings', and when the winter came they had to be taken out. The work went on and on.

No one was better at solving problems than Poirot. With his decision to employ a valet, this unending toil passed forever into the capable hands of George. Poirot's linen, however, was still sent out, and in 'The Dream' we catch a glimpse of a spirited war with his laundress – 'That miserable woman who ruins my collars!'

Having taken on board the amiable bow, the gleaming moustaches, and the spotless clothes of this odd little stranger, the next thing immediately apparent to anyone of the island race was the fact that Poirot was a foreigner – a gallant little Belgian, to be sure, but suspiciously French-like for all that. Those exaggerated gestures, those idioms so extravagant to the English ear – 'Oh dear,' thought Rhoda Dawes in *Cards on the Table*, confronted by a Poirot in a particularly Gallic mode, 'He's going to be French and it does embarrass me so.'

Though Rhoda, gingerly sipping blackberry *sirop*, was spared, one of the most embarrassing things about Poirot was his habit of embracing and kissing in moments of excitement. 'Suddenly clasping me in his arms, he kissed me warmly on both cheeks,' wrote Hastings, shaken, in *The Mysterious Affair at Styles*. 'Ah, you are a brave man! If we were not in the street, I would embrace you!' cried Poirot in *The Big Four* to Mr Ingles, a retired civil servant. Mr Ingles looked relieved.

Alien as well was Poirot's repertoire of dramatic shrugs, lightning movements, and unexpected noises. In *The Murder of Roger Ackroyd*, for example, his innuendoes to Caroline Sheppard were expressed by 'his eyebrows and his shoulders'. In *Sad Cypress*, in a poignant moment, 'He spread out his hands in a wide, appealing foreign gesture'. In 'The Under Dog' he broke 'into a fantastic little dance'. In *The Mysterious Affair at Styles*, in moments of joy, he both gambolled 'wildly' on a lawn and 'swayed backwards and forwards, apparently suffering the keenest agony'. In *The Big Four* he 'uttered an excited yelp, reminiscent of a Pomeranian dog', and in *Murder in Mesopotamia* his throat clearing caused Nurse Leatheran to observe: 'I've always noticed that foreigners can make the oddest noises'.

In meditative moments Poirot became inscrutable. Hastings particularly resented his habit of abandoning a scene of action for an armchair, 'furiously to think'. There he would sit, an aloof little cat, stroking his chin and caressing his moustaches.

Of course nothing displayed Poirot's foreignness more than his French accent and exclamations – '*Sacré mille tonnerres!*', '*Nom d'un nom d'un nom!*' – and his idiosyncratic use of the English language. Examples abound: 'I will not derange you further' . . . 'I perceive that you think Lady Astwell has in her bonnet the buzzing bee' . . . 'Among the sleeping dogs there is one on whom I shall put my foot, and by shooting the arrows into the air, one will come down and hit a glass-house!'

'I speak the English very well,' he once declared, 'except when I am excited – but hardly so as to deceive the ear.' Poirot was right. His English was memorably adequate and he understood every nuance in return. Moreover, in these mixed metaphors there was a method, as he explained to Mr Satterthwaite in *Three Act Tragedy*:

> 'Why do you sometimes speak perfectly good English and at other times not?'
>
> Poirot laughed.
>
> 'Ah, I will explain. It is true that I can speak the exact, the idiomatic English. But, my friend, to speak the broken English is an enormous asset. It leads people to despise you. They say, 'A foreigner; he can't even speak English properly.' It is not my policy to terrify people; instead, I invite their gentle ridicule.'

When the Big Four Syndicate prepared a dossier on its enemy, it pinpointed two of Poirot's most ingrained traits and possible weaknesses – a 'finicky tidiness' and an 'overweening vanity'.

Everyone needs something to cling to. With Poirot it was tidiness. Asked Nick Buckley in *Peril at End House*:

> 'Are you very tidy, M. Poirot?'
>
> 'Ask my friend Hastings here.'
>
> The girl turned an inquiring gaze on me.
>
> I detailed some of Poirot's minor peculiarities – toast that had to be made from a square loaf – eggs matching in size – his objection to golf as a game 'shapeless and haphazard' whose only redeeming feature was the tee boxes! I ended by telling her the famous case which Poirot had solved by his habit of straightening ornaments on the mantelpiece.

With Poirot impeccable clothes were only the beginning. Such was his mania that he tidied up wherever he happened to be, especially in moments of agitation. 'I do not like confusion,' was his cry, heading straight towards the nearest cluttered bookcase or mantelpiece for therapy. When John Cavendish threw a match into a flowerbed in *The Mysterious Affair at Styles*, Poirot 'retrieved it and buried it neatly.' When gazing upon the Pyramids in 'The Adventure of the Egyptian Tomb' he observed:

> 'It is true that they, at least, are of a shape solid and geometrical, but their surface is of an unevenness most unpleasing. And the palm-trees I like them not. Not even do they plant them in rows!'

Nor did his worries stop with inanimate objects. 'I never cease trying to persuade Hastings to part his hair in the middle instead of on the side. See what an air – lopsided and unsymmetrical – it gives him,' he scolded in *Peril at End House*, and in *The Mysterious Affair at Styles* Cynthia Murdoch reported: 'He made me take the brooch out of my tie the other day, and put it in again, because he said it wasn't straight.'

Nothing gave him more pleasure than catching an untidy criminal. In 'How Does Your Garden Grow?', for example, he rejoiced to find a few shells of the wrong size in a flower-bed border, and in 'The Adventure of Johnnie Waverly' he gloated over dust in the corners.

His other great obsession was himself. 'The fellow is the most conceited little devil I ever met,' said Sir Charles Cartwright in *Three Act Tragedy*: Poirot was forever bragging that he had 'the finest brain in Europe' and knew everything. Though on occasion he adopted a mock-modest air, no one enjoyed fame more than he. 'Even in our remote country village we have heard of you,' declared an admirer in *Peril at End House* to audible purrs.

A failure stung Poirot to the heart. 'It is impossible. I *cannot* be wrong!' he would cry, and then would follow a short bout of true and disarming humility: 'I am a triple imbecile, a miserable animal; thirty-six times an idiot.' As a rule, however, vanity was one of Poirot's outstanding characteristics and, like his mutilation of the English metaphor, it had its uses. In *Three Act Tragedy* he observed:

> 'An Englishman he says often, 'A fellow who thinks as much of himself as that cannot be worth much.' That is the English point of view. It is not at all true. And so, you see, I put people off their guard. Besides,' he added, 'it has become a habit.'

His adopted milieu also found disconcerting the unashamed way he told falsehoods and pried into other people's business. We are told in *Five Little Pigs*:

> It has been said of Hercule Poirot by some of his friends and associates, at moments when he has maddened them most, that he prefers lies to truth and will go out of his way to gain his ends by means of elaborate false statements rather than trust to the simple truth.

Hastings was always taking him to task for this. 'More lies, I suppose?' he exclaimed in *Dumb Witness* when, in the course of a few hours, Poirot changed his name, posed as a prospective house buyer, invented a couple of relatives, and claimed to be writing the biography of a deceased admiral. 'You are really very offensive sometimes, Hastings,' Poirot replied with dignity. 'Anyone would think I enjoyed telling lies.' As a pragmatist he rejoiced in his belief that the end often justified the means. 'A lot of additional pain and grief is caused by honesty,' he once said. The fact is that Poirot loved subterfuge and often resorted to it for pure pleasure. In *Dumb Witness* he said with relish: '. . . *if* one is going to tell a lie at all, it might as well be an artistic lie, a romantic lie, a convincing lie!'

Equally distressing to Hastings was Poirot's addiction to listening at doors, peering through keyholes, and reading other people's letters. In *Lord Edgware Dies* he calmly read a letter while the Duke of Merton was actually writing it ('in my early days in the police force in Belgium I learned that it was very useful to read handwriting upside down').

> 'Poirot,' I cried. 'You can't do a thing like that, overlook a private letter.'
>
> 'You say the imbecilities, Hastings. Absurd to say I "cannot do" a thing which I have just done!'
>
> 'It's not – not playing the game.'

He could also pick locks and pockets. 'You see,' he said in 'Wasps' Nest',

> 'one of the advantages, or disadvantages, of being a detective is that it brings you into contact with the criminal classes. And the criminal classes, they can teach you some very interesting and curious things.'

'Nice mind you've got, Poirot, I must say,' said his friend Mr Bonnington in 'Four-and Twenty-Blackbirds'. 'All this police work saps your ideals.' In fact this was not so. Poirot was naturally a sceptical man – it was one of the reasons he was such a good detective – but he had a firm code of his own. 'When a person has been murdered,' he said in *Evil Under the Sun*, 'it is more important to be truthful than to be decent.' Order and reason, truth revealed and justice done were his passions. Accused of being sentimental in *One, Two, Buckle My Shoe*, he replied indignantly:

> 'It is not I who am sentimental! That is an English failing! It is in England that they weep over young sweethearts and dying mothers and devoted children. Me, I am logical.'

He resolutely believed in cause and effect. 'You have no doubt heard the Spanish proverb,' he said in 'The Apples of the Hesperides', '*Take what you want – and pay for it, says God*'; and in *Peril at End House* he told a clergyman:

> 'Evil never goes unpunished, Monsieur. But the punishment is sometimes secret.'

'I have a thoroughly bourgeois attitude to murder,' he declared on one occasion and, on another: 'A human being who has exercised the right of private judgement and taken the life of another human being is not safe to exist amongst the community,' but unlike his contemporary, Jane Marple, he was never heard advocating capital punishment. He had, after all, served many years with the police in Belgium, where convicted murderers were never executed but could be sentenced to a lifetime of solitary confinement.

Always he was pragmatic. 'Let us not discuss the Bomb,' he said to Colin Lamb in *The Clocks*. 'If it has to be, it has to be, but let us not discuss it.' In *Dead Man's Folly* an angry young man demanded to know Poirot's attitude towards life:

> 'You are rather old-fashioned in your views, I think. Let's hear what your slogan would be.'
>
> 'I do not need to formulate one of my own. There is an older one in this country which contents me very well.'
>
> 'What is that?'
>
> '*Put your trust in God, and keep your powder dry.*'

In the matter of God, it was Poirot's opinion that people could have 'too much religion or a lamentable lack of religion'. Brought up as a *bon catholique*, he had a habit of making the sign of the cross on momentous occasions, and twice he can be seen in church. In *Taken at the Flood*, in Warmsley Vale,

> In front of Poirot, set back a little, was the Roman Catholic Church of the Assumption, a small modest affair, a shrinking violet compared to the aggressiveness of St Mary's which stood arrogantly in the middle of the Square facing the Cornmarket, and proclaiming the dominance of the Protestant religion.

> Moved by an impulse Poirot went through the gate and along the path to the door of the Roman Catholic building. He removed his hat, genuflected in front of the altar and knelt down behind one of the chairs.

In *One, Two, Buckle My Shoe*, in the course of one of his most perplexing cases, Poirot accompanied his weekend host to church, where he seems to have got along very well with the Anglican liturgy:

> Hercule Poirot essayed a hesitant baritone.
>
> '"The proud have laid a snare for me,"' he sang, '"and spread a net with cords: yea, and set traps in my way – "'
>
> His mouth remained open.
>
> He *saw it* – saw clearly the trap into which he had so nearly fallen!
>
> A snare cunningly laid – a net with cords – a pit open at his feet – dug carefully so that he could fall into it . . .
>
> For the first time, Hercule Poirot was looking at the case *the right way up* . . .
>
> As one in a dream, [he] rose to praise the Lord in the *Te Deum*.

And no doubt Poirot praised the Lord in a collegial spirit, for he appears to have regarded the Almighty as more or less an equal. In *The Mystery of the Blue Train*, castigating a slippery witness,

> He leant forward and struck the table a blow with his fist; his eyes flashed with anger.
>
> 'Yes, yes, it is as I say. You tell your lies and you think nobody knows. But there are two people who know. Yes – two people. One is *le bon Dieu* – '
>
> He raised a hand to heaven, and then settling himself

back in his chair and shutting his eyelids, he murmured comfortably:

'And the other is Hercule Poirot.'

This table-banging and evoking of *le bon Dieu* was not an uncommon occurrence as Poirot had a quick temper, though sometimes – as with so much else in his repertoire – he created tantrums deliberately. In *The Mysterious Affair at Styles* Hastings was upset to hear 'a frightful row going on below. I could hear Poirot shouting and expounding,' thereby revealing the disappearance of an important clue to the whole household. 'Once again,' Hastings wrote, 'I could not help regretting that my friend was so prone to lose his head in moments of excitement.' When Poirot was really angry he was apt to attack furniture. In *Evil Under the Sun* he exclaimed:

> 'I enrage myself at an imbecile. I say, "I would like to kick him." Instead I kick the table. I say, "This table, it is the imbecile, I kick him so." And then, if I have not hurt my toe too much, I feel much better and the table is not usually damaged.'

Another characteristic was his 'steady appraising gaze'. When he wished, this could intimidate. In *Lord Edgware Dies*, questioning a frightened young woman about her beloved cousin in danger, he said bluntly: 'You do not want to see him hanged then?', a remark 'that shocked me in its crudity,' Hastings recalled. In *Peril at End House*, begged to hush up a case, Poirot said imperiously: 'You cannot silence me now,' raising his forefinger in a threatening gesture. But such moments were rare. Ordinarily Poirot was the soul of *politesse*. A prima donna at climactic moments, when offstage – particularly in the early stages of a case – he was apt to be deceptively unobtrusive, his voice lulling and gentle, his manner watchful and composed.

'Everything interests me,' he often said. Sometimes people were surprised at his mania for trivia. Recalled Nurse Leatheran of a conversation in *Murder in Mesopotamia*:

> 'I like all the information there is,' was Poirot's reply.
>
> And really, that described his methods very well. I found later that there wasn't anything – no small scrap of insignificant gossip – in which he wasn't interested.

Even if he had never become a detective, Poirot's insatiable curiosity would have been a hallmark. 'I am a gossip,' he said chattily in *Dead Man's Folly*. 'I like to hear all about people.'

Entertaining, hospitable, full of irony, he was a good companion and could shake with 'the most exquisite mirth', 'his high Gallic laugh' filling the room. As Hastings knew to his cost, he was a terrible tease. 'M. Poirot,' said Jane Olivera in *One, Two, Buckle My Shoe*, 'I never know whether you're serious or not.' He was, of course, a memorable conversationalist and *raconteur*. In *After the Funeral*:

> Graphically, with many gestures, he set forth the story . . . but with such embellishments as his exuberant nature suggested. One almost felt that Hercule Poirot had himself been an eye-witness of the scene.

An enormously important part of Poirot's character was his kindness, and his cases are sprinkled with sympathetic advice to the unhappy and great acts of charity. In *The Mystery of the Blue Train*, for example, it is recalled how he once shielded a misled schoolgirl from suffering the consequences of a robbery, and in 'The Arcadian Deer' he put all business aside to reunite a village garage mechanic with a lost love. In moments of crisis or anxiety he could be a real refuge. In *Evil Under the Sun*, Christine Redfern, a young woman in distress,

> . . . wept stormily and bitterly against Poirot's accommodating shoulder. She said: 'I can't bear it . . . I can't bear it . . .'
>
> Poirot patted her arm. He said soothingly: 'Patience – only patience.'

Despite his dismissal of sentimentality as 'an English failing', Poirot was a cautious romantic and matchmaking was his great hobby. It may be recalled that he had promised himself the pleasure of one day arranging a marriage 'of great suitability' for Hastings, who eluded all this by marrying Cinderella Duveen. Never one to be discouraged, Poirot pressed on, and his record at playing Cupid over the years almost equalled his success at solving crimes. 'Murder, I have often noticed,' he remarked in *The ABC Murders*, 'is a great matchmaker.'

Many of his romantic interventions sprang from his determination to impose order on chaos. 'It is droll the way they arrange the marriages over here,' he observed in 'The Adventure of the Christmas Pudding'.[3] 'No order. No method. Everything left to chance.' Such haphazard proceedings were anathema to Poirot. 'To arrange a good marriage, one must take more than romance into consideration,' he lectured in *Dead Man's Folly*. *Death in the Clouds* is an excellent example of Poirot as matrimonial agent. At the end of the case he was able to say:

> 'In a year's time there will be an announcement: "A marriage is arranged and will shortly take place

> between Lord Horbury and the Hon. Venetia Kerr." And do you know who will have arranged that marriage? Hercule Poirot! There is another marriage that I have arranged too.'
>
> 'Lady Horbury and Mr Barraclough?'
>
> 'Ah, no, in that matter I take no interest.' He leaned forward. 'No, I refer to a marriage between M. Jean Dupont and Miss Jane Grey.'

To arrange all this required the skilful detachment of decent young Stephen Horbury ('a sporting, out-of-door kind of man without anything spectacular in the way of brains') from his unsuitable and philandering wife ('And now, Lady Horbury, will you permit me to give you some advice? Why not arrange with your husband a discreet divorce?') so he might marry his far more suitable neighbour and live happily ever after with 'hunting, tea and muffins, the smell of wet earth and leaves, children'.

To ensure a match between pretty Jane Grey and the young archaeologist who Poirot decided would make her a suitable husband required removing her from the clutches of the wrong man ('with the object of preventing a precipitate marriage, I took Mademoiselle Jane to Paris as my secretary') and making a substantial donation to the archaeologist's forthcoming expedition to Persia so Jane could join it.

After this it should come as no surprise, in *Sad Cypress*, to find Poirot and the stately housekeeper, Mrs Bishop,

> . . . engaged in pleasant conversation on a really interesting theme – no less than the selection of a suitable future husband for Princess Elizabeth.

And with all this matchmaking, what of Poirot himself?

This is a ticklish subject, for in all his cases there is never a mention that he ever seriously considered marriage or any relationship like it. Alas, then, for Amy Leatheran's wonderings in *Murder in Mesopotamia* 'if M. Poirot had a wife, and if he went on in the way you always hear foreigners do, with mistresses and things like that.' From the very beginning, like Sherlock Holmes, Poirot was destined to live as a bachelor.[4] And there is not much point, either, in looking speculatively at Poirot's relationship with Hastings, or pouncing significantly on his occasional notice of male beauty – 'Here,' he thought in 'The Arcadian Deer', 'was one of the handsomest specimens of humanity he had ever seen, a simple young man with the outward semblance of a Greek god.' What evidence there is of Poirot's thoughts on love and sex points towards women and, from all reports, they were thoughts from afar, for Poirot was doomed, like Sherlock Holmes, to love the unobtainable. As Irene Adler was always to Holmes *the* woman, so to Poirot was the Countess Vera Rossakoff. 'What woman was there,' he mused in *One, Two, Buckle My Shoe*,

> who could hold a candle to Countess Vera Rossakoff? A genuine Russian aristocrat, an aristocrat to her fingertips! And also, he remembered, a most accomplished thief – One of those natural geniuses –

At times he contrived to appear sad about all this. 'I, Madame, am not a husband,' he said to an inquirer in *Dead Man's Folly*:

> 'Alas!' he added.
>
> 'I'm sure there's no alas about it. I'm sure you're quite delighted to be a carefree bachelor.'

'No, no, Madame, it is terrible all that I have missed in life.'

Or did he really believe this? The *ménage* he so lovingly created exactly suited his tastes and obsessions. Could any woman have borne it? 'Once, Mademoiselle,' he told a young neighbour in 'The Third-Floor Flat', 'I loved a beautiful young English girl, who resembled you greatly – but alas! – she could not cook. So perhaps everything was for the best.'

Many of Poirot's friends and clients were women. He enjoyed their company and liked springing to his feet, kissing their hands and being gallant and protective whether they wanted to be protected or not. He was especially kind to orphaned young women, such as Katherine Grey in *The Mystery of the Blue Train* and Elinor Carlisle in *Sad Cypress*. '*Pauvre petite*,' he would worry.

Like Miss Marple and her formulae to explain gentlemen, Poirot was full of assumptions about women. Unlike Miss Marple, he also insisted on giving advice. '*Les femmes*,' he would generalize loftily, 'they are marvellous! They invent haphazard – and by miracle they are right' . . . 'It is very necessary for a woman to lie sometimes. Women must defend themselves, and the lie, it can be a good weapon' . . . 'Let me tell you something, Mademoiselle, in the course of my experience I have known five cases of women murdered by devoted husbands, and twenty-two of husbands murdered by devoted wives. *Les femmes*, they obviously keep up appearances better' . . . 'The heart of a woman in love will forgive many blows' . . . and so on.

Sex, in Poirot's opinion, was the 'great force of nature' but we are never permitted to presume that he matched action to words. '*Dieu merci*, I am not of an ardent temperament,' he exclaimed in 'The Mystery of the Baghdad

Chest', 'It has saved me from many embarrassments'; and in 'The Incredible Theft', confronted by a coquettish maid who told him, 'If I meet Monsieur on the stairs, be well assured that I shall not scream', he replied, 'My child . . . I am of advanced years. What have I to do with such frivolities?' And yet – and yet – those of us wishing Hercule Poirot his share of frivolities can, perhaps, take comfort in words once spoken to Hastings: 'Do you not know, my friend, that each of us is a dark mystery, a maze of conflicting passions and desires and aptitudes?'

Despite the 'advanced years' he spoke of to the maid in 'The Incredible Theft', Poirot enjoyed phenomenally good health. From time to time, as the decades went by, the day when he would be finally and utterly old was imminently predicted by both friends and enemies, which is hardly surprising when one considers that he arrived in England at a pensionable age in 1916 and lived until the 1970s.[5] If asked, I am sure Poirot would have attributed his fine health to the unremitting precautions he took against the English climate. Hastings summed this up in *Curtain*:

> He had always been, in my opinion, extremely fussy about his health. Distrusting draughts, wrapping up his neck in silk and wool, showing a horror of getting his feet damp, and taking his temperature and retiring to bed at the least suspicion of a chill – 'For otherwise it may be for me a *fluxion de poitrine*.' In most little ailments, he had, I knew, always consulted a doctor immediately.

A picture of Poirot dealing with influenza is provided in 'The Mystery of Hunter's Lodge': 'He was now sitting up in bed, propped up with pillows, his head muffled in a woollen shawl, and was slowly sipping a particularly noxious *tisane*', his misery somewhat lightened by:

> '. . . a little paragraph to myself in *Society Gossip*. But yes! Here it is: "Go it – criminals – all out! Hercule Poirot – and believe me, girls, he's some Hercules! – our own pet society detective can't get a grip on you. 'Cause why? 'Cause he's got *la grippe* himself!"'

Besides colds, Poirot's other great fear was of seasickness – and later airsickness – which reduced him to a 'wraith of his former self'. In 'The Kidnapped Prime Minister', when crossing the Channel with Hastings, Poirot performed 'gymnastic endeavours' as a counter-measure:

> 'Leave me, my friend. See you, to think, the stomach and the brain must be in harmony. Laverguier has a method most excellent for averting the *mal de mer*. You breathe in – and out – slowly, so – turning the head from left to right and counting six between each breath.'

Apart from this affliction, and the recollection in *Taken at the Flood* of 'sitting, very sick in my stomach' during an air raid, Poirot's digestion was a sturdy one. As he remarked on more than one occasion in the course of his demanding career, 'Mercifully I have an excellent stomach.'

There are hints that Poirot had been more prone to illness earlier in life. In 'The Chocolate Box', reminiscing to Hastings about past cases, he recalled: '*La bonne chance*, it cannot always be on your side . . . Twice have I been stricken down with illness just as I was on the point of success'; and in *Peril at End House* he shuddered when the conversation turned to nursing homes: 'It is not amusing there, the floors of green linoleum, the conversation of the nurses – the meals on trays, the ceaseless washing.'

In Poirot's early years in England his doctor was a bustling, collaborating sort of man named Dr Ridgeway who lived just around the corner from 14 Farraway Street. Later Poirot seems to have preferred to patronize Harley Street specialists, though more for consultations on murder cases than for any ill health of his own. His doctors must have marvelled in their turn at this ageless patient who never needed spectacles, whose hearing was as keen as a cat's, and whose only problems were his phobia about chills, the corns on his feet from his deplorably tight shoes, and 'a certain protuberance in his middle'. In later years, perhaps, they may have lectured him on the dangers of the tiny Russian cigarettes he liked to smoke, though I am sure anyone having the temerity to do so would have received a reproving account of how, in *The Big Four*, a cigarette saved his life.

There is never a mention of Poirot and false teeth. With great trepidation he visited his dentist for a 'twice-yearly overhaul', to be told, as in *One, Two, Buckle My Shoe*: 'Gums are in pretty good condition . . . Just a couple of fillings – and a trace of decay on that upper molar.' Perhaps his good teeth were due to a habit observed in a restaurant in *Death in the Clouds*? – 'Very delicately, so as not to offend English susceptibilities, Poirot used a toothpick.'

For a shock Poirot believed in brandy, for a cold or a headache hot *tisanes*, and for a drowning, as in *Cards on the Table*, he 'stood by' to administer artificial respiration. He himself had occasional accidents, but these were minor and usually self-inflicted to serve some devious purpose. In *Peril at End House* a heavy fall and a supposedly turned ankle brought 'a decidedly pretty girl' to his aid, and in *Murder in Mesopotamia* his loud lamentations when 'I steb the toe' tested a key theory of his on the case. On two occasions his sufferings bordered on martyrdom. From the days of the Big Four case he carried, well hidden by his moustaches, a small scar on his upper lip from an injury deliberately suffered in the interests of disguise; and in 'The Under Dog', to obtain blood as bait for an incriminating trap, he ordered George to stab his fingers with a scarf pin.

From the days of poultices to the era of tranquillizers Poirot defied his age until close to the end, and his occasional complaints of feeling old and mournful tended to be experiments in retirement gone wrong rather than anything medically amiss. Running nimbly up and down stairs, walking briskly to every goal, for him image was all. 'At my age,' he explained in *Three Act Tragedy*, 'one's preoccupation is to arrange one's goods well in the shop window.'

In this, as in almost everything else, he succeeded. In *The Mystery of the Blue Train*, regarding this self-possessed complete little man who enjoyed life immensely, did exactly what he liked, and kept a great many secrets to himself, young Katherine Grey mused that 'there was something very attractive about M. Hercule Poirot.' Millions would agree with her. It is not the easiest run in life to be an eccentric and diminutive alien. Poirot did it very well – and to well-deserved applause.

NOTES

1 In films, over the years, Poirot has been played in different ways by Austin Trevor, Tony Randall, Albert Finney and Peter Ustinov. It is this biographer's opinion, however, that Poirot himself would have found much to approve of in David Suchet's recent portrayal in the London Weekend television series, *Agatha Christie's Poirot*.

2 The second version.

3 The first version.

4 In recalling a discussion with a playwright on the adaptation of *The Murder of Roger Ackroyd* to the stage, Agatha Christie

wrote firmly, 'I much disliked his first suggestion, which was to take about twenty years off Poirot's age, call him Beau Poirot and have lots of girls in love with him.'

5 'In due course I saw what a terrible mistake I had made in starting with Hercule Poirot so *old*,' wrote Agatha Christie in her autobiography, though in doing so she created a heartening model for everyone over sixty-five.

8

The English World of Hercule Poirot

'Oh, you English! With *nous autres* it is different.'
—Hercule Poirot, Murder on the Links

It is 1939 and Poirot is visiting his dentist:

> It was a room furnished in quiet good taste and, to Hercule Poirot, indescribably gloomy. On the polished (reproduction) Sheraton table were carefully arranged papers and periodicals. The (reproduction) Hepplewhite sideboard held two Sheffield plated candlesticks and an epergne. The mantelpiece held a bronze clock and two bronze vases. The windows were shrouded by curtains of blue velvet. The chairs were upholstered in a Jacobean design of red birds and flowers.
>
> In one of them sat a military-looking gentleman with a fierce moustache and a yellow complexion. He looked at Poirot with an air of one considering some noxious insect. It was not so much his gun he looked as though he wished he had with him, as his Flit spray.

There is no doubt that in the English garden Poirot appeared as an aberrant insect. In the foreground people are playing tennis, but here, on the rose bush, is something strange. From his vantage on the rose bush there lay before Poirot a landscape made to order, a mildly precious realm of good taste periodically invaded by murderers. 'Hopelessly bourgeois', Poirot enjoyed all this very much. '*Je suis un peu snob*,' he murmured in *The Hollow*. In the English garden and drawing-room – be it Mayfair, the suburbs or the country – he found his natural hunting and gathering ground. There was, as that Old Etonian, Hastings, pointed out, 'nothing of the Socialist about Poirot'. His *entrée*, despite his alien manners and clothes, was his enthralling ability to solve insoluble crimes and unmask and repel the invaders. For this he expected rich clients to pay handsomely, and when their troubles were over many of them became his patrons. In *Five Little Pigs* Meredith Blake, an 'English country gentleman of straitened means and outdoor tastes', gazed in bewilderment upon a caller bearing letters of introduction:

> As he had often felt lately, things were not what they used to be. Dash it all, private detectives used to be private detectives – fellows you got to guard wedding presents at country receptions, fellows you went to, rather shamefacedly, when there was some dirty business afoot and you had to get the hang of it.
>
> But here was Lady Mary Lytton-Gore writing: 'Hercule Poirot is a very old and valued friend of mine. Please do all you can to help him, won't you?' And Mary Lytton-Gore wasn't – no, decidedly she wasn't – the sort of woman you associate with private detectives and all that they stand for. And Admiral Cronshaw wrote: 'Very good chap – absolutely sound. Grateful if you will do what you can for him. Most entertaining fellow – can tell you lots of good stories.'
>
> And now here was the man himself. Really a most

> impossible person – the wrong clothes, button boots, an incredible moustache! Not his, Meredith Blake's, kind of fellow at all. Didn't look as though he'd ever hunted or shot – or even played a decent game.

Though Poirot was very fond of the English upper classes, and happily ate at their tables and solved their crimes, he remained his own man. Here he is in *The Hollow*, donning his officious dark clothes and grey Homburg hat for Sunday luncheon in the country:

> He knew well enough the kind of clothes that were worn in the country on a Sunday in England, but he did not choose to conform to English ideas. He preferred his own standards of urban smartness. He was not an English country gentleman and he would not dress like an English country gentleman.

On occasions this detachment saved him from pitfalls. In 'Double Clue', for example, observing the agonies of toadying Mr Hardman who refused to believe that his jewels had been stolen by either a countess, a *grande dame* or a millionaire, Poirot remarked to Hastings: 'He has one law for the titled, and another law for the plain, this Mr Hardman. Me, I have not yet been ennobled, so I am on the side of the plain.'

'Hercule Poirot does not hunt down tramps,' he declared in one drawing-room case and, in another, a 'small, ironic voice' in his inner ear chanted, 'Look among the respectable people—'. Poirot's looking among the respectable people for over fifty years is wonderful entertainment and a small slice of social history. He was fond, for example, of invoking the metaphor of the old school tie to explain the English. 'Miss Lawson,' he remarked to Hastings in *Dumb*

Witness of a hired companion suspected of eavesdropping, 'she is not an old school tie, *mon cher*.' 'Now Monsieur Fanthorp,' he said in *Death on the Nile*:

> 'I perceive that you wear the same tie that my friend Hastings wears.'
>
> Jim Fanthorp looked down at his neckwear with some bewilderment.
>
> 'It's an O.E. tie,' he said.
>
> 'Exactly. You must understand that, though I am a foreigner, I know something of the English point of view. I know, for instance, that there are "things which are done" and "things which are not done".'

The English, in Poirot's experience, did not accept bribes, respond readily to direct questions, display their emotions, believe that anyone not born a lady or gentleman could ever become one, or properly understand geography beyond their own island. In *Dumb Witness* he spoke of 'your insular prejudice against the Argentines, the Portuguese and the Greeks'.

Prior to the Second World War there were many casual remarks about Jews. 'A tinge of Jewish blood is not a bad thing,' said Mary Cavendish briskly in *The Mysterious Affair at Styles*. 'It leavens . . . the stolid stupidity of the ordinary Englishman.'

Poirot enjoyed explaining the English. 'What,' asked Dr Constantine, a Greek, 'does a *pukka sahib* mean?' as Colonel Arbuthnot exited in *Murder on the Orient Express* with the words: 'About Miss Debenham . . . you can take it from me that she's all right. She's a *pukka sahib*.' 'It means,' explained Poirot kindly, 'that Miss Debenham's father and brothers were at the same kind of school as Colonel Arbuthnot was.'

'Ah, she is very, very English,' he said, mimicking the 'drawling, well-bred tones' of the Honourable Venetia Kerr in *Death in the Clouds* to the delight of Jane Grey, a hairdresser:

> 'She is the kind that any shopkeeper on the Riviera will give credit to – they are very discerning, our shopkeepers. Her clothes are very well cut, but rather like a man's. She walks about as though she owns the earth; she is not conceited about it; she is just an Englishwoman. She knows which department of England different people come from. It is true; I have heard ones like her in Egypt. "What? The Etceteras are here? The Yorkshire Etceteras? Oh, the Shropshire Etceteras."'

Of those not of the 'Etceteras' but still solidly British Poirot particularly approved. In *Five Little Pigs*, interviewing a shrewd old governess, he reflected:

> Miss Williams' life had been interesting to her – she was still interested in people and events. She had that enormous mental and moral advantage of a strict Victorian upbringing . . . she had done her duty in that station of life to which it had pleased God to call her, and that assurance encased her in an armour impregnable to the slings and darts of envy, discontent and regret.

And he was no doubt pleased with Dr Sheppard's description of his old friend Roger Ackroyd:

> Of course, Ackroyd is not really a country squire. He is an immensely successful manufacturer of (I think) wagon wheels. He is a man of nearly fifty years of age, rubicund

> of face and genial of manner. He is hand and glove with the vicar, subscribes liberally to parish funds (though rumour has it that he is extremely mean in personal expenditure), encourages cricket matches, Lads' Clubs, and Disabled Soldiers' Institutes. He is, in fact, the life and soul of our peaceful village of King's Abbot.

Poirot never could appreciate the English mania for the country life ('the country,' reminisced Rosamund Darnley in *Evil Under the Sun*: 'a big shabby house – horses, dogs – walks in the rain – wood fires – apples in the orchard – lack of money – old tweeds – evening dresses that went on from year to year – a neglected garden – with Michaelmas daisies coming out like great banners in the Autumn . . .'). He was far more interested in what went on *inside* English houses – in the Misses Tripps' cottage in *Dumb Witness*, for instance, a cottage 'so extremely old-world and picturesque that it looked as though it might collapse any minute':

> The interior was very rich in old oak beams – there was a big open fireplace and such very small windows that it was difficult to see clearly. All the furniture was of pseudo-simplicity – ye olde oake for ye cottage dweller – there was a good deal of fruit in wooden bowls and large numbers of photographs.

Or in an elegant bed-sitting-room encountered in 'Murder in the Mews':

> The walls were silver and the ceiling emerald green. There were curtains of a modernistic pattern in silver and green. There was a divan covered with a shimmering emerald green silk quilt and numbers of gold and silver cushions. There was a tall antique walnut bureau, a

walnut tallboy and several modern chairs of gleaming chromium. On a low glass table there was a big ashtray full of cigarette stubs.

Or in a friend's house in *Three Act Tragedy*:

> Mr Satterthwaite's house was on Chelsea Embankment. It was a large house and contained many beautiful works of art. There were pictures, sculpture, Chinese porcelain, prehistoric pottery, ivories, miniatures and much genuine Chippendale and Hepplewhite furniture. It had an atmosphere about it of mellowness and understanding.

Until the 1940s there hovered in the background of these houses an unobtrusive multitude, the servants. As a crucial barometer in Poirot's English world they deserve more than a passing glance. The number in each household varied, of course, depending on the owners' incomes. At the Misses Tripps' 'A child of fourteen or thereabouts opened the door and with difficulty squeezed herself against the walls sufficiently to allow us to pass inside'; while in *Hercule Poirot's Christmas*, at Gorston Hall, Superintendent Sugden reported:

> 'There are eight servants in the house, six of them are women and of those six, five have been here for four years and more. Then there's the butler and the footman. The butler has been here for close on forty years – bit of a record that, I should say. The footman's local, son of the gardener and brought up here . . . The only other person is Mr Lee's valet attendant. He's comparatively new . . .'

In murder cases much could be learned from the Servant's Hall – but only if its inhabitants would co-operate. 'The domestics had withdrawn tactfully,' wrote Hastings in *Peril at End House*, but often they withdrew in possession of the very facts and opinions Poirot wanted to know. Extracting these demanded his most persuasive wiles, for many of the servants he encountered – particularly those at the top of the pecking order – were, if anything, more class-conscious than their employers. In *After the Funeral* Lanscombe the butler was 'courteous but distant'. He clearly 'regarded this upstart foreigner as the materialization of the Writing on the Wall. This was What We are Coming to!' In *Mrs McGinty's Dead* 'An imperturbable manservant opened the door and was loath to admit Hercule Poirot. In his view Hercule Poirot was the kind of caller who is left outside. He clearly suspected that Hercule Poirot had come to sell something.' In *Sad Cypress* the initial responses of Mrs Bishop, the housekeeper, 'were frosty and she eyed him with disfavour and suspicion.'

In a number of cases Poirot never did win over the servants and had to tack his way cautiously around them, but more often they capitulated. A cook-housekeeper in 'Four-and-Twenty Blackbirds' is a good example:

> Mrs Hill was inclined to be stiff and suspicious at first, but the charming geniality of this strange-looking foreigner would have had its effect on a stone. Mrs Amelia Hill began to unbend.

In the world below stairs it was the butlers – the lofty Tredwells – who were the *grands seigneurs*. At the Angkatells, in *The Hollow*, the door was opened by the magnificent Gudgeon. Loyal, discreet and forgiving, Gudgeon was the perfect butler. It may be recalled that it was he who polished a murder weapon belonging to the family because 'I fancied it might be dusty, sir', so it will come as no surprise to learn how he dealt with Lady Angkatell's fondness for reading *News of the World*. 'We pretend,' she said, 'we get it for the servants, but Gudgeon is very understanding and never takes it out until after tea.'

In *Hercule Poirot's Christmas* we are given an insight into a butler's mind as Tressilian circles the dinner table, decanter in hand:

> Mrs Alfred, he noted, had got on her new flowered black and white taffeta. A bold design, very striking, but she could carry it off, though many ladies couldn't. The dress Mrs George had on was a model, he was pretty sure of that. Must have cost a pretty penny! He wondered how Mr George would like paying for it! Mr George didn't like spending money – he never had. Mrs David now, a nice lady, but didn't have any idea of how to dress. For her figure, plain black velvet would have been the best. Figured velvet, and crimson at that, was a bad choice. Miss Peela, now, it didn't matter what she wore; with her figure and her hair she looked well in anything. A flimsy cheap little white gown it was, though . . . 'Hock or claret?' murmured Tressilian in a deferential whisper in Mrs George's ear.

Very occasionally – and usually when murder was about – a butler's mask might slip. Gudgeon himself uttered 'an unbutlerlike noise' when he glimpsed a body in the swimming pool, and in 'Dead Man's Mirror', when Sir Gervase Chevenix-Gore was late for dinner for the first time in twenty years:

> The notes of a gong sounded from the hall, then the butler opened the door and announced:
>
> 'Dinner is served.'

> And then, almost before the last word, 'served,' had been uttered, something very curious happened. The pontifical domestic figure became, just for one moment, a highly astonished human being . . .

As the years went by there were fewer and fewer butlers to whom Poirot could hand his coat, hat and walking stick. In the 1950s old Lanscombe, tottering around Enderby Hall, saw clearly the passing of a regime:

> The third blind in the White Boudoir refused to go up as it should. It went up a little way and stuck. The springs were weak – that's what it was – very old, these blinds were, like everything else in the house. And you couldn't get these old things mended nowadays. Too old-fashioned, that's what they'd say, shaking their heads in that silly superior way – as if the old things weren't a great deal better than the new ones! *He* could tell them that! Gimcrack, half the new stuff was – came to pieces in your hand. The material wasn't good, or the craftsmanship either. Oh yes, *he* could tell them.

Evolution was also at work in another part of Enderby Hall.

> Looking into the kitchen with a word of admonition, Lanscombe was snapped at by Marjorie the cook. Marjorie was young, only twenty-seven, and was a constant irritation to Lanscombe as being so far removed from what his conception of a proper cook should be. She had no dignity and no proper appreciation of his, Lanscombe's, position. She frequently called the house 'a proper old mausoleum' and complained of the immense area of the kitchen, scullery and larder saying that it was a 'day's

walk to get round them all.' . . . Janet, who stood by the kitchen table, refreshing herself with a cup of tea, was an elderly housemaid who, although enjoying frequent acid disputes with Lanscombe, was nevertheless usually in alliance with him against the younger generation as represented by Marjorie. The fourth person in the kitchen was Mrs Jacks who 'came in' to lend assistance where it was wanted . . .

A grander scene greeted Hercule Poirot when he visited the kitchen at Kings Lacy in 'The Adventure of the Christmas Pudding':[1]

There was a moment's pause and then Mrs Ross came forward in a stately manner to meet him. She was a large woman, nobly built with all the dignity of a stage duchess. Two lean grey-haired women were beyond in the scullery washing up and a towhaired girl was moving to and fro between the scullery and the kitchen. But these were obviously mere myrmidons. Mrs Ross was the queen of the kitchen quarters.

The tow-haired girl glimpsed 'moving to and fro between the scullery and the kitchen' was Annie Bates. 'There's always hope when there's a kitchen maid,' said Inspector Grange in *The Hollow*:

'Heaven help us when domestic staffs are so reduced that nobody keeps a kitchen maid any more . . . They're so kept down and in their place by the cook and the upper servants that it's only human nature to talk about what they know to someone who wants to hear it.'

It is interesting to note that Poirot, to reward Annie Bates for warning him of a possible danger, promised to send her a present from London. 'What would you like?' he asked. 'A real posh slap-up vanity box,' replied Annie. Poirot had clearly mellowed over the years, for in an earlier version of 'The Adventure of the Christmas Pudding', published thirty-seven years before, he gave Annie's counterpart no choice of presents but told her:

> 'When I return to London, I will send you an excellent book on *le ménage*, also the Lives of the Saints, and a work upon the economic position of women.'

Mrs Hill, Gudgeon, Tressilian, Annie Bates *et al* are but a sample of the cooks, housekeepers, butlers, valets, governesses, footmen, kitchen maids, parlourmaids, ladies' maids, chauffeurs, gardeners, under-gardeners, aged faithfuls, daily helps and *au pairs* (though scarcely a nanny, oddly) that abounded in Poirot's English world. One category, the paid companion, was made particularly memorable by Amy Carnaby, one of the most remarkable people Poirot ever met. The plight of these indigent respectable women who were, as it was observed in *After the Funeral*, 'dependent for existence on the fears and whims of employers', is described in several cases. In *Dumb Witness*, for example, Miss Emily Arundell had a reputation for treating a succession of companions 'with great generosity' one moment and bullying them 'unmercifully' the next, but with Miss Army Carnaby the worm turned.

Outwardly the most timid of women, in 'The Nemean Lion' Miss Carnaby single-handedly organized a number of her downtrodden colleagues into a protection racket for lapdogs and was well on her way to building up a modest retirement fund when Poirot caught up with her. As she explained:

'Yes, it's difficult for a gentleman to understand, I expect. But you see, I'm not a clever woman at all, and I've no training and I'm getting older – and I'm so terrified for the future. I've not been able to save anything . . . and as I get older and more incompetent there won't be anyone who wants me.'

Poirot was impressed by Miss Carnaby's words and in due course wrote her the following letter:

Dear Miss Carnaby,

Allow me to enclose a contribution to your very deserving fund before it is finally wound up.

Yours very truly,

Hercule Poirot.

When Miss Carnaby turned up again it was with 'The most extraordinary ideas! For instance, yesterday, a really most *practical* scheme for robbing a post office came into my head. I wasn't thinking about it – it just came! And another very ingenious way for evading custom duties. I feel convinced – quite convinced – that it would work'. Poirot hastily recruited her as a legitimate undercover agent for the case of 'The Flock of Geryon'.

With exceptions such as his friend Ariadne Oliver and his secretary Miss Lemon, women in Poirot's milieu who had to earn their own living tended to have a difficult time. If one was in the Servants' Hall there was at least the possibility of rising within that hierarchy, or if one was safely buttressed by the Establishment one could be as cheeky and adventuresome as one chose, but outside these spheres life could be precarious unless a husband came along or a rich relative died.

In wartime things could be different. During the First World War, in *The Mysterious Affair at Styles*, Cynthia Murdoch enjoyed immensely her work at a Red Cross Hospital and proudly showed Hastings through the dispensary. In the Second World War Lynn Marchmont served with distinction in North Africa and Sicily, but when it was over, in *Taken at the Flood*, she read sad advertisements in the daily newspapers:

> 'Ex W.A.A.F. *seeks post where initiative and drive will be appreciated.*' '*Former WREN seeks post where organizing ability and authority are needed.*'

'"Oh! brave new world," thought Lynn grimly . . . Her way ahead lay clear. Marriage to her Cousin Rowley Cloade.'

Women who entered the male domain of politics tended to be looked at askance. In *Appointment with Death* one of the party journeying to the Caves at Petra was a Member of Parliament:

> Lady Westholme threw herself with vigour into political life, being especially active at Question time. Cartoons of her soon began to appear (always a sure sign of success). As a public figure she stood for the old-fashioned values of Family Life, welfare work amongst Women, and was an ardent supporter of the League of Nations. She had decided views on questions of Agriculture, Housing and Slum Clearance. She was much respected and almost universally disliked!

By contrast, in 'The Augean Stables' Mrs Ferrier, who was in the public eye as the wife of the Present Prime Minister and the daughter of a past one, 'was looked up to by the whole nation and was a most valuable asset to the party':

> Poirot looked at her with attention. He saw a tall woman still handsome, with character and intelligence in her face. Mrs Ferrier was a popular figure. As the wife of the Prime Minister, she naturally came in for a good share of limelight. As the daughter of her father, her popularity was even greater. Dagmar Ferrier represented the popular ideal of English womanhood.
>
> She was a devoted wife, a fond mother, she shared her husband's love of country life. She interested herself in just those aspects of public life which were generally felt to be proper spheres of womanly activity.

Poirot, uttering time-worn clichés about women one moment, and vigorously defending the emancipated 'new women' the next, reflected his times. However, like many of his English contemporaries he took it for granted that a woman's most appropriate sphere was the domestic milieu – a place of great interest to Poirot himself, as we shall in due course see.

But for all the people Poirot met in his discovery and exploration of the English, there was one who stands above all as his most useful example and informant. I refer, of course, to Captain Arthur Hastings.

NOTE

1 The second version.

9

Captain Arthur Hastings, OBE

'This is my friend, Captain Hastings. He assists me in my cases.'

—Hercule Poirot, Lord Edgware Dies

'*Mon ami* Hastings', 'my poor Hastings', 'my colleague, Captain Hastings'. Though a constant in Poirot's epic life for only seven years, and an intermittent companion for twelve years after that, the importance of being Hastings in the history of detective literature should not be underestimated. Besides his contribution as Poirot's most trusted adviser on the English, Hastings set a style in recording the great detective's achievements that has addicted readers ever since. Poirot himself perceived him as a major influence and counted him his dearest friend. 'If only,' he would sigh in the years following his friend's departure, '*ce cher Hastings* were available'; or he would exclaim, in the excitement of a chase, 'How my dear friend Hastings would have enjoyed this!'

Of Poirot's exploits, twenty-six stories and eight books are narrated by Hastings, but so enthralled was he with his subject, and so full of proper English reticence about himself, that he tells us practically nothing about his own early life. We know that he went to Eton, but the only member of his family ever mentioned is his great-aunt Mary whose handwriting, he once recalled, had been 'exactly as though a spider had got into an ink pot and were walking over a sheet of notepaper!' It is possible that Hastings was orphaned at an early age, for one of the first things we learn about him is that he had 'no near relations or friends'. Perhaps great-aunt Mary had been his guardian?

Old Etonian though he was, Hastings always had his living to earn and, it may be recalled, he first met Poirot during a business trip to Belgium for Lloyd's of London. While Hastings had always nurtured a secret ambition to be an amateur detective in the tradition of Sherlock Holmes, his encounter with the Belgian Police Force's most famous detective provided an exhilarating new model. Thereafter, beneath his boyish and bluff exterior, there burned in Arthur Hastings a passion for detection *à la Hercule Poirot*. Quite how he went about practising his new hobby is never revealed, but we find him, in the early pages of *The Mysterious Affair at Styles*, confiding his admiration for Poirot to Mary Cavendish, a person he was trying hard to impress. 'My system is based on his – though of course I have progressed rather further,' he told her.

Upon the outbreak of the Great War, Hastings offered his services to his country and was commissioned into the army with the rank of captain. Early in 1916 he was wounded:

> I had been invalided home from the Front; and, after spending some months in a rather depressing Convalescent Home, was given a month's sick leave . . . I was trying to make up my mind what to do, when I ran across John

> Cavendish. I had seen very little of him for some years. Indeed, I had never known him particularly well. He was a good fifteen years my senior, for one thing, though he hardly looked his forty-five years. As a boy, though, I had often stayed at Styles, his mother's place in Essex.
>
> We had a good yarn about old times, and it ended in his inviting me down to Styles to spend my leave there.

As we know, it was at the post office at Styles St Mary on 17 July 1916 that Hastings had his ecstatic reunion with Poirot 'whom I have not seen for years', and it was at Styles Court, as dawn was breaking the next day, that its mistress, Emily Inglethorp, was taken violently ill and died. In a flash Hastings's hobby came into its own. 'Do you know what I think,' he whispered to Mary Cavendish, 'I believe she has been poisoned!', and by six o'clock that morning he was ransacking the library at Styles 'until I discovered a medical book which gave a description of strychnine poisoning.' Within the hour he was banging on the door of Leastways Cottage, the home of Mrs Inglethorp's little colony of Belgian refugees. This was one of the most exciting moments of Hastings's life. Not only was his master at hand, but he, Arthur Hastings, had an authentic murder to lay at his feet!

In the earliest moments of this first collaboration the pattern of the relationship between Poirot and Hastings was set. As Hastings poured forth the confusing details of Mrs Inglethorp's death and his own theories on it, Poirot dressed himself, arranged his moustaches 'with exquisite care', smiled kindly upon his excited pupil and said:

> '. . . I am pleased with you. You have a good memory, and you have given me the facts faithfully. Of the order in which you present them, I say nothing – truly, it is

deplorable! But I make allowances – you are upset . . . Excuse me, *mon ami*, you dressed in haste, and your tie is one one side. Permit me.' With a deft gesture, he rearranged it.

What was really being rearranged, of course, was Arthur Hastings's life, for within hours of the murder at Styles there fell upon him not the mantle of Sherlock Holmes, but that of the loyal and credulous Dr Watson instead. 'It is not my habit to explain until the end is reached,' Poirot told him firmly as they hurried towards Styles Court. So began Hastings's joyful and bewildered new vocation, and so began, a few months later, his famous first narrative, *The Mysterious Affair at Styles*:

> The intense interest aroused in the public by what was known at the time as 'The Styles Case' has now somewhat subsided. Nevertheless, in view of the world-wide notoriety which attended it, I have been asked, both by my friend Poirot and the family themselves, to write an account of the whole story.

By the time Hastings wrote these words he and Poirot were in London, Hastings at a 'half-fledged Army job' at the War Office and Poirot busily establishing himself as a private detective.

Three years later Hastings the Narrator was at it again. Picking up his pen, chewing his pipe stem, and breathing heavily, he began the first of a series of short memoirs of Poirot's cases:

> Pure chance led my friend Hercule Poirot, formerly chief of the Belgian force, to be connected with the Styles

> Case. His success brought him notoriety, and he decided to devote himself to the solving of problems in crime. Having been wounded on the Somme and invalided out of the Army, I finally took up my quarters with him in London. Since I have a first-hand knowledge of most of his cases, it has been suggested to me that I select some of the most interesting and place them on record.

In the intervening time, and over the course of many future cases, Poirot and his resident pupil became indispensable to each other. 'I had a friend – a friend who for many years never left my side,' Poirot was later to tell Dr Sheppard in *The Murder of Roger Ackroyd*; and years again after that, in *Lord Edgware Dies*, Hastings was still saying 'Poirot! You are not going to leave me behind. I always go with you.' They made an odd couple, the dandified little foreign detective and his bluff-looking English friend. Though about thirty years old when his adventures with Poirot began, Hastings's naïvety and enthusiasm always made him seem younger than he actually was, and very much younger than Poirot. He was also much taller, with a 'straight back' and 'broad shoulders'. Poirot moved like a cat, while Hastings was apt to rush upstairs two at a time and knock things over. Poirot's moustache was flamboyant, while Hastings's was a conventional 'toothbrush'. Poirot drank *tisanes* and *sirops*, while Hastings preferred whisky and soda. Poirot was artful and eccentric, while Hastings was gullible, faithfully played by the rules, and had 'a horror of doing anything conspicuous'.

Despite their great friendship, they constantly exasperated each other. 'Let us hear M. le Capitaine Hastings on the case,' Poirot might say, and then gleefully pounce on Hastings's impulsive and misled conclusions. 'Never, never will you use the brains the good God has given you,' he might cry or, as in *Peril at End House*, launch into a full-scale lecture:

> 'You have an extraordinary effect on me, Hastings. You have so strongly the *flair* in the wrong direction that I am almost tempted to go by it! You are that wholly admirable type of man, honest, credulous, honourable, who is invariably taken in by any scoundrel. You are the type of man who invests in doubtful oil fields, and nonexistent gold mines.'

And he delighted in keeping poor Hastings in the dark. 'I don't quite see what you are driving at, Poirot,' Hastings would complain when dragged without explanation off a train or dispatched on some inexplicable errand. In *Mrs McGinty's Dead* Poirot recalls his disciple's

> '. . . incredulous wonder, his open-mouthed appreciation of my talents – the ease with which I misled him without uttering an untrue word, his bafflement, his stupendous astonishment when he at last perceived the truth that had been clear to me all along.'

When goaded to retaliate, Hastings could be almost as patronizing. Often this took the form of digs at Poirot's age. 'The idea crossed my mind,' he ruminated in *The Mysterious Affair at Styles*, 'that poor old Poirot was growing old. Privately I thought it lucky that he had associated with him someone of a more receptive type of mind.' In *Peril at End House*, sixteen years later, he was saying much the same thing: 'Poor old Poirot. He was perplexed by this case – I could see that. His powers were not what they were.'

His friend's habits of eavesdropping, prying, and dissembling never failed to horrify him. 'The English character is adverse to lying on a wholesale scale', he was apt to observe primly when recounting some particularly outrageous deception of Poirot's. Not surprisingly, his own considerable vanity was often offended by Poirot's taunts and lectures. 'He always displayed a ridiculous distrust of my capacities,' he wrote accusingly in *The Big Four*. In 'The Adventure of "The Western Star"' he threw a tantrum:

> 'It's all very well,' I said, my anger rising, 'but you've made a perfect fool of me! From beginning to end! No, it's all very well to try and explain it away afterwards. There really is a limit!'
>
> 'But you were so enjoying yourself, my friend, I had not the heart to shatter your illusions.'
>
> 'It's no good. You've gone a bit too far this time.'
>
> '*Mon Dieu*! but how you enrage yourself for nothing, *mon ami*!'
>
> 'I'm fed up!' I went out, banging the door.

Though running battles were the order of the day with Hastings and Poirot, they did nothing to shake their friendship. 'His loyalty to me is absolute,' said Poirot in *Dumb Witness*. Inspector Japp, whom Hastings disliked, put it more baldly. 'Where the master goes, there the dog follows,' he once said in what, as Hastings rightly remarked, 'I could not think was the best of taste.'

It says much for Hastings's honesty that, as Poirot's chronicler, he recorded so many belittling remarks about himself. Indeed, the debt we owe him as scribe has been sadly overlooked. It can't always have been easy, in the years he shared rooms with Poirot, to be ever an unpaid companion and factotum, forever on call to read the newspapers aloud, run for taxis, and work out railway timetables. He had, as well, to hold down a job of his own – though, admittedly, Hastings was fortunate in having employers who gave him astonishing latitude – and on top of all this there was always the task on hand of writing up Poirot's latest case. One imagines Hastings who, after all, was far from studious, toiling away in every spare moment at the sitting-room table at what Poirot lightly called the 'record of my little successes'. Said peppery old Miss Peabody to Hastings in *Dumb Witness*:

> 'Can you write decent English?'
> 'I hope so.'
> 'H'm – where did you go to school?'
> 'Eton.'
> 'Then you can't.'

But Hastings did write decent, if somewhat turgid, English, and so successful was he in recording bewildering progressions of events, conversations *en bloc*, and Gallic eccentricities, that his books were avidly read and garnered Poirot much celebrity. In *The Murder of Roger Ackroyd* a suitably impressed Dr Sheppard told Poirot: 'Well, as a matter of fact I've read some of Captain Hastings's narratives'; and in *The Big Four* Dr Quentin, another country physician, exclaimed: '. . . M. Poirot? You see, I've read all about your methods, and I may say I'm an enormous admirer of yours.'[1]

In the summer of 1923, to Poirot's great surprise, a significant new person appeared in Arthur Hastings's life. Hastings, who had been working for some time as 'a sort of private secretary . . . to an M.P.', was on his way back to London from 'transacting some business in Paris' when he fell impetuously in love with Dulcie Duveen, a most unlikely person. At the very least, as Poirot had often observed, 'Always you have had a penchant for auburn hair!'

In Hastings's compartment on the Calais express on that fateful day there was one other passenger, a very young woman with 'a pretty, impudent face' who, as the train started, suddenly stuck her head out of the window and shouted 'Hell!' Hastings was shocked. Somehow, this young woman explained, her sister had been left behind on the platform. He looked at her carefully. 'The girl,' he decided, 'was certainly all that I most disliked.' She was small and dark, she wore a lot of make-up, she was clearly prepared to talk to strange men in trains, and she was reading a comic book. Nevertheless, he reasoned, 'that was no reason why I should make myself ridiculous by my attitude. I prepared to unbend. After all, she was decidedly pretty.' Before long she was telling Hastings:

> 'I'm an actress. No – not the kind you're thinking of, lunching at the Savoy covered with jewellery, and with their photograph in every paper saying how much they love Madame So and So's face cream. I've been on the boards since I was a kid of six – tumbling.'
>
> 'I beg your pardon,' I said puzzled.
>
> 'Haven't you seen child acrobats?'
>
> 'Oh, I understand.'
>
> 'I'm American born, but I've spent most of my life in England. We got a new show now – '
>
> 'We?'
>
> 'My sister and I. Sort of song and dance, and a bit of patter, and a dash of the old business thrown in. It hits them every time.'

To his amazement Hastings then found himself telling this extraordinary girl all about himself and his friend Poirot:

'. . . a very marvellous little man. Time and again he has proved to be right where the official police have failed.'

My companion listened with widening eyes.

'Isn't that interesting now? I just adore crime. I go to all the mysteries on the movies. And when there's a murder on I just devour the papers.'

With these words Hastings's fate was sealed. 'My companion seemed to have an intuitive knowledge of what was in my mind,' he wrote, and later when Dulcie – or Cinderella as she preferred to be called – inexplicably reappeared and disappeared again in *Murder on the Links*, he found himself confiding his new preoccupation to Poirot:

'I may be old-fashioned, but I certainly don't believe in marrying out of one's class. It never answers.'

'I agree with you, *mon ami*. Ninety-nine times out of a hundred, it is as you say. But there is always the hundredth time! Still, that does not arise, as you do not propose to see the lady again.'

His last words were almost a question, and I was aware of the sharpness with which he darted a glance at me.

Alas for Poirot! Before he could turn around '*la petite acrobate*' and her improbable prince had sailed away to a 'ranch across the seas' with Cinderella's twin sister, Bella, and *her* new husband – a second match born from this unsettling case. Poirot put on the best face he could under the circumstances and even claimed, rather lamely, that in retrieving the lost Cinderella he had arranged a marriage for Hastings after all. '*Mon ami! Vive l'amour*! It can perform miracles,' he exclaimed. 'It defeats even Hercule Poirot!'

Argentina? In *The Mysterious Affair at Styles* an impassioned remark by Mary Cavendish – 'I want to be – free!' – had immediately conjured up in Hastings's mind 'a sudden vision of broad spaces, virgin tracts of forest, untrodden lands . . .' This was exactly the picture that Englishmen like Hastings had of Argentina at that time. *Las pampas*, the Argentine prairie, was romantically famous for its enormous cattle ranches and, on a more practical level, British investors had been taking a profitable interest in Argentine railways and banks since well before the turn of the century. To prospective immigrants the flourishing Argentine appeared, unofficially, to be almost part of the British Empire. It was to a promising land, then, that the adventurous Cinderella and the suddenly starry-eyed Hastings set their course.

At the time of their marriage Cinderella appeared to be 'little more than seventeen', Hastings was about twenty years older, and one quails to think how little they could have known about cattle. It is a fair guess that neither of them had much money, so one suspects that it was Jack Renauld, Cinderella's rich new brother-in-law, who staked them to their ranch.

Cinderella's first taste of being left in charge came about a year and a half later when Hastings departed 'hurriedly as a result of certain business complications' to spend 'some months' in England. In London, like a homing pigeon, he made straight for 'the old address' and stayed there for almost a year. It was, as it turned out, the year of Poirot's epic confrontation with the Big Four and Hastings clearly could not tear himself away. 'You are a staunch friend, Hastings. It is to serve me that you remain on here,' said Poirot, though once or twice he did inquire after 'little Cinderella'. 'I haven't gone into details, of course, but she understands. She'd be the last one to wish me to turn my back on a pal,' Hastings assured him.

It soon transpired that the long arm of the Big Four could reach even as far as a ranch in Argentina for, in the midst of all the other excitements of the case, Hastings received the following cable from his foreman:

> 'Mrs Hastings disappeared yesterday, feared been kidnapped by some gang calling itself big four cable instructions have notified police but no clue as yet.'

I am sure that Cinderella and Hastings – his 'deep tan' long gone – had much to discuss when he finally returned home. What, one wonders, did the feisty Cinderella have to say when Hastings told her of the occasion when he had been duped into apparently sacrificing both their lives to save Poirot's?

Poirot himself had understandably been very moved by this:

> 'You like not that I should embrace you or display the emotion, I know well. I will be very British. I will say nothing – but nothing at all. Only this . . . the honours are all with you, and happy is the man who has such a friend as I have!'

Hastings had indeed displayed much courage in *The Big Four* and was suitably rewarded by a grateful England, for the next time we see his name officially listed it is as Captain Arthur Hastings, OBE in the play *Black Coffee*, his only adventure with Poirot that he himself did not narrate.

In 1932 he returned yet again from 'those clear open

spaces' to visit Poirot and immediately found himself gathering material for another short story, 'The Mystery of the Baghdad Chest', and a new book, *Peril at End House*. 'How I wish I had been with you,' he said wistfully on being told of a case that had occurred in his absence:

> 'I too,' said Poirot. 'Your experience would have been invaluable to me.'
>
> I looked at him sideways. As a result of long habit, I distrust his compliments but he appeared perfectly serious. And after all, why not? I have a very long experience of the methods he employs.
>
> 'What I particularly missed was your vivid imagination, Hastings,' he went on dreamily. 'One needs a certain amount of light relief. My valet, Georges, an admirable man with whom I sometimes permitted myself to discuss a point, has no imagination whatever.'

But some of Poirot's comments were not so subtle, and he and Hastings were soon at it again. In *Peril at End House* Hastings angrily exclaimed:

> 'Do you suppose I'd have made a success of my ranch out in the Argentine if I was the kind of credulous fool you make out?'
>
> 'Do not enrage yourself, *mon ami*. You have made a great succes of it – you and your wife.'
>
> 'Bella,' I said, 'always goes by my judgement.'
>
> 'She is as wise as she is charming,' said Poirot.'[2]

Despite such *contretemps*, Hastings's appetite for playing Watson was whetted all over again, for he stayed on to hunt with Poirot in his next case, *Lord Edgware Dies*. From this he was 'suddenly recalled to the Argentine' and did not return to England for several years. With these two major cases fresh in his mind, he doubtless spent most of his evenings in the intervening time writing furiously.

Hastings may well have needed the extra income he earned by his pen, for in the 1930s Argentina, like most other countries, found itself in difficulties. Of his next trip he wrote solemnly:

> It was in June of 1935 that I came home from my ranch in South America for a stay of about six months. It had been a difficult time for us out there. Like every one else, we had suffered from world depression. I had various affairs to see to in England that I felt could only be successful if a personal touch was introduced. My wife remained to manage the ranch.

As before, the ostensible reason for Hastings's trip seems to have been forgotten as soon as he entered Poirot's sitting-room, though admittedly the *ABC Murders*, just under way, turned out to be an exceptionally exciting investigation. Six months later, in 1936, Hastings was back again in time to join in on an interesting country case, *Dumb Witness*.

After this, for reasons never explained, many years were to pass before the faithful Hastings would record another of Poirot's cases or hear again his hunting cry: '*Vive le sport.*' At the conclusion of *Dumb Witness* he sailed away in the company of Bob, the charming wire-haired terrier he had inherited during his visit, and we hear no more of him for a very long time. One imagines him at last settled down and, of an evening, wistfully poring over the latest book of Poirot's exploits just sent from England.

Oddly, over the years these two fast friends seemed at times to drift out of touch. 'It is a long time since I have had news of him,' said Poirot in *The Clocks* in the early 1960s. 'What an absurdity to go and bury oneself in South America, where they are always having revolutions.' He still missed Hastings very much – 'My first friend in this country – and still to me the dearest friend I have.'

In *Lord Edgware Dies* Hastings allowed himself to record an emotional moment:

> Then, as we sipped our coffee, Poirot smiled affectionately across the table at me.
>
> 'My good friend,' he said. 'I depend upon you more than you know.'
>
> I was confused and delighted by these unexpected words. He had never said anything of the kind to me before. Sometimes, secretly, I had felt slightly hurt. He seemed almost to go out of his way to disparage my mental powers . . .
>
> 'Yes,' he said dreamily, 'you may not always comprehend just how it is so – but you do often and often point the way.'
>
> I could hardly believe my ears.
>
> 'Really, Poirot,' I stammered, 'I'm awfully glad. I suppose I've learnt a good deal from you one way or another – '
>
> He shook his head
>
> '*Mais non, ce n'est pas ça*. You have learnt nothing.'
>
> 'Oh!' I said, rather taken aback.
>
> 'That is as it should be . . . I do not wish you to be a second and inferior Poirot. I wish you to be the supreme Hastings. And you are the supreme Hastings. In you, Hastings, I find the normal mind almost perfectly illustrated . . .'
>
> I looked across the table at him. He was smoking his tiny cigarettes and regarding me with great kindliness.

'*Ce cher Hastings*,' he murmured. 'I have indeed much affection for you.'

I was pleased but embarrassed and hastened to change the subject.

Notes

1 Besides Hastings's thirty-four accounts, three other Poirot cases were recounted by first-person narrators: Dr Sheppard of *The Murder of Roger Ackroyd*, Amy Leatheran of *Murder in Mesopotamia*, and Colin Lamb of *The Clocks*.

2 Celebrated sleuth though he was, Poirot apparently did not notice Hastings's mistake in calling Cinderella by her sister Bella's name. What *was* going on at the ranch?

10

The Domestic Poirot

The flat was a modern one. The furnishings of the room were modern, too. The armchairs were squarely built, the upright chairs were angular. A modern writing-table was set squarely in front of the window and at it sat a small, elderly man. His head was practically the only thing in the room that was not square.

—'Dead Man's Mirror'

Poirot was an interior person; he loved his comforts and intensely enjoyed ruling and ordering his own small kingdom. He was always happiest at home, his desk symmetrically arranged, his wardrobe in perfect order, and the world beating a path to his door. It never seems to have occurred to him to carry out his practice as a private detective from any place other than his sitting-room. There he received his clients, dispatched his agents, and held court. It was the centre of his web.

It will be remembered that Poirot's earliest years in England were spent in 'rooms' shared with Hastings, a comfortable arrangement hallowed by several generations of Victorian and Edwardian gentlemen. As tenants under a system halfway between lodgings and a separate establishment, each had his own bedroom and shared between them a sitting-room, to which their landlady brought their meals and their visitors.

As will be recalled, Poirot's first set of rooms – in which Hastings soon joined him on a more or less permanent basis – was of a modest ambience and administered by a landlady of decidedly brusque habits. Nevertheless the two friends enjoyed many happy times there. A cosy picture is provided by Hastings in 'The Chocolate Box':

> Poirot and I sat facing the hearth, our legs stretched out to the cheerful blaze. Between us was a small table. On my side of it stood some carefully brewed hot toddy; on Poirot's was a cup of thick, rich chocolate which I would not have drunk for a hundred pounds! Poirot sipped the thick brown mess in the pink china cup, and sighed with contentment.

On at least one occasion – 'The Affair at the Victory Ball' – this first set of rooms was used to stage an elaborate reconstruction of a crime. Wrote Hastings:

> The preparations greatly intrigued me. A white screen was erected at one side of the room, flanked by heavy curtains at either side. A man with some lighting apparatus arrived next, and finally a group of members of the theatrical profession, who disappeared into Poirot's bedroom, which had been rigged up as a temporary dressing-room.[1]

Afterwards 'a recherché little supper', prepared, one suspects, by hands other than the landlady's, was served to five bemused guests.

With their incomes rising, Poirot's and Hastings's next set of rooms was at 14 Farraway Street, an address 'not aristocratic' and somewhere in central London. Here their surroundings were better appointed, and their landlady, Mrs Pearson – 'that excellent Mrs Funnyface of yours', Poirot's doctor once called her – was a person of a more soft-spoken and tidy disposition.

It was while living at Farraway Street that Poirot came into his own as the *dernier cri*. Of his clients he boasted in 'The Adventure of "The Western Star"': 'One says to another: "*Comment*? You have lost your gold pencil-case? You must go to the little Belgian. He is too marvellous!" Everyone goes! *Courez*! And they arrive! In flocks, *mon ami*!'

Hastings loved to stand at this sitting-room window and watch new clients arrive. From below would come the sound of the bell and, after a short interval, steps on the stairs, a tap on the sitting-room door, and the voice of Mrs Pearson, or that of 'the little maid servant', announcing a visitor. 'Enter then,' Poirot would call. Upon doing so, the visitor would have seen a very tidy sitting-room with, if the weather even threatened to be chilly, the windows tightly shut, a fire of logs or coal burning in the grate, and two comfortable armchairs 'well drawn up to the fire'. On the wall by the fireplace hung a holder for matches, on the mantelpiece sat 'a magnificent model of a foxhound', a trophy of Poirot's victory over Inspector Giraud of the Paris *Sûreté*, and a framed photograph of a recent prime minister inscribed with the words: '*To my discreet friend, Hercule Poirot – from Alloway*.' Elsewhere in this room was Poirot's writing-table, a telephone, a waste-paper basket, a bookcase, and, by the window, the table and chairs where Poirot and Hastings ate their meals. On one of the walls hung a framed cheque for a guinea, the fee with which Mrs Todd tried to dismiss Poirot in 'The Adventure of the Clapham Cook', and on the wall by the door was a light switch that Poirot, fearing a booby trap by the Big Four, once turned on with an old galosh.

At Farraway Street Poirot's bedroom was again off the sitting-room. In 'The Veiled Lady' Poirot stationed Japp behind the door to listen in on a conversation, and in *The Big Four* an escapee from a mental asylum climbed in through one of its two windows and was followed, a few hours later, by an assassin who murdered the poor man as he lay upon the bed.

This room seems to have been comparatively large, no doubt to accommodate Poirot's commodious wardrobe. 'The top of a wardrobe,' he once told Hastings, 'is an excellent place for brown paper and cardboard boxes. I have kept them there myself. Neatly arranged, there is nothing to offend the eye.' On the bedroom mantel sat an eight-day clock.

A bathroom and Hastings's bedroom were on the same floor. 'I was just out of my bath,' recalled Hastings in *The Big Four*, 'and indulging in pleasurable thoughts of breakfast when I heard Japp's voice in the sitting-room. I threw on a bathrobe and hurried in.'

These, then, were 'the old familiar surroundings' of which Hastings was to speak so nostalgically in later years. Not long after Hastings's departure Poirot also moved away from Farraway Street, and one rather imagines pleasant Mrs Pearson wondering, as she readied their rooms for newcomers, if Hastings and Poirot – one off to South America with an acrobat and the other off to the country to raise vegetable marrows – had both taken leave of their senses.

In the village of King's Abbot, as we know, Poirot lived for close to a year in almost complete seclusion, devoting himself entirely to his strange agricultural mission. At the end of this time – about the year 1926 – he emerged to solve the murder of Roger Ackroyd, thus permitting us to see something of The Larches, the house he had taken in King's Abbot.

Apart from the vegetable marrows in their walled garden, the most distinctive feature of this establishment during Poirot's regime was his ancient Breton housekeeper. Apparently speaking no English, wearing an 'immense Breton cap', and employed in a strange country by a hermit, one cannot help wondering what sort of life she led. 'I believe,' said Caroline Sheppard of her mysterious neighbour, 'Mr Porrot', 'that he's got one of those new vacuum cleaners.' While it is easy to imagine Poirot as one of the first in England to own a vacuum cleaner, it is harder to imagine this ancient housekeeper actually using it.

It will come as no surprise to learn that the little sitting-room at The Larches was 'arranged with formal precision'. In *The Murder of Roger Ackroyd* Dr Sheppard describes a call:

> Poirot sprang up to meet me, with every appearance of pleasure. 'Sit down, my good friend,' he said. 'The big chair? This small one? The room is not too hot, no?'
>
> I thought it was stifling, but refrained from saying so. The windows were closed, and a large fire burned in the grate.
>
> 'The English people, they have a mania for the fresh air,' declared Poirot. 'The big air, it is all very well outside, where it belongs. Why admit it to the house?'

The finale of this famous case took place in this room, a stage carefully set for what Poirot liked to call 'my little performance':

On the table were various *sirops* and glasses. Also a plate of biscuits. Several chairs had been brought in from the other room.

Poirot ran to and fro rearranging things. Pulling out a chair here, altering the position of a lamp there, occasionally stooping to straighten one of the mats that covered the floor. He was specially fussy over the lighting. The lamps were arranged in such a way as to throw a clear light on the side of the room where the chairs were grouped, at the same time leaving the other end of the room, where I presumed Poirot himself would sit, in a dim twilight.

When, at the end of the Ackroyd affair, Poirot abandoned the marrows and re-entered the world, he went off for a short time to live with considerable flair in a hotel on the French Riviera. It was during this period that the imperturbable and 'intensely English' George, previously the valet of the late Lord Edward Frampton, agreed to become Poirot's man-servant after reading in *Society Snippets* that the little detective had been received with much graciousness at Buckingham Palace. Thereafter, the doors where Poirot lived were answered with 'a low murmured colloquy', hot chocolate appeared as if by magic, and his trousers were always perfectly pressed.

George (or Georges as Poirot often called him) hovered in the background for the rest of Poirot's life. Laconic, unemotional, and endlessly efficient, George's last name is never revealed and the only aspect of his private life that we ever learn is that he had an aged father who lived in Eastbourne.

Besides anticipating Poirot's every wish, answering the door and the telephone, waiting on guests, running errands, and endlessly ironing, pressing and sponging, 'my good George' was a useful, if somewhat diffident, conveyor of information. In *Third Girl*:

> Master and servant looked at each other. Communication was sometimes fraught with difficulties for them. By inflexion or innuendo or a certain choice of words George would signify that there was something that might be elicited if the right question was asked.

Often the 'something' had to do with social status. 'Good evening, sir,' said George to Poirot in *Mrs McGinty's Dead*:

> 'There is a – gentleman waiting to see you.'
>
> He relieved Poirot deftly of his overcoat.
>
> 'Indeed?' Poirot was aware of that very slight pause before the word *gentleman*. As a social snob, George was an expert.

Contrary to what one might expect, George, in his wooden way, patently enjoyed being a gentleman's gentleman to a *bourgeois* detective. Perhaps he enjoyed the novelty of it all. In 'The Apples of the Hesperides' it is observed that 'It was the habit of Hercule Poirot to discuss his cases with his capable valet, George', even though, as Poirot pointed out in *Peril at End House*, George had 'no imagination whatever'. It was as a captive audience and a weathervane that George was so valuable and, when pressed into more active service, he was no mean detective himself. In 'The Lernean Hydra':

> Poirot said, 'Have you seen this compact before, Georges?'
>
> George stepped forward.
>
> 'Yes, sir. I observed this person . . . purchase it at Woolworth's on Friday the 18th. Pursuant to your instructions I followed this lady whenever she went out. She took a bus over to Darnington on the day I have mentioned

> and purchased this compact. She took it home with her. Later the same day she came to the house in which Miss Moncrieffe lodges. Acting as by your instructions, I was already in the house. I observed her go into Miss Moncrieffe's bedroom and hide this in the back of the bureau drawer. I had a good view through the crack of the door. She then left the house, believing herself unobserved.'

When Poirot returned from the Riviera in the late 1920s to take up his life in London once again, he briefly lived – presumably in the interests of a case – without the ministrations of George and under the assumed and unlikely name of O'Connor. During this interlude he established himself on the fifth floor of a building of flats, a self-contained existence which was a considerable departure from his previous domestic arrangements. In the adventure that ensued, 'The Third-Floor Flat', we never actually see anything of Poirot's own flat and its 'view over London', and we find him next ensconced with George in new surroundings described by Hastings on a visit in 1932 by an old familiar term: 'our rooms'. Of the sitting-room there is mention made of a clock and roses on the mantelpiece, of Poirot's 'accustomed chair', and, in *Lord Edgware Dies*, a glimpse through Hastings's eyes of the room itself:

> I have often recalled that day in Poirot's prim, neat little sitting-room when, striding up and down a particular strip of carpet, my little friend gave us his masterly and astounding résumé of the case.

Poirot apparently gave up these rooms for another 'retirement' to Monte Carlo, for on a visit back to London in

Three Act Tragedy we find him staying in a 'slightly florid suite at the Ritz'. As well as an investigation of a set of murders, this visit may also have been used for serious flat hunting, for by 1935, in 'How Does Your Garden Grow?', Poirot is firmly re-established as a private detective in London and has acquired the formidable Miss Lemon – complete with her own small office – as his secretary. It is clear that by now the words 'rooms' and 'prim' can no longer be applied, for when next Hastings visited Poirot:

> I found him installed in one of the newest type of service flats in London. I accused him (and he admitted the fact) of having chosen this particular building entirely on account of its strictly geometrical appearance and proportions.

This modernist building was Whitehaven Mansions, and as soon as one hears of it one wants to know where it was. One set of clues seems to point towards Chelsea. In *Cards on the Table* Poirot walked home 'in the direction of King's Road' from Mrs Lorrimer's house at 111 Cheyne Lane in Chelsea, and was able to 'come round immediately' when summoned back to Cheyne Lane next morning. More substantial evidence, however, points to Mayfair. In *Evil Under the Sun* Poirot's address appears in the register of the Jolly Roger Hotel as 'Whitehaven Mansions, London, W1', and in making his way home on the underground in 'The Capture of Cerberus' he 'ascended to ground level and stepped out into the hubbub of Piccadilly Circus'.

On reaching home, in *Mrs McGinty's Dead*:

> Poirot turned into the courtyard of his block of flats. As always his heart swelled in approval. He was proud of

> his home. A splendid symmetrical building. The lift took him up to the third floor where he had a large luxury flat with impeccable chromium fittings, square armchairs, and severely rectangular ornaments. There could truly be said not to be a curve in the place.

In this flat Poirot lived happily, surrounded by perfect order, for the rest of his life. As before, what would have met a caller's eyes?

The caller, having arrived by lift at the third floor and pressed the 'trilling' bell of Flat 203, would have been treated to the sight of 'that impeccable manservant, George'. If one was known to George, 'a smile of welcome' might flit briefly across his wooden face, but if one was not known, or had no appointment to see Poirot, one would have been invited to take a seat in the 'square white lobby' while George retired to convey one's reason for calling and apparent social status to Poirot. If the reply was favourable, one's coat would have been hung on the hall-stand, one's umbrella deposited in the umbrella stand, and one would have been led down a 'narrow hall' and ushered with formality into the sitting-room. There one would have been greeted with 'punctilious courtesy' by Poirot if one was a stranger or adversary, or with delight if one was a friend. 'He came towards me on twinkling patent-leather shod feet with outstretched hands,' wrote Colin Lamb in *The Clocks*. Greetings over, one would have been invited to 'Pray sit down'.

'Nice place you have here, M. Poirot,' remarked Charles Arundell approvingly in 1936 in *Dumb Witness*. Charles was a rakish young man about town and must have been astonished to find this elderly detective living in an Art Deco flat. Its 'shining' sitting-room, which 'gleamed with chromium', is described in *The Labours of Hercules*:

> A square room, with good square modern furniture – even a piece of good modern sculpture representing one cube placed on another cube and above it a geometrical arrangement of copper wire.

Electric radiators set in the walls fought off the slightest vestige of cold or damp. The 'square fireplace' was seldom used ('A coal fire,' in Poirot's opinion, 'was always shapeless and haphazard!') but its chromium-plated curb added to the effect.

On the mantelpiece sat a clock, over it hung a mirror, and on either side of the hearth sat two square armchairs each placed at 'a definite geometrical angel'. A sofa and a number of upright chairs completed the seating arrangements.

Poirot was particularly fond of his 'handsome modern desk', which sat near the window. 'Its squareness and solidity were more agreeable to him than the soft contours of antique models,' observed Hastings on one occasion; on another, 'Its contents, I need hardly say, were all neatly docketed and pigeon-holed so that he was able at once to lay his hand upon the paper he wanted.' Its drawers, of course, were locked.

In a small alcove stood a table (probably the antique table with claw feet mentioned in *Third Girl* and banished to the alcove because of its age), and other small square tables were carefully placed around the room. On one of them sat a telephone and directory, and on another a box of cigarettes.

At the windows hung curtains (perhaps made from the purple and gold material Poirot purchased in Assuan in *Death on the Nile?*) and on the walls hung etchings. 'These are awfully good,' said Anne Meredith in *Cards on the Table*, getting up to examine them. To match the decor one would have expected these etchings to be severe and modern, though contradictorily in 'The Dream' Poirot's taste in art is described as 'always somewhat bourgeois' and tending towards the 'opulent and florid'.

Also in the sitting-room was a large bookcase. Poirot could become very upset – as in 'The Adventure of "The Western Star"' – if a book was improperly shelved:

> See you not that the tallest books go in the top shelf, the next tallest in the row beneath, and so on. Thus we have order, *method*, which, as I have often told you, Hastings – '
>
> 'Exactly,' I said hastily, and put the offending volume in its proper place.

The collection on these shelves was eclectic and reflected Poirot's English immersion. It included a *Peerage* and a *Who's Who* (though George was easily as good as both), a bible, books on psychology, an 'ancient tattered' edition of *The Magic of the Egyptians and Chaldeans*, several 'volumes of the Middle Ages' (supposedly useful for counteracting black magic), *First Steps in Russian* (supposedly useful for understanding Countess Rossakoff), *Alice Through the Looking Glass*, a well-thumbed book of English nursery rhymes, the novels of Dickens, a bit of Trollope, *Under the Fig Tree* (the gift, in *Death on the Nile*, of the novelist Mrs Otterbourne), an anthology of English poetry, the works of Tennyson, the works of Wordsworth, and Poirot's favourites, the plays of Shakespeare.

The bookcase also held a collection of reference files (in 'The Apples of the Hesperides' Poirot took down 'a file labelled with the letter D and opened it at the words *Detective Agencies – Reliable*'); many books on criminology ('there is no doubt whatever in my mind as to who murdered Charles Bravo'); and an important collection of detective fiction ('I give American crime fiction on the whole a pretty high place. I think it is more ingenious, more imaginative, than English writing'). As well as the classics, Poirot's detective library also included works by contemporary authors such as his friend Ariadne Oliver and his fan Daniel Clancy, a quivering young mystery writer encountered in *Death in the Clouds*. Altogether this large collection of crime was the basis for Poirot's own book, his 'analysis of great writers of detective fiction'.

Besides the all-important sitting-room, Flat 203 contained seven other rooms: a 'tiny' dining-room, sometimes called 'the other room' (on display was the fatal knife from *Murder on the Orient Express*), Miss Lemon's typing room, Poirot's bedroom, a second bedroom for guests, George's bedroom, a bathroom and a kitchen. All of these rooms were under the care of a regular cleaning woman whose name we are never told, though we do learn, in *The Clocks*, that during an absence her replacement brought one of her children with her, which was 'strictly against orders'.

Who did the cooking? George could make a very acceptable *omelette fines herbes* if lunch was needed, and 'provide a meal of square crumpets richly buttered, symmetrical sandwiches, and other suitable components of a lavish English afternoon tea', and he almost certainly made the coffee and warmed the rolls for Poirot's breakfast, but the more substantial meals – when Poirot did eat at home – were undoubtedly prepared in a kitchen below, for one of the attractions of an establishment of service flats such as Whitehaven Mansions was that its tenants could eat at a restaurant on the premises or have their meals sent upstairs to their own dining-rooms. That a certain amount of arranging went on in this system is evidenced by a conversation in *After the Funeral*:

'I don't know,' muttered Mr Entwhistle reminiscently, 'how you manage to get hold of an escalope like that! It melted in the mouth!'

'I have a friend who is a Continental butcher. For him I solve a small domestic problem. He is appreciative – and ever since then he is most sympathetic to me in the matters of the stomach.'

In a later chapter we will see something of Poirot's business, or detective, day, but what might be called his domestic day began with George depositing 'a tray of early-morning coffee by his master's bedside'. Upon rising, Poirot performed a meticulous *toilette* which took about three-quarters of an hour and from which he emerged, 'neat, spruce and dandified' to breakfast 'exact to the minute' at nine. 'Poirot clung firmly to the Continental breakfast,' wrote Hastings in *Peril at End House*, a case set in the 1930s. This was just as well, since in the previous decade Poirot seems to have waged war with the English breakfast. 'It is really insupportable,' he complained in 'The Disappearance of Mr Davenheim', 'that every hen lays an egg of a different size!' In *Murder on the Links* he became enraged at the toast:

'Ah, *par example, c'est trop fort!*' he cried.

'What is it?'

'This piece of toast. You remark him not?' He whipped the offender out of the rack, and held it up for me to examine.

'Is it square? No. Is it a triangle? Again no. Is it even round? No. Is it of any shape remotely pleasing to the eye? What symmetry have we here? None.'

'It's cut from a cottag loaf, Poirot,' I explained soothingly.

Poirot threw me a withering glance.

When he reverted to a more familiar *petit déjeuner* his criticisms became less passionate. In *Third Girl*:

> Hercule Poirot was sitting at the breakfast table. At his right hand was a steaming cup of chocolate. He had always had a sweet tooth. To accompany the chocolate was a *brioche*. It went agreeably with chocolate. He nodded his approval. This was from the fourth shop he had tried. It was a Danish *pâtisserie* but infinitely superior to the so-called French one nearby. That had been nothing less than a fraud.

As he drank his chocolate (or occasionally coffee):

> Hercule Poirot arranged his letters in a neat pile in front of him. He picked up the topmost letter, studied the address for a moment, then neatly slit the back of the envelope with a little paper-knife that he kept on the breakfast table for that express purpose and extracted the contents.

His letters skimmed, Poirot turned his attention to the newspapers. In the early days, when they shared rooms together, Poirot and Hastings 'pleaded guilty rather shamefacedly' to regularly reading what Poirot called 'your pretty little English scandal-papers', and it was Hastings's custom to read aloud at breakfast the more sensational headlines from the *Daily Megaphone*, *Society Gossip*, the *Daily Blare*, the *Daily Newsmonger*, and so on. In later years Poirot seems to have developed more sober tastes though still maintaining, in *Sad Cypress*, 'the newspapers, they are so inaccurate, I never go by what they say.' In *The Murder of Roger Ackroyd* he subscribed to the *Daily Budget*, in *Third Girl* he took the *Morning News*, the *Daily Comet* and *The Times*, though in 'The Augean Stables', 'blushing slightly', he admitted to a passing acquaintance with the scandalmongering *X-Ray News*.

The newspapers folded neatly away, Poirot's working day began. If he remained at home and appointments allowed the time, George often brought him a mid-morning cup of chocolate. Lunch was 'at twelve-thirty if possible but certainly not later than one o'clock', and was often followed by a quiet half-hour in one of his square-backed armchairs with coffee (well sugared) at his elbow.

Throughout the day these cups of coffee and chocolate were supplemented by the *tisanes* and *sirops* to which he was equally addicted. In the days before George, Poirot prepared his own herbal teas – usually camomile – over a spirit lamp. Hastings found this whole procedure 'disgusting'. He was not alone in his aversion to *tisanes*. 'They were nauseating to taste and pungent to smell,' declared Colin Lamb in *The Clocks*. To Poirot they were a panacea for everything. In 'The Under Dog':

> . . . Poirot pulled the bell for George.
>
> 'A cup of *tisane*, George. My nerves are much disturbed.'
>
> 'Certainly, sir,' said George. 'I will prepare it immediately.'
>
> Ten minutes later he brought a steaming cup to his master. Poirot inhaled the noxious fumes with pleasure.

A glass of *sirop* – especially *sirop de cassis* ('Blackcurrant to you and me,' wrote Colin Lamb) – was Poirot's favourite social drink. He often urged it on his guests who, if they had drunk it before, usually refused, as did Inspector Japp in 'The Capture of Cerberus':

> 'No thanks, I won't have any of your fancy *sirops*. I have to take care of my stomach. Is that whisky I see over there? That's more the ticket!'

Poirot had lots of visitors. In the course of a typical day George answered the door many times and would no sooner get back to the kitchen when he was apt to be summoned forth again by the sitting-room bell. In *Mrs McGinty's Dead*:

> Poirot pressed his guest with refreshments. A *grenadine? Crème de Menthe? Benedictine? Crème de Cacao?* . . .
>
> At this moment George entered with a tray on which was a whisky bottle and a siphon. 'Or beer if you prefer it, sir?' he murmured to the visitor.
>
> Superintendent Spence's large red face lightened.
>
> 'Beer for me,' he said.

Also on hand were sherry, brandy, port and, at heady moments, cocktails. In *The Labours of Hercules* Dr Burton sipped appreciatively at a glass of Château Mouton Rothschild, and in *The ABC Murders* an impromptu case conference was treated to sandwiches and wine. A less satisfied guest was Dr Sheppard in *The Murder of Roger Ackroyd*:

> Poirot greeted me hospitably. He had placed a bottle of Irish whisky (which I detest) on a small table, with a soda water siphon and a glass. He himself was engaged in brewing hot chocolate.

Though Poirot himself intensely disliked tea ('your English

poison', he called it), and sighed with relief when a visitor preferred something else, he recognized occasions when only tea would do. For a nervous witness in *One, Two, Buckle My Shoe*:

> Profiting by a long experience of the English people, Poirot suggested a cup of tea. Miss Nevill's reaction was all that could be hoped for.
>
> 'Well, really, M. Poirot, that's *very* kind of you. Not that it's so very long since breakfast, but one can always do with a cup of tea, can't one?'
>
> Poirot, who could always do without one, assented mendaciously.

In later years Poirot virtually capitulated in his war against tea. In *Hallowe'en Party*, in the late 1960s:

> Though personally deprecating *le five o'clock* as inhibiting the proper appreciation of the supreme meal of the day, dinner, Poirot was now getting quite accustomed to serving it.
>
> The resourceful George had on this occasion produced large cups, a pot of really strong Indian tea and, in addition to the hot and buttery square crumpets, bread and jam and a large square of rich plum cake.

Occasionally Poirot hosted small dinner parties. In *Death in the Clouds*, for example, he invited two French colleagues and Inspector Japp to dine:

> By common consent, no mention of the case was made during the very excellent meal which the little Belgian provided for his friends.

'After all, it is possible to eat well in England,' murmured Fournier appreciatively, as he made delicate use of a thoughtfully provided toothpick.

'A delicious meal, M. Poirot,' said Thibault.

'Bit Frenchified, but damn good,' pronounced Japp.

In evenings at home, and if there was no case on hand to concern him, Poirot liked to read. A picture of him in his armchair is sketched in *The Clocks*:

> On either side of him on the floor was a neat pile of books. More books stood on the table at his left side. At his right hand was a cup from which steam rose.

Evenings may also have been the time that he wrote, for, besides his enormous reputation as a detective, Poirot also enjoyed a modest success as an author – though his works, including his *Magnum Opus*, seem lost to bibliography. In *Death on the Nile* a fellow passenger, Mr Ferguson, said cheekily:

> 'What's the matter with you, Monsieur Poirot? You seem very deep in thought.'
>
> Poirot roused himself with a start.
>
> 'I reflect, that is all. I reflect.'
>
> 'Meditation on Death. Death, the Recurring Decimal, by Hercule Poirot. One of his well-known monographs.'
>
> 'Monsieur Ferguson,' said Poirot, 'You are a very impertinent young man.'

In *Peril at End House* Poirot demanded of Nick Buckley:

> 'You know my name, eh?'
>
> 'Oh! Yes.'

She wriggled uncomfortably. A hunted look came into her eyes. Poirot observed her keenly.

'You are not at ease. That means, I suppose, that you have not read my books.'

'Well – no – not all of them. But I know the name of course.'

Poirot usually retired to bed about midnight. He liked to have a bottle of mineral water on the table beside him and the windows tightly closed:

> Hercule Poirot had been brought up to believe that all outside air was best left outside, and that night air was especially dangerous to the health.

As a rule, Poirot slept lightly. Sometimes, if preoccupied with a case, he slept badly. In *After the Funeral*, for example:

> Elusive snatches of conversation, various glances, odd movements – all seemed fraught with a tantalizing significance in the loneliness of the night. He was on the threshold of sleep, but sleep would not come.

When he finally did fall asleep on this particular night he dreamt of crimson paint, wax flowers, and nuns, and awoke with a solution to the case.

Shortly after the end of the Second World War Poirot bought a weekend cottage even though, as he confessed to himself in *The Hollow*, he did not really like the country:

> The weekend cottage – so many of his friends had extolled it – he had allowed himself to succumb, and had purchased Resthaven, though the only thing he had liked

> about it was its shape which was quite square like a box. The surrounding landscape he did not care for, though it was, he knew, supposed to be a beauty spot. It was, however, too wildly asymmetrical to appeal to him . . .
>
> The best thing about Resthaven, he considered, was the small vegetable garden neatly laid out in rows by his Belgian gardener, Victor. Meanwhile, Françoise, Victor's wife, devoted herself with tenderness to the care of her employer's stomach.

By this time Poirot had clearly abandoned thoughts of actually gardening himself and, in his brief ownership of Resthaven, the ominous words *vegetable marrows* are never uttered. Always, however, a well-cultivated kitchen garden or a neat herbaceous border caught the eye of the domestic Poirot. Despite his disclaimers about nature, he had a considerable knowledge of flowers. 'Do you know the name of this rose?' he asked Peter Lord in *Sad Cypress*. 'It is Zephyrine Droughin, my friend—', an observation that was to prove an important break in the case.

The fact remains, however, that at heart Poirot was an urban animal. Like The Larches in King's Abbot, Resthaven, with its neat hedges and prim sitting-room containing 'two of everything', was soon given up and Poirot resumed his year-round residence in London.

In the 1960s Whitehaven Mansions – which was beginning to be overshadowed by trendier neighbours – received cosmetic surgery. Wrote Colin Lamb in *The Clocks*:

> It had been quite a long time since I had visited Whitehaven Mansions. Some years ago it had been an outstanding building of modern flats. Now there were many other more imposing and even more modern blocks of buildings flanking it on either side. Inside, I noted, it

had recently had a facelift. It had been repainted in pale shades of yellow and green.

And in Flat 203 he found an agitated Poirot:

> 'I am disturbed. I am much disturbed. They make the renovations, the redecorations, even the structural alteration in these flats.'
>
> 'Won't that improve them?'
>
> 'It will improve them, yes – but it will be most vexatious to me. I shall have to disarrange myself. There will be a smell of paint!' He looked at me with an air of outrage.

Happily, these renovations seem to have retained Whitehaven Mansions' delicious 1930s look, for a few years later, in *Hallowe'en Party*, Ariadne Oliver described Poirot's flat as 'ultramodern, very abstract, all squares and cubes'. Inexplicably – and even before these events – the Mansions underwent a temporary change of name. In *Cat Among the Pigeons* Poirot's visitors found him living in *Whitehouse* Mansions and, depending on what edition one consults, George answered the door of Flat 28 or Flat 228. This may account for Ariadne Oliver's confusion in the 1970s in *Elephants Can Remember* when, on her way to visit Poirot, she remarked to a friend:

> 'I think it's Whitefriars Mansion. I can't quite remember the name of it, but I know where it is.'
>
> 'Oh, flats. Rather modern ones. Very square and geometrical.'
>
> 'That's right,' said Mrs Oliver.

From this geometrical haven Poirot went bravely forth to challenge a world lamentably askew.

Note

1 In 'The Mystery of Hunter's Lodge' the rooms seem to have been redealt. Poirot's bedroom is no longer off the sitting-room but on the floor above.

11

The Expeditionary Poirot

> They commented on a new guest who had just arrived, trying to guess his nationality. Harold thought a moustache like that must be French – Elsie said German – and Mrs Rice thought he might be Spanish.
>
> —'The Stymphalean Birds'

In London, if one is to believe Poirot's complaints, his professional and social obligations required him to emerge far too often from his comfortable flat. Sometimes, to his great disapproval, this happened several times a day. His misgivings about going outdoors bore a direct relation to the weather, however. Wind and rain – the precursors of disarranged moustaches and wet feet – were viewed with despair from the sitting-room window, while a sunny day tended to bring forth a Poirot full of expeditionary zeal.

Poirot spent a great deal of time in taxis. Occasionally he took the Tube. In 'The Capture of Cerberus':

> The train started off again with a jerk, Poirot was thrown against a stout woman with knobbly parcels, said, '*Pardon!*' bounced off again into a long angular man whose attaché case caught him in the small of the back. He said,

> '*Pardon!*' again. He felt his moustaches becoming limp and uncurled. *Quel enfer!*

Once, in *Cards on the Table*, he was seen clambering aboard a bus, and now and then one might have spied him walking. In *One, Two, Buckle My Shoe*, meditations on the case at hand:

> . . . occupied Hercule Poirot on his homeward way until he reached Regent's Park. He decided to traverse a part of the park on foot before taking a taxi. By experience, he knew to a nicety the moment when his smart patent-leather shoes began to press painfully on his feet.
>
> It was a lovely summer's day and Poirot looked indulgently on courting nursemaids and their swains, laughing and giggling while their chubby charges profited by nurse's inattention.
>
> Dogs barked and romped.
>
> Little boys sailed boats.
>
> And under nearly every tree was a couple sitting close together.
>
> 'Ah! *Jeunesse, jeunesse*,' murmured Hercule Poirot, pleasurably affected by the sight.

Poirot loved London, and not all his expeditions around it had to do with crime. As he once exclaimed to Hastings, '*Mon Dieu*, I cannot always be talking blood and thunder!' and so we learn of him attending an exhibition of Snuff-Boxes in *Cards on the Table*, a sale of authors' manuscripts in *The Clocks*, and the exhibitions at the Royal Academy in *The Labours of Hercules*.

He was particularly fond of the theatre and supper afterwards at the Savoy, though in *Dumb Witness* Hastings remembered a critical occasion:

> I made the slight mistake of taking Poirot to a crook play. There is one piece of advice I offer to all my readers. Never take a soldier to a military play, a sailor to a naval play, a Scotsman to a Scottish play, a detective to a thriller . . . Poirot never ceased to complain of faulty psychology, and the hero detective's lack of order and method nearly drove him demented.

With the order and method of Shakespeare he had no such quarrel, as a good many of his cases testify, and in any performance of *Othello* he was particularly gripped by the character of Iago. *Peril at End House* provides an example of many such musings:

> 'Jealousy may not, necessarily, be a sexual emotion. There is envy – envy of a possession – of supremacy. Such a jealousy as drove the Iago of your great Shakespeare to one of the cleverest crimes (speaking from the professional point of view) that has ever been committed.'

Poirot was forever quoting, misquoting, and evoking Shakespeare. In *Taken at the Flood* he explained to Inspector Spence:

> '. . . you have here two different kinds of crime – and consequently you have, you must have, two different murderers. Enter First Murderer, and enter Second Murderer.'
>
> 'Don't quote Shakespeare,' groaned Spence.

Poirot much preferred the theatre to the cinema. At a loose end, in the opening pages of *Mrs McGinty's Dead*:

> He turned into Shaftesbury Avenue. Should he cross it and go on to Leicester Square and spend the evening

at a cinema? Frowning slightly, he shook his head. The cinema, more often than not, enraged him by the looseness of its plots – the lack of logical continuity in the argument – even the photography which, raved over by some, to Hercule Poirot seemed often no more than the portrayal of scenes and objects so as to make them appear totally different from what they were in reality.

On most evenings Poirot could, if he chose, go 'faultlessly and beautifully apparelled' into London society. As Hastings pointed out in 'The Mystery of the Baghdad Chest', 'Poirot, whilst bemoaning social engagements and declaring a passion for solitude, really enjoyed these affairs enormously. To be made a fuss of and treated as a lion suited him down to the ground.'

As a celebrity he was much in demand. In 'Dead Man's Mirror', wishing to discuss a case with a particular friend, he had merely to take a pile of invitation cards from his desk and: 'His face brightened. "A *la bonne heure*! Exactly my affair! He will certainly be there."' Before long:

> A Duchess greeted M. Hercule Poirot in fulsome tones:
>
> 'So you could manage to come after all, M. Poirot! Why, that's splendid.'
>
> 'The pleasure is mine, madame,' murmured Poirot bowing.
>
> He escaped from several important and splendid beings – a famous diplomat, an equally famous actress and a well-known sporting peer – and found at last the person he had come to seek, that invariably 'also present' guest, Mr Satterthwaite.

In 'The Mystery of the Spanish Chest' he was to be seen at a lively cocktail party:

> The door of Lady Chatterton's delightful house in Cheriton Street was ajar and a noise as of animals mutinying at the zoo sounded from within. Lady Chatterton who was holding two ambassadors, an international rugger player and an American evangelist in play, neatly jettisoned them with the rapidity of sleight of hand and was at Poirot's side.
>
> 'M. Poirot, how wonderful to see you! No, don't have that nasty martini. I've got something special for you – a kind of *sirop* that the sheikhs drink in Morocco.'

On several occasions Poirot visited nightclubs – most notably when Countess Rossakoff ran one of her own – but he was not fond of dancing and much preferred more sedentary pleasures. In *The Big Four* it is mentioned that he had once played chess, but in his English years he played bridge. In *Lord Edgware Dies* a game of bridge ended 'in a heavy financial gain' to Poirot and Sir Montagu Corner, and in *Cards on the Table* he and Colonel Race won over Ariadne Oliver and Superintendent Battle. Poirot was a steady, if cautious, player:

> '*Je crois bien* – a grand slam vulnerable doubled. It causes the emotions, that! Me, I admit it, I have not the nerve to go for the slams. I content myself with the game.'

But more than anything else Poirot enjoyed going out to eat. 'We will dine first, Hastings,' he announced in *Lord Edgware Dies*, 'and, until we drink our coffee, we will not discuss the case further.' It was his *modus operandi*.

As a sought-after guest, Poirot was often to be seen at dinner parties. These were apt to prove memorable for more than just the food and company. In *Cards on the Table*, it will be recalled, Poirot was invited to an elegant dinner by a famous host, the wealthy and cunning Mr Shaitana. This proved to be Mr Shaitana's last dinner party, but at least it began in the best traditions of Park Lane:

> The butler threw the door open.
>
> 'Dinner is served,' he murmured.
>
> . . . The dinner was delicious and its serving perfection. Subdued light, polished wood, the blue gleam of Irish glass. In the dimness, at the head of the table, Mr Shaitana looked more than ever diabolical.

Not all Poirot's invitations were issued by the rich and famous. In *Hickory Dickory Dock* he had a splendid dinner at a hostel for students presided over by Mrs Hubbard, Miss Lemon's sister:

> Dinner was at seven thirty and most of the students were already seated when Mrs Hubbard came down from her sitting-room (where sherry had been served to the distinguished guest) followed by a small elderly man with suspiciously black hair and a moustache of ferocious proportions which he twirled contentedly.
>
> 'These are some of our students, M. Poirot. This is M. Hercule Poirot who is kindly going to talk to us after dinner.'
>
> Salutations were exchanged and Poirot sat down by Mrs Hubbard and busied himself with keeping his moustaches out of the excellent *minestrone* which was served by a small active Italian man-servant from a big tureen.

In the evening after dinner, or at a supper party after the theatre, a host or hostess might persuade Poirot to have something to drink beyond coffee and liqueurs. In

Lord Edgware Dies he drank champagne – 'possibly a glass too much' in Hastings's opinion – and occasionally he accepted a dry martini, but no one could induce him to drink 'your English national drink', whisky and soda. In *Three Act Tragedy* he exclaimed:

> 'The sherry, I prefer it to the cocktail, and a thousand thousand times to the whisky. *Ah, quelle horreur*, the whisky. But drinking the whisky, you ruin – absolutely ruin – the palate. The delicate wines of France, to appreciate them, you must never, never – Ah, *qu'est-ce qu'il y a?*'

The strange sound that interrupted him was a choking cry from a guest who 'stood swaying, his face convulsed. The glass dropped from his hand onto the carpet; he took a few steps blindly, then collapsed.' This sort of thing often happened at parties Poirot attended.

Eating in good restaurants was one of his passions. In the early pages of *Death on the Nile*:

> M. Gaston Blondin, the proprietor of that modish little restaurant Chez Ma Tante, was not a man who delighted to honour many of his *clientèle* . . . Only in the rarest cases did M. Blondin, with gracious condescension, greet a guest, accompany him to a privileged table, and exchange with him suitable and apposite remarks.
>
> On this particular night, M. Blondin had exercised his royal prerogative three times – once for a Duchess, once for a famous racing peer, and once for a little man of comical appearance with immense black moustaches, who, a casual onlooker would have thought, could bestow no favour on Chez Ma Tante by his presence there.
>
> M. Blondin, however, was positively fulsome in his attentions. Though clients had been told for the last half

hour that a table was not to be had, one now mysteriously appeared, placed in a most favourable position. M. Blondin conducted the client to it with every appearance of *empressement*.

'But naturally, for *you* there is *always* a table, Monsieur Poirot! How I wish that you would honour us oftener.'

The *Jardin des Cygnes*, the *Vieille Grand-mère*, the Ritz, The Savoy, Claridges, the Carlton, the Gallant Endeavour, the Cheshire Cheese – they all knew Poirot well. In busy cases he used them as retreats for himself or as meeting places with others. In periods of retirement, such as occurred in *Mrs McGinty's Dead*, they became his *raison d'être*:

. . . Always a man who had taken his stomach seriously, he was reaping his reward in old age. Eating was now not only a physical pleasure, it was also an intellectual research. For in between meals he spent quite a lot of time searching out and marking down possible sources of new and delicious food . . .

'Alas,' murmured Poirot to his moustaches, 'that one can only eat three times a day . . .'

Escargots, *consommé*, *omelette aux champignons*, *sole à la Normandie*, chicken *en casserole*, *blanquette de veau*, steak and kidney pudding, *petit pois à la française*, *baba au rhum*, blackberry and apple tart, 'a cheese of Port Salut', a Stilton, *café noir* and Benedictine – turning his critical attention to each menu, Poirot lunched and dined his way through Soho and Mayfair and Chelsea.

At the dictates of a case, he sometimes found himself eating and drinking in less elegant establishments. In 'The Lost Mine', for example, his stomach, usually reliable in matters of food, quailed before the 'peculiar dishes' served him in an opium den. In *Third Girl* he ordered coffee and received 'a cup of pale beige fluid' at the Merry Shamrock Café. In *Death in the Clouds* he sought out a murder witness in the bar of the matey Crown and Feathers.

In London, coffee à la Merry Shamrock Café could usually be avoided, but away from home, and at the mercy of haphazard country houses, obscure village inns or uncertain hotels, who knew what uncontrollable discomforts lay in wait? Often, when preparing for a trip, 'An expression of conscious heroism spread over Poirot's face.'

Packing – even when the summons was urgent – was, of course, a careful affair. In his early years in England Poirot seems to have embarked on overnight forays surprisingly lightly. In 'The Tragedy at Marsdon Manor' Hastings watched him 'strapping up his small valise', and in 'The Kidnapped Prime Minister' he found him 'busy packing a minute suitcase with quick, deft movements'. In *The ABC Murders* Hastings attempted the packing himself:

> I put a few things together in a suitcase whilst Poirot once more rang up Scotland Yard.
>
> A few minutes later he came into the bedroom and demanded:
>
> '*Mais qu'est-ce que vous faites là?*'
>
> 'I was packing for you. I thought it would save time.'
>
> '*Vous éprouvez trop d'émotion, Hastings.* It affects your hands and your wits. Is that a way to fold a coat? And regard what you have done to my pyjamas. If the hairwash breaks what will befall them?'
>
> 'Good heavens, Poirot,' I cried, 'this is a matter of life and death. What does it matter what happens to our clothes?'
>
> 'You have no sense of proportion, Hastings. We cannot catch a train earlier than the time that it leaves, and

to ruin one's clothes will not be the least helpful in preventing a murder.'

In later years packing became the responsibility of George. 'There is drama there, at Mon Repos. A human drama and it excites me,' exclaimed Poirot in 'The Under Dog' as he prepared to answer an urgent call to the country. 'Shall I pack dress clothes, sir?' came George's single-minded reply.[1]

In England, especially in the more frenetic Hastings years, Poirot usually travelled on trains. These varied from great monsters hissing 'superbly, throwing off clouds of steam' to one wryly recollected by Hastings in *The Big Four*: 'We went back to London on a milk train in the early hours of the morning, and a most uncomfortable journey it was.' When on an expense account – and always in his later, affluent years – Poirot travelled first class. As a rule he liked trains, but he never hesitated to jump off one at the next station if he suddenly decided he should be going somewhere else. Occasionally Hastings, often deputized to work out impromptu timetables, attempted to divert him on to a bus. In 'Double Sin' this brought on a tirade:

> 'My friend, why this passion for the motor coach? The train, see you, it is true? The tyres, they do not burst; the accidents, they do not happen. One is not incommoded by too much air. The windows can be shut and no draughts admitted.'

He had similar reservations about cars. In *Dumb Witness*, persuaded to travel in Hastings's second-hand Austin:

> On the way to London we talked very little. I am not fond of talking and driving, and Poirot was so busy protecting

his moustaches with his muffler from the disastrous effects of wind and dust that speech was quite beyond him.

As the years went by, Poirot became more reconciled to the automobile, particularly when whisked away to the country in a rich client's Rolls-Royce. Although he certainly never drove a car himself, from time to time he hired a limousine. In *After the Funeral* Susan Banks glimpsed:

> . . . a big Daimler which was preparing to go out. It was chauffeur driven and inside it, very much muffled up, was an elderly foreign gentleman with a large moustache.

For a short time in the late 1930s Poirot actually owned a car, but he seems to have given it up after a trying incident in 'The Arcadian Deer':

> He was annoyed. His car – an expensive Messarro Gratz – had not behaved with that mechanical perfection which he expected of a car. His chauffeur, a young man who enjoyed a handsome salary, had not succeeded in putting things right. The car had staged a final refusal in a secondary road a mile and a half from anywhere with a fall of snow beginning. Hercule Poirot, wearing his usual smart patent leather shoes, had been forced to walk that mile and a half to reach the riverside village of Hartly Dene – a village which, though showing every sign of animation in summertime, was completely moribund in winter.

The meal that the stranded Poirot was subsequently served at the Black Swan in Hartly Dene confirmed all his suspicions about country hostelries. On this occasion, however, he ate in a somewhat mellow mood.

> An hour later, his feet stretched out toward the comfortable blaze, Hercule Poirot reflected leniently on the dinner he had just eaten. True, the steak had been both tough and full of gristle, the Brussels sprouts had been large, pale, and definitely watery, the potatoes had had hearts of stone. Nor was there much to be said for the portion of stewed apple and custard which had followed. The cheese had been hard and the biscuits soft. Nevertheless, thought Hercule Poirot, looking graciously at the leaping flames, and sipping delicately at a cup of liquid mud euphemistically called coffee, it was better to be full than empty, and after tramping snowbound lanes in patent leather shoes, to sit in front of a fire was Paradise!

'I suffer,' Poirot was sure to exclaim 'in acute self-pity' when staying at a country inn. At bedtime, as in 'The Apples of the Hesperides', things could get very miserable indeed:

> In the saloon bar of Jimmy Donovan's Hotel, Hercule Poirot sat uncomfortably against the wall. The hotel did not come up to his ideas of what a hotel should be. His bed was broken – so were two of the window panes in his room – thereby admitting that night air which Hercule Poirot distrusted so much. The hot water brought him had been tepid and the meal he had eaten was producing curious and painful sensations in his inside.

Coffee in the country – even in the large hotels in Brighton and on the Devon and Cornish coasts where he sometimes holidayed – was a particularly sore point with Poirot. 'Only in England,' he scolded in *The Big Four*, 'is the coffee so atrocious . . . on the Continent they understand how important it is for the digestion that it should be properly made.' In *Taken at the Flood*, at the Stag Inn:

> He stood for a moment in the hall looking from the glass enclosed empty office to the door labelled in firm old-fashioned style COFFEE ROOM. By experience of country hotels Poirot knew well that the only time coffee was served there, was somewhat grudgingly for breakfast and that even then a good deal of watery hot milk was its principal component. Small cups of a treacly and muddy liquid called Black Coffee were served not in the COFFEE ROOM but in the Lounge. The Windsor Soup, Vienna Steak and Potatoes, and Steamed Pudding which comprised Dinner would be obtainable in the COFFEE ROOM at seven sharp.

Tea, of course, was always a threat. In *Sad Cypress*, a country case:

> Nurse Hopkins was hospitable with the teapot, and a minute later Poirot was regarding with some dismay a cup of inky beverage.
>
> 'Just made – nice and strong!' said Nurse Hopkins.
>
> Poirot stirred his tea cautiously and took one heroic sip.

To help it down he invariably requested three, four and sometimes even five lumps of sugar, and ate whatever was the sweetest. 'A sandwich, M. Poirot?' asked Miss Brewis in *Dead Man's Folly*:

'Those are tomato and these are pâté. But perhaps,' said Miss Brewis, thinking of the four lumps of sugar, 'you would rather have a cream cake?'

Poirot would rather have a cream cake, and helped himself to a particularly sweet and squelchy one.

'You stick out in a country place,' Inspector Spence once told him. Spence was right – the countryside was simply not Hercule Poirot's milieu. 'Brrrr!' he complained during an outing in *Peril at End House*. 'The grass, it is damp to the feet! I shall suffer for this – a chill. And no possibility of obtaining a proper *tisane*!' If it was absolutely necessary to sit down on such occasions he always did so on a rock or a stump – never on the ground – and only after carefully spreading out a handkerchief. His one cautious concession to the country was an occasional walk, and if the matter at hand was urgent Hastings could, to his astonishment, find himself recording Poirot advancing across the countryside 'at a great pace'.

Poirot deplored fox hunting, distrusted horse racing, and had a horror of golf. 'You do not play the golf, M. Poirot?' he was asked in *Murder on the Links*:

> 'I? Never! What a game!' He became excited. 'Figure to yourself, each hole it is of a different length. The obstacles, they are not arranged mathematically. Even the greens are frequently up one side! There is only one pleasing thing – the how do you call them? Tee boxes! They, at least, are symmetrical.'

Of course he was never seen swimming, sunbathing, or in any kind of sports clothes,[2] but it must be put to his credit that in *Evil Under the Sun* he organized a very fine picnic. If Hastings had been there I am sure he would have been immediately suspicious of a Poirot saying engagingly,

'I am most anxious to see something of Dartmoor', but the picnic, in 'a delightful heathery spot free from prickly furze', was a great success.

As a celebrated Big House detective, Poirot received many an invitation 'almost royal in its character, to dine and sleep'. On at least one occasion – a visit to Sandringham in the early 1940s – the invitation *was* royal. Did the corgis take to him, one wonders? Alas, we are permitted no details.

In winter, before accepting rural hospitality, Poirot was apt to conduct private inquiries of his own as to the existence of central heating, but as a rule these visits, often of a working nature, were his most comfortable expeditions to the country, despite a pall sometimes cast by recent inexplicable deaths and the presence of police constables searching the shrubbery. At Exsham House in *One, Two, Buckle My Shoe*:

> The vast wealth that owned it was only indicated by the smoothness with which this apparent simplicity was produced. The service was admirable – the cooking English, not Continental – the wines at dinner stirred Poirot to a passion of appreciation. They had a perfect clear soup, a grilled sole, saddle of lamb with tiny young garden peas, and strawberries and cream.

In *The Hollow*, on the evening of a day which has seen the murder of a weekend guest:

> They had the cold ducks for supper. After the ducks there was a caramel custard which, Lady Angkatell said, showed just the right feeling on the part of Mrs Medway.
>
> Cooking, she said, really gave great scope to delicacy of feeling.

'We are only, as she knows, moderately fond of caramel custard. There would be something very gross, just after the death of a friend, in eating one's favourite pudding. But caramel custard is so easy – slippery if you know what I mean – and then one leaves a little on one's plate.'

Poirot preferred to spend Christmas quietly in London and close to his electric radiators. 'Me – I am not an Englishman,' he said in. 'The Adventure of the Christmas Pudding'.[3] 'In my country, Christmas, it is for the children'; and the mere thought of 'a large, cold, stone manor house' at that time of year hardly bore thinking of. Nevertheless, three times in his English career Poirot went against his better judgement and accepted invitations to Christmas in the country. The most memorable of these was spent with a delightfully hospitable family, the Laceys. Fortunately, 'The temperature of the long drawing-room at Kings Lacey was a comfortable sixty-eight', and the food that appeared in the dining-room was the best of old-fashioned fare. After Christmas dinner, Poirot – on a case as usual – paid a visit to the kitchen to wheedle information from the cook:

'But you are a genius, Mrs Ross! A genius! *Never* have I tasted such a wonderful meal. The oyster soup—' he made an expressive noise with his lips '—and the stuffing. The chestnut stuffing in the turkey, that was quite unique in my experience.'

'Well, it's funny that you should say that, sir,' said Mrs Ross graciously. 'It's a very special recipe, that stuffing. It was given me by an Austrian chef that I worked with many years ago. But all the rest,' she added, 'is just good, plain English cooking . . .'

'I am sure, Mrs Ross, you could manage anything! But

> you must know that English cooking – *good* English cooking, not the cooking one gets in the second-class hotels or the restaurants – is much appreciated by gourmets on the Continent, and I believe I am correct in saying that a special expedition was made to London in the early eighteen hundreds, and a report sent back to France of the wonders of the English puddings. 'We have nothing like that in France,' they wrote. 'It is worth making a journey to London just to taste the varieties and excellencies of the English puddings.'

On a holiday in Devon, in *Evil Under the Sun*, a jocular acquaintance, Horace Blatt, said to Poirot:

> 'I know the cut of a fellow's jib. A man like you would be at Deauville or Le Touquet or down at Juan les Pins. That's your – what's the phrase? – spiritual home.'
>
> Poirot sighed. He looked out of the window. Rain was falling and mist encircled the island. He said: 'It is possible that you are right!'

Horace Blatt *was* right. Though commissions occasionally took Poirot abroad, most of his trips to the Continent and the Middle East were intended as escapes to sun and pleasure, and when in this mode he liked to present himself as a man firmly retired. 'My time is all holidays nowadays,' he remarked airily in *Three Act Tragedy*. 'I have succeeded. I am rich. I retire. Now I travel about, seeing the world.'

The world for Poirot was anything that could be reached by train or by the shortest possible voyage on the Mediterranean. It is true that he once contemplated a trip by sea to South America, but once that was abandoned he surrendered completely to his conviction that he could never survive more than four days of *mal de mer*. Nor, in his later years, was flying any sort of an alternative. One or two experiences were enough. 'I do not take aeroplanes,' he said firmly in *Dead Man's Folly*. 'They make me sick.'

The 1930s was the great era of Poirot's trips abroad, and from the moment he set foot in Victoria Station he travelled in style. His trains, the pride of the Belgian-based *Compagnie Internationale des Wagons Lits*, were the great ones of Europe – the glamorous 'Millionaire's Train', or *le train bleu*, which cradled its passengers from Calais to Nice in enamelled blue and gold sleeping cars, and the legendary trains of the Orient Express which offered passengers three routes across Europe in cars with inlaid panelling, velvet upholstery, and crystal chandeliers.[4] The food, of course, was wonderful, and the murders that were apt to occur when Poirot was aboard a luxurious train were never allowed to interfere with it. In the dining-car in *The Mystery of the Blue Train* Poirot 'dexterously polished one of the forks' in anticipation of *cordon bleu* delights to come, and in *Murder on the Orient Express* he 'found himself in the favoured position of being at the table which was served first and with the choicest morsels'.

Poirot's travels took him over much of Europe, but his favourite destination was the French Riviera, where at times he took up residence at the best of hotels. It was here, at restaurants and parties, and when 'jauntily placing the minimum stake on the even numbers' at the casino at Monte Carlo, that his smart white clothes came into their own.

In Paris he liked to stay at the Ritz and dine in the evenings at restaurants such as the Samovar, whose proprietor, Count Alexis Pavlovitch, 'prided himself on knowing everything that went on in the artistic world'.

But not all his visits to Europe were so comfortable. For Poirot, who had no head for heights and quailed at ladders, an unforgettable case was 'The Erymanthian Boar', which required him to stay at a hotel which could only be reached by a funicular railway, was occupied by a gang determined to kill off the other guests, and where decent coffee was not to be had because of the difficulty of boiling water at high altitudes. 'Problem at Sea', when he should have known better, saw him seasick, of course, on a Mediterranean cruise, and of certain events in 'The Adventure of the Egyptian Tomb' Hastings could only write sadly:

> I cut short his lamentations, by suggesting that we should start for the camp. We were to ride there on camels, and the beasts were patiently kneeling, waiting for us to mount, in charge of several picturesque boys headed by a voluble dragoman.
>
> I pass over the spectacle of Poirot on a camel. He started by groans and lamentations and ended by shrieks, gesticulations and invocations to the Virgin Mary and every saint in the calendar. In the end, he descended ignominiously and finished the journey on a diminutive donkey.

Four of Poirot's major cases of the 1930s coincided with commissions or holidays in the Middle East[5]. Poirot thoroughly enjoyed these expeditions and added a smattering of Arabic to his repertoire of languages, though in *Dumb Witness* Hastings observed tartly:

> Poirot's travellings in the East, as far as I knew, consisted of one journey to Syria extended to Iraq, and which occupied perhaps a few weeks. To judge by his present

> conversation one would swear that he had spent most of his life in jungles and bazaars and in intimate converse with fakirs, dervishes, and mahatmas.

In *Death on the Nile* and *Appointment with Death* he fled the English winter to holiday in Egypt and Palestine. In anticipation he observed happily: 'One can even voyage there now, I believe, by train, escaping all sea travel except the Channel.' In Assuan he stayed at the Cataract Hotel, and in Jerusalem at the famous Solomon, his arrival as a celebrity duly noted by the local newspaper. At both the main topic of conversation was of murders recently perpetrated.

'Decidedly, wherever I go, there is something to remind me of crime! Poirot once exclaimed, and it is a fact that wherever he travelled, in England or abroad, the murder statistics shot up amazingly. This phenomenon did not go unnoticed. In *Evil Under the Sun* Mrs Gardener, an American guest at the Jolly Roger, knew from the transatlantic tourist set all about Poirot's reputation for presiding over ruined holidays:

> 'I've just got to confess one thing, M. Poirot. It gave me a kind of a *turn* meeting you here – not that I wasn't just thrilled to meet you, because I was, Mr Gardener knows that. But it just came to me that you might be here – well, *professionally*. You know what I mean? Well, I'm just terribly sensitive, as Mr Gardener will tell you, and I just couldn't bear it if I was to be mixed up in crime of any kind. You see – '
>
> Mr Gardener cleared his throat. He said: 'You see, M. Poirot, Mrs Gardener is very sensitive.'
>
> The hands of Hercule Poirot shot into the air. 'But let me assure you, Madame, that I am here simply in the

same way that you are here yourself – to enjoy myself – to spend the holiday.'

A pious hope! All of Mrs Gardener's fears were, of course, soon realized.

'Sometimes,' said Poirot in *One, Two, Buckle My Shoe*, 'I return for a short while to my own country – Belgium'. He took sanctuary there in 'an isolated white villa' in *The Big Four*, but beyond this (and the fact that he sent presents such as gloves, calendars and bonbons to his relatives at Christmas) we hear nothing further of Belgium. No doubt, as the years went by, the family and surroundings he had left there grew ever more distant – for when it was time to go home, it was to his beloved Whitehaven Mansions and his friends in England that Hercule Poirot's thoughts turned.

NOTES

1 Despite carefulness all around, surprises could occur. In *Murder on the Orient Express* Poirot opened one of his valises to find, neatly folded, a woman's scarlet silk kimono embroidered with dragons.

2 Though in Nice, in *The Mystery of the Blue Train*, he was seen 'yesterday at the tennis'. It is elementary, however, to deduce that he was there as a spectator.

3 The second version.

4 For these details I am grateful to Dennis Sanders's and Len Lovallo's useful and interesting *The Agatha Christie Companion*.

5 *Murder in Mesopotamia*, *Murder on the Orient Express*, *Death on the Nile* and *Appointment with Death*.

12

'My Friend Poirot'

'Poirot's friends are so many and so varied, and range from dustmen to dukes.'

—Arthur Hastings, 'Double Sin'

To the end of his life Poirot was a cordial and hospitable man, and his sitting-room, over which a pleasant air of open house reigned, was always an interesting place to be – especially if one was a good listener and had an interest in crime. There are a number of references over the years to *aficionados* like Dr Hawker, Poirot's near neighbour in 'The Adventure of the Italian Nobleman', who liked to 'drop in sometimes of an evening and have a chat with Poirot, of whose genius he was an ardent admirer'; or Solly Levy, mentioned in *Hallowe'en Party*, with whom Poirot spent many happy hours 'reviving their never-ending controversy about the real culprit in the Canning Road Municipal Baths murder'.

With luck, if one was a visitor, one could forestall invitations to drink blackcurrant *sirop* until George arrived with the whisky, and with even greater luck one might be on hand for developments in an actual case – the arrival of a client from the country, for example, with a story of some disturbing event in the family, or a police inspector ostensibly dropping by for old time's sake but really in search of advice. Or, of an evening, if one was a good friend of Poirot's, one might find oneself making decisions about food and wine, for Poirot loved to eat with friends in restaurants.

This *bonhomie* notwithstanding, in really important matters Poirot was a loner. The only truly close friend he seems to have had – at least in England – was Hastings, and devoted to Hastings though Poirot undoubtedly was, he seldom made him his real confidant, as Hastings frequently pointed out with chagrin. Poirot *always* had a hidden agenda.

No one knew this better than little 'ferret-faced' Inspector Jimmy Japp of Scotland Yard, Poirot's companion-in-arms and rival from the days of Styles to the eve of the Second World War. Indeed, their association went back even further, for the two of them had hunted together in Poirot's former preserve of Belgium. In 1904 Inspector Japp, with Poirot's help, had run down the famous forger Abercrombie in Brussels, and later in Antwerp they had 'nailed' 'Baron' Altara, a criminal who had 'eluded the clutches of half the police in Europe'.

It must have come as something of a shock to Japp to find Poirot of the Belgian police turning up as a private detective in his own backyard, and by the same token it must have seemed strange to Poirot to suddenly find himself without the resources of his own police department. In this situation both men, like clever cats, fell on their feet. For his part Japp learned to tolerate more or less gracefully the intrusion of Poirot into many a Scotland Yard case, and in return he received the best professional advice in Europe. Japp generally got the official credit for the results of these unorthodox collaborations, a fact that always annoyed Hastings. 'He always was an offensive kind of devil,' he said of Japp in *The ABC Murders*, and in *Lord Edgware Dies* he wrote:

> I had not the indulgence for Japp that Poirot had. It was not so much that I minded his picking Poirot's brains. After all, Poirot enjoyed the process, it was a delicate flattery. What did annoy me was Japp's hypocritical pretence that he was doing nothing of the kind. I liked people to be straightforward. I said so, and Poirot laughed.
>
> 'You are the dog of the bulldog breed, eh, Hastings? But you must remember that the poor Japp, he has to save his face. So he makes his little pretence. It is very natural.'

In exchange for this uncharacteristic self-effacement, Poirot craftily enjoyed an unfettered call on the resources of Scotland Yard for almost a quarter of a century. Could these greasy fingerprints be of significance? – 'We will send them to our good friend Inspector Japp of Scotland Yard.' How did Poirot gain admittance to a perfectly strange household? – 'It was most simple. I called, presented a fictitious card and one of Inspector Japp's official ones.' Was a local inspector inclined to be timid? – 'I assure you that if you can get through to Scotland Yard you will receive full authority.'

Though indulgently fond of the Inspector,[1] Poirot never ceased to deplore the misled school of detection to which he belonged. In 'The Plymouth Express':

> 'That good inspector believes in matter in motion,' murmured Poirot as our friend departed. 'He travels; he measures footprints; he collects mud and cigarette-ash! He is extremely busy! He is zealous beyond words! And

if I mentioned psychology to him, do you know what he would do, my friend? He would smile! He would say to himself: 'Poor old Poirot! He ages! He grows senile!' Japp is 'the younger generation knocking on the door'. And *ma foi*! They are so busy knocking that they do not notice that the door is open!'

That invariably Poirot bested him in every case did nothing to discourage Japp's belief that he himself was the smartest bear in the woods. Wrote Hastings in 'The Plymouth Express':

> Japp was an old friend of ours, and greeted Poirot with a sort of affectionate contempt.
>
> 'And how are you, monsieur? No bad feelings between us, though we *have* got our different ways of looking at things. How are the "little grey cells", eh? Going strong?'
>
> Poirot beamed upon him. 'They function, my good Japp; assuredly they do!'

Though 'jaunty and dapper' with his friends, when in charge of a case, 'a kind of wooden shutter of officialdom came down from Japp's expressive countenance', much to Poirot's amusement. In court he gave evidence 'succinctly and briefly'; behind the scenes he was apt to jump to conclusions and bully suspects. 'That is the severity of your official demeanour, my good Japp,' Poirot would protest, as he intervened to save his friend yet again from disastrous conclusions based upon circumstantial evidence.

Though Japp appears in twenty-one of Poirot's cases, and lends the services of Scotland Yard offstage in several more, he seldom spoke of his private life. A rare glimpse of him at leisure is provided by Hastings in 'The Market Basing Mystery':

> 'After all, there's nothing like the country, is there?' said Inspector Japp, breathing in heavily through his nose and out through his mouth in the most approved fashion.
>
> Poirot and I applauded the sentiment heartily. It had been the Scotland Yard inspector's idea that we should all go for the weekend to the little country town of Market Basing. When off duty, Japp was an ardent botanist, and discoursed upon minute flowers possessed of unbelievably lengthy Latin names (somewhat strangely pronounced) with an enthusiasm even greater than that he gave to his cases.

Japp was a sociable fellow and during Poirot's early years in England he dropped by regularly. 'Ah, here is Japp! I recognize his knock,' Poirot would say, and 'Here I am Moosior Poirot,' Japp would reply, bounding into the room with some heavy-handed joke – 'Just going to have breakfast, I see' was his greeting in *Lord Edgware Dies*. 'Not got the hens to lay square eggs for you yet, M. Poirot?' Food was always a critical element in Poirot's and Japp's relationship. 'We will go now to the Cheshire Cheese where Japp meets us for an early dinner,' said Poirot to Hastings in *Peril at End House*. 'Upon my word, you take the cake!' cried Japp to Poirot in 'Murder in the Mews'. 'Come out and have a spot of lunch?' A delightful breakfast scene occurred during their Market Basing weekend:

> . . . we sat down to breakfast on Sunday morning in the parlour of the village inn, with the sun shining, the tendrils of honeysuckle thrusting themselves in at the

window, we were all in the best of spirits. The bacon and eggs were excellent, the coffee not so good, but passable and boiling hot.

'This is the life,' said Japp. 'When I retire, I shall have a little place in the country. Far from crime, like this!'

In due course Japp apparently did retire – presumably to sun and honeysuckle and his ardent botanical pursuits – and Poirot went on detecting for three more decades, an irony in view of Japp's remarks over the years about Poirot's advanced age. 'Old friend of mine,' he explained to a fellow inspector in 'Murder in the Mews'. 'Not half as balmy as he looks, mind you. All the same he's getting on now.'

In Peril at *End House* Hastings recorded a mellowing Japp:

'I let you in on some pretty good cases in the old days, didn't I?' This, I realized, was Japp's way of acknowledging indebtedness to Poirot who had solved many a case which had baffled the Inspector.

'They were the good days – yes.'

'I wouldn't mind having a chat with you now and again even in these days. Your methods may be old-fashioned but you've got your head screwed on the right way, M. Poirot.'

At Scotland Yard Japp was outranked by another friend of Poirot's, Superintendent Battle. In *Cards on the Table*, when introductions were being performed:

A big, square, wooden-faced man moved forward. Not only did an onlooker feel that Superintendent Battle was carved out of wood – he also managed to convey the impression that the wood in question was the timber out of a battleship.

Superintendent Battle was supposed to be Scotland Yard's best representative. He always looked stolid and rather stupid.

'I know M. Poirot,' said Superintendent Battle.

And his wooden face creased into a smile and then returned to its former unexpressiveness.

This 'solid, comfortable-looking man with a broad red face and a large handsome moustache' (a moustache that even Poirot viewed with respect) came into Mr Shaitana's drawing-room with a well-documented reputation of his own. Two lively books, *The Secret of Chimneys* and *The Seven Dials Mystery*, had already recorded two of Superintendent Battle's cases and, after his collaboration with Poirot in *Cards on the Table*, *Murder is Easy*[2] and *Towards Zero* were to record two more.

Of all the police officers he met over his long career, Superintendent Battle was probably the one Poirot admired most. 'What is your style, Superintendent?' he once asked him, and back came a reply from a detective equally astute:

> 'A straightforward, honest, zealous officer doing his duty in the most laborious manner – that's my style. No frills. No fancy work. Just honest perspiration. Stolid and a bit stupid – that's my ticket.'

Battle's deceptively simple demeanour made him one of Scotland Yard's trump cards. To him were assigned cases of the most 'delicate political nature'. He was especially good, in his soothing, yeomanlike way, at coping with the aristocracy. In *The Seven Dials Mystery*, for example, he absorbed with equanimity the fact that a murder suspect had bought a pistol at Harrods. In *The Secret of Chimneys* he explained:

> 'Well, you see . . . most of my work has lain amongst these people. What they call the upper classes, I mean. You see, the majority of people are always wondering what the neighbours will think. But tramps and aristocrats don't – they just do the first thing that comes into their heads, and they don't bother to think what anyone thinks of them.

In Poirot's world it seems to have been almost *de rigueur* that detectives and police officers were bachelors, but Superintendent Battle was an exception to this convention. He and Mrs Battle were the parents of five children. Their youngest, Sylvia, played a small but important part in events in *Towards Zero*, and Colin Lamb, the brilliant young secret service agent who shared honours with Poirot in *The Clocks*, was almost certainly their son operating under an assumed name. No doubt Superintendent Battle also served as a role model for his nephew, James Leach, who became a provincial police inspector.

'Never give in. That's my motto,' he once declared. 'The good square Superintendent Battle,' Poirot said of him admiringly. Battle, in turn, had great respect for Poirot. 'I wish I knew what keeps putting Hercule Poirot into my head,' he mused when events in *Towards Zero* took a perplexing turn. 'You mean that old chap – the Belgian – comic little guy?' asked his nephew.

> 'Comic, my foot,' said Superintendent Battle. 'About as dangerous as a black mamba and a she-leopard – that's

Appointment with Death, was precipitated by a letter of introduction he carried from Colonel Race to Colonel Carbury in Transjordania, it is not recorded that Poirot and Race ever worked together again, though one can be almost sure that they kept in touch. In the 1940s, in *Sparkling Cyanide*,[4] Colonel Race – still 'a tall, erect, military figure, with sunburnt face, closely cropped iron-grey hair, and shrewd dark eyes' – solved a murder case so extraordinarily similar to 'Yellow Iris', an investigation Poirot undertook in the 1930s, that one cannot help speculating that a good deal of discreet discussion must have gone on about it in the sitting-room at Whitehaven Mansions.

An early different sort of friend was that diminutive social butterfly, Mr Satterthwaite, an associate of Poirot's in *Three Act Tragedy* and a helpful purveyor of gossip in 'Dead Man's Mirror'. Like Superintendent Battle and Colonel Race, Mr Satterthwaite has a distinct place of his own on Christie bookshelves, for in 1930 there was published *The Mysterious Mr Quin*, a memorable collection of twelve short stories devoted to Mr Satterthwaite and the periodic visits he received from a mysterious *commedia dell'arte* figure, Harley Quin. Two other short stories published elsewhere, 'The Love Detectives' and 'The Harlequin Tea Set', tell even more of this strange period of Mr Satterthwaite's life when he became the bewildered pawn and agent of Quin, an elusive benevolence determined to explore the riddles of death and right the misfortunes of lovers.

These episodes were well behind Mr Satterthwaite by the time he became the friend of the rational Poirot, whose eyebrows, one suspects, would have risen very high indeed if ever told of these strange visitations and goings-on. A weekend guest of Sir Charles Cartwright in

Three Act Tragedy, Mr Satterthwaite had, for some years, reverted to his natural vocation:

> He was, he felt, always in the stalls watching the play, never on the stage taking part in the drama. But, in truth, the role of onlooker suited him very well.

A man in his sixties and independently wealthy, Mr Satterthwaite was an inveterate snob, but a kindly one, and much cherished by the many millionaires, duchesses, and gourmets he counted among his friends. 'Dear me, how interesting all this is,' he was apt to exclaim. His bachelor home in Chelsea was beautiful, his art collection famous, and his Rolls-Royce gleamed as it transported him on his wonderful gossipy rounds. He was devoted to the opera, he was a keen amateur photographer, and he was the author of an elegant book, *Homes of My Friends*. The pattern of his life was described in *The Mysterious Mr Quin*:

> Every year regularly on the second Sunday in January, Mr Satterthwaite left England for the Riviera. He was far more punctual than any swallow. In the month of April he returned to England. May and June he spent in London, and had never been known to miss Ascot. He left town after the Eton and Harrow match, paying a few country house visits before repairing to Deauville or Le Touquet. Shooting parties occupied most of September and October, and he usually spent a couple of months in town to wind up the year. He knew everybody and it may safely be said that everybody knew him.

'My good friend Mr Satterthwaite,' Poirot called him, and the conversations between these two small and observant men make interesting reading. It was not for nothing that Mr Satterthwaite was a sympathetic listener who 'knew instinctively when the elements of drama were at hand'. To him Poirot confided more of his past life than to any other, including Hastings.

In the course of his career Poirot made a number of friendships of a more casual nature which often proved useful in subsequent cases or provided him with dining companions. Three of these – Mr Entwhistle, Mr Endicott and Mr Enderby – were lawyers with confusingly similar names.[5]

Another such friend, and a good friend of Mr Satterthwaite's as well, was Colonel Johnson, 'a big, red-faced man with a barrack-room voice and a hearty manner'. He and his 'missus' were hospitable people. In *Three Act Tragedy* he genially presided over a murder investigation as Chief Constable of Yorkshire and, some four years later, as Chief Constable of Middleshire, he invited Poirot for Christmas. Other intermittent friends were Alexander Simpson, who owned an art gallery in Mayfair and for whom Poirot retrieved a famous painting, and Dr Burton, a Fellow of All Souls, Oxford, whose chance remark inspired Poirot to emulate the Labours of Hercules. A sad friend was John Harrison, who lived in the country and was rescued by Poirot from a terrible deed in 'Wasps' Nest'; and a giddy friend was young Tony Chapell of 'Yellow Iris' who introduced Poirot to his nightclubing friends as 'Poirot the police hound!':

> 'He's got an appointment with a body, I believe, or is it an absconding financier, or the Rajah of Borrioboolagah's great ruby?'
>
> 'Ah, my friend, do you think I am never off duty? Can I not, for once, seek only to amuse myself?'

'Perhaps you've got an appointment with Carter here. The latest from Geneva. International situation now acute. The stolen plans *must* be found or war will be declared tomorrow!'

Another cheeky friend, and a great admirer of Poirot's methods, was a likeable young doctor, John Stillingfleet. In 'The Dream' he greeted Poirot 'with a remarkable lack of medical decorum' as 'old horse'; in *Sad Cypress* it was his energetic insistence that brought Poirot into the case; and in *Third Girl* he flew off to Australia an engaged man thanks to the matchmaking of old 'Moustaches'. 'I wonder if you'll ever commit a crime, Poirot?' Stillingfleet once said.

'I bet you could get away with it all right. As a matter of fact, it would be *too* easy for you – I mean the thing would be off as definitely too unsporting.'

'That,' said Poirot, 'is a typically English idea.'

From time to time Poirot renewed acquaintance with old friends from his past life with the Belgian police. Such 'an old crony' was Pierre Combeau of Paris who, in *The Big Four*, obligingly pulled the communication cord on a train and 'made a scene' so that Poirot and Hastings, disguised as 'two loafers in dirty blue blouses' could jump off. In 'The Erymanthian Boar' Poirot did a great favour for an old friend, Lementeuil, the Swiss Commissaire of Police, in capturing a gang of thieves on a mountain top. On the Riviera M. Papopolous, Poirot's 'dear friend' of seventeen years' standing and a man renowned for his discretion in dealing in jewels, was persuaded to part with useful information in *The Mystery of the Blue Train*. And in *Murder on the Orient Express* there occurred a joyful reunion with an old Belgian friend, M. Bouc, 'a short stout elderly man, his hair cut *en brosse*'. On this occasion, with the train crowded, M. Bouc, a director of the *Compagnie Internationale des Wagons Lits*, generously gave up his own sleeping compartment so that Poirot could be sure of a restful night.

In his latter years Poirot's most stalwart and helpful friend was undoubtedly Superintendent Albert Spence. Fortuitously, Spence entered Poirot's life at about the time Inspector Japp seems to have retired, and over a period of almost twenty-five years he proved to be a valuable source of police contacts and information. Though of the Oastshire Police when Poirot first worked with him in *Taken at the Flood*, Spence had once been of the Scotland Yard fraternity. 'Chief Inspector Japp . . . always said you have a tortuous mind,' he told Poirot on one ticklish occasion. His character and tactics as a police officer were quite different from Japp's, however. Methodical, sceptical and fair-minded, he had 'a quiet Oastshire voice', a reassuring wry smile, and an easy manner with witnesses. His face was:

> . . . a typical countryman's face, unexpressive, self-contained, with shrewd but honest eyes. It was the face of a man with definite standards who would never be bothered by doubts of himself or by doubts of what constituted right and wrong.

In the Mrs McGinty case it will be recalled that Superintendent Spence took the unorthodox step of asking Poirot to re-investigate privately a murder charge already prepared for the courts. As Spence had suspected, a miscarriage of justice was well under way, and for its prevention he was always grateful. 'You did me a good turn then, Poirot; a very good turn. I went to you for help and you didn't let me down,' he told him years later in *Hallowe'en Party*. Thereafter he stood ready to do all he could to help Poirot. Even after he retired to live in a 'modern, perky little house' with his sister (Spence was, of course, a bachelor) he continued to wield a modest influence. In *Hallowe'en Party* the senior partner of an old-fashioned law firm was astonished to find 'a dandy, a fop, a foreigner', most 'unsuitably attired as to the feet in patent leather shoes', calling with a letter of introduction from Superintendent Spence, formerly of Scotland Yard.

Like so many of Poirot's friends, Spence, a 'square, solid bulk' of a man, loved to eat, though his tastes differed greatly from Poirot's. In *Mrs McGinty's Dead*:

> Hercule Poirot and Superintendent Spence were celebrating at the *La Vieille Grand'mère*.'
>
> As coffee was served Spence leaned back in his chair and gave a deep sigh of repletion.
>
> 'Not at all bad grub here,' he said approvingly. 'A bit frenchified, perhaps, but after all where *can* you get a decent steak and chips nowadays?'

In *Hallowe'en Party* Poirot told Ariadne Oliver:

> 'At six o'clock I drink tea and eat sausages with my friend Spence and his sister again in their house and we discuss.'

Fond as he was of Poirot, in such discussions the straightforward Superintendent Spence could often be found wagging 'a heavy forefinger' at Poirot's convoluted ways. 'Motive,' said Poirot in *Taken at the Flood*, 'has led us astray':

'If A has a motive for killing C and B has a motive for killing D – well, it does not seem to make sense, does it, that A should kill D and B should kill C?'

Spence groaned. 'Go easy, M. Poirot, go easy. I don't even begin to understand what you are talking about with your As and Bs and Cs.'

Thus Inspector Japp, Superintendent Battle, Colonel Race, Mr Satterthwaite, Superintendent Spence, *et al.* But, lest the reader think that all Poirot's good friends were men, it is time to turn our attention to two who decidedly were not – Countess Vera Rossakoff and Ariadne Oliver.

Notes

1 In the course of the Poirot saga Japp rose in rank from Detective Inspector to Chief Inspector.
2 Also published under the title *Easy to Kill.*
3 Also published under the title *Anna the Adventuress.*
4 Also published under the title *Remembered Death.*
5 In *Hickory Dickory Dock* Mr Endicott thanked Poirot for his help in the 'Abernethy business', an earlier case that sounds suspiciously like *After the Funeral* in which the Abernethie family had a lawyer named Mr Entwhistle.

13

Countess Rossakoff and Mrs Oliver

'My dear – my *very* dear friend! What a joy to see you again!'

—Countess Vera Rossakoff, 'The Capture of Cerberus'

In England Poirot made two significant women friends, the adventurer Countess Vera Rossakoff and the author Ariadne Oliver. As no recorded case of Poirot's ever brought them together, it is unlikely that these two – so different in every way – would otherwise have met. It is not easy to picture Countess Rossakoff at a literary luncheon, or Mrs Oliver in a night-club, but if one is determined to imagine them together a marginally possible time would have been in the late 1930s when Countess Rossakoff lived for a short while in London, and a marginally possible place would have been at a Mayfair hairdressers. Hair was a subject that passionately interested them both, so perhaps one morning, while the Countess's 'luxuriant henna-red hair' was being revived, in the very next chair sat Ariadne Oliver having her untidy grey hair coaxed into 'a pseudo-Marquise style'. And if the two of them had happened to fall into conversation, I suspect the Countess would have whiled away the time dramatically complaining about her current misunderstandings with the police, and Mrs Oliver, attentive and astonished, would have nodded her head vigorously and exclaimed: 'Now if a woman were the head of Scotland Yard – '

It was while working on a jewel-robbery case, 'The Double Clue', in the early 1920s that Poirot first encountered Countess Rossakoff. Like Poirot, the Countess was a refugee. 'The Countess Rossakoff is a very charming Russian lady, a member of the old régime,' was how Poirot's client described her as he reviewed the guests who had attended a party at which his collection of antique jewellery had disappeared. At first Poirot was inclined to be sceptical. '*Parbleu*! . . . Any woman can call herself a Russian Countess,' he told Hastings, but so smitten was he when he actually met the Countess that his doubts all melted away. In a vivid passage Hastings described her unheralded arrival at their rooms:

> Without the least warning the door flew open, and a whirlwind in human form invaded our privacy, bringing with her a swirl of sables (it was as cold as only an English June day can be) and a hat rampant with slaughtered ospreys.

To probe the robbery further, Poirot and Hastings called on her at her suite at the Carlton Hotel next morning, and within minutes the quick-witted Countess, 'arrayed in a marvellous négligé of barbaric design', abandoned all attempts to hoodwink Poirot. 'Ah, but you are the clever little man! Superb!' she exclaimed, handing back the jewels. He was enthralled:

> 'What a woman!' cried Poirot enthusiastically as we descended the stairs. '*Mon Dieu, quelle femme*! Not a word of argument – of protestation, of bluff! One quick

> glance, and she had sized up the position correctly. I tell you, Hastings, a woman who can accept defeat like that – with a careless smile – will go far!'

From that moment on, though their paths crossed only a few more times, Countess Rossakoff was the hopeless passion of Poirot's life. 'A woman in a thousand – in a million!' he called her, worshipping from afar. Observed Hastings drily: 'Small men always admire big, flamboyant women – .'

Following the ticklish matter of the jewels, the Countess departed from the Carlton and was seen no more by Poirot until she surfaced in Paris a few years later in *The Big Four*, demurely dressed in 'the heavy mourning that denotes a French widow'. 'That she was arrayed against us, on the side of our bitterest enemies, never seemed to weigh in his judgement,' wrote a shaken Hastings. The Countess, as it turned out, was playing a desperate game of her own. In their final battle with the Four she saved Poirot and Hastings from destruction, and in return Poirot reunited her with her little son whom she had thought dead.

Countess Rossakoff a mother? '*What?*' cried Hastings. Replied Poirot airily:

> 'But yes! You know my motto – Be prepared. As soon as I found that the Countess Rossakoff was mixed up with the Big Four, I had every possible inquiry made as to her antecedents. I learnt that she had had a child who was reported to have been killed, and I also found that there were discrepancies in the story which led me to wonder whether it might not, after all, be alive. In the end, I succeeded in tracing the boy, and by paying out a big sum I obtained possession of the child's person. The poor little fellow was nearly dead of starvation. I placed him

> in a safe place, with kindly people, and took a snapshot of him in his new surroundings. And so, when the time came, I had my little *coup de théâtre* all ready!'[1]

There is a hint on the last page of *The Big Four* that Poirot was trying to summon up courage to propose marriage to the Countess, but whether he lost his nerve, or she turned him down, we shall never know. He did, however, shortly thereafter retreat to the country to grow marrows and did not see her again until to his astonishment, one evening in the late 1930s, he spied her in London on a passing escalator. By this time Gothic adventures such as *The Big Four* were well in Poirot's past, but still, in his heart, no woman could ever compare with the Countess Rossakoff:

> All these young women who surrounded him – so alike, so devoid of charm, so lacking in rich, alluring femininity! He demanded a more flamboyant appeal. Ah! to see a *femme du monde*, *chic*, sympathetic, *spirituelle* – a woman with ample curves, a woman ridiculously and extravagantly dressed!

In 'The Capture of Cerberus', on the escalator at Piccadilly Circus, Poirot fell in love with the Countess all over again:

> Though it was something like twenty years since he had seen her last the magic still held. Granted that her make-up now resembled a scene-painter's sunset, with the woman under the make-up well hidden from sight, to Hercule Poirot she still represented the sumptuous and the alluring.

'I lead a life of the extreme, the most virtuous dullness. It is not so?' the Countess demanded of Poirot when he finally caught up with her. It was most certainly not. Dressed in magnificent scarlet, she had carved out a new career as the manager of a spectacular night-club whose entrance was guarded by an alarming animal named Cerberus, 'the largest and ugliest and blackest dog Poirot had ever seen'. On *Hell's* walls:

> . . . Orpheus and his jazz band played, while Eurydice looked hopefully toward the grill. On the opposite wall Osiris and Isis seemed to be throwing an Egyptian underworld boating party. On the third wall some bright young people were enjoying mixed bathing in a state of nature.

The Countess was overjoyed to see Poirot, and when he asked after Niki, the pathetic little boy of the long-ago snapshot:

> The Countess's face lit up with enthusiastic motherhood.
>
> 'The beloved angel! So big now, such shoulders, so handsome! He is in America. He builds there – bridges, banks, hotels, department stores, railways, anything the Americans want!'
>
> Poirot looked slightly puzzled.
>
> 'He is then an engineer? Or an architect?'
>
> 'What does it matter?' demanded the Countess.
>
> 'He is adorable! He is wrapped up in iron girders, and machinery, and things called stresses.'

In his visits to *Hell* it did not take Poirot long to perceive that the Countess was in grave danger on two fronts: she was about to be used as the scapegoat of a drug ring, and she was soon to become the mother-in-law of

Alice Cunningham, a most unsympathetic young woman engaged to marry the far-off Niki. 'I am writing a book on criminal psychology,' Miss Cunningham told Poirot:

'I find the night life of this place very illuminating. We have several criminal types who come here regularly. I have discussed their early life with some of them. Of course, you know all about Vera's criminal tendencies – I mean that she steals?'

'Why, yes – I know that,' said Poirot, slightly taken aback.

'I call it the Magpie complex myself. She takes, you know, always glittering things. Never money. Always jewels. I find that as a child she was petted and indulged but very much shielded. Life was unendurably dull for her – dull and safe. Her nature demanded drama – it craved for *punishment*. That is at the root of her indulgence in theft. She wants the importance, the notoriety of being *punished*!'

Poirot objected: 'Her life can surely not have been safe and dull as a member of the *ancien régime* in Russia during the Revolution?'

A look of faint amusement showed in Miss Cunningham's pale blue eyes.

'Ah,' she said. 'A member of the *ancien régime*? She has told you that?'

'She is undeniably an aristocrat,' said Poirot staunchly, fighting back certain uneasy memories of the wildly varying accounts of her early life told him by the Countess herself.

'One believes what one wishes to believe,' remarked Miss Cunningham, casting a professional eye on him.

Poirot gallantly saved Countess Rossakoff from all this,

and received a great deal of tearful gratitude in return. With her thoughts on her son, the Countess cried:

> 'And but for you his mother would be in prison – in *prison* – with her hair cut off – sitting in a cell – and smelling of disinfectant . . .'
>
> Surging forward, she clasped Poirot in her arms and embraced him with Slavonic fervour . . . The dog Cerberus beat his tail upon the floor.

Shortly after this episode the Countess Rossakoff disappeared once more – probably to America where, as Poirot managed to learn, Niki eventually became engaged to the daughter of a steel magnate. She did not appear in Poirot's life again, but his admiration for her never faltered. In *One, Two, Buckle My Shoe* he asked himself mournfully:

> . . . who could hold a candle to Countess Vera Rossakoff? A genuine Russian aristocrat, an aristocrat to her finger tips! And also, he remembered, a most accomplished thief – One of those natural geniuses –
>
> With a sigh, Poirot wrenched his thoughts away from the flamboyant creature of his fantasy.

Though not the stuff of romantic fantasy, the manifestly substantial Ariadne Oliver was arguably the most interesting of Poirot's friends and collaborators. Not only did she provide him with all sorts of refreshing theories on crime, but she provides Agatha Christie's readers with unforgettable insights into the agonies of writing detective novels.

'Am I interrupting, or anything?' a caller asked in *Cards on the Table*:

> 'Well, you are and you aren't,' said Mrs Oliver. 'I *am* working, as you see. But that dreadful Finn of mine has got himself terribly tangled up. He did some awfully clever deduction with a dish of French beans, and now he's just detected deadly poison in the sage-and-onion stuffing of the Michaelmas goose, and I've just remembered that French beans are over by Michaelmas.'

Poirot first met Mrs Oliver (as she was almost invariably called) at a literary dinner, but he did not really know her until they were brought together at Mr Shaitana's seminal dinner party in 1937. 'Let me introduce you – do you know Mrs Oliver?' said their Mephistophelean host, and 'the showman in him enjoyed the little start of surprise that Poirot gave,' for Mrs Oliver was an extremely well-known crime writer and a celebrity in her own right:

> She was not unduly modest. She thought the detective stories she wrote were quite good of their kind. Some were not so good and some were much better than others. But there was no reason, so far as she could see, to make anyone think she was a noble woman. She was a lucky woman who had established a happy knack of writing what quite a lot of people want to read. Wonderful luck that was, Mrs Oliver thought to herself.

Of her younger life we know that she had a grandmother and a great-aunt Alice, that she was sent to Paris to be 'finished', and that, in her own words, 'I was quite determined to be a nun and later on I thought I'd be a hospital nurse.' She first appeared in the Christie arena in the early 1930s, already middle-aged, widowed, and a 'world-famous novelist' in a short story, 'The Case of the

Discontented Soldier'.[2] At that time she was a member of the staff of the extraordinary Parker Pyne, a retired civil servant turned detective-therapist whose speciality was putting worrisome predicaments to rights. In the personal columns of the morning papers his advertisement regularly appeared:

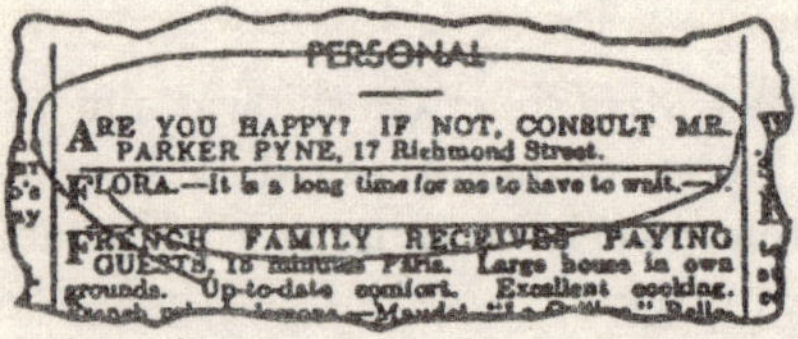
PERSONAL

ARE YOU HAPPY? IF NOT, CONSULT MR. PARKER PYNE, 17 Richmond Street.

FLORA.—It is a long time for me to have to wait.—

FRENCH FAMILY RECEIVES PAYING GUESTS, 15 minutes Paris. Large house in own grounds. Up-to-date comfort. Excellent cooking.

At 17 Richmond Street Mrs Oliver sat in a room at the top of the house 'at a table on which were a typewriter, several notebooks, a general confusion of loose manuscripts and a large bag of apples' thinking up happy endings for Mr Pyne's clients – mere child's play for someone who had already written 'forty-six successful works of fiction, all best sellers in England and America, and freely translated into French, German, Italian, Hungarian, Finnish, Japanese, and Abyssinian.'[3] Mrs Oliver's job with Parker Pyne was only an interlude, however, and she soon took up her life as a full-time author once again.

Like Poirot and so many of his friends, in the matter of age Mrs Oliver led a charmed life. Over a span of forty years the only thing about her that seemed to change significantly was the way she did her hair. In *Elephants Can Remember*:

> Mrs Oliver looked at herself in the glass . . . The trouble with Mrs Oliver was – and she admitted it freely – that her styles of hairdressing were always being changed. She

had tried almost everything in turn. A severe pompadour at one time, then a windswept style where you brushed back your locks to display an intellectual brow, at least she hoped the brow was intellectual. She had tried tightly arranged curls, she had tried a kind of artistic disarray. She had to admit that it did not matter very much today what her type of hairdressing was, because today she was going to do what she very seldom did – wear a hat.

Mrs Oliver was large, had 'an agreeable bass voice', 'fine eyes' (sometimes concealed by massive glasses), and was 'handsome in a rather untidy fashion'. On at least one occasion Poirot was called upon to extricate her from her small two-seater car, from which she emerged shaking herself 'rather like a large Newfoundland dog'. She often felt insecure about her clothes and with endearing reason. At a large dinner in *Dead Man's Folly* she is described in 'iron-grey satin . . . like an obsolete battleship', and in *Cards on the Table*:

> She gave a deep sigh, pushed back her country hat to an unfashionable angle, looked down with approval at the tweeds she had remembered to put on [and] frowned a little when she saw that she had absent-mindedly retained her London high-heeled patent leather shoes . . .

When necessary, Mrs Oliver could speak in 'a business-like committee-meeting manner', but she drew the line at making speeches. 'I know what I can do and I know what I can't. I can't make speeches. I get all worried and nervy and I should probably stammer or say the same thing twice.' When complimented on her writing she invariably turned 'purple with embarrassment'. 'I only write very plain murders,' she would say apologetically. Because she was a celebrity people were forever trying to interview her 'about such subjects as student unrest, socialism, girls' clothing, should sex be permissive, and many other things . . .' Though to her 'politics had always been anathema', on one subject – the equality of women – Mrs Oliver was prepared to speak out. 'But I wasn't going to be out of it and let those three men have all the fun to themselves,' she declared of the murder investigation in *Cards on the Table*, and she was perfectly prepared to endure all sorts of amused tolerance at her suggestion that it was time a woman headed Scotland Yard. 'Women *know* about crime,' she insisted.

Though she had many friends, and so many godchildren that she could hardly remember them all, Mrs Oliver was happiest when at home with:

> A deal table, her typewriter, black coffee, apples everywhere . . . What bliss, what glorious and solitary bliss! What a mistake for an author to emerge from her secret fastness. Authors were shy, unsociable creatures, atoning for their lack of social aptitude by inventing their own companions and conversations.

When Poirot first knew Mrs Oliver she lived in Harley Street on the top floor of a smart block of flats she airily described as 'all among the nursing homes', but later she seems to have moved to a house in Eaton Terrace. Wherever she lived her drawing-room and workroom were always exotically wallpapered. In time 'a riot of birds and vegetable life' gave way to a fruit pattern which had the effect, Poirot thought, of 'rather like being in a cherry orchard'. No doubt he was also disconcerted to find, on occasion, that Mrs Oliver's drawing-room was 'very untidy'. This was caused by her habit of strewing apple cores and papers wherever she went, despite a series of protective and elderly maids – Milly, in *The Pale Horse*, 'an efficient dragon who guarded her mistress from the onslaughts of the outside world'; Edith, in *Third Girl*, who rushed overdue manuscripts to the post office; and Maria, in *Elephants Can Remember*, who 'always approved and gave praise'. 'You look ever so smart,' she would say reassuringly as Mrs Oliver fared forth to social ordeals.

She also had a series of secretaries. One of them, in *Cards on the Table*, 'was so competent that it used to depress me . . . Then I tried having a thoroughly incompetent secretary, but, of course, that didn't answer very well, either.' Years later, in *Elephants Can Remember*, she mourned the departure of a secretary who had suited her perfectly ('If I don't get Sedgwick back, I shall go mad, thought Mrs Oliver to herself. I can't deal with this thing if I don't have Sedgwick'), and she regarded her new secretary, Miss Livingstone, with unease: 'Every line of her face said, "I am very efficient." But she wasn't really, Mrs Oliver thought.'

Enormously successful, Mrs Oliver had a love-hate attitude towards her calling. 'I'm in agony,' she would cry, tugging her hair violently, but shortly after finishing one book she would begin another. 'One actually has to *think*, you know,' she explained in *Cards on the Table*:

> 'Some days I can only keep going by repeating over and over to myself the amount of money I might get for my next serial rights. That spurs you on, you know. So does your bank-book when you see how much overdrawn you are.'

In *Mrs McGinty's Dead* there is an interesting scene in

which Mrs Oliver encounters some of her books in a Penguin display at a village post office:

> '*The Affair of the Second Goldfish*,' she mused, 'that's quite a good one. *The Cat it was who Died* – that's where I made a blowpipe a foot long and it's really six feet. Ridiculous that a blowpipe should be that size, but someone wrote from a museum to tell me so. Sometimes I think there are people who only read books in the hope of finding mistakes in them. What's the other one of them? Oh! *Death of a Débutante* – that's frightful tripe! I made sulphonal soluble in water and it isn't, and the whole thing is wildly impossible from start to finish. At least eight people die before Sven Hjerson gets his brainwave.'

Poirot must have blanched a bit when Mrs Oliver launched into tirades against her famous detective, Sven Hjerson:

> 'Why a Finn when I know nothing about Finland? Why a vegetarian? Why all the idiotic mannerisms he's got? These things just *happen*. You try something – and people seem to like it – and then you go on – and before you know where you are, you've got someone like that maddening Sven Hjerson tied to you for life. And people even write and say how found you must be of him. Fond of him? If I met that bony, gangling, vegetable-eating Finn in real life, I'd do a better murder than any I've ever invented.'

Sometimes, however, she was driven to protect him. In *Mrs McGinty's Dead* she argued furiously with a playwright who, in adapting one of her books to the stage, proposed to turn Sven Hjerson into a Norwegian resistance fighter:

> 'But, darling, if he's sixty, you can't have the tension between him and the girl – what's her name? Ingrid. I mean, it would make him just a nasty old man!'
>
> 'It certainly would.'
>
> 'So you see, he *must* be thirty-five,' said Robin triumphantly.
>
> 'Then he can't be Sven Hjerson. Just make him a Norwegian young man who's in the Resistance Movement.'
>
> 'But darling Ariadne, the whole *point* of the play is Sven Hjerson. You've got an enormous public who simply *adore* Sven Hjerson, and who'll flock to see Sven Hjerson. He's *box office*, darling!'
>
> 'But people who read my books *know* what he's like! You can't invent an entirely new young man in the Norwegian Resistance Movement and just *call* him Sven Hjerson.'
>
> 'Ariadne darling, I *did* explain all that. It's not a *book*, darling, it's a *play*. And we've just got to have glamour! And if we get this tension, this antagonism between Sven Hjerson and this – what's-her-name? – Karen – you know, all against each other and yet really frightfully attracted – '
>
> 'Sven Hjerson never cared for women,' said Mrs Oliver coldly.
>
> 'But you *can't* have him a *pansy*, darling. Not for *this* sort of play. I mean it's not green bay trees or anything like *that*. It's thrills and murders and clean open-air fun.'

Always a stern critic, in his own book Poirot gave Mrs Oliver a mixed review, despite their long friendship. 'I do not wholly approve of her works, mind you,' he told Colin Lamb in *The Clocks*:

> 'The long arm of coincidence is far too freely employed. And, being young at the time, she was foolish enough to make her detective a Finn, and it is clear that she knows nothing about Finns or Finland except possibly the works of Sibelius.
>
> Still, she has an original habit of mind, she makes an occasional shrewd deduction, and of later years she has learnt a good deal about things which she did not know before.'

It has not gone unnoticed that both Poirot's and Mrs Oliver's first names had their origins in Greek mythology. Ariadne, the daughter of King Minos, gave her cruel hero, Theseus, a ball of thread to guide him from the labyrinth after slaying the Minotaur. Some have seen a parallel in all this to the help Mrs Oliver gave Poirot in the six investigations in which they worked together – though Mrs Oliver, if she had been asked, would have scoffed at such an idea. 'Yes, I suppose it is a Greek name,' she said in *Hallowe'en Party*. 'But nothing Ariadne-like has ever happened to me. I've never been deserted on a Greek island by my own true love or anything like that.' Lovers she and Poirot certainly were not, but between the large and untidy Mrs Oliver and the small and orderly Poirot there flourished a lively friendship:

> 'When my friend, Mrs Oliver, asks me to do anything, I always have to do it,' said Poirot.
>
> 'What nonsense,' said Mrs Oliver.

Their friendship was such that each could be sure of

finding exactly the right kind of encouragement and comfort-foods in each other's sitting-rooms. In *Elephants Can Remember*:

'Coffee,' said Poirot. 'Let coffee be prepared and some petits fours. I rather think I ordered some in lately from Fortnum and Mason.'

'A liqueur of any kind, sir?'

'No, I think not. I myself will have some *Sirop de Cassis*.'

'Yes, sir.'

Mrs Oliver arrived exactly on time. Poirot greeted her with every sign of pleasure.

Such was Poirot's affection for Mrs Oliver that for her he broke a lifetime's cardinal rule. To her goes the honour of being the only adult – apart from servants – that Poirot ever addressed by first name. 'And who are you?' he asked a distraught telephone caller in *Hallowe'en Party*:

The voice, a female one, seemed surprised.

'Don't you know?' it said incredulously.

'Yes, I know,' said Hercule Poirot. 'You are my friend Ariadne.'

Much of their sleuthing together sprang from Mrs Oliver's habit of discovering murder mysteries that had nothing to do with the one she was currently writing. In rushing with them to Poirot she greatly enlivened his old age, although, as with his other colleagues, he often deplored her methods and conclusions. He had to concede, nevertheless, that her 'original if untidy mind' sometimes inspired him. In *Dead Man's Folly*:

'It is extraordinary,' said Poirot, and his voice was awed. 'Always you give me ideas. So also did my friend Hastings whom I have not seen for many, many years. You have given me now the clue to yet another piece of my problem.'

In addition to her cases with Poirot, Mrs Oliver did some worthwhile sleuthing on her own in a most interesting book, *The Pale Horse*, published in 1961.[4] In it she unerringly put her finger on the secret of her success:

'Oh *Chelsea*!' said Mrs Oliver. 'Everything happens there, I believe. Beatniks and sputniks and squares and the beat generation. I don't write about them much because I'm so afraid of getting the terms wrong. It's safer, I think, to stick to what you know.'

'Such as?'

'People on cruises, and in hotels, and what goes on in hospitals, and on parish councils – and sales of work – and music festivals, and girls in shops, and committees and daily women, and young men and girls who hike round the world in the interests of science, and shop assistants – '

'You enjoy life altogether, don't you?' someone once asked her. 'Yes, I do,' she replied. 'I suppose it's the feeling that one never knows what might be going to happen next.'

Ah, this Mrs Oliver of blessed memory!

Notes

1 It has, of course, been speculated that Poirot was the father of Countess Rossakoff's son. Taking all that we know about Poirot into consideration, this seems very unlikely. At the

very least, it is well documented that he was carefully chaperoned by Hastings at the Carlton Hotel.

2 This story, and another in which Mrs Oliver is mentioned, 'The Case of the Rich Woman', were first published in magazines in 1932. They were later included in a collection, *Parker Pyne Investigates*, published in 1934 (also published under the title *Mr Parker Pyne, Detective*).

3 The prolific Mrs Oliver was famously absent-minded. Several years later she told Superintendent Battle she had written a mere thirty-two books. By 1961, in *The Pale Horse*, she thought she had written 'fifty-five at least'.

4 In *The Pale Horse* Mrs Oliver encountered Hugh and Rhoda Despard, whom she and Poirot had first met some twenty-five years before in *Cards on the Table*, as well as the unforgettable Mrs Dane Calthrop and the Rev. Dane Calthrop, friends of Miss Jane Marple in *The Moving Finger*.

14

The Available Poirot

'But you're right at the top of the tree, aren't you, M. Poirot? . . . I mean you're the sort of person royalty calls in, or the Home Office or duchesses.'

—Gladys Nevill, One, Two, Buckle My Shoe

From the moment he set his pointed shoes upon the soil of England, it must have been painfully clear to Poirot that he had to begin earning his living all over again. Gone was his comfortable life in Brussels with imminent prospects of a handsome retirement. Instead, as he later told Hastings, he suddenly found himself 'existing by charity in a foreign land'.

As we know, after a brief period of haven in the cottage at Styles, Poirot solved the sensational murder of his benefactor with great flourish and shortly thereafter took up residence in London as a private detective. Though his practice began modestly, it says as much for Poirot's business acumen as it does for his detective skills that within a few years he became the most fashionable – and expensive – private detective in London. Such was his success that he never seems to have given a thought to returning to Belgium, and such was his curiosity that he undertook many cases for which he earned no money at all. In 'Double Sin' Hastings describes these early years:

> My little friend was a strange mixture of Flemish thrift and artistic fervour. He accepted many cases in which he had little interest owing to the first instinct being predominant.
>
> He also undertook cases in which there was a little or no monetary reward sheerly because the problem involved interested him.

By the mid-1920s Poirot had earned enough money to declare – as he would continue to declare for the rest of his life – that there was no need for him ever to accept a case again. Clearly he was a master of the art of attracting a wealthy clientele, charging it expensive fees, and managing his money wisely. How did he do it?

There are one or two hints that in the very early days of private practice Poirot may have advertised his services, but before long the rich and anxious who came knocking at his door arrived there because they had heard of him from their network of friends and acquaintances. In *Murder in Mesopotamia*, for example, the archaeologist, Dr Leidner, called in Poirot to investigate the murder of his wife because 'I once heard a Mr Van Aldin speak of him in very high terms.' Ten years after that, in *Death on the Nile*, old Miss Van Schuyler, 'making a Royal Progress bedward', paused to say, 'I have only just realized who you are, Monsieur Poirot. I may tell you that I have heard of you from my old friend Rufus Van Aldin.'

All this occurred, of course, because Poirot himself delivered the goods. He patently solved difficult and embarrassing mysteries better than anyone else, and he was far more discreet about it than the police – or so his clients hoped. 'Leave it in the hands of Hercule Poirot,' he was apt to tell them reassuringly. 'Have no fears. I will discover the truth.' He invariably did, and sometimes no one was more astonished and dismayed than the client.

Another source of lucrative cases was the entrée his reputation gave him to inner circles of power. Over the years he carried out a number of commissions for prime ministers, the Home Office, foreign governments, and large business houses, but in time he seems to have become bored with these politicians and insurance companies. In *Peril at End House* he waved away an urgent summons from Whitehall:

> 'In all generosity I say: Let the young men have a chance. They may possibly do something creditable. I doubt it, but they may. Anyway they will do well enough for this doubtless tiresome affair of the Home Secretary's.'

Some of his most interesting and satisfying cases were those undertaken on his own initiative and with no prospect of fees. 'Many unlikely people came to consult Poirot,' Hastings once wrote primly of clients who were not distinguished by birth or fortune. An even unlikelier lot – whether poor or rich – were those whom Poirot ruthlessly adopted as clients whether they wanted to be clients or not. '*Pas un sou*!' he cried imperiously in *Lord Edgware Dies*. 'When a case interests me, I do not touch money.'

Just such a case was *Peril at End House*, in which Poirot gallantly offered his services to an elfin and independent young woman who had been inexplicably shot at by an unknown assailant. Hastings described the scene:

> 'You mustn't be alarmed, Miss Buckley. We will protect you.'

> 'How frightfully nice of you,' said Nick. 'I think the whole thing is perfectly marvellous. Too, too thrilling.'
>
> She still preserved her airy detached manner, but her eyes, I thought, looked troubled.
>
> 'And the first thing to do,' said Poirot, 'is to have the consultation.'
>
> He sat down and beamed upon her in a friendly manner.

If one hired Poirot as one's detective this consultation usually took place in his sitting-room. If desperate, a client might arrive at any time of day or night – 'the door of our sitting-room flew open,' wrote Hastings, 'and a distracted female precipitated herself into the room.' If the matter at hand was less urgent, one would make an appointment in advance and, in due course, find oneself waiting to be ushered into Poirot's presence. In *Third Girl*:

> He lifted his cup. 'Show her in after five minutes.'
>
> 'Yes, sir.' George withdrew.
>
> Poirot finished the last sip of chocolate. He pushed aside his cup and rose to his feet. He walked to the fireplace and adjusted his moustaches carefully in the mirror over the chimney piece. Satisfied, he returned to his chair and awaited the arrival of his visitor.

When seated, if the visitor was a new client, out would come his or her story – or, at least, the story the client wanted Poirot to hear. 'M. Poirot. You're the only man in the world who can help me . . .' a newcomer might begin. In this process a good deal of sizing-up went on on both sides. 'You are making up your mind – are you not? – whether I am a mere mountebank or the man you need,'

Poirot asked Carla Lemarchant who came to consult him in *Five Little Pigs*:

> She smiled. She said, 'Well, yes – something of that kind. You see, M. Poirot, you – you don't look exactly the way I pictured you.'
>
> 'And I am old, am I not? Older than you imagined?'
>
> 'Yes, that too.' She hesitated. 'I'm being frank, you see. I want – I've got to have – the best.'
>
> 'Rest assured,' said Hercule Poirot, 'I *am* the best!'

For his part, Poirot's acceptance of a case, particularly when he was well established, was not a foregone conclusion. In *The Big Four* Hastings observed:

> The time when his cases had drawn him from one end of England to the other was past. His fame had spread, and no longer would he allow one case to absorb all his time. He aimed more and more, as time went on, at being considered a 'consulting detective' – as much a specialist as a Harley Street physician.

This eminence, and his never-ending threats to retire, allowed Poirot to adopt a lofty stance when refusing a would-be client. 'I must decline the case,' he told an American magnate in 'The Plymouth Express', 'because you have not been frank with me.' In *Murder on the Orient Express* he turned down a huge commission because: 'If you will forgive me for being personal – I do not like your face, M. Ratchett.'

When he did agree to act he was apt to include conditions which sometimes returned to haunt his client. 'I accept,' he told Alfred Lee in *Hercule Poirot's Christmas*, 'but you comprehend, Mr Lee, there can be no drawing back. I am not the dog one sets on to hunt and then recalls because you do not like the game he puts up!'

With such acceptances came money. How much was it? 'I ask myself only – is this affair sufficiently interesting for me to undertake?' he might say grandly, but the fact remains that Poirot's Mayfair flat, his expensive clothes, the salaries of George and Miss Lemon, his eventful holidays to the Mediterranean, and his occasional flings at ownership of Messarro Gratzs and weekend cottages all had to be paid for.

'You realize that my fees are high?' he warned on more than one occasion, but the delicate subject of what they would actually be was not openly discussed. A laughably small fee, such as the guinea Mrs Todd paid him in 'The Adventure of the Clapham Cook', or an impressively large one, such as the twenty thousand dollars offered him in the early 1930s in *Murder on the Orient Express*, might be mentioned as extraordinary, but as a rule financial arrangements were phrased in emotional rather than businesslike terms. 'Spare no expense!' he might be directed. 'My poor father – killed by someone – killed with the utmost brutality! You *must* find out, M. Poirot.' Or: 'All the dollars were made for my little girl – and now she's gone, I'll spend my last cent to catch the damned scoundrel that did it!' Such was Poirot's reputation that he was generally given *carte blanche*. No doubt, when such cases were wound up, a substantial statement of account, neatly typed on Poirot's 'thick and expensive' writing-paper would shortly follow. 'Nobility, *chère Madame*,' he once remarked to a client attempting to bargain, 'will not pay steamer and railway and air travel fares. Nor will it cover the cost of long telegrams and cables, and the interrogations of witnesses.'

All this said, and taking into account the many cases

for which he has never received a fee, the fact remains that Poirot did earn a great deal of money. 'You must be a millionaire by now,' exclaimed Japp in *Lord Edgware Dies*. 'What do you do with the money? Save it?' 'Assuredly I practise the thrift,' replied Poirot. He lived well but he also knew precisely where every penny went. There is a tiny scene in *Dumb Witness* in which, having torn up a letter just written, he 'carefully placed the wetted stamp face downwards on the blotting-paper to dry'.

In 'Double Sin' Hastings accused him of meanness when he attempted to obtain a reduction in their railway fares. 'My friend,' replied Poirot, 'it is not the meanness. It is the business sense.' He saved his money and he invested it with care. In recounting the case of 'The Lost Mine', Hastings recorded the following conversation:

'It is a curious thing,' I observed, 'but my overdraft never seems to grow any less.'

'And it perturbs you not? Me, if I had an overdraft, never should I close my eyes all night,' declared Poirot.

'You deal in comfortable balances, I suppose!' I retorted.

'Four hundred and forty-four pounds, four and fourpence,' said Poirot with some complacency. 'A neat figure, is it not?'

'It must be tact on the part of your bank manager. He is evidently acquainted with your passion for symmetrical details. What about investing, say, three hundred of it in the Porcupine oil-fields? Their prospectus, which is advertised in the papers today, says that they will pay one hundred per cent dividends next year.'

'Not for me,' said Poirot, shaking his head. 'I like not the sensational. For me the safe, the prudent investment – *les rentes*, the consols, the – how do you call it? – the conversion.'

> 'Have you never made a speculative investment?'
>
> 'No, *mon ami*,' replied Poirot severely. 'I have not.'

Poirot's professional expenses ranged from disbursements of petty cash (a 'crisp piece of paper' pressed into the hand of an informative valet, or the purchase of 'two postcards, a book of stamps, and a piece of local pottery' to win the confidence of a postmistress) to major outlays. 'There are moments,' he was on record as saying, 'when economy should be abandoned.' Though he saved a great deal of money by his habitual expedient of using his sitting-room as his place of business, he never stinted on the handsome commissions he paid out to the best freelance agents and investigators money could buy. 'It is not for Hercule Poirot to run up and down the evil-smelling streets of Limehouse like a little dog of no breeding. Be calm. My agents are at work,' he said with dignity in 'The Lost Mine'. Over the years he hired all sorts of irregulars – an actor to impersonate a window cleaner in order to see and tell all, or a tramp who had a way with dogs to kidnap Countess Rossakoff's terrible black hound. On occasion he even displaced the ever-available George when he felt someone with more specialized skills was needed. In *The ABC Murders* he told a visitor:

> 'You may have noticed I had a new manservant to-day – a friend of mine – an expert sneak thief. He removed your pistol from your pocket, unloaded it, and returned it all without your being aware of the fact.'

Two of Poirot's favourite and most expensive investigators were Joseph Aarons and Mr Goby. By profession Joseph Aarons was a theatrical agent, but he was always ready to sleuth for Poirot. 'He, without doubt, will be able to put us in the way of finding out what we want to know,' Poirot once told Hastings confidently. Aarons was one of Poirot's agents in his clashes with the Big Four, and in *Murder on the Links* he solved the mystery of the disappearance of Hastings's darling Cinderella. In 'Double Sin' Poirot interrupted a holiday to go to his aid:

> '*Eh bien*, Hastings, Joseph Aarons finds himself at Charlock Bay. He is far from well, and there is a little affair that it seems is worrying him. He begs me to go over and see him. I think, *mon ami*, that I must accede to his request. He is a faithful friend, the good Joseph Aarons, and has done much to assist me in the past.'

We have met the enigmatic Mr Goby before in these pages, 'a small shrunken little man, so nondescript as to be practically non-existent'. His services as a purveyor of information were extremely expensive, but his army of informants, spread all over England and the Continent, always produced gratifying results. It may be remembered that Mr Goby had a disconcerting habit of directing all his remarks to inanimate objects. In *After the Funeral* he arrived to report to Poirot:

> 'I've got what I could for you,' he told the fire curb in a soft confidential whisper. 'I sent the boys out. They do what they can – good lads – all of them, but not what they used to be in the old days. They don't come that way nowadays. Not willing to learn, that's what it is. Think they know everything after they've only been a couple of years on the job.
>
> And they work to time. Shocking the way they work to time.'

He shook his head sadly and shifted his gaze to an electric plug socket.

After the Hastings era, the most constant of Poirot's assistants was Felicity Lemon, his impressively efficient secretary. 'How I miss my friend Hastings,' Poirot once mourned:

'He had such an imagination. Such a romantic mind! It is true that he always imagined wrong – but that in itself was a guide.'

Miss Lemon was silent. She had heard about Captain Hastings before, and was not interested. She looked longingly at the typewritten sheet in front of her.

Miss Lemon was irredeemably unromantic and seldom wrong. She was, moreover, the one person capable of intimidating Poirot. Though they often annoyed each other, he trusted her utterly:

She was a woman without imagination, but she had an instinct. Anything that she mentioned as worth consideration usually was worth consideration.

Like Ariadne Oliver, Miss Lemon had once been employed by the remarkable detective, Parker Pyne. She appeared briefly as his secretary – 'a forbidding-looking young woman with spectacles' – in two of his commissions, 'The Case of the Middle-Aged Wife' and 'The Case of the Distressed Lady'. These short stories first appeared in 1932,[1] but by 1935, just three years later, she was firmly established as Poirot's secretary in 'How Does Your Garden Grow?' In this case she is described as 'forty-eight and of unprepossessing appearance', which seems a distinctly unfair leap in time for poor Miss Lemon.

As with George, little can be discovered about Felicity Lemon apart from her employment by Poirot. There is a mention that her family once lived at Croydon Heath, and in *Hickory Dickory Dock* we meet her likeable sister, Mrs Hubbard, but apart from this we know nothing of her life beyond her small typing room. Perhaps this was where her true passion lay? 'It was well known that the whole of Miss Lemon's heart and mind was given, when she was not on duty, to the perfection of a new filing system which was to be patented and bear her name.'

Miss Lemon was invaluable to Poirot. 'She was never tired, never upset, never inaccurate . . . She knew everything, she coped with everything. She ran Hercule Poirot's life for him.' She answered his phone, took impeccable dictation, paid his bills, answered many of his letters, and arranged his engagements. 'You have made the necessary researches for me, the appointments, the necessary contacts?' he asked her in *Third Girl*. '"Certainly," said Miss Lemon. "It is all here." She handed him a small brief-case.'

From time to time Poirot wrested Miss Lemon away from her typewriter to play detective. 'Sublimely incurious by nature', she took a dim view of these assignments. To her they seemed such a waste of time. As one would expect, however, she performed such outside duties with perfect efficiency. In 'How Does Your Garden Grow?' she travelled at Poirot's request to the village of Charman's Green to interview a fishmonger – and reported to her employer afterwards at the Green Cat tea-rooms.

Miss Lemon was still typing Poirot's letters beautifully and filing his papers flawlessly in the early 1970s in his penultimate case, *Elephants Can Remember*.[2] 'My much valued secretary, Miss Lemon . . .' Though she must be well over one hundred by now, somehow one imagines

Miss Lemon still going strong and being very good with electronic messages.

Typically, Poirot's working day began 'at ten o'clock precisely [when] he entered the room where Miss Lemon . . . sat awaiting her instructions', pad and pencil at the ready for dictation, the scheduling of appointments, and the acceptance or rejection of invitations. If a case so required, 'cautiously worded' advertisements would be drafted asking informants or mislaid relatives to communicate with Poirot's solicitors, or the wording of telegrams – sometimes in code – decided upon. Poirot loved to send telegrams. 'We have not seen M. Poirot today,' Father Lavigny remarked in *Murder in Mesopotamia*. 'I told him that Poirot had said he was going to be busy all day sending off telegrams,' wrote Nurse Leatheran in her memoir.

He also liked the telephone. 'Allô. Allô . . . Ah, good morning . . . Yes, it is I myself, Hercule Poirot.' He was particularly fond of long-distance telephone calls. 'It is romantic, you know, the transatlantic telephone. To speak so easily to someone nearly halfway across the globe.'[3]

These tasks concluded, Poirot then embarked on the main work of his day, and most of his days were very busy. 'I am always punctual,' he liked to point out. 'The exactitude – always I observe it.' On a hot summer's day in *Lord Edgware Dies*, for example, Poirot and Hastings attended a useful luncheon party at Claridge's from which 'Poirot had to leave early, as he had an appointment. He was investigating the strange disappearance of an ambassador's boots, and had a rendezvous fixed for half-past two.' At twenty minutes to five he returned to his sitting-room, having solved the mystery of the ambassador's boots with time to spare for a quick investigative visit to a hairdressers. No sooner was he home than the telephone rang with news of the main case at hand. 'A few minutes later we were jumping into a taxi. Poirot's face was very grave. "I am afraid, Hastings," he said.' At their destination, a maisonette in Kensington, Poirot's fears were realized. The telephone caller lay dead, sprawled across a dining-room table. Then followed 'the arrival of the police, the questioning of the other people in the house, the hundred and one details of the dreadful routine following upon a murder.'

Back home again, Poirot paced the sitting-room. 'I could almost feel the waves of his furious concentration of thought,' wrote Hastings. Presently Hastings dozed off and was awakened about nine o'clock by a cry. Poirot's green eyes were shining: 'I have been foolish. I have been blind. But *now* – *now* – we shall get on!' And so they did, rushing by taxi to possible new evidence. After this foray they found themselves crossing Euston Road when the chance remark of a passer-by gave Poirot a blinding inspiration. Recalled Hastings:

> Reaching the pavement I turned back to see Poirot standing in the middle of the road with buses bearing down on him from either side. Instinctively I put my hands over my eyes. There was a jarring of brakes, and some rich bus driver language. In a dignified manner Poirot walked to the curb. He looked like a man walking in his sleep.

Arriving home, Poirot flew to the telephone to summon yet another witness. With her departure he finally called it a day: 'Nothing more this evening, my friend. Tomorrow morning, early, we will ring up Japp.'

In *Hallowe'en Party*, some thirty-six years later, Poirot's working day was almost as busy (though at least during this one he later found time for an evening meal):

'This afternoon my friend Spence is making an appointment for me to talk with the local Inspector at a suitable hour. I should also like a talk with the doctor here. And possibly the headmistress at the school . . .'

'Do you know what you sound like?' said Mrs Oliver. 'A computer. You know. You're programming yourself. That's what they call it, isn't it? I mean you're feeding all these things into yourself all day and then you're going to see what comes out.'

But there were times when Poirot seemingly did no work at all. Clients and assistants alike were apt to be seized with exasperation or panic upon discovering their great detective building houses out of cards or sitting aimlessly in an armchair. 'He made mysterious absences, talked very little, frowned to himself, and consistently refused to satisfy my natural curiosity,' complained Hastings in *The ABC Murders*. In 'The Kidnapped Prime Minister', as precious time ticked by, Hastings could hardly contain himself:

> And for five long hours the little man sat motionless, blinking his eyelids like a cat, his green eyes flickering and becoming steadily greener and greener. The Scotland Yard man was obviously contemptuous, Major Norman was bored and impatient, and I myself found the time pass with wearisome slowness.

In 'The Under Dog' a client, Lily Margrave, 'smoothed her gloves out on her knee with a nervous gesture' at the sight of Poirot:

> His occupation at the moment struck her as particularly childish. He was piling small blocks of coloured wood

one upon the other, and seemed far more interested in the result than in the story she was telling.

In contrast to these private withdrawals to knit together the strands of a case, Poirot, when called upon to be a detective in the public eye, could be very professional indeed. Not surprisingly, a good deal of his time was taken up by inquests and trials. As he said in *Five Little Pigs*, 'In the Assize Court, as on the playing fields of Eton, and in the hunting country, the Englishman likes the victim to have a sporting chance.' Many a day was spent thus:

'Hercule Poirot.'

Hercule Poirot entered the box, took the oath, twirled his moustache and waited, with his head a little on one side. He gave his name and address and calling.

'M. Poirot, do you recognize this document?'

'Certainly.'

And many an evening was spent dutifully talking about his profession. In *Third Girl*:

'*Bonjour*, Madame – you are well, I hope?'

'Oh, I'm all right.' Ariadne Oliver's voice came through in its usual cheerful accents . . . 'It's rather early to ring you up, but I want to ask you a favour.'

'Yes?'

'It is the annual dinner at our Detective Authors' Club; I wondered if you would come and be our Guest Speaker this year. It would be very very sweet of you if you would.'

'When is this?'

'Next month – the twenty-third.'

A deep sigh came over the telephone.

In *Hickory Dickory Dock* a notice appeared on the bulletin board of a student youth hostel:

> *M. Hercule Poirot, the celebrated private detective, has kindly consented to give a talk this evening on the theory and practice of successful detection, with an account of certain celebrated criminal cases.*

No doubt, when he returned home from such engagements, he would find on his desk a small pile of Miss Lemon's impeccably typed letters awaiting his signature, and yet more incoming letters to read. 'The evening post arrived about ten o'clock,' noted Hastings in *The ABC Murders*, but often the available Poirot's day did not end there. Sometimes Japp dropped by late at night for a chat, or the telephone would ring again. In 'Yellow Iris':

> Poirot rose, glancing at his watch as he did so. The time was close to half past eleven. He wondered who was ringing him up at this hour. It might, of course, be a wrong number.
>
> 'And it might,' he murmured to himself . . . 'be a millionaire newspaper proprietor, found dead in the library of his country house, with a spotted orchid clasped in his left hand and a page torn from a cookery book pinned to his breast.'

NOTES

1 And were later collected in *Parker Pyne Investigates*, 1934.

2 Oddly, despite all their years of service together, there is no record that George and Miss Lemon ever spoke to one another.

3 At Whitehaven Mansions in the 1930s Poirot's telephone number was Trafalgar 8137, a unique privilege in view

of the fact that for all other mortals no such London exchange existed. Poirot's neighbours would have had to make do with the Whitehall exchange and, indeed, Poirot's own telephone number was once given as Whitehall 7272 which is intriguingly similar to Whitehall 1212, the famous old Scotland Yard number.

15

The Detective Poirot

'. . . yet I am only taking you all on a journey – my journey towards the truth.'

—Hercule Poirot, Murder in Mesopotamia

Detective: One whose occupation it is to discover matters artfully concealed.

—The Oxford English Dictionary

'Your mistress lies dead, and it is necessary that we should know all,' Poirot tells a servant in *The Mysterious Affair at Styles*. 'Nothing can bring her back to life, but we do hope, if there has been foul play, to bring the murderer to justice.'

At these solemn words, uttered by a little man in magician's attire, the reader's attention gives a sudden lurch. The hunt is up and there is a wonderful promise of suspense and conundrum to come. 'The dog hunts rabbits. Hercule Poirot hunts murderers' – in thirty-three books and fifty-six stories he practised his craft for all to see. The most important thing, surely, about Poirot, and the greatest fun in reading him, is that he was a superb detective.

Before the investigation came the crime. In the margins of the Poirot canon are any number of felonies short of homicide: kidnappings, blackmailings, robberies, espionage, drug peddling, embezzlements, frauds, forgeries, unlawful impersonations, confidence rackets, and so on, but at the centre are the murders – and the murderers. Inept murderers rarely warranted Poirot's attention. The ones he pursued selected themselves by their sheer cleverness. Those chosen had, along the way, cunningly eluded all the usual authorities or had been so adroit that their crimes had gone unnoticed in the first place. Matching his wits against them was the great joy of Poirot's life. 'How do you know the murderer is of the first class?' asked Amy Leatheran in *Murder in Mesopotamia*. 'Because,' replied Poirot, 'if he were not, the whole truth would be plain to me at this instant – and it is not.'

Poirot's murderers occasionally committed their deeds – particularly second or third murders – in the heat of the moment, but as a rule their crimes were carefully premeditated and their prey – usually friends or relatives – were dispatched, in Poirot's words, 'for gain, for fear or for love'. Sometimes their victims were genuinely mourned (in some later cases children were victims) but more often they were apt to be unlikeable people whose *coups de grâce* were greeted with sighs of relief. Whether as victims, murderers or witnesses, all hands involved tended to be members, or servants, of the upper classes.

Within these closed and seemingly secure circles the murderers struck in many ways. Sometimes the dinner table or a box of chocolates provided splendid opportunities. Over the years Poirot investigated a score or more of poisonings by arsenic, cyanide, strychnine, morphine, nicotine, prussic acid, adrenaline, procaine, dixitoxin or deadly germs. Knives, stilettos and daggers claimed some victims, and scarves, belts and clothes-lines dispatched others. There were several deaths from falls or drownings, a number of skulls crushed by heavy objects, and a good many fatal shootings. Two very bizarre murder weapons were a booby-trapped chess piece and an infected shaving brush. These dreadful deeds were often artfully camouflaged. Suicides were made to look like murders, murders made to look like suicides, and innocent people carefully framed. But, as Poirot pointed out, 'Motive and opportunity are not enough . . . there must also be the criminal temperament!' And luck. 'I tell you, my friends,' he declared in *The ABC Murders*, 'however carefully planned, no crime can be successful without luck!'

As a rule, when Poirot sniffed murder in the air he would go to almost any lengths to stop it ('It is much easier to catch a murderer than it is to prevent a murder,' he said in *The Labours of Hercules*), but if murderers there had to be, Poirot liked them to be worthy of his mettle. 'I tell you, my friend . . . This was a reasoned crime – a sane crime,' he observed with respect in *Appointment with Death*. 'This is not a crime well ordered and regular, such as a detective delights in,' he complained in *Murder on the Links*. In due course he adopted further criteria. 'I consider your crime not an English crime at all – not above-board – not *sporting*—' he lectured the perpetrator of the ABC Murders.

To catch murderers, as Hastings pointed out in *Murder on the Links*, Poirot employed two crucial weapons:

> 'Order' and 'Method' were his gods. He had a certain disdain for tangible evidence, such as footprints and cigarette ash, and would maintain that, taken by themselves, they would never enable a detective to solve a problem. Then he would tap his egg-shaped head with absurd complacency, and remark with great satisfaction, 'The

true work, it is done from *within*. *The little grey cells* – remember always the little grey cells, *mon ami*!'

Oh, those repositories of all order and method, the little grey cells of Hercule Poirot![1] First introduced as a phenomenon in *The Mysterious Affair at Styles* ('He tapped his forehead. "These little grey cells . . ."'), they were evoked so often by their owner in the earlier years of his English career that in *Lord Edgware Dies* Hastings protested:

> I am afraid that I have got into the habit of averting my attention whenever Poirot mentions his little grey cells. I have heard it all so often before.

In this matter Poirot seems to have taken Hastings's advice for once, and in his later career we hear less and less about grey cells. For his part Japp rather missed the constant refrain. 'Exert those cellular arrangements of yours I used to hear so much about,' he urged Poirot in *The ABC Murders*.

By the rigorous employment of 'sanity, logic, order and method', it was Poirot's unshakeable belief – as it had been the belief of his predecessor, Sherlock Holmes – that no murderer could escape. Unlike the hawkish Holmes, however, Poirot tended to avoid waging direct war against an adversary. He preferred, instead, to surround a suspect with a wide and carefully constructed net and sit in it, awaiting twitches.[2]

Which brings us next, in this examination of the detective Poirot, to psychology. Like the grey cells, in reading Poirot we tend to hear more about psychology in the 1920s and early 1930s than thereafter, but when he was its devotee no case could pass without a good dose of it:

'Order and method! That is the first stage. To arrange the facts with neatness and precision. The next stage – '

'Yes?'

'The next stage is that of the psychology.'

Poirot's psychology was of the interactionist school. He passionately believed that the key to the identity of a murderer lay in the crime itself – ('It is not the mere act of killing; it is what lies *behind* it that appeals to the expert') and in the character of the victim ('Because the victim was the kind of person he or she was, *therefore* was he or she murdered!'). When properly ordered grey cells discerned the inevitable pattern of psychological cause and effect in a case, it only remained to fit the appropriate suspect to the crime, regardless of apparently conflicting evidence. The crucial thing, to his tidy mind, was to see this method faithfully through, and the clues he built his deductions on were not so much tangible ones – the end of a cigarette or the print of a shoe – as the fleeting impressions and ideas from something let slip in a conversation, or glimpsed in a momentary expression of surprise on an onlooker's face. 'Women,' he said grandiloquently in *The Murder of Roger Ackroyd*,

> 'observe subconsciously a thousand little details, without knowing that they are doing so. Their subconscious mind adds these little things together – and they call the result intuition. Me, I am very skilled in psychology. I know these things.'

In *Murder on the Links* Hastings protested:

> 'But surely the study of fingerprints and footprints, different kinds of mud, and other clues that comprise

the minute observation of details – all these are of vital importance?'

'But certainly. I have never said otherwise. The trained observer, the expert, without doubt he is useful! But the others, the Hercule Poirots, they are above the experts! To them the experts bring the facts. Their business is the method of the crime, its logical deduction, the proper sequence and order of the facts; above all, the true psychology of the case. You have hunted the fox, yes?'

'I have hunted a bit, now and again,' I said, rather bewildered by this abrupt change of subject. 'Why?'

'*Eh bien*, this hunting of the fox, you need the dogs, no?'

'Hounds,' I corrected gently. 'Yes, of course.'

'But yet,' Poirot wagged his finger at me, 'You did not descend from your horse and run along the ground smelling with your nose and uttering loud *Ow Ows?*'

As Hastings and countless readers have learned over the years, Poirot had his own way of handling a case and, once started, he never gave up. 'Good morning, mademoiselle,' he greeted a surprised observer in 'Dead Man's Mirror' who had just discovered a muffled-up little man pacing around the herbaceous border beneath her bedroom window. 'You now behold a detective – a great detective, I may say – in the art of detecting!'

How did the great detective pursue his art? A case of the utmost complexity is *The Murder of Roger Ackroyd*, and to track Poirot's progress in it through the eyes and pen of its narrator, Dr James Sheppard, is one of the great treats of detective fiction.

A promising setting is provided by the village of King's Abbot. 'Our hobbies and recreations,' wrote Dr Sheppard, 'can be summed up in one word, "gossip".' In these pleasant surroundings an extraordinary event occurs, the inexplicable murder of King's Abbot's most prominent resident, Roger Ackroyd. Enter Hercule Poirot, who can rarely resist a case but likes to be persuaded:

> 'Miss Ackroyd,' I said, 'wants you to – to – '
>
> 'To find the murderer,' said Flora in a clear voice.
>
> 'I see,' said the little man. 'But the police will do that, will they not?'
>
> 'They might make a mistake,' said Flora. 'They are on their way to make a mistake now, I think. Please, M. Poirot, won't you help us?'

At the police station those in charge – who, after all, have had to deal with the actual blood and gore of the case – greeted Poirot's arrival with less than enthusiasm. Said the chief constable:

> 'Mr Ackroyd's family must, of course, do what they see fit . . . But we cannot have the official investigation hampered in any way. I know M. Poirot's great reputation of course, he added courteously.

This 'of course' was the harbinger of things to come. The Ackroyd case occurred comparatively early in Poirot's English career, when dealings with the police could still be ticklish.[3] In time Poirot would have most of the chief constables of England at his beck and call, and in London his sitting-room would become a sort of outpost of Scotland Yard, but in King's Abbot of the 1920s, he had to tread carefully. He generally liked the English police – he was, after all, 'an old Belgian police dog' himself – and he thought them 'a brave and intelligent force of men'. On this occasion he said smoothly:

'Above all things, I have a horror of publicity. I must beg, that in the case of my being able to contribute something to the solution of the mystery, my name may not be mentioned.'

Inspector Raglan's face lightened a little.

So the hunt was on. Often, in a post-Hastings case, one of Poirot's first actions was to recruit an assistant or two from within the situation. In *The Murder of Roger Ackroyd* he recruited Dr Sheppard:

'Do you really wish to aid me? To take part in this investigation?'

'Yes, indeed,' I said eagerly. 'There's nothing I should like better. You don't know what a dull old fogey's life I lead. Never anything out of the ordinary.'

'Good, we will be colleagues then.'

Briefed by Dr Sheppard, Poirot's first step was to assess critically the obvious evidence – 'the blue letter you speak of, where was it when you left the room?' . . . 'will you kindly indicate to me the exact position of the dagger?' . . . 'how was the fire? Was it low?' 'We have cleared away the manufactured clues'. 'Now for the real ones', he was apt to say at this stage.

In finding these his patience was inexhaustible. Somehow, despite his many admonitions against the foxhound school of detection, if it was Poirot crawling on his hands and knees across the floor of a summer-house, or groping in a fish-pond, such activities magically became legitimate and part of 'the method'.

To discover the antecedents, the *bona fides* or otherwise, of the people involved, there also began the *tête à têtes*, 'the little gossips', at which Poirot, retentive as blotting-paper, was so adroit. 'In the sporting phrase,' as he was to say in *Murder in Mesopotamia*, 'I run my eye over the possible starters.' 'It is always wise,' he once coached Hastings, 'to suspect everybody until you can prove logically, and to your own satisfaction, that they are innocent.'

One mode that Poirot often adopted was what Japp called his 'Father Confessor manner'. With what 'engaging candour', his voice 'coaxing, almost tender', his manner 'persuasive and a little more foreign than he need have been', could Hercule Poirot question witnesses! 'See now, Mademoiselle,' he said endearingly to Flora Ackroyd, 'it is Papa Poirot who asks you this. The Old Papa Poirot who has much knowledge and much experience.' Or: 'Reconstruction of the crime, they call it, do they not?' asked Parker, Roger Ackroyd's butler, observing Poirot's mysterious ways. 'Ah! he knows something, the good Parker,' cried Poirot admiringly. 'He has read of these things.' Or: 'M. Poirot! M. Poirot! Oh, do believe me,' cried Miss Russell, Roger Ackroyd's housekeeper, breaking down. 'Poirot got up and came to her. He patted her reassuringly on the shoulder. "But yes – but yes, I will believe. I had to make you speak, you know."' 'It shows you,' he said years later in *After the Funeral*:

> 'the dangers of *conversation*. It is a profound belief of mine that if you can induce a person to talk to you for long enough, *on any subject whatever*, sooner or later they will give themselves away.'

Another method was more aggressive. 'With your help I propose to examine a witness,' said Poirot to Dr Sheppard. 'We will question him, we will put such fear into him that the truth is bound to come out.' At what he lightly called a 'little reunion', he sat 'at the head of the table, like the chairman of some ghastly board meeting', and said severely:

> 'I mean to arrive at the truth. The truth however ugly in itself, is always curious and beautiful to the seeker after it . . . *Messieurs et mesdames*, I tell you, I mean to *know*. And I shall know – in spite of you all.'

And so this case, like many before and many to come, progressed relentlessly, if at times obscurely, towards the truth. There is nothing in detective literature so paradoxically soothing and suspenseful as watching Hercule Poirot, in the thick of a case, cleverly and mysteriously stirring the pot. In King's Abbot, that summer, there were many contradictions to be found, and many doubts and incriminations to be encouraged. The local intelligence corps had to be worked through and the police kept on his side. 'I was beginning to understand Poirot's methods,' wrote Dr Sheppard hopefully as he followed in his wake. 'Every little irrelevancy had a bearing upon the whole.' Later, when *The Murder of Roger Ackroyd* was published, Hastings, far away in South America, must surely have felt a twinge of sympathy for Dr Sheppard on reading these words.

At this stage of a case Poirot, in action more akin to a grasshopper than a foxhound, was apt to appear at his most foreign and incompetent. 'He shook his head, puffed out his chest, and stood blinking at us,' wrote Dr Sheppard. 'Bit gone here,' said Inspector Raglan, tapping his forehead. 'I've thought so for some time. Poor old chap, so that's why he had to give up and come down here.'

Gradually, provoked by fear or guilt, people start to loosen up. Changes are rung on first stories. Hidden conflicts surface. Sometimes a second, or even a third murder occurs. Suddenly we are on shifting sands. Nothing is as we first thought. The first murder had been a great surprise and the day not long enough to talk of it, but now we are apt to eye everyone suspiciously.

When a case reached this juncture, Poirot tended to play his cards very close to his chest, a habit that could prove extremely irritating to his colleagues. 'He would throw out hints and suggestions,' complained Dr Sheppard, 'but beyond that he would not go.' Said Poirot, when the plot in the Ackroyd case was becoming very thick indeed:

> 'And, as you know, my friend, I much dislike to have to explain my little ideas until the time comes.'
>
> I smiled a little.
>
> 'My friend Hastings, he of whom I told you, used to say of me that I was a human oyster. But he was unjust. Of facts, I keep nothing to myself. But to everyone his own interpretation of them.'

So intense did his own concentration on these known facts become in the final stages of a case that Poirot often shut himself completely away. 'I want to think,' he insisted in *Three Act Tragedy*. 'I ask of you twenty-four hours in which to think.' 'We are in darkness,' he said in *Murder on the Links*:

> 'A hundred conflicting points confuse and worry us. That is well. That is excellent. Out of confusion comes forth order.'

Though not detailed in *The Murder of Roger Ackroyd*, our yardstick case, we can be sure that towards the end of it Poirot carefully shut all the windows of his sitting-room, built up a fire in the grate, and gave himself over to complete immobility. With him would have gone food for the grey cells – his microscopic notebook, his neat lists of queries and trivia (tactfully compiled in his adopted language), and a puzzle box in his mind of clues, nuances, irrelevant remarks, coincidences, unrelated facts, stirrings of recognition, oddities, psychological hunches, and 'little ideas'. Why was a bit of cambric and a goose quill found in the summer-house? Who lifted the lid of the silver table? Why was a marriage kept secret? This was the stuff of Poirot's meditations, his 'furiously to think', as he built his card houses and primed himself with hot chocolate.

The task of Poirot's reveries was to hunt like a magpie through this accumulation of facts and thoughts, separating out this one, rejecting that one, holding up something for a closer look, sharply tapping something else to hear how it sounded. His genius lay in his ability to see what everyone else had seen and make new patterns and connections. 'Arrange your facts. Arrange your ideas,' he once counselled Hastings. 'And if some fact will not fit in – do not reject it but consider it closely. Though its significance escapes you, be sure that it *is* significant.'

In his progress towards the truth in his cases, Poirot was, of course, up against murderers who had done everything possible to lay false trails. Though he prided himself on his logical mind, a sure Poirot touch at a critical moment was the abandonment of logic – a tactic no murderer could possibly foresee. Poirot described such a leap in *Elephants Can Remember*:

> 'The proofs are there, the motive, the opportunity, the clues, the *mise en scène*, it's all there. A complete blueprint, as you might say. But all the same, those whose profession it is, *know*. They know that it's all

wrong, just like a critic in the artistic world knows when a picture is all wrong.'

Suddenly – amid groans and mutterings – the key deception, the hitherto unseen link would be perceived and Poirot would know the murderer. In *Murder on the Orient Express*:

> . . . his eyebrows began to move slowly up his forehead. A little sigh escaped him. He murmured beneath his breath.
>
> 'But after all, why not? And if so – why, if so, that would explain everything.'
>
> His eyes opened. They were green like a cat's. He said softly: '*Eh bien.*'

Obtaining the evidence to support a theory sometimes required setting a trap. This is the most suspenseful moment of many a Poirot case, particularly as those who are privy to the trap (including the readers) tend to have conflicting views as to who is to be caught. Poirot's theatrical streak came wonderfully to the fore on such occasions. The more elaborate the trap, the more he relished it. In one case, with the connivance of a guest, he staged a mock death to flush out the murderer. In another he hired an actor to play a ghost. Sometimes – though he claimed not to be very brave – he staked himself out as the bait. 'What I did,' he said with importance in *Evil Under the Sun*, 'was exceedingly dangerous – but I do not regret it. I succeeded!'

In some cases the trap was sprung during the grandest scene of all – the unveiling by the master magician of the solution to the case. For such a dénouement Poirot liked to assemble together the entire cast of suspects as audience.

'And then,' as he explained in *After the Funeral*, 'I make my little speech. And I sit back and see what happens . . .' In *The Murder of Roger Ackroyd* Dr Sheppard describes the opening moments of Poirot's 'little performance':

> 'The number is complete,' said Poirot. 'Everyone is here.' There was a ring of satisfaction in his tone. And with the sound of it I saw a ripple of something like uneasiness pass over all those faces grouped at the other end of the room.

In that company 'of well-bred masks for faces' was the murderer who, confident that all suspicions had been redirected elsewhere, contrived an air appropriate to a drawing-room court of inquiry. Poirot, simultaneously playing prosecution and defence, then conducted his captive audience step by step towards the solution, with frequent stops to examine red herrings drawn across his way. And, at exactly the right moment – and at considerable risk, as his hypothesis might still lack evidence – he played his trump card. 'A new note crept into his voice,' it is recounted in one case. 'He was no longer a ridiculous little man with an absurd moustache and dyed hair, he was a hunter very close to his quarry.' 'Having lulled [him] into security,' Poirot once said of a murderer, 'I turned on him and did my utmost to make him lose his self-control.'

Thus might a trap be sprung. 'You damned interfering murdering lousy little worm!' cried one killer at such a moment, his face 'transformed, suffused with blood, blind with rage . . . He hurled himself forward, his fingers stretching and curling, his voice raving curses, as he fastened his fingers round Hercule Poirot's throat . . .'

At such times – as in most crises – Poirot was well prepared. At the ready, other players waited in the wings.

Typically, with the drawing-room in confusion and the murderer unmasked, 'two detectives from Scotland Yard emerged from the next room.'

Sometimes, however, Poirot conducted a finale quite differently, and Scotland Yard's time-honoured formula – 'I warn you that anything you say may be used as evidence' – was never uttered at all. In several cases he unashamedly took the law into his own hands and played judge and jury. Occasionally a murderer who, in his opinion, had performed a justifiable act was allowed to go free. Sometimes, following a private interview with Poirot, a timely suicide would occur. 'I have my own way of regarding things,' he said in *Death in the Clouds*:

> 'What should you say the most important thing was to bear in mind when you are trying to solve a murder?'
>
> 'Finding the murderer,' said Jane.
>
> Norman Gale said: 'Justice.'
>
> Poirot shook his head.
>
> 'There are more important things than finding the murderer. And justice is a fine word, but it is sometimes difficult to say exactly what one means by it. In my opinion, the important thing is to clear the innocent.'

In looking back on the Ackroyd case, Dr Sheppard wrote:

> Every one had a hand in the elucidation of the mystery. It was rather like a jigsaw puzzle to which every one contributed his own little piece of knowledge or discovery. But their task ended there. To Poirot alone belongs the renown of fitting those pieces into their correct place.

Or, as Poirot himself once said, 'Lay the mystery on my shoulders.'

NOTES

1 According to H.R.F. Keating in *Agatha Christie: First Lady of Crime*, the term 'grey cells' is used in lieu of the word 'brain' by an entire African tribe.

2 The careers of Sherlock Holmes and Hercule Poirot slightly overlap. Poirot solved the mysteries of Styles in 1916 (though an account of them did not appear until 1921). Holmes's *His Last Bow* appeared in 1917. Poirot, though he owed so much to Sherlock Holmes, was surprisingly unappreciative of his talents, though full of admiration for his creator. In *The Clocks* Colin Lamb recorded Poirot's thoughts on Holmes:

> '*The Adventures of Sherlock Holmes*', he murmured lovingly and uttered reverently the one word, '*Maître*!'
>
> 'Sherlock Holmes?' I asked.
>
> 'Ah, *non, non*, not Sherlock Holmes! It is the author, Sir Arthur Conan Doyle, that I salute. These tales of Sherlock Holmes are in reality farfetched, full of fallacies and most artificially contrived. But the art of the writing – ah, that is entirely different. The pleasure of the language, the creation above all of that magnificent character, Dr Watson. Ah, that was indeed a triumph.'

3 A recurring antagonist during this period was the officious Inspector Miller who, much to Inspector Japp's amusement, openly sneered at Poirot's methods. Of him Poirot said: 'He's what they call the sharp man, the ferret, the weasel'.

16

The Curtain Falls

'This, Hastings, will be my last case. It will be too, my most interesting case – and my most interesting criminal.'

—Hercule Poirot, CURTAIN

'You really are the limit, Poirot.'

—Arthur Hastings, CURTAIN

The famous *Curtain*,[1] published in 1975, was indeed Poirot's last case and saw yet one more return of Arthur Hastings from Argentina to relate, as in the beginning, the deeds of the master. For Hastings this drama began with the arrival of a letter from Poirot in the spring of 1974. Posted in the Essex village of Styles St Mary, it bore the stamp of the very post office at which Poirot and Hastings had been reunited in 1916:

> And does it not intrigue you, my friend, to see the address from which I write? It recalls old memories, does it not? Yes, I am here, at Styles. Figure to yourself, it is now what they call a guest house. Run by one of your so British old Colonels – very 'old school tie' and 'Poona' . . .
>
> I saw their advertisement in the paper, and the fancy took me to go once again to the place which first was

my home in this country. At my age one enjoys reliving the past.

Then, figure to yourself, I find here a gentleman, a baronet who is a friend of the employer of your daughter. (That phrase it sounds a little like the French exercise, does it not?)

Immediately I conceive a plan. He wishes to induce the Franklins to come here for the summer. I in my turn will persuade you and we shall be all together, *en famille*. It will be most agreeable. Therefore, *mon cher Hastings*, *dépêchez-vous*, arrive with the utmost celerity. I have commanded for you a room with bath (it is modernized now, you comprehend, the dear old Styles) and disputed the price with Mrs Colonel Luttrell until I have made an arrangement *très bon marché*.

The Franklins and your charming Judith have been here for some days. It is all arranged, so make no histories.

A bientôt,
Yours always, Hercule Poirot.

Poirot's letter was a most welcome diversion for poor Hastings as it arrived at a very sad time in his life. His wife, the 'merry, laughing' Cinderella, had recently died and 'lay now in Argentine soil, having died as she would have wished, with no long drawn-out suffering, or feebleness of old age'. Hastings at once began packing for England:

The prospect was alluring, and I fell in with my old friend's wishes without demur. I had no ties and no settled home. Of my children, one boy was in the Navy, and the other married and running the ranch in the Argentine. My

> daughter Grace was married to a soldier and was at present in India. My remaining child, Judith, was the one whom secretly I had always loved best, although I had never for one moment understood her.[2]

Thus, within a few weeks, Hastings found himself once again gazing upon Styles Court, the scene of the sensational Inglethorp murder of so long ago. 'The park was much as I remembered it,' he wrote, 'but the drive was badly kept and much overgrown with weeds growing up over the gravel. We turned a corner and came in view of the house. It was unaltered from the outside and badly needed a coat of paint.'

Inside, Hastings was ushered upstairs to the very room he had occupied years before. It appeared virtually unaltered, though part of it, as a sign of changed times, had been partitioned off to make a small bathroom. In due course, when he had encountered the lukewarm water that trickled from the taps of the new Styles, Hastings was to remember:

> . . . the clouds of steam which had gushed from the hot tap of the one bathroom Styles had originally possessed, one of those bathrooms in which an immense bath with mahogany sides had reposed proudly in the middle of the bathroom floor. Remembered, too, the immense bath towels, and the frequent shining brass cans of boiling hot water that stood in one's old-fashioned basin.

Directly across the corridor from Hastings was the room that had once been Lawrence Cavendish's and had now been assigned to Poirot. 'With my heart beating slightly faster', Hastings rapped on the door.

A sad sight met his eyes:

> My poor friend. I have described him many times. Now to convey to you the difference. Crippled with arthritis, he propelled himself about in a wheeled chair. His once plump frame had fallen in. He was a thin little man now. His face was lined and wrinkled. His moustache and hair, it is true, were still of a jet black colour, but candidly, though I would not for the world have hurt his feelings by saying so to him, this was a mistake. There comes a moment when hair dye is only too painfully obvious. There had been a time when I had been surprised to learn that the blackness of Poirot's hair came out of a bottle. But now the theatricality was apparent and merely created the impression that he wore a wig and had adorned his upper lip to amuse the children!

Poor Hercule Poirot. And even worse, as Hastings was eventually to learn, Poirot's black hair now *was* a wig, and – the final indignity – the famous moustache *fake*! How could all this have happened in just the two or three years that had passed since last we saw him happily collaborating with Ariadne Oliver in that busy and interesting case, *Elephants Can Remember*? 'When the very young girls come and talk to you kindly, oh so kindly – it is the end!' he said mournfully to Hastings. His body crippled, his heart, as a doctor was soon to confide to Hastings, about to 'go out – phut – at any moment', there he sat in his wheelchair, nothing more than that 'dear old Belgian fellow' to the rest of the world, and cared for by a bovine new valet, Curtiss, a replacement for the faithful George, who had been summoned away by family illness. 'I am a wreck,' Poirot told Hastings. 'Mercifully I can feed myself, but otherwise I have to be attended to like a baby. Put to bed, washed and dressed. *Enfin*, it is not amusing that.'

'Nothing is so sad,' Hastings wrote, 'as the devastation

wrought by age.' In this respect he himself was still faring rather well. From his wheelchair Poirot surveyed his longtime pupil critically, 'his head a little to one side':

> 'Yes, just the same – the straight back, the broad shoulders, the grey of the hair – *très distingué*. You know, my friend, you have worn well. *Les femmes*, they still take an interest in you? Yes?'
>
> 'Really, Poirot,' I protested.

Then, as in the old days, the meeting was briskly called to order:

> 'Just now,' said Poirot, 'you asked why I had come here. You may not have observed that I gave you no answer. I will give you the answer now. I am here to hunt down a murderer.'
>
> I stared at him with even more astonishment. For a moment I thought he was rambling.
>
> 'You really mean that?'
>
> 'But certainly I mean it. For what other reason did I urge you to join me? My limbs, they are no longer active, but my brain, as I told you, is unimpaired. My rule, remember, has been always the same – sit back and think. That I still can do – in fact it is the only thing possible for me. For the more active side of the campaign I shall have with me my invaluable Hastings.'
>
> 'You really mean it?' I gasped.
>
> 'Of course I mean it. You and I, Hastings, *are going hunting once again*.'

Unlocking his dispatch case, Poirot produced a pile of notes and newspaper clippings, his research on five recent murders, all apparently solved. In studying their circumstances, however, the cunning old spider had detected a common thread:

> 'I intend, Hastings, to be very careful in what I say. Let me put it this way. There is a certain person – X. In none of these cases did X (apparently) have any motive in doing away with the victim. In one case, as far as I have been able to find out, X was actually two hundred miles away when the crime was committed. Nevertheless I will tell you this. X was on intimate terms with Etherington, X lived for a time in the same village as Riggs, X was acquainted with Mrs Bradley. I have a snap of X and Freda Clay walking together in the street, and X was near the house when old Matthew Litchfield died. What do you say to that?'
>
> I stared at him. I said slowly: 'Yes, it's a bit too much. Coincidence might account for two cases, or even three, but five is a bit too thick. There must, unlikely as it seems, be some connection between these different murders.'
>
> 'You assume, then, what I have assumed?'
>
> 'That X is the murderer? Yes.'
>
> 'In that case, Hastings, you will be willing to go with me one step farther. Let me tell you this. *X is in this house.*'

Quite naturally, Hastings wanted to know who X was. He should have known better.

> To my intense annoyance Poirot shook his head very decidedly. 'That my friend, I do not tell.'
>
> 'Nonsense. Why not?'
>
> Poirot's eyes twinkled. 'Because, *mon cher*, you are still the same old Hastings. You have still the speaking countenance. I do not wish, you see, that you should sit

> staring at X with your mouth hanging open, your face saying plainly: "This – this that I am looking at – is a murderer."'
>
> 'You might give me credit for a little dissimulation at need.'
>
> 'When you try to dissimulate, it is worse. No, no, *mon ami*, we must be very incognito, you and I. Then, when we pounce, we pounce.'

So began their last great adventure, with Poirot pretty well confined to his room and Hastings in the dark. 'I realized at once,' he wrote, 'that my part was destined to be a far more active one than usual. I had to be, as it were, Poirot's eyes and ears'. Besides reporting on everything that went on downstairs, Hastings persisted, to Poirot's annoyance, in trying to spot the culprit. 'I have not demanded your presence here, Hastings,' he thundered *ex cathedra*, 'in order to watch you clumsily and laboriously following the way I have already trodden.' Instead:

> 'You are active, you can get about, you can follow people about, talk to them, spy upon them unobserved—' (I nearly uttered an indignant protest, but quelled it. It was too old an argument) – 'You can listen to conversations, you have knees that will still bend and permit you to kneel and look through keyholes – '
>
> 'I will not look through keyholes,' I interrupted hotly. Poirot closed his eyes. 'Very well, then. You will not look through keyholes. You will remain the English gentleman and someone will be killed. It does not matter, that. Honour comes first with an Englishman. Your honour is more important than somebody else's life. *Bien*! It is understood.'
>
> 'No, but dash it all, Poirot – '

'The days passed,' wrote Hastings. Though it was summer, an air of dampness and dejection seemed to hang over the recycled Styles. Some of this unease was probably caused by the food, for Styles, as Poirot pointed out, 'is not, you comprehend, the Ritz':

> '. . . the cooking, it is English at its worst. Those Brussels sprouts so enormous, so hard, that the English like so much. The potatoes boiled and either hard or falling to pieces. The vegetables that taste of water, water, and again water. The complete absence of the salt and pepper in any dish – '

In the interests of the case Hastings diligently appeared at every meal, smoked in the smoking room, played bridge in the drawing-room, and accompanied on expeditions any fellow guest who wanted a companion. In between he rushed upstairs to the room at the end of the hall to report.

The people assembled that summer at Styles were a classic collection. First there were the Luttrells, who owned and ran Styles as a retirement enterprise. Colonel Luttrell was a 'very tall, attenuated old man, with a cadaverous face, mild blue eyes and a habit of irresolutely tugging at his little white moustache'. He was much hounded by his wife, in Poirot's opinion. Mrs Luttrell managed everything, and had 'curly white hair, pink cheeks, and a pair of cold pale blue eyes'.

As to the guests, Hastings firmly believed that the one who could be most trusted was Sir William Boyd Carrington, a retired 'Governor of a province in India, where he had been a signal success. He was also renowned as a first-class shot and big game hunter. The sort of man,' Hastings reflected sadly, 'that we no longer seemed to breed in these degenerate days.' Then there was Norton, a grey-haired man with a boyish face and a stammer, who was devoted to bird-watching and hurried about with field-glasses and cries of 'There's a pair of n-nesting black caps down by the sycamore.' And there was Miss Elizabeth Cole, 'a tall, still handsome woman of thirty-three or four' who sometimes played Bach and Mozart to Poirot on the drawing-room piano when he felt well enough to come down, and on whom he had his eye as a possible match for Hastings. And there was Major Allerton, 'a good-looking man in the early forties, broad-shouldered, bronzed of face, with an easy way of talking, most of what he said holding a double implication. He had the pouches under his eyes that come with a dissipated way of life.' Wrote Hastings severely, 'I knew instinctively that Allerton was a rotter,' and he became very angry indeed when he began to suspect that Allerton had dishonourable intentions toward Judith Hastings, his daughter.

Ostensibly, Judith's presence was the reason Poirot had suggested to her father that the three of them spend the summer *en famille* as, by coincidence, her work had brought her to Styles not long after Poirot's arrival. 'Judith is tall,' reported a rather intimidated Hastings, 'she holds her head high, she has level dark brows, and a very lovely line of cheek and jaw, severe in its austerity.' Judith had already been living some time in England where she had obtained a B.Sc. and clearly had her consciousness raised by the new wave of feminism. 'Is it very bad?' she asked absent-mindedly when 'Uncle Hercule' complained of the Styles cuisine. Scolded Poirot:

> 'You should not have to ask that, my child. Is it that you think of nothing but the test tubes and the microscopes? Your middle finger it is stained with methyline blue. It is

> not a good thing for your husband if you take no interest in his stomach.'
>
> 'I dare say I shan't have a husband.'
>
> 'Certainly you will have a husband. What did the *bon Dieu* create you for?'
>
> 'Many things, I hope,' said Judith.

Her employer was a brilliant scientist, Dr John Franklin, 'a tall, angular young man of thirty-five, with a decided jaw, reddish hair, and bright blue eyes'. He and his invalid wife had come to Styles for a summer of country air, and in an old studio in the garden he pursued, with Judith's help, his research into a rare tropical disease. His wife, Barbara Franklin, spent her days decoratively 'on a day bed, propped up with pillows, and wearing a very dainty négligé of white and pale blue'. Her attendant, Nurse Craven, was, Hastings noted approvingly, 'a tall, good-looking young woman with a fine colour and a handsome head of auburn hair'.

'My narrative of the days spent at Styles must necessarily be somewhat rambling,' wrote Hastings. Upstairs, perched in his wheelchair, Poirot brooded:

> 'I am terribly afraid. And I am powerless – or nearly so. And the days go by. There is danger, Hastings, and it is very close.'

It was indeed, for an accidental shooting followed by two murders sent Styles rocketing into the headlines once again, and those who compose obituaries would, in due course, scramble to the international wire services with an even more sensational story – the death by heart attack of the legendary Hercule Poirot.[3]

'It is with a heavy heart that I take up my pen to write

these the last words . . .' Thus did Dr Watson announce to the world the 'death' of Sherlock Holmes in 'The Final Problem'. For the devotees of Hercule Poirot, however, there was not to be even the consolation of a faint question mark, for Hastings left no doubt, in that second summer of mysteries at Styles, that the life of their dear and elegant little Belgian detective had come to an irrevocable end:

> '*Cher ami*!' Poirot had said to me as I left the room.
>
> They were the last words I was ever to hear him say. For when Curtiss came to attend to his master he found that master dead . . .

Poirot was buried – very neatly one may be sure – in Styles St Mary, 'the spot', wrote the stricken Hastings, 'where he had lived when he first came to this country'. This was not the first funeral Hastings had arranged for his friend. Years before, in the case of *The Big Four*, he had been deliberately led to believe that 'the unique, the inimitable' Hercule Poirot was dead. The words he wrote then could equally have described the final funeral at Styles:

> It was a solemn and moving ceremony, and the extraordinary number of floral tributes passed belief. They came from high and low alike, and bore striking testimony to the place my friend had made for himself in the country of his adoption. For myself, I was frankly overcome by emotion as I stood by the grave side and thought of all our varied experiences and the happy days we had passed together.

No doubt, as before, the dashing Countess Rossakoff sent an enormous wreath of crimson roses to the funeral of her little friend, and no doubt there were gathered at the graveside, with Hastings and Judith and the other surviving guests, a surprised and saddened Miss Lemon, and Mrs Oliver, and Superintendent Spence, and Mr Goby, and many others of Poirot's friends and associates.

'I could hardly imagine life without Poirot . . .' wrote Hastings.

And what of George? '*Talk to my valet George*', commanded a posthumous note that fluttered into Hastings's hand as he sorted through Poirot's dispatch box.

And what of X? 'In the duel between Poirot and X, X had won,' Hastings had concluded bitterly, completely forgetting, in his grief, one of the last smiles of Hercule Poirot and his words: 'But you and I, Hastings, go on, working underground, like moles. And, sooner or later, *we get* X.'

And so they did. Such style, Poirot.

NOTES

1 *Curtain: Poirot's Last Case* has a curious 'back to the future' air. Agatha Christie wrote it and *Sleeping Murder*, a Miss Marple case, in the early years of World War Two 'in anticipation of my being killed in the raids, which seemed to be in the highest degree likely as I was working in London'. Though it describes the very last events in Poirot's life – already in its longevity a phenomenon – *Curtain* presents its readers with a further puzzle by its lack of references and touchstones to Poirot's life between the early 1940s and 1974. As a result we find such intriguing zigzags in the timewarp as an old lady speaking of the 1916 Styles case as having occurred merely 'twenty years ago . . .'

2 It is possible that Hastings, who would have lived through the Peronist era of 1946 to 1955, may have been glad to take a holiday at this particular time for more than one reason. These were tense days in Argentina. 1973 saw the

return of Juan Perón, and July of 1974 saw his death and the assumption of power by his widow, Isabel.

3 When news of Poirot's death was revealed with the publication of *Curtain* in 1975, a number of obituaries appeared. The most handsome of these – though it contained a number of inaccuracies – was published on the front page of *The New York Times* of 6 August, 1975 beside W. Smithson Broadhead's portrait of Poirot.

A Poirot Bibliography

Books

'Miss Lemon, where are you now that I need you?' must be the cry of any Poirot bibliographer. Listed here are most of the first appearances in print in the English language of the various editions of novels, short story collections, plays and omnibus volumes wholly or in part devoted to Hercule Poirot. Many of these editions have been reissued numerous times and are still in print.

(PB) indicates a paperback edition.

The ABC Murders:

London: Collins, 1936.
New York: Dodd, Mead, 1936.
London: Crime Club, 1939.
New York: Pocket Books, 1941. (PB)
Harmondsworth (UK): Penguin, 1948. (PB)
London: Pan, 1958. (PB)
London: Fontana, 1962. (PB)
London: Collins, 1976 (Greenway edition).
New York: Pocket Books, 1976. (PB)
London: Collins, 1980.
Boston: G.K. Hall Large Print Books, 1988.
London: Collins, 1990 (centenary edition).

London: HarperCollins, 1996 (diamond anniversary edition). (PB)

See also omnibus Volumes *Agatha Christie Omnibus; Five Complete Hercule Poirot Novels; Murder-Go-Round; Surprise Endings by Hercule Poirot.*

The Adventure of the Christmas Pudding and a Selection of Entrées: (short stories):

London and Don Mills (Canada): Collins, 1960.
London: Fontana, 1963. (PB)
London: Pan, 1971. (PB)
London: Collins, 1981.

After the Funeral:

London: Collins, 1953.
London: Fontana, 1956. (PB)
Leicester (UK): Ulverscroft Large Print Edition, 1968.

See also omnibus volume *A Poirot Quintet.*
Also published under the title *Funerals are Fatal:*

New York: Black, 1953.
New York: Dodd, Mead, 1953. (Red Badge Detective).
New York: Pocket Books, 1954. (PB)

See also omnibus volume *Murder-Go-Round.*

Agatha Christie Crime Collection (includes *Lord Edgware Dies; Murder in Mesopotamia; The Murder of Roger Ackroyd; Mrs McGinty's Dead*):

London: Hamlyn, 1969. 2 vols.

Agatha Christie Murder by the Box (includes *The Regatta Mystery and Other Stories*):

New York: Berkley, 1988. (PB)

An Agatha Christie Omnibus (includes *The Mysterious Affair at Styles; Murder on the Links; Poirot Investigates*):
London: John Lane, 1931.

Agatha Christie Omnibus (includes *The Mysterious Affair at Styles; Perit at End House The ABC Murders; One, Two, Buckle My Shoe*):
London: Diamond Books, 1993.

The Agatha Christie Omnibus of Crime (includes *The Mystery of the Blue Train; The Murder of Roger Ackroyd*):
London: Collins, 1932.

Agatha Christie's Best Loved Sleuths (includes *Murder in Three Acts; Murder on the Links; There is a Tide*):
New York: Berkley, 1988. (PB)

Agatha Christie's Crime Reader (includes selections from *Poirot Investigates*):
Cleveland (US): World Publishing, 1944.

Agatha Christie's Detectives: Five Complete Novels (includes *Dead Man's Folly; Sad Cypress*):
New York: Avenel, 1982.
New York: Chatham River Press, 1985.

Agatha Christie's Poirot, Book 1 (10 short stories):
London: Fontana, 1993. (PB)
Also published under the title
Hercule Poirot's Casebook:
London: Fontana, 1989. (PB)

Agatha Christie's Poirot, Book 2 (8 short stories):
London: Fontana, 1990. (PB)

Agatha Christie's Poirot, Book 3 (10 short stories):
London: Fontana, 1991. (PB)

Agatha Christie's Poirot, Book 4 (8 short stories:
London: Fontana, 1993. (PB)

Alibi (dramatization by Michael Morton of *The Murder of Roger Ackroyd*):
London: French, 1929.

Appointment with Death:
London: Collins, 1938.
New York: Dodd, Mead, 1938.
New York: Grosset & Dunlap, 1938.
New York: Dell, 1946. (PB)
Harmondsworth (UK): Penguin, 1948. (PB)
London: Pan, 1957. (PB)
London: Fontana, 1960. (PB)
New York: Dell, 1971 (New Dell Edition).
Leicester (UK): Ulverscroft Large Print Edition, 1975.
New York: Berkley, 1984. (PB)
See also omnibus volume *Make Mine Murder*.

The Best of Poirot (contains *Murder on the Orient Express*; *Cards on the Table*; *Hercule Poirot's Christmas*; *Five Little Pigs*; *The Labours of Hercules*):
London: Collins, 1980.

The Big Four:
London: Collins, 1927.
New York: Dodd, Mead, 1927.
Harmondsworth (UK): Penguin, 1957. (PB)
London: Pan, 1961. (PB)
New York: Avon, 1964. (PB)
London: Fontana, 1965. (PB)

New York: Dell, 1965. (PB)
Leicester (UK): Ulverscroft Large Print Edition, 1974.
New York: Berkley, 1984. (PB)
See also omnibus volume *1920s Agatha Christie, Volume 3.*

Black Coffee; a Play in Three Acts:
London: Ashley, 1934.
London: French, 1952.
London and New York: French, 1961.

Blood Will Tell: see *Mrs McGinty's Dead*

Cards on the Table:
London: Collins, 1936.
New York: Dodd, Mead, 1937.
New York: Dell, 1949. (PB)
London: Pan, 1951. (PB)
London: Fontana, 1957. (PB)
London: Collins, 1968 (Greenway edition).
New York: Dodd, Mead, 1968 (Greenway edition).
Leicester (UK): Ulverscroft Large Print Edition, 1969.
New York: Dell, 1970 (New Dell edition). (PB)
New York: Berkley, 1984. (PB)
London: Collins, 1990 (centenary edition).
London: HarperCollins, 1996 (diamond anniversary edition). (PB)
See also omnibus volumes *The Best of Poirot; Five Complete Hercule Poirot Novels; Surprise Endings by Hercule Poirot.*
Also published as a play: *Agatha Christie's Cards on the Table*, adapted by Leslie Darbon:
London and New York: French, 1982.

Cat Among the Pigeons:
London: Collins, 1959.
New York: Dodd, Mead, 1960.

New York: Pocket Books, 1961. (PB)
London: Fontana, 1962. (PB)
Leicester (UK): Ulverscroft Large Print Edition, 1964.
New York: Dodd, Mead, 1986 (Winterbrook edition).

Christie Classics (includes *The Murder of Roger Ackroyd*):
New York: Dodd, Mead, 1957.

The Clocks:
London: Collins, 1963.
New York: Dodd, Mead, 1964.
New York: Pocket Books, 1965. (PB)
London: Fontana, 1966. (PB)
Leicester (UK): Ulverscroft Large Print Edition, 1969.
New York: Bantam, 1988 (Hardcover Collection).

Crime in Cabin 66 (short story):
London: Vallancey, 1944. (PB)
Also published under the title *The Mystery of the Crime in Cabin 66*:
London: Todd, 1943. (PB)
New York: Bantam, 1943. (PB)

Curtain:
London: Collins, 1975.
New York: Dodd, Mead, 1975.
Leicester (UK): Ulverscroft Large Print Edition, 1976.
New York: Pocket Books, 1976. (PB)
London: Fontana, 1977. (PB)
Mattituck, N. Y.: Amereon, no date.
See also omnibus volume *Curtain and the Mysterious Affair at Styles*.

Curtain and the Mysterious Affair at Styles:
New York: Doubleday, 1975.

Dead Man's Folly:
London: Collins, 1956.
New York: Dodd, Mead, 1956.
London: Book Club, 1957.
New York: Pocket Books, 1957. (PB)
London: Fontana, 1960. (PB)
London: Pan, 1966. (PB)
Leicester (UK): Ulverscroft Large Print Edition, 1967.
London: Fontana, 1970 (PB)
See also omnibus volume *Agatha Christie's Detectives*.

Dead Man's Mirror and Other Stories: see *Murder in the Mews and Three Other Poirot Cases*

Death in the Air: see *Death in the Clouds*

Death in the Clouds:
London: Collins, 1935.
London: Fontana, 1957. (PB)
London: Pan, 1964. (PB)
Leicester (UK): Ulverscroft Large Print Edition, 1967.
London: Collins, 1973 (Greenway edition).
New York: Dodd, Mead, 1974 (Greenway edition).
Also published under the title *Death in the Air*:
New York: Dodd, Mead, 1935.
New York: Triangle, 1939.
New York: Avon, 1946. (PB)
New York: Popular Library, 1961. (PB)
New York: Berkley, 1984. (PB)
See also omnibus volume *Murder on Board*.

Death on the Nile:
London: Collins, 1937.
New York: Dodd, Mead, 1938.

New York: Grosset & Dunlap, 1939.
New York: Avon, 1944. (PB)
London: Pan, 1949. (PB)
Harmondsworth (UK): Penguin, 1953. (PB)
London: Fontana, 1960. (PB)
New York: Bantam, 1963. (PB)
London: Collins, 1969 (Greenway edition).
New York: Dodd, Mead, 1970 (Greenway edition).
Leicester (UK): Ulverscroft Large Print Edition, 1971.
London: Collins, 1978 (Film edition).
London: Collins, 1990 (centenary edition).

See also omnibus volumes *Five Complete Hercule Poirot Novels; Masterpieces of Murder; Perilous Journeys of Hercule Poirot; A Poirot Quintet.*

Double Sin and Other Stories (short stories):
New York: Dodd, Mead, 1961.
Roslyn, NY: Black, 1961 (Detective Book Club).
New York: Pocket Books, 1962. (PB)
New York: Dell, 1964. (PB)
New York: Berkley, 1984 (PB)

Dumb Witness:
London: Collins, 1937.
London: Pan, 1949. (PB)
London: Fontana, 1958. (PB)
London: Pan, 1969. (PB)
Leicester (UK): Ulverscroft Large Print Edition, 1973.
London: Fontana, 1975. (PB)

Also published under the title: *Poirot Loses a Client:*
New York: Dodd, Mead, 1937.
Cleveland (US): World Publishing, 1944.
New York: Avon, 1945. (PB)
New York: Dell, 1965. (PB)

New York: Berkley, 1985. (PB)
See also omnibus volume: *A Poirot Quintet.*

Elephants Can Remember:
London: Collins, 1972.
New York: Dodd, Mead, 1972.
Boston: G.K. Hall Large Print Books, 1973.
New York: Dell, 1973. (PB)
London: Fontana, 1975. (PB)
London: Collins, 1978 (Greenway edition).
New York: Dodd, Mead, 1979 (Greenway edition).
New York: Berkley, 1984. (PB)

Evil Under the Sun:
London: Collins, 1941.
New York: Dodd, Mead, 1941.
New York: Pocket Books, 1945. (PB)
London: Fontana, 1957. (PB)
London: Pan, 1963. (PB)
Leicester (UK): Ulverscroft Large Print Edition, 1971.
New York: Dodd, Mead, 1981 (Greenway edition).
Boston: G.K. Hall Large Print Books, 1988.
See also omnibus volume *Murder International.*

Five Complete Hercule Poirot Novels (contains *Thirteen at Dinner; Murder on the Orient Express; The ABC Murders; Cards on the Table; Death on the Nile*):
New York, Avenel, 1980.

Five Little Pigs:
London: Collins, 1942.
London: Pan, 1953. (PB)
London: Fontana, 1959. (PB)
Leicester (UK): Ulverscroft Large Print Edition, 1982.

Also published under the title *Murder in Retrospect*:
New York: Dodd, Mead, 1942.
New York: Dell, 1948. (PB)
New York: Berkley, 1988.
See also omnibus volumes *The Best of Poirot: Murder Preferred*.

Four Great Detective Novels (includes *The Murder of Roger Ackroyd*):
London: Odhams, 1938?

Funerals are Fatal: see *After the Funeral*

Hallowe'en Party:
London: Collins, 1969.
New York: Dodd, Mead, 1969.
New York: Pocket Books, 1970. (PB)
London: Fontana, 1972. (PB)
Leicester (UK): Ulverscroft Large Print Edition. 1987.

Hercule Poirot, Master Detective (includes *The Murder of Roger Ackroyd: Murder in the Calais Coach: Thirteen at Dinner*):
New York: Dodd, Mead. 1936.

Hercule Poirot's Casebook (short stories):
New York: Dodd, Mead, 1984. (50 short stories).
See also *Agatha Christie's Poirot, Book 1*.

Hercule Poirot's Christmas:
London: Collins. 1938.
London: Fontana, 1957. (PB)
London: Pan, 1967. (PB)
London: Collins. 1973. (Greenway edition).

New York: Dodd, Mead, 1974 (Greenway edition).
Leicester (UK): Ulverscroft Large Print Edition, 1987.
Also published under the title *Murder for Christmas*:
New York: Dodd, Mead, 1939.
New York: Grosset & Dunlap, 1940.

Also published under the title *A Holiday for Murder*:
New York: Avon, 1947. (PB)
New York: Bantam, 1962. (PB)
See also omnibus volume: *The Best of Poirot*

Hercule Poirot's Early Cases: see *Poirot's Early Cases*

Hickory Dickory Death: see *Hickory Dickory Dock*

Hickory Dickory Dock:
London: Collins, 1955.
London: Fontana, 1958. (PB)
London: Pan, 1967. (PB)
Leicester (UK): Ulverscroft Large Print Edition, 1987.
Also published under the title *Hickory Dickory Death*:
New York: Dodd, Mead, 1955.
New York: Pocket Books, 1956. (PB)
Toronto: Bantam Books, 1984 (Hardcover Collection).
See also omnibus volume *The Nursery Rhyme Murders*.

A *Holiday for Murder*: see *Hercule Poirot's Christmas*

The Hollow:
London: Collins, 1946.
New York: Dodd, Mead, 1946.
New York: Pocket Books, 1948. (PB)
London: Pan, 1950. (PB)
London: Fontana, 1957. (PB)

Leicester (UK): Ulverscroft Large Print Edition, 1974.
London: Pan, 1975. (PB)
New York: Berkley, 1984. (PB)
Also published under the title *Murder After Hours*:
New York: Dell, 1954. (PB)

The Labours of Hercules (short stories):
London: Collins, 1947.
New York: Dodd, Mead, 1947.
Toronto: Collins, 1947.
New York: Dell, 1951. (PB)
Harmondsworth (UK): Penguin, 1953. (PB)
London: Fontana, 1961. (PB)
London: Collins, 1967 (Greenway edition).
New York: Dodd, Mead, 1967 (Greenway edition).
Leicester (UK): Ulverscroft Large Print Edition, 1978.
New York: Berkley, 1988. (PB)
See also omnibus volume *The Best of Poirot*.

Lord Edgware Dies:
London: Collins, 1933.
Harmondsworth (UK): Penguin, 1948. (PB)
London: Fontana, 1954. (PB)
London: Collins, 1969 (Greenway edition).
Leicester (UK): Ulverscroft Large Print Edition, 1970.
New York: Dodd, Mead, 1970 (Greenway edition).
Also published under the title *Thirteen at Dinner*:
New York: Dodd, Mead, 1933.
New York: Dell, 1944. (PB)
New York: Berkley, 1985. (PB)
New York: Dodd, Mead, 1986 (Winterbrook edition).
See also omnibus volumes: *Agatha Christie Crime Collection; Five Complete Hercule Poirot Novels; Hercule Poirot, Master Detective; Murder-Go-Round; 3 Christie Crimes*.

Make Mine Murder (includes *Appointment with Death; Peril at End House; Sad Cypress*):
New York: Dodd, Mead, 1962.

Masterpieces of Murder (includes *The Murder of Roger Ackroyd; Death on the Nile*):
New York: Dodd, Mead, 1977.

The Mousetrap and Other Stories: see *Three Blind Mice and Other Stories*

Mrs McGinty's Dead:
London: Collins, 1952.
New York: Dodd, Mead, 1952.
New York: Pocket Books, 1953. (PB)
London: Fontana, 1955. (PB)
London: Pan, 1970. (PB)
Also published under the title *Blood Will Tell*:
New York: Black, 1951.
See also omnibus volume *Agatha Christie Crime Collection*.

Murder After Hours: see *The Hollow*

Murder for Christmas: see *Hercule Poirot's Christmas*

Murder-Go-Round (includes *Thirteen at Dinner; The ABC Murders; Funerals are Fatal*):
New York: Dodd, Mead. 1972.

Murder in Mesopotamia:
London: Collins, 1936.
New York: Dodd, Mead, 1936.
New York: Dell, 1944. (PB)
Harmondsworth (UK): Penguin, 1955. (PB)

London: Fontana. 1962. (PB)
Leicester (UK): Ulverscroft Large Print Edition, 1969.
London: Collins. 1978 (Greenway edition).
New York: Berkley, 1984. (PB)

See also omnibus volumes *Agatha Christie Crime Collection: Perilous Journeys of Hercule Poirot; Spies Among Us.*

Murder in Retrospect: see *Five Little Pigs*

Murder in the Calais Coach: see *Murder on the Orient Express*

Murder in the Mews and Three Other Poirot Cases (short stories):
London: Collins, 1937.
London: Fontana, 1958. (PB)
Harmondsworth (UK): Penguin, 1961. (PB)
London: Collins, 1967.
London: Pan, 1976. (PB)
Leicester (UK): Ulverscroft Large Print Edition, 1986.

Also published under the title *Dead Man's Mirror and Other Stories*:
New York: Dodd, Mead, 1937.
New York: Dell, 1958. (PB)
New York: Berkley, 1984. (PB)

Murder in Three Acts: see *Three Act Tragedy*

Murder International (includes *Evil Under the Sun*):
New York: Dodd, Mead, 1965.

The Murder of Roger Ackroyd:
London: Collins, 1926.
New York: Dodd, Mead, 1926.

New York: Grosset & Dunlap, 1927.
London: Collins, 1939 (Canterbury Classics).
New York: Pocket Books, 1939. (PB)
New York: Triangle, 1943.
Harmondsworth (UK): Penguin, 1948. (PB)
London: Fontana, 1957. (PB)
London: Collins, 1964 (Modern Author Series).
London: Collins, 1967 (Greenway edition).
New York: Dodd, Mead, 1967 (Greenway edition).
Leicester (UK): Ulverscroft Large Print Edition, 1972.
Boston: G.K. Hall Large Print Books, 1988.

See also omnibus volumes *Agatha Christie Crime Collection; The Agatha Christie Omnibus of Crime; Christie Classics; Four Great Detective Novels; Hercule Poirot, Master Detective; Masterpieces of Murder; 1920s Agatha Christie, Volume 3; A Poirot Quintet; 3 Christie Crimes.*

Retold by George F. Wear:
London: Oxford University Press, 1948 (Tales Retold for Easy Reading).
New York and London: Garland, 1976.

Murder on Board (includes *The Mystery of the Blue Train; Death in the Air*):
New York: Dodd, Mead, 1974.

Murder on the Links:
London: John Lane, 1923.
New York: Dodd, Mead, 1923.
Harmondsworth (UK): Penguin, 1936. (PB)
New York: Dell, 1949. (PB)
London: Corgi Books, 1954. (PB)
London: Bodley Head, 1960.
London: Pan, 1960. (PB)
London: Hodder & Stoughton, 1968.

Leicester (UK): Ulverscroft Large Print Edition, 1977.
London: Panther, 1978. (PB)

See also omnibus volumes *An Agatha Christie Omnibus*; *Agatha Christie's Best Loved Sleuths*; *1920s Agatha Christie, Volume 1*; *Two Detective Stories in One Volume*.

Murder on the Orient Express:
London: Collins, 1934.
Harmondsworth (UK): Penguin, 1948. (PB)
London: Fontana, 1959. (PB)
New York: Pocket Books, 1960. (PB)
Leicester (UK): Ulverscroft Large Print Edition, 1965.
London: Collins, 1968 (Greenway edition).
New York: Dodd, Mead, 1968 (Greenway edition).
Leicester (UK): Ulverscroft Large Print Edition, 1978.
New York: Scholastic, 1988. (PB)

Also published under the title *Murder in the Calais Coach*:
New York: Dodd, Mead, 1934.
New York: Spivak, 1934 (abridged edition).
New York: Pocket Books, 1940. (PB)

See also omnibus volumes *The Best of Poirot*; *Five Complete Hercule Poirot Novels*; *Hercule Poirot, Master Detective*; *3 Christie Crimes*.

Murder Preferred (includes *The Patriotic Murders*; *Murder in Retrospect*):
New York and Toronto: Dodd, Mead, 1960.

The Mysterious Affair at Styles:
London and New York: John Lane, 1921 (c 1920).
London: John Lane, 1926.
New York: National Book, 1920s.
Harmondsworth (UK): Penguin, 1936. (PB)
New York: Avon, 1945. (PB)

London: Pan, 1954. (PB)
London: Bodley Head, 1960.
New York: Bantam, 1961. (PB)
London: Longmans, 1965.
New York: Dodd, Mead, 1976 (Commemorative edition).
New York: G.K. Hall Large Print Books, 1976.
London: Panther, 1978. (PB)
London: Collins, 1990 (centenary edition).
London: HarperCollins, 1995 (75th anniversary edition). (PB)

See also omnibus volumes *An Agatha Christie Omnibus; Agatha Christie Omnibus; Curtain and The Mysterious Affair at Styles; 1920s Agatha Christie, Volume 1; Two Detective Stories in One Volume.*

The Mystery of the Baghdad Chest:
London: Todd, 1943. (PB)
London: Vallancey, 1945? (PB)

The Mystery of the Blue Train:
London: Collins, 1928.
New York: Dodd, Mead, 1928.
New York: Grosset & Dunlap, 1928.
New York: Pocket Books, 1940. (PB)
Harmondsworth (UK): Penguin, 1948. (PB)
New York: Pocket Books, 1956. (PB)
London: Fontana, 1958. (PB)
London: Collins, 1972 (Greenway edition).
New York: Dodd, Mead, 1973 (Greenway edition).
Leicester (UK): Ulverscroft Large Print Edition. 1976.
New York: Bantam, 1987 (Hardcover Collection).

See also omnibus volumes *The Agatha Christie Omnibus of Crime; Murder on Board; 1920s Agatha Christie,*

Volume 3; Perilous Journeys of Hercule Poirot; A Poirot Quintet.

The Mystery of the Crime in Cabin 66:
London: Todd, 1943. (PB)
New York: Bantam, 1943. (PB)
See also *Crime in Cabin 66*

1920s *Agatha Christie, Volume 1* (includes *The Mysterious Affair at Styles; Murder in the Links*):
London: HarperCollins, 1995.

1920s Agatha Christie, Volume 2 (includes *Poirot Investigates*):
London: HarperCollins, 1995.

1920s Agatha Christie, Volume 3 (includes *The Murder of Roger Achroyd; The Big Four The Mystery of the Blue Train*):
London: HarperCollins, 1996.

The Nursery Rhyme Murders (includes *Hickory Dickory Death*):
New York: Dodd, Mead, 1970.

One, Two, Buckle My Shoe:
London: Collins, 1940.
London: Pan, 1956. (PB)
London: Fontana, 1959. (PB)
Leicester (UK): Ulverscroft Large Print Edition. 1973.
London: Pan, 1975. (PB)
Also published under the title The Patriotic Murders:
New York: Dodd, Mead, 1941.

New York: Grosset & Dunlap, 1941.
New York: Pocket Books, 1944. (PB)
New York: Berkley, 1988. (PB)
See also ominibus volumes *Agatha Christie Omnibus*; *Murder Preferred*. Also published under the title *An Overdose of Death*:
New York: Dell, 1953. (PB)

An Overdose of Death: see *One, Two, Buckle My Shoe*

The Patriotic Murders: see *One, Two, Buckle My Shoe*

Peril at End House:
London: Collins, 1932.
New York: Dodd, Mead, 1932.
New York: Modern Age Books, 1938.
New York: Pocket Books, 1942. (PB)
Harmondsworth (UK): Penguin, 1948. (PB)
London: Fontana, 1961. (PB)
Leicester: Ulverscroft Large Print Edition, 1978.
Boston: G.K. Hall Large Print Books, 1988.
See also omnibus volumes *Agatha Christine Ominibus*; *Make Mine Murder*.
Also published as *Peril at End House; A Play in Three Acts*, adapted by Arnold Ridley:
London: French, 1945.

Perilous Journeys of Hercule Poirot (includes *The Mystery of the Blue Train: Death on the Nile; Murder in Mesopotamia*):
New York: Dodd, Mead, 1954.

Poirot and the Regatta Mystery:
London: Todd, 1943. (PB)
London: Vallancey, 1944? (PB)

Poirot Investigates (short stories):
London: John Lane, 1924.
New York: Dodd, Mead, 1925.
London: Pan, 1955. (PB)
New York: Avon, 1956. (PB)
London: Bodley Head, 1958.
New York: Bantam, 1961. (PB)
London: Triad Grafton, 1983. (PB)
London: Collins, 1987.
See also omnibus volumes *An Agatha Christie Omnibus*, *Agatha Christie's Crime Reader*; *1920s Agatha Christie, Volume 2*; *Triple Threat*.

Poirot Knows the Murderer (short stories):
London and New York: Polybooks, 1946? (PB)

Poirot Lends a Hand (short stories)
London and New York: Polybooks, 1946? (PB)

Poirot Loses a Client: see *Dumb Witness*

Poirot on Holiday (short stories):
London: Todd, 1943. (PB)

A Poirot Quintet (includes *The Murder of Roger Ackroyd; The Mystery of the Blue Train; Dumb Witness; After the Funeral; Death on the Nile)*:
London: Collins, 1977.

Poirot's Early Cases (short stories):
London: Collins, 1974.
London: Fontana, 1975. (PB)
Also published under the title *Hercule Poirot's Early Cases*:
New York: Dodd, Mead, 1974.

New York: G.K. Hall Large Print Books, 1975.
Mattituck, NY: Amereon, no date.

Problem at Pollensa Bay and Christmas Adventure (short stories):
London: Todd, 1943. (PB)

Problem at Pollensa Bay and Other Stories (short stories):
London: HarperCollins, 1991.

The Regatta Mystery and Other Stories (short stories):
New York: Dodd, Mead, 1939.
New York: Spivak, 1939 (abridged edition).
New York: Grosset & Dunlap, 1940.
New York: Avon, 1946. (PB)
New York: Dell, 1964. (PB)
New York: Berkley, 1984. (PB)
See also omnibus volume *Agatha Christie Murder by the Box.*

Sad Cypress:
London: Collins, 1940.
New York: Collier, 1940.
New York: Dodd, Mead, 1940.
New York: Dell, 1946. (PB)
London: Fontana, 1959. (PB)
Leicester (UK): Ulverscroft Large Print Edition, 1965.
London: Crime Club, 1974.
New York: Berkley, 1984.
See also omnibus volumes *Agatha Christie's Detectives; Make Mine Murder.*

Spies Among Us (includes *Murder in Mesopotamia*):
New York: Dodd, Mead, 1968.

Surprise Endings by Hercule Poirot (includes *The ABC Murders: Murder in Three Acts; Cards on the Table*):
New York: Dodd, Mead, 1956.

Surprise! Surprise! A Collection of Mystery Stories with Unexpected Endings, ed. Raymond T. Bond (short stories):
New York: Dodd, Mead, 1965.
New York: Dell. 1966. (PB)

Taken at the Flood:
London: Collins, 1948.
London: Fontana, 1961. (PB)
London: Pan, 1965. (PB)
Leicester (UK): Ulverscroft Large Print Edition, 1971.
Also published under the title *There is a Tide . . .*:
New York: Dodd, Mead, 1948.
New York: Pocket Books, 1949. (PB)
New York: Dell, 1955. (PB)
New York: Berkley, 1984. (PB)
New York: Bantam, 1987. (Hardcover Collection)
See also omnibus volume *Agatha Christie's Best Loved Sleuths*.

There is a Tide . . .: see *Taken at the Flood*

Third Girl:
London: Collins, 1966.
New York: Dodd, Mead, 1967.
Leicester (UK): Ulverscroft Large Print Edition, 1968.
New York: Pocket Books, 1968. (PB)
London: Fontana, 1976. (PB)
London: Collins, 1980 (Greenway edition).
London: Pan, 1982. (PB)

Thirteen at Dinner: see *Lord Edgware Dies*

13 for Luck! A Selection of Mystery Stories for Young Readers (short stories):
New York and Toronto: Dodd, Mead, 1961.
New York: Dell, 1965. (PB)
London: Collins, 1966.

Three Act Tragedy:
London: Collins, 1935.
London: Fontana, 1957. (PB)
London: Pan, 1964. (PB)
London: Collins, 1972 (Greenway edition).
New York: Dodd, Mead, 1973 (Greenway edition).
Leicester (UK): Ulverscroft Large Print Edition, 1975.
London: Pan, 1983. (PB)
Also published under the title *Murder in Three Acts*:
New York: Dodd, Mead, 1934.
Cleveland (US): World Publishing, 1944.
New York: Avon, 1945. (PB)
New York: Popular Library, 1961. (PB)
New York: Berkley, 1984. (PB)
New York: Bantam, 1988 (Hardcover Collection).
See also omnibus volumes: *Agatha Christie's Best Loved Sleuths*; *Surprise Endings by Hercule Poirot*.

Three Blind Mice and Other Stories (short stories):
New York: Dodd, Mead, 1950.
New York: Dell, 1980. (PB)
New York: Berkley, 1984. (PB)
New York: Dodd, Mead, 1985 (Winterbrook edition).
Boston: G.K. Hall Large Print Books, 1988.
Also published under the title *The Mousetrap and Other Stories*:

New York: Dell, 1952. (PB)

3 Christie Crimes (includes *The Murder of Roger Ackroyd; Murder in the Calais Coach; Thirteen at Dinner*):
New York: Grosset & Dunlap, 1937.

Triple Threat (includes *Poirot Investigates*):
New York: Dodd, Mead, 1943.

Two Detective Stories in One Volume (includes *The Mysterious Affair at Styles; Murder on the Links*):
New York: Dodd, Mead, 1940.

Two New Crime Stories, by Agatha Christie and E. Phillips Oppenheim (includes 'The Under Dog'):
London: Readers Library, 1929?

Two Thrillers, by Agatha Christie and E. Phillips Oppenheim (includes 'The Under Dog'):
London: Daily Express Fiction Library, 1936?

The Under Dog and Other Stories (short stories):
New York: Black, 1926.
New York: Dodd, Mead, 1951.
New York: Pocket Books, 1955. (PB)
New York: Dell, 1965. (PB)
New York: Berkley, 1986. (PB)
New York: Bantam, 1988. (Hardcover Collection)

The Veiled Lady and The Baghdad Chest (short stories):
London: Hodgson, 1944. (PB)
Also published under the title *The Veiled Lady and The Mystery of the Baghdad Chest*:
London and New York: Polybooks, 1944. (PB)

While the Light Lasts and Other Stories (short stories):
London: HarperCollins, 1997.

Witness for the Prosecution and Other Stories (short stories):
New York: Dodd, Mead, 1948.
New York: Dell, 1956, (PB)

SHORT STORIES

Listed here are Poirot short stories as they appear in Christie bibliography. Many of these were first published in periodicals, sometimes with differing titles and occasionally in variant forms. A number have been anthologized elsewhere.

'The Adventure of Johnnie Waverly'
Agatha Christie's Poirot, Book 1
Hercule Poirot's Casebook
Hercule Poirot's Early Cases
The Mousetrap and Other Stories
Poirot's Early Cases
Surprise! Surprise!
Three Blind Mice and Other Stories

Also published under the title 'The Kidnapping of Johnnie Waverly'

'The Adventure of the Cheap Flat'
An Agatha Christie Omnibus
Agatha Christie's Crime Reader
Agatha Christies Poirot, Book 2
Hercule Poirot's Casebook
Poirot Investigates
Triple Threat

Also published under the title 'Poirot Indulges a Whim'

'The Adventure of the Christmas Pudding' (first version) see 'Christmas Adventure'

'The Adventure of the Christmas Pudding' (second version) — *The Adventure of the Christmas Pudding and a Selection of Entrées*

Also published under the title 'The Theft of the Royal Ruby'

'The Adventure of the Clapham Cook — *Agatha Christie's Poirot, Book 1*
Hercule Poirot's Casebook
Hercule Poirot's Early Cases
Poirot's Early Cases
The Under Dog and Other Stories

Also published under the title 'The Mystery of the Clapham Cook'

'The Adventure of the Egyptian Tomb' — *An Agatha Christie Omnibus*
Agatha Christie's Crime Reader
Agatha Christie's Poirot, Book 4
Hercule Poirot's Casebook
Poirot Investigates
Triple Threat

'The Adventure of the Italian Nobleman' — *An Agatha Christie Omnibus*
Agatha Christie's Poirot, Book 4

	Hercule Poirot's Casebook *Poirot Investigates* *Triple Threat*
'The Adventure of the King of Clubs' see 'The King of Clubs'	
'The Adventure of "The Western Star"'	*An Agatha Christie Omnibus* *Agatha Christie's Crime Reader* *Agatha Christie's Poirot, Book 2* *Hercule Poirot's Casebook* *Poirot Investigates* *Triple Threat*
'The Affair at the Victory Ball'	*Agatha Christie's Poirot, Book 3* *Hercule Poirot's Casebook* *Hercule Poirot's Early Cases* *Poirot's Early Cases* *The Under Dog and Other Stories*
'The Apples of the Hesperides'	*Hercule Poirot's Casebook* *The Labours of Hercules*

Also published under the title 'The Poison Cup'

'The Arcadian Deer'	*Hercule Poirot's Casebook* *The Labours of Hercules* *Surprise! Surprise!*

Also published under the title 'The Vanishing Lady'

'The Augean Stables'	*Hercule Poirot's Casebook* *The Labours of Hercules*

'The Birds of Ill Omen' see 'The Stymphalean Birds'

By Road or Rail' see 'Double Sin'

'The Capture of Cerberus'	*Hercule Poirot's Casebook* *The Labours of Hercules*

Also published under the title 'Meet Me in Hell'

'The Case of the Drug Peddler' see 'The Horses of Diomedes'

'The Case of the Kidnapped Pekinese' see 'The Nemean Lion'

'The Case of the Missing Will'	*An Agatha Christie Omnibus* *Agatha Christie's Poirot, Book 4* *Hercule Poirot's Casebook* *Poirot Investigates* *Triple Threat*

'The Case of the Veiled Lady' see 'The Veiled Lady'

'The Chocolate Box'	*Agatha Christie's Poirot, Book 4* *Hercule Poirot's Casebook* *Hercule Poirot's Early Cases*

	Poirot Investigates (US edition) *Poirot's Early Cases* *Triple Threat*

Also published under the titles 'The Clue of the Chocolate Box' and 'The Time Hercule Poirot Failed'

'Christmas Adventure'	*Poirot Knows the Murderer* *Problem at Pollensa Bay and Christmas Adventure* *While the Light Lasts and Other Stories*

Also published under the title 'The Adventure of the Christmas Pudding (first version)

'The Clue of the Chocolate Box' see 'The Chocolate Box'

'The Cornish Mystery'	*Agatha Christie's Poirot, Book 2* *Hercule Poirot's Casebook* *Hercule Poirot's Early Cases* *Poirot's Early Cases* *Surprise! Surprise!* *The Under Dog and Other Stories*
'The Cretan Bull'	*Hercule Poirot's Casebook* *The Labours of Hercules*

Also published under the title 'Midnight Madness'

'Crime in Cabin 66' see 'Problem at Sea'

'The Curious Disappearance of the Opalsen Pearls' see 'The Jewel Robbery at the Grand Metropolitan'

'Dead Man's Mirror'
Agatha Christie's Poirot, Book 4
Dead Man's Mirror and Other Stories
Hercule Poirot's Casebook
Murder in the Mews and Three Other Poirot Cases
An expanded version of 'The Second Gong'

'The Disappearance of Mr Davenheim'
An Agatha Christie Omnibus
Agatha Christie's Poirot, Book 2
Hercule Poirot's Casebook
Poirot Investigates
Triple Threat
Also published under the title 'Mr Davenby Disappears'

'The Disappearance of Winnie King' see 'The Girdle of Hyppolita'

'The Double Clue'
Agatha Christies Poirot, Book 3
Double Sin and Other Stories
Hercule Poirot's Casebook
Hercule Poirot's Early Cases
Poirot's Early Cases
Also published under the title 'The Dubious Clue'

'Double Sin' — *Agatha Christie's Poirot, Book 2*
Double Sin and Other Stories
Hercule Poirot's Casebook
Hercule Poirot's Early Cases
Poirot's Early Cases
Surprise! Surprise!

Also published under the title 'By Road or Rail'

'The Dream' — *The Adventure of the Christmas Pudding and a Selection of Entrées*
Agatha Christies Poirot, Book 1
Hercule Poirot's Casebook
The Regatta Mystery and Other Stories

'The Dubious Clue' see 'The Double Clue'

'The Erymanthian Boar' — *Hercule Poirot's Casebook*
The Labours of Hercules

Also published under the title 'Murder Mountain'

'The Flock of Geryon' — *Hercule Poirot's Casebook*
The Labours of Hercules

Also published under the title 'Weird Monster'

'Four-and-Twenty Blackbirds' — *The Adventure of the Christmas Pudding and a Selection of Entrées*

	Agatha Christie's Poirot, Book 1 *Hercule Poirot's Casebook* *The Mousetrap and Other Stories* *Three Blind Mice and Other Stories*

Also published under the title 'Poirot and the Regular Customer'

'The Girdle of Hyppolita'	*Hercule Poirot's Casebook* *The Labours of Hercules* *13 for Luck!*

Also published under the titles 'The Girdle of Hippolyte' and 'The Disappearance of Winnie King'

'The Horses of Diomedes'	*Hercule Poirot's Casebook* *The Labours of Hercules*

Also published under the title 'The Case of the Drug Peddler'

'How Does Your Garden Grow?'	*Agathe Christie's Poirot, Book 3* *Hercule Poirot's Casebook* *Poirot's Early Cases* *The Regatta Mystery and Other Stories*

'In the Third Floor Flat' see 'The Third Floor Flat'

'The Incredible Theft'	*Agatha Christie's Poirot, Book 1* *Dead Man's Mirror* *Hercule Poirot's Casebook*

	Murder in the Mews and Three Other Poirot Cases

An expanded version of 'The Submarine Plans'

'The Invisible Enemy' see 'The Lernean Hydra'

'The Jewel Robbery at the Grand Metropolitan'	*An Agatha Christie Omnibus* *Agatha Christie's Poirot, Book 4* *Hercule Poirot's Casebook* *Poirot Investigates* *Triple Threat*

Also published under the title 'The Curious Disappearance of the Opalsen Pearls'

'The Kidnapped Prime Minister'	*An Agatha Christie Omnibus* *Agatha Christie's Poirot, Book 2* *Hercule Poirot's Casebook* *Poirot Investigates* *Triple Threat*

'The Kidnapping of Johnnie Waverly' see 'The Adventure of Johnnie Waverly'

'The King of Clubs'	*Agatha Christie's Poirot, Book 1* *Hercule Poirot's Casebook* *Hercule Poirot's Early Cases* *Poirot's Early Cases* *The Under Dog and Other Stories*

Also published under the title 'The Adventure of the King of Clubs'

'The Lemesurier Inheritance'	*Hercule Poirot's Casebook* *Hercule Poirot's Early Cases* *Poirot's Early Cases* *The Under Dog and Other Stories*
'The Lernean Hydra'	*Hercule Poirot's Casebook* *The Labours of Hercules*

Also published under the title 'The Invisible Enemy'

'The Lost Mine'	*Agatha Christie's Poirot, Book 2* *Hercule Poirot's Casebook* *Hercule Poirot's Early Cases* *Poirot Investigates* (US edition) *Poirot's Early Cases* *Triple Threat*
'The Market Basing Mystery'	*Hercule Poirot's Casebook* *Hercule Poirot's Early Cases* *Poirot's Early Cases* *13 for Luck!* *The Under Dog and Other Stories*

'Meet Me in Hell' see 'The Capture of Cerberus'

'Midnight Madness' see 'The Cretan Bull'

'The Million Dollar Bank Robbery' see 'The Million Dollar Bond Robbery'

'The Million Dollar Bond Robbery'	*An Agatha Christie Omnibus* *Agatha Christie's Crime Reader* *Agatha Christie's Poirot, Book 3* *Hercule Poirot's Casebook* *Poirot Investigates* *Triple Threat*

Also published under the title 'The Million Dollar Bank Robbery'

'Mr Davenby Disappears' see 'The Disappearance of Mr Davenheim'

'Murder in the Mews'	*Agatha Christie's Poirot, Book 1* *Dead Man's Mirror and Other Stories* *Hercule Poirot's Casebook* *Murder in the Mews and Three Other Poirot Cases*

'Murder Mountain' see 'The Erymanthian Boar'

'The Mystery of Hunter's Lodge'	*An Agatha Christie Omnibus* *Agatha Christie's Crime Reader* *Agatha Christie's Poirot, Book 3* *Hercule Poirot's Casebook*

	Poirot Investigates *Triple Threat*
'The Mystery of the Baghadad Chest'	*Agatha Christie's Poirot Book 3* *Hercule Poirot's Casebook* *The Mystery of the Baghdad Chest* *Poirot Knows the Murderer* *The Regatta Mystery and Other Stories* *The Veiled Lady and the Baghdad Chest* *The Veiled Lady and the Mystery of the Baghdad Chest* *While the Light Lasts and Other Stories*

An expanded version was published under the title 'The Mystery of the Spanish Chest'

'The Mystery of the Clapham Cook' see 'The Adventure of the Clapham Cook'

'The Mystery of the Crime in Cabin 66' see 'Problem at Sea'

'The Mystery of the Plymouth Express' see 'The Plymouth Express'

'The Mystery of the Spanish Chest'	*The Adventure of the Christmas Pudding and a Selection of Entrées*

An expanded version of 'The Mystery of the Baghdad Chest'

'The Nemean Lion' — *Hercule Poirot's Casebook*
The Labours of Hercules
13 for Luck!

Also published under the title 'The Case of the Kidnapped Pekinese'

'The Plymouth Express' — *Agatha Christie's Poirot, Book 3*
Hercule Poirot's Casebook
Hercule Poirot's Early Cases
Surprise! Surprise!
The Under Dog and Other Stories

Also published under the title 'The Mystery of the Plymouth Express'

'Poirot and the Crime in Cabin 66' see 'Problem at Sea'

'Poirot and the Regatta Mystery' — *Poirot and the Regatta Mystery*
Poirot Lends a Hand
Poirot on Holiday

Also published under the title 'The Regatta Mystery'

'Poirot and the Regular Customer' see 'Four-and-Twenty Blackbirds'

'Poirot Indulges a Whim'

see 'The Adventure of the Cheap Flat'

'The Poison Cup' see 'The Apples of the Hesperides'

'Problem at Sea'
Agatha Christie's Poirot, Book 1
Crime in Cabin 66
Hercule Poirot's Casebook
Hercule Poirot's Early Cases
The Mystery of the Crime in Cabin 66
Poirot Knows the Murderer
Poirot on Holiday
Poirot's Early Cases
The Regatta Mystery and Other Stories

Also published, sometimes in slightly different versions, under the titles 'Crime in Cabin 66', 'The Mystery of the Crime in Cabin 66', and 'Poirot and the Crime in Cabin 66'

'The Regatta Mystery' see 'Poirot and the Regatta Mystery'

'The Second Gong'
Witness for the Prosecution and Other Stories

An expanded version was published under the title 'Dead Man's Mirror'

'The Stymphalean Birds'
Hercule Poirot's Casebook
The Labours of Hercules

Also published under the titles 'The Birds of Ill Omen' and 'The Vulture Women'

'The Submarine Plans' — *Hercule Poirot's Early Cases*
Poirot's Early Cases
The Under Dog and Other Stories

An expanded version was published under the title 'The Incredible Theft'

'The Theft of the Royal Ruby' — *Agatha Christie's Poirot, Book 3*
Double Sin and Other Stories
Hercule Poirot's Casebook

Also published under the title 'The Adventure of the Christmas Pudding' (second version)

'The Third Floor Flat' — *Agatha Christie's Poirot, Book 1*
Hercule Poirot's Casebook
Hercule Poirot's Early Cases
The Mousetrap and Other Stories
Poirot's Early Cases
Surprise! Surprise!
Three Blind Mice and Other Stories

Also published under the title 'In the Third Floor Flat'

'The Time Hercule Poirot Failed' see 'The Chocolate Box'

'The Tragedy at Marsdon Manor' — *An Agatha Christie Omnibus*
Agatha Christie's Crime Reader
Agatha Christie's Poirot, Book 3

	Hercule Poirot's Casebook *Poirot Investigates* *Triple Threat*
'Triangle at Rhodes'	*Agatha Christie's Poirot, Book 1* *Dead Man's Mirror and Other Stories* *Hercule Poirot's Casebook* *Murder in the Mews and Three Other Poirot Cases*
'The Under Dog'	*The Adventure of the Christmas Pudding and a Selection of Entrées* *Agatha Christie's Poirot, Book 4* *Hercule Poirot's Casebook* *Two New Crime Stories* *Two Thrillers* *The Under Dog and Other Stories*
'The Vanishing Lady' see 'The Arcadian Deer'	
'The Veiled Lady'	*Agatha Christie's Poirot, Book 2* *Hercule Poirot's Casebook* *Hercule Poirot's Early Cases* *Poirot Investigates* (US edition) *Poirot Lends a Hand* *Poirot's Early Cases*

Poirot Films and Television

~

Films

1931 *Alibi* (Twickenham Studios) with Austin Trevor as Hercule Poirot: adapted from *The Murder of Roger Ackroyd*.

1931 *Black Coffee* (Twickenham Studios) with Austin Trevor as Hercule Poirot: adapted from the play.

1934 *Lord Edgware Dies* (Real Art Studios) with Austin Trevor as Hercule Poirot: adapted from *Lord Edgware Dies/Thirteen at Dinner*.

1966 *The Alphabet Murders* (MGM) with Tony Randall as Hercule Poirot: adapted from *The ABC Murders*.

1974 *Murder on the Orient Express* (EMI/Paramount) with Albert Finney as Hercule Poirot: adapted from *Murder on the Orient Express/Murder in the Calais Coach*.

1978 *Death on the Nile* (EMI/Paramount) with Peter Ustinov as Hercule Poirot: adapted from the novel.

1982 *Evil Under the Sun* (EMI/Paramount) with Peter Ustinov as Hercule Poirot: adapted from the novel.

1988 *Appointment with Death* (The Cannon Group Inc.) with Peter Ustinov as Hercule Poirot: adapted from the novel.

TELEVISION

Starring Peter Ustinov (Warner Brothers Television):

1985 *Thirteen at Dinner*; adapted from *Lord Edgware Dies*

1986 *Dead Man's Folly*

Murder in Three Acts; adapted from *Three-Act Tragedy*

Starring Ian Holm (ITV):

1986 *Murder by the Book*; original drama in which Poirot meets Agatha Christie (Peggy Ashcroft)

Starring Alfred Molina (Daniel H Blatt Productions):

2001 *Murder on the Orient Express*

Starring David Suchet (ITV):

1989 The Adventure of the Clapham Cook

Murder in the Mews

The Adventure of Johnny Waverly

Four-and-Twenty Blackbirds

The Third Floor Flat

Triangle at Rhodes

Problem at Sea

The Incredible Theft

The King of Clubs

The Dream

1990 *Peril at End House*

The Veiled Lady

The Lost Mine

The Cornish Mystery

The Disappearance of Mr Davenheim

Double Sin

The Adventure of the Cheap Flat

The Kidnapped Prime Minister

The Adventure of the Western Star

The Mysterious Affair at Styles

1991 How Does Your Garden Grow?
The Million Dollar Bond Robbery
The Plymouth Express
Wasp's Nest
The Tragedy at Marsden Moor
The Double Clue
The Mystery of the Spanish Chest
The Theft of the Royal Ruby
The Affair at the Victory Ball
The Mystery of Hunter's Lodge
1992 *Death in the Clouds*
One, Two, Buckle My Shoe
1993 The Adventure of the Egyptian Tomb
The Under Dog
Yellow Iris
The Case of the Missing Will
The Adventure of the Italian Nobleman
The Chocolate Box
Dead Man's Mirror
The Jewel Robbery at the Grand Metropolitan
1995 *Hercule Poirot's Christmas*
Hickory Dickory Dock
1996 *The Murder on the Links*
1997 *Dumb Witness*
2000 *The Murder of Roger Ackroyd*
Lord Edgware Dies
2001 *Murder in Mesopotamia*
2002 *Evil Under the Sun*
2004 *Five Little Pigs*
Sad Cypress
Death on the Nile
The Hollow

References

The Blue Book Magazine. Chicago: 1923–1925.

Christie, Agatha. *An Autobiography*. London: Collins, 1977.

Christie, Agatha. 'The Harlequin Tea Set' and 'The Love Detectives' in *Problem at Pollensa Bay and Other Stories*. London: Collins, 1991.

Christie, Agatha. *The Man in the Brown Suit*. London: John Lane. 1924. Also published serially, as *Anna the Adventuress* in *The Evening News*. London: 1924.

Christie, Agatha. *The Moving Finger*. London: Collins, 1943.

Christie, Agatha, *Murder is Easy*. London: Collins. 1939.

Christie, Agatha. *The Mysterious Mr Quin*. London: Collins, 1930.

Christie, Agatha. *The Pale Horse*. London: Collins, 1961.

Christie, Agatha. *Parker Pyne Investigates*. London: Collins, 1934.

Christie, Agatha. *Partners in Crime*. London: Collins, 1929.

Christie, Agatha. *The Secret of Chimneys*. London: John Lane, 1925.

Christie, Agatha. *The Seven Dials Mystery*. London: Collins, 1929.

Christie, Agatha. *Sparkling Cyanide*. London: Collins, 1945.

Christie, Agatha. *Towards Zero*. London: Collins, 1944.

Doyle, Sir Arthur Conan. 'The Final Problem' in *The Memoirs of Sherlock Holmes*. London: Newnes, 1894.

Doyle, Sir Arthur Conan. *His Last Bow*. London: Murray, 1917.

Hart, Anne. *The Life and Times of Miss Jane Marple*. New York: Dodd, Mead, 1985. London: Macmillan, 1986. Reissued as *Agatha Christie's Miss Marple*. London: HarperCollins, 1997.

Keating, H.R.F., ed. *Agatha Christie: First Lady of Crime*. London: Weidenfeld and Nicolson, 1977.

Morgan, Janet. *Agatha Christie: a Biography*. London: Collins, 1984.

Lask, Thomas. 'Hercule Poirot is Dead: Famed Belgian Detective.' *The New York Times*, August 6, 1975.

Sanders, Dennis and Lovallo, Len. *The Agatha Christie Companion*. New York: Delacorte Press, 1984. London: W.H. Allen, 1985.

The Sketch: a Journal of Art and Actuality. London: 1923.

Also by Anne Hart

AGATHA CHRISTIE'S MISS MARPLE

'I have had a lot of experience in solving different little problems that have arisen.'

Most of the 'little problems' tackled by Miss Jane Marple occurred in the pretty rural village of St Mary Mead and came in the shape of murder, robbery and blackmail. In the 40 years of her career, she even solved cases as far afield as London and the Caribbean. But though she usually masqueraded as 'everybody's favourite great aunt', what was she *really* like?

In this authorized biography of the world's most famous female sleuth, Anne Hart combs through the 12 novels and 20 short stories in which Miss Marple appeared, uncovering clue after clue and amassing all the evidence to solve the most difficult case of them all – the mystery of Miss Marple.

'A great treat for Agatha Christie addicts' *Daily Mail*

'Elegantly arranged and presented' *Daily Telegraph*